GEORGE V. HIGGINS
WONDERFUL YEARS, WONDERFUL YEARS

ZEBRA BOOKS
KENSINGTON PUBLISHING CORP.

ZEBRA BOOKS

are published by

Kensington Publishing Corp.
475 Park Avenue South
New York, NY 10016

First Zebra Books printing: October, 1989

Printed in the United States of America

1

The hotel was old and made of wood, three white clapboard stories set back on a long curving gravel drive among pines, oaks and maples in the foothills of the Berkshires. The trees concealed it from view from the Mohawk Trail.

Four white columns supported the *porte cochère,* and the double doors leading into the foyer were painted dark green with tarnished brass hardware; the knockers were a pair of lion's heads. The floor of the foyer and lobby was red flagstone. It was furnished with white wicker. The oak registration desk was at the rear center of the lobby. Off to the left in the shadows was the entrance to the bar, small and cramped; off to the right was the dining room: twelve octagonal oak tables and seventy-two oak chairs. The tables in the morning were set with white paper placemats and pewter jam pots, in the evening with white tablecloths frayed at the edges and mended in places. The menu advised that boxed lunches consisting of sandwiches and pastries would be prepared on request at a charge of two-fifty per guest.

To the left behind the registration desk there was an open hallway roofed in translucent greyish glass that led abruptly into a long solarium. The roof sloped away from the main building, the green iron framework rusting in places and slowly leaking at the joints, the large rectangles of glass darkened by the stains and detritus of pine needles and leaves that had fallen and remained to rot undisturbed under years of rain and winter snow. The shadowy outlines of small broken branches showed through the glass. The two glass walls facing south and west were soiled from the foliage decomposing on the roof.

The solarium was crowded with potted palms and ominous plants with broad leaves yellowed and browned at the edges. The air was heavy and moist. The flagstone floor was alternately slick and sticky underfoot. In the center there was a small unpainted iron fountain, its four-foot basin shaped like an open flower fluted at the edges. A hidden electric pump endlessly circulated five gallons of water through the center column, silently pushing it to spill into three progressively larger fluted receptacles. There were four small goldfish and some pennies in the bottom basin. Six dark green wicker chairs faced the fountain, with small circular tables between each pair.

At the rear of the solarium, there was a bower of palms and two sets of iron shelving holding stout short plants with spreading leaves. In the center there was an iron stand that held a large domed iron cage painted yellow. Inside was a big parrot, its body and wings bright green, its head masked in yellow under its green crest. The parrot had angry golden eyes closed to slits most of the time; it stirred only fitfully, ruffling its feathers and resettling itself. It did not talk. There was a small hand-lettered sign taped to the bottom of its cage: "DO NOT FEED — BITES."

"In the winter, skiers," Arbuckle said, facing the fountain, "or so the brochure says. Supposedly they've got this great network of cross-country trails, and supposedly there's good downhill only about eight miles away. Didn't mean squat to me."

"It doesn't seem like the kind of place . . ." Morse said.

". . . that skiers'd line up to get into," Arbuckle said. "No, I agree with you there. And the picture on the front the pamphlet, it shows these people getting out their car at the door? It's a Seventy-three Chevy ragtop. So I think it's probably been a while, they printed that thing up. But the place is cheap, compared the lodges, and you get your real serious types, I imagine they're too pooped to do much at night anyway. In the fall you've got your leaf-peepers. They'll stay anywhere. And in the summer, well, they brag they've got a pool out back, but I took a look at it, and it's about as big as your toilet bowl. Except with green stuff in it. Fishing? Maybe golf? I don't know. There must be courses around. Tanglewood? Quite a drive. And I can tell you, after three nights, they don't come here for the food. Pot roast *à la* pot roast — that's the chef's specialty."

"Is anybody else here?" Morse said. "You seen anybody else?"

"Three old ladies show up at meals," Arbuckle

7

said. "Separately, at meals. They nod to each other, sit down, eat, and leave. Residents, I think, permanent residents. One of them's been reading *Rage of Angels* since I got here. She brings it down with her every night. I think she's covered maybe forty pages—not much more'n that. She reads like a buddy I had the *Tecumseh*—one book'd last him a year. Sunday night there was an older man, maybe forty-five, fifty, and a woman in her late twenties, early thirties. They had a thing of red wine, and they touched fingers now and then and looked sad. Neither one of them had a ring. Two drinks in the bar, White Label and water, and up they went to bed."

"End of the affair?" Morse said. "Couldn't pick a better place."

"That's sort of what I thought," Arbuckle said. "It's pretty nearly perfect, wouldn't you say? End of the goddamned world."

Morse surveyed the solarium. "I don't know," he said. "The first thing, of course, the first thing you've got to wonder's how you're going to get her up here. Going to take some doing." He paused. "Probably have to knock her out again."

" 'Scuse me," Arbuckle said, "but I was under the impression that was not a problem. He called me in, well, Edith did, I got the clear impression that'd been disposed of—how to get her here, I mean. Hospital wanted her out, said she's not sick anymore and she's taking up a bed. So: 'Eugene, check out the joint.' And I did. The way I understood it, only question was whether this was the kind of place he wanted, put her in—she gonna be at least comfortable here. He asks me that, or she does, when I go to pick her up, well, it ain't no Caesar's Palace but I guess it fits the bill. She gonna give me trouble?"

"Nothing's ever cut-and-dried with Nell," Morse said. "You've been around, you've had enough experience by this time, know it's never that neat."

"Yeah," Arbuckle said, "well, that's something to look forward to. Why're they letting her out then, she's still acting up? Doesn't make any sense. First I spend four joyous days, three quiet nights, making mine hosts very nervous. Now you're telling me I'm in for a rerun of *I Want to Live?* I'm gonna be the guy, locks her in the chamber, and then turns on the gas?"

"Calm down," Morse said. "You won't have to do anything. They'll give her an industrial dose of Thorazine. Whatever it is. She'll be all zonked out 'fore she even comes out of the building. Probably sleep the whole way up. And even if she doesn't, you know how slow it makes her talk. She'll be all right. All right's she ever gets, anyway. Zombied. And either Fanny or Jo'll be along, she does start to thrash around."

"Poor lady," Arbuckle said. "She'll fit right in here."

"You didn't, exactly?" Morse said.

"They didn't have any trouble, me staying one night," Arbuckle said. "I didn't say anything, except to ask, they had a room." He snorted. "Unless the old ladies're bunking together, which I tend to doubt, myself, them and the lovers were the only other guests, which'd mean they had forty-two rooms, I could find a use for them. Forty-two other rooms with short mattresses and thin blankets. My

9

wallet's thicker'n the pillow, which is nice when I want to buy something but not so hot, I want to sleep. I think they assumed I'd been driving all day and just got tired and decided, finish the trip in the morning. Guy at the desk seemed kind of surprised, I didn't check out after breakfast. Looked at me funny, you know? I was gonna say to him: 'No, I'm not on the run—just taking a little time off. For a rest.' But I figured: I deny it, he's gonna have a whole army of cops here in ten minutes. So: kept my mouth shut, for a change."

"What'd you do, all day?" Morse said.

"Tried to keep a grip on my sanity," Arbuckle said. "One thing, somebody puts you here 'cause you're nuts. But another thing, you got most of your marbles when you come here, part your job, like to leave with the same number. But it wasn't easy. I sat around the lobby—they don't get a paper here until the local afternoon comes out, and it's fascinating stuff, I guess, you know the background on the zoning fight between Mister Macalester and Cold Springs developers. Macalester says the new Cold Springs condos'll fuck up the traffic in town. Cold Springs says they won't. Macalester's buddy, Mister Desmond, he says Cold Springs'll screw up the solid-waste disposal. Cold Springs says it won't. Or you happen to be wondering what Lambert's got for back-to-school. Tried to get a rise out the parrot but I guess he's mute or something. Bored speechless, maybe. Although I did hear him screech once—awful goddamned shriek. At least I think it was him; I wasn't in the sunroom at the time. Could've been the owner, someone asking about lunch. 'You should talk the old ladies, at least,' I told him. The bird, I mean. 'See they'd like a fourth for bridge, or something.' Nothing. I went for walks around the grounds—very pleasant, I must say, you like birds and shit like that. Which she told me once, Nell did, she does. Squirrels. Must have close to a million squirrels here. Big fat bastards, grey ones, and these mean little red ones that the grey ones stay away from. Must be oaks or hickories or something else around here with nuts on them—I don't know from trees much, either. Proprietor told me, like he was my mother or something—maybe Agnes in a bad mood—that no, they don't serve lunch. Pointed to the fine print onna menu. I drove into town after that, had a cheeseburger in the coffee shop. After pissing him off by agreeing his suspicion I'm staying on another night."

"It was probably the gold neck chain that got him," Morse said. "Don't see many of those here, I'd guess."

"Could've been," Arbuckle said. "He wanted to ask me what the hell I was up to, but he didn't quite dare."

"Probably thinks you're from the State," Morse said.

"That's what I thought," Arbuckle said. "Everybody's got a scam. 'Holding back on the meals taxes, chum?' That's what I wanted to say. 'That wetback you got, back there in the kitchen? He got his employment Green Card? How 'bout them two chambermaids? Paying the minimum wage? Sure you're turning over, all the withholding taxes?' Just for some excitement. But I didn't. I think the prop was

11

glad today, you finally showed up. Relieved, you know? Like maybe now I'd leave." He sighed. "Nothing I'd like better."

Morse nodded. He took a leather memo pad from his inside jacket pocket. "You're finished today," he said. "Just let me get some stuff down here, and you can go pack, get out and go back."

"I don't have to report him, direct?" Arbuckle said.

"You can if you want to," Morse said. "I was more or less assuming, since I had to anyway, and you've been cooped up here this long, you'd just as soon knock off, go back, get drunk or laid or something."

"Oh, I don't want," Arbuckle said. "You want to let me out of this, I'm more'n willing, friend."

Morse nodded. "No entertainment, then?"

"The big event here," Arbuckle said, "is when someone shows the gumption to turn on the TV set. In the bar. It's an old Hitachi and I think they get their signal parcel post or something. Two channels, one of which must be ABC — *Monday Night Football*. Watched the Rams play the Raiders. Went in there after dinner, probably seven, seven-thirty. Sat there by myself maybe twenty, thirty minutes, meditating on my sins. Like the priest used to tell me to do. Owner comes in like he's annoyed. Points out there's a pad on the counter, next the register. Just fix what I want and write it down and sign it. I apologized. Said I saw him doing the honors, previous night, the couple was in there with me. Thought that was policy. He said, No, that's just Sunday nights. Weekends. Rest of the week, honor system. Which I think's another way of saying he's

12

not going to stand around out here watching one person drink, he can be back in his own hole, sleeping. So I got into the bourbon moderately good, wrote down four drinks, which was true, but left out they were doubles—thought I deserved that, the labor. And when nine o'clock came, turned on the game. Local paper had that, at least. That was my big night here—getting swacked alone."

"You should've brought a book," Morse said, making notes. "I hope she does, at least. That last feature's not one that's going to please him. Or Fanny and Josephine, either."

"Phil," Arbuckle said, "inna first place, I didn't think this detail was gonna be like in the service, you know? Or the brig. I associate, you know, stocking up on books with getting ready to go someplace for a long quiet time that I don't have any choice about staying there. And I can't possibly get out. And inna second place, the bar? The owner'll change that, I know. You offer him some money, he'll lock that bar up tighter'n a fried-fish fart. Hell, he'd probably do it for nothing. He's got the two teenagers with the kind of acne that the only way they'll ever get cured is to skin them, and they come in afternoons and change the beds—four beds—vacuum and dust. And then they serve the dinners, and wash up afterwards. He's got the cook. He's got himself. Caught a glimpse of another guy out by the pool yesterday, probably about forty, looked like a corpse, lying in the sun. Soon's he saw me, got out of the chaise lounge, grabbed his towel and skedaddled. That's the whole crew. He's just barely getting by here. He'll do anything for money."

"Boyfriend?" Morse said.

"Boyfriend," Arbuckle said, "idiot brother, stray dog, vagabond—who the hell knows? Or cares? He doesn't bother anybody. Point is: the money. You couldn't make enough off this operation, keep the parrot in chow. Which is probably why the bird's not talking—he's hungry. Conserving energy. You say to this guy you'll cover his losses, closing the bar, he's not there, and offer him fifty, a hundred a week, which he hasn't seen his whole life out of income from this place, he'll jump at it like a dog for meat." He paused. "Unless you—he—*wants* her served. Might be another way, out of his troubles."

"I don't think I'll mention that," Morse said, making notes. "He wouldn't go for it. Phones in the rooms?"

"Nope," Arbuckle said. "I asked about that, by way of no harm, and he got all huffy with me: 'None of our rooms have phones, sir,' he said. 'Few of our guests would desire them.' Meaning, I suppose, that nobody who comes here knows anybody, that'd be worried about them enough to call. You come to this place, maybe you're not all alone in the world, but you're close enough, pal, close enough."

"Good," Morse said. "Nothing like old Nell and a phone of her own. Nero with a flamethrower—that's old Nell with a phone in her hand." He shook his head. "I sure don't envy Fanny and Jo. He pays them all right, and I suppose if you're an ex-nun at fifty, you take what you can get. But I wouldn't want their jobs, four days a week of Nell."

" 'Ex-nun, ex-con, they got no choice'—that what you're saying, Philly?" Arbuckle said.

"Oh ease up, all right?" Morse said. "That's not what I meant. I know you're jumpy, don't like this, but that's not what I meant."

"I know," Arbuckle said.

"It's just something, we got to do," Morse said. "Just something that's got to be done."

"It's still kind of a shame, though, isn't it?" Arbuckle said. "I only met her, the only times I've seen her's been when something like this's up, but those times she seemed like a very nice woman—kind of dazed, but pretty and happy and all. But there she is, got everything wrapped, whole fucking world on the half-shell, and everything's all out of whack."

Morse shrugged. "She doesn't like what he does," he said. "She found out about it, and she told him to stop, and naturally he couldn't. He'd never see another contract. She took it the wrong way. Thought he was choosing between her and what he does, when he hasn't got a choice—he's got no choice at all. And she cracked. I guess that's the way it happens sometimes. Everybody's got their personal limit of shit, and then something happens, over the limit, and they crack. Like trying to reach too far from your ladder, when you oughta get down and just move it—there's a point where you go too far, and it slips, and down you go, crash to the ground. Prolly sick all along, but bang, one more thing happens, and they go out of control. Blooey."

"Yeah," Arbuckle said, "but is she that dangerous? Does she really know that much, that she could hurt him if she talked? He doesn't tell her things, does he? Now that she's like this?"

"I assume he doesn't," Morse said. "Not anymore.

15

I assume he hasn't told her anything for years. Does she know about things? She knows about some things, or she did, anyway. Some times, all right? Some times there was just too much money involved, so he couldn't keep it a secret. You know Buster Feeley?"

"No," Arbuckle said. "Never heard of him."

"I'm not far ahead of you," Morse said. "I met Buster Feeley maybe five times in my life. The first one was a night in a bar on Broadway in South Boston, and I recognized him from his description, the one I had of him. And I went up to him, I had this envelope, and I said: 'You Buster Feeley?' And he said, he was drinking a Bally draft ale, and he said: 'Yeah.' And I took the envelope out my coat and I said: 'This's for Sonny.' And he took it, and he said: 'Thanks.' And he put it in his pocket. And he said: 'You wanna beer?' Well, Ken didn't tell me much, but I know what's in that envelope and I'm going to be pleasant because this guy may be important. So I said: 'No, I can't. I'm a drunk. But I'll have a cup of coffee.' And he looked at me. 'Son of a bitch,' he said. 'Lots of guys are. Very few guys admit it. Have a Coke, or a ginger or something. Coffee's horrible here.' So I had a Coca-Cola. And he told me three dirty jokes about niggers, and I see this guy's not important at all—he's just an errand boy, like me. Only I, at least, am smart. And I left."

"So what?" Arbuckle said.

"Buster was the collector," Morse said. "There was fifty thousand dollars in that envelope. I know because I got it from the bank that day, cashing in fifty K in certificates of deposit."

"For who?" Arbuckle said.

"Look, all right?" Morse said. "I know but I don't want to. You don't, and believe me, you don't want to."

"Okay," Arbuckle said. "I make it a habit, take good advice. Mrs. Farley knows?"

"Most likely," Morse said. "That cash came from joint CDs. She hadda sign off on them. And if she didn't know, flat-out, it was going, Brian Mooney, well, she knew enough to know it was something Sonny Donovan wanted, and Ken was giving it to him. 'Course that was over twenty years ago. Whether she still remembers it? I dunno. And of course the Statute's run—they couldn't prosecute it now, even it was illegal then."

"What?" Arbuckle said. "What was illegal then?"

"Oh," Morse said, "Mooney was a shitbum, see? He had some kind of a no-show job Sonny got him down at Parks, Parks and Recreation. And Sonny, I think this was his third term, he's running, and there's talk going around, like there always was, that Sonny's getting free and easy with the city's money, and most of his friends seem to be doing pretty well, all a sudden. So this young bombthrower, the City Council, he decides he's gonna take old Sonny down a peg, and he's Mister Integrity. So Sonny, he looks at this Brendan Rooney character, with his rosary hanging out his pocket and his lovely wife and three children all marching to Mass together, and I don't know, he thought the guy could beat him, but he didn't feature finding out Election Night, he could. So he gets ahold this bozo Mooney, and says: 'Mooney, run for mayor. That makes the primary, you know, Rooney and Mooney plus me.' Which half the stewbums they had voting then couldn't see the ballot anyway, good enough to read it, and all they hadda do was just pick the longest name. Which was Donovan, of course. And Mooney says: 'Me? For mayor? I haven't got no money.' And Sonny says: 'Don't worry. I got a friend with money.' And that's what the dough was for—twenty-five for Brian, he's being kind enough to make a big fool of himself, and twenty-five for signs and stuff, to make it look legit.

"Now, was that illegal? I dunno—most likely. But see, that wouldn't matter to them, these guys after Sonny now. All they got on their minds is just smearing old enemies—getting even now for good beatings they took then. Any bad stuff they could dig up that'd dress Ken like a crook, well, you destroy his reputation and you don't need, put him in jail. And, you've never seen her when she is really nuts. Or pickled for that matter. She'll say anything. And anything she says'll damage him. Anything. True or not, it wouldn't matter. Because it'd attract attention to him, just because she's his wife and she's the one saying it. And he can't afford that. Maybe all that happens is, he can't get bonded now. Or maybe what she has to say smokes out some other person, knows about more recent things, for which they can put him in jail. Those grand juries don't care if the witness's sane. Or sober, for that matter. All they care is what they know, or say they know, at least." He hesitated. "And you and me, Bucky, you know . . . well, you know what we can do. Same she can do, my friend: what he tells us to, is what. What he tells us to."

"Yeah," Arbuckle said, "I suppose. Well, she can talk to the parrot, I guess."

2

Arbuckle sat in the driver's seat of a silver-grey Chrysler station wagon parked in front of the main entrance of the Hall Institute Hospital in Westwood. Fanny Clancy sat beside him. The rear cargo area was filled with luggage. Fanny was a slender woman dressed in a grey tweed suit. Her dark hair was cut short around her small face.

"Agnes tells me, Bucky," she said, "you've got yourself a girlfriend."

Arbuckle nodded. He smiled. "Yeah," he said, "I have. It's kind of nice."

"Quite young and quite pretty, was what Agnes said," she said.

"Yup," Arbuckle said. "Sharon's a beautiful kid. I hadda, Mister Farley sent me this errand, pick up some blueprints for him? Phil Morse was busy. And so I went this drafting business up in Braintree, and I go in and ask the plans, and there's this very pretty girl in there that's waiting on people. So, and I don't know what the devil got into me, you know? Because, well, I'm kind of old. And this is a very pretty kid. But what the hell, huh? You don't ask, you never find out. Maybe she likes the old goats. So, nothing to lose, I say: 'How 'bout a drink after work?' And she kind of squints at me, and says: 'Yeah.' And that's how I pulled that one off. Usual way. Story of my life. Dumb luck. And we started going out."

"Well," Fanny said, "that must make you feel good." She paused. "Although Agnes certainly isn't all that keen on you bringing the girlfriend home, your place. For the night, I mean."

"Yeah," Arbuckle said. "Well, Agnes can just stop sitting in the dark in the study, nights, spying on when I come and whether there's anyone with me, it bothers her so much. It does make me feel good, and that's why I do it, and I don't care what Agnes thinks. You know what I hadda do? I swear, she's getting strange. The older she gets, the funnier she gets. I been working Mister Farley for twelve years, all right? Twelve damned years. I mind my own business, he minds his own business, everyone gets along great. Now, you know what I do? I subscribe, *Playboy*. There's something wrong with this? And I keep the magazine. I got stacks of them. That's what happens to you, you serve on submarines. In the first place, there's no place to throw it out. Inna second place, somebody else might like to have it, and he will trade you something. So you pack-rat. And I just never got around, throwing the old *Playboys* out. And one night I come home, and I put the car the garage, and I go up my room to change, and

22

they've been *moved around*. So I look around, I mean: really look around. And I'm very neat. I always put my skivvies in the drawer the same way, always fold them the same way. And my shirts and stuff. And *they've* been moved. Not much, but they've been moved, and then whoever did it tried to put them back. And the same with the bed. I make the bed every morning. And it's always, it's like I can't get over thinking that some bastard's gonna pull an inspection on me. So: hospital corners — you dropped a quarter on the blanket, it'd bounce, you know? And somebody's been at that, too. Peeking under my blankets, see if there's stains on my sheets.

"Well, it hadda be Agnes," he said. "Somebody was in my room and poking through my stuff, and it hadda be her, and it really tacked me off. Because that's another thing subs do, you serve on them long enough — you got so little space, your own, you get kind of nutty about it. Anyone comes in it, boy, you really get pissed off. And it hadda be her, because she's the one's got all the keys, everything inna place. And I say to myself: 'Awright, what're you gonna do here? You gonna go out and make a big performance? What good's that gonna do? Isn't gonna stop her. Or are you gonna be sensible for once?' And I decided: I'd be sensible. So I went down the store, and I bought a new lock, and I yanked the old lock out and put the new lock in. It was easy. And I didn't say anything.

"Three nights," he said, "three nights go by before I'm home for dinner. He isn't. And I go up the main house and there's Agnes, and she looks like she had trouble with her bowels about a week. And I know

23

what's bothering her. So I say: 'Hey, Agnes, got any eggs?' And she says: 'Where you been?' And I say: 'With Mister Farley.' And she gives me the glare, you know how she does, and I tell you, Fanny, there's never been a harder fried egg'n the two I got that night. I can't figure it out. I wasn't hacking, Agnes. I didn't dump on her, you know? Why's Sharon make her mad? I got lucky. We're pals. Why's it piss her off?"

"She's jealous," Fanny said. "She never had that luck. She thinks you feel good, and she envies you."

"Yeah," Arbuckle said, "but what she doesn't realize is it don't make me feel good *all* the time. When I'm with Sharon, everything's fine. But I worry, you know, when I'm not. I think she's gonna get sick an old fart like me, and pick up some young stud that rides a motorcycle. I did that a guy once. He, his wife was about twelve years younger'n he was, and they were having some trouble. He was on a sub with me, and we get back for shore leave, and they had this big blowout, right in front of me. Regular dogfight. And I said: 'Right. So long.' And I went off to New York. And then we get back to the ship, and we went back out to sea, and we did the cruise and came back, and she's started divorce. And he said he didn't care. Said he was sick and tired, trying to keep her entertained all the time. But he didn't really mean that. And I knew it. And we go out again, and come in again, and they're divorced. And he says: 'Good. Maybe now some peace and quiet.' And I knew he didn't mean that, either. I knew he was just — oh, I don't know. He really felt bad about it. Wanted to get back with her.

"But I still called her, didn't I? And when he finally got around to making his move, well, I was in his place. That was on the *George Washington*. He got a transfer, *Ethan Allen*. Couldn't stand to be with me. I didn't blame him, either."

"So, what happened with her?" Fanny said.

"Oh, the jail thing," Arbuckle said. "That was the worst part of that whole thing, when they put me in the jug. Cost me Gina. I don't blame her. I don't blame her at all. She came up to Portsmouth to see me, you know, I told her she should stop. And finally she did, and she found another guy. It was the best thing."

"That's too bad," Fanny said.

"Yeah," Arbuckle said. "She was a beautiful woman. I really liked her, too. But everybody gets bad luck. You try to ride it out, and that's the best that you can do. I caught some better breaks'n the Farleys did, I think. At least mine got over with, and stayed that way. Theirs just goes on and on."

Fanny sighed. "I know," she said. "It seems like God, I don't know, just allows things to go on too long. Like it doesn't matter how long you live, you survive, there's never going to be any relief."

"I really hate this deal," Arbuckle said. "The guy's so good to me. Jeez, I wanted to refuse, I couldn't. But cripes, you know? I still dread it. This's just an awful thing. And this time, instead of thirty miles, forty miles, or like that time we hadda take her up that place, Methuen, this time we got over a hundred miles of it. I don't know how the hell the two of you stand it. And one of you even hadda choice, not ride out with us. Whaddaya, like punishment or something?"

"No," she said, "it isn't that. But we thought, well, the one who doesn't stay there tonight for the rest of this week's going to have to drive herself out there, the next shift. And since it is so isolated, it might be best to learn the route with you today.

"And the other thing is," she said, "we both came out here yesterday to see her, and talk with her doctors, Doctor Wendell, and we thought it might be better, more reassuring for her, if both of us were with her, when you drove her out."

"Is she still bad?" Arbuckle said. "I admit, I don't understand this. If she's still rocky, how the hell come they're letting her out? Why not just keep her in?"

"Bucky," Fanny said, "the conference we had with the doctors? Doctor Frontenac and Doctor Wendell? I've been working for Mister Farley now for more than six years. During that time I've been to eight of those pre-release conferences. Jo's been to eleven. And I said to her when we came out: 'I've heard this all before. The doctor'd had laryngitis, I could've made the whole presentation myself, almost word for word.' And Jo said: " 'Mrs. Farley's made good progress, and there's no reason to believe she can't continue to improve if she's scrupulous about taking her medication." Don't you just love the meaningful glances they give us, when they say that? "You guys watch her like hawks, there's an outside chance she won't go off the deep end again." That's what they always say, what the doctors always say.'

"And Jo is right," Fanny said. "You have to translate what they tell you. What they were saying is that

26

Nell Farley's been released nineteen times in twenty-one years of persistent mental illness. The medications've changed, because medicine has changed. But each time some doctor's discharged her as having made progress toward recovery, and told her she'll get even better if she faithfully takes her medicine, sooner or later she's been back. Because each time she's faithfully done as she's been told. Sometimes for three months. Sometimes for six months. Sometimes for more than a year. Until she decides that she's cured. Every single damned time: sooner or later she decides she is cured. And she goes off the drugs, and onto the vodka, and it's off to the races again.

"They've got all her records," Fanny said. "Every new doctor she gets's got all her old doctors' records. And notes, and frustrations. They know just as well as we do what the pattern is. But they can't do anything more for her. She's a manic-depressive. She has intervals of paranoid schizophrenia. She cannot metabolize alcohol. Those conditions can't be changed. They can be controlled, but not permanently changed. It's like amputees: there are prosthetic devices for them. We can usually locate some appliance that will enable a paraplegic at least to get around some. But we can't restore such patients fully to their previous able-bodied condition. And we can't completely restore patients with serious mental illness, either. All the doctors can do is hope for function. If they said they'd keep their patients until they changed them back again, they'd have to put on a new wing every week. So they bring them back as far as they can, and then they cross their fingers and

27

they let them out.

"That's what the truth of it is," Fanny said. "That's what all the pious jargon means. It means that until they find a magic bullet that actually, permanently, cures the condition, with *one* application, done in the hospital, while the patient's still under supervision and can't figure out a way to thwart the procedure, then the best things these doctors can do is get the administrators to install revolving doors and express check-in counters." She sighed. "They don't recover. They don't ever recover. They get better, but they don't recover. They're mentally ill, and that's how they stay."

"Was she there, for all of that?" Arbuckle said.

"Oh, sure," Fanny said. "Always. It's sort of like when you were a kid, and you had to go to the principal's office and your parents had to come. And the principal tells you, and your mother and your father, what you have to do to avoid further punishment. And bad report cards, and more visits to the principal's office. And the principal really means it. You know she really means it. He really means it, if it's a man. I used to be a principal, and I really meant it. If the kid got out of line again, the kid would be punished. 'I will bounce you,' I would say, and some of the little urchins didn't believe me. And they'd get out of line again. And I would bounce them.

"That made believers out of some of them," Fanny said. "Not all of them, though, and that's where the difference is. When you're in your right mind, and somebody tells you that you'd better change your ways or something bad will happen, you do every-

28

thing you can to prevent that bad thing from happening. But when you're talking to somebody who's only temporarily in their right mind, the only thing you can be sure of is that when they go off again, they will *want* the bad thing to happen."

"She does this on purpose?" Arbuckle said. He shuddered. "Cripes, this happened to me, even once, I'd do anything the world, stop it happening again. People locking you up? Giving you stuff? You got no control of your life? It's an awful thing. Just awful. I know. I was there. Not the same thing, but still the same."

"Sure," Fanny said, "but you're in your right mind. When these *victims* have their heads on straight, they steer the straight and narrow. But when they begin to slip, first of all there's this exhilaration. The closer they get to relapse, the more exhilaration they feel. You said you had a bike?"

"Uh huh," Arbuckle said. "I had an old Indian."

"When I was in high school," Fanny said, "I had a boyfriend. And he had a Harley. I never drove it. But he sure did. And I used to think, riding behind him, the only thing I wanted him to do was make that thing go faster. Isn't that strange? No, that's young. But you're supposed to get over that. You're supposed to come around to the understanding that if you keep on doing what you're doing, you're going to get demolished. And that's what people like Nell don't do. *This woman is crowding sixty.* She's nuts. When she goes nuts again, she will be fearless. It will be an overwhelming feeling. She'll be cured. She'll be able to do anything. Stop taking orders from people and start doing what she likes. And since by then she'll be at least halfway back down the road to the booby hatch, whatever she wants to do will almost certainly be terribly harmful to her. Because she's crazy, see? The decisions she will make in the course of her relapse will be certain to be choices that will make her worse. She will make the wrong choices because she is crazy, and the choices that she makes will make her crazier. Jo and I won't be able to stop her.

"So," Fanny said, "in a sense: yes, they do it on purpose. But they're not in a condition to select purposes wisely. Their judgment is gone. All shot to hell. She sat there yesterday, very prim and polite, very eager to agree to any condition that the doctors might impose. Making promises to me and Jo, patting our hands, telling us how this is absolutely the last time we'll have one of these interviews, hugged us with tears in her eyes when we promised to come back today, gave us her usual list of things that she wanted from home. And it was absolutely identical to the performance we all went through the last time. And the time before that, and the time before that. And so on into the night. It could've been a recording. A videotape. It wasn't talk at all, not really—it was sounds uttered in a ritual, and if you didn't know what they all meant, secretly, it would've been meaningless. Unless you were so innocent you took them at face value. The poor, suffering, woman."

"Doesn't she . . ." Arbuckle said. "Doesn't she know that?"

"Dimly, maybe," Fanny said. "The doctors call it 'massive denial.' What the patients tell you is that things that really happened, never really happened.

Or that things that never happened really did—they saw them. And they really believe what they say. You can't talk them out of it. You see why the therapists get a little wacky, themselves? Is what they do the cause of the blockage? Or is it because the people who do things that put them into therapy're so mortified they black things out? Nobody really knows.

"What they do know is that's one way, that they're able to 'get better.' By convincing themselves they never were that sick, never did all the awful things they did. That's why the doctors get so frustrated. If they try to demolish that denial, and succeed, they're retarding the patient's improvement. If they don't try, or they do try and fail, they're quite aware that a relapse is just a matter of time. So they take them as far as they can, and then they let them out. Hoping for the best, and praying a lot." Fanny glanced toward the hospital entrance and opened the passenger door. "As they're doing right now," she said. "Come on, Bucky . . . showtime."

Nell Farley emerged from the hospital gripping Josephine Demers by the right hand. Each of them was carrying a green suitcase. Josephine was blocky in a green wool suit, with a settled look about her. She deliberately walked slowly. Nell was petite and slight, with curly black hair. She wore a beige suit and she took each step very carefully, concentrating on where she placed her feet. "Tell me," Fanny said softly, so that only Arbuckle could hear her, "where are the simple joys of maidenhood?"

Nell looked up at the sky and smiled, and squeezed Josephine's hand. Josephine smiled in return. Fanny and Arbuckle stood on the passenger side of the station wagon, holding the right-side doors open. Nell looked at them and smiled, tears forming in her blue eyes as she continued her slow progress.

When Nell and Josephine reached the wagon, Nell said very slowly: "Oh, Bucky. And, Fanny." Without detaching Nell's grip, Josephine produced a handkerchief from her right jacket pocket and transferred it into Nell's left hand. Nell recoiled slightly, released Josephine's hand, and held the handkerchief up, feeling with the tips of her fingers as though uncertain of its use.

"Wipe your eyes, dear," Jo said, "your mascara's going to run."

Nell formed a circle with her mouth. She nodded. She raised the handkerchief to her face and blotted the tears. "It's just," she said, "I'm, so glad, to see, all of you. Again. How many months? It was, summer, when I came. Summer when I came. And now, the leaves are changing. But, my friends, have not. You still care for me." She put her suitcase down and advanced to Fanny. She embraced her.

"It'll be much better, now, Nell," Fanny said, patting her on the back. Nell sobbed. "Much, much better now. We're going to do everything the doctors said, and everything will be all right. Now let's let Bucky put the rest of your things in the car, and we'll be on our way."

Nell stepped back from Fanny. She approached Arbuckle and hugged him. Initially he did not raise his arms from his sides, but after a few seconds, he hugged her loosely. "Nice to have you, uh, back, Mrs. Farley," he said, his voice unusually gruff.

Nell stepped back from Arbuckle. She shifted her gaze to Fanny. "You said," Nell said, in a tearful voice, "you, said: 'Rest. Of my things.' "

Fanny began guiding Nell slowly to the right rear passenger door. "Why yes, Nell," she said. "We went to the house yesterday, and Agnes helped us get all the things you said you wanted. Asked us to bring. And they're all in the back. And there are these two cases, with the rest of your things, and that's what Bucky's putting in."

Nell resumed sobbing as she slid into the car. "But, the rest. Of my things. These are all, my things? All of my things? In this car?" She looked out, appealing. "I'm never going back. Am I? Never? Going back? To my lovely home? And my hus, band? That's what you're, telling me. What you're telling me."

Fanny shut the door gently as Arbuckle locked the two suitcases in the cargo area and Josephine entered the left rear seat. "Now Nell," Fanny said, "you know what the doctors said. You've made a lot of progress. But you've still got a lot of recovering to do. And you need a quiet place to do it. Where you can rest and not have any distractions from your biggest job. Which is getting better. And Mister Farley's found a lovely place. And Bucky's been there and can tell you all about it on the way." Arbuckle got into the driver's seat.

Nell reached forward and put her left hand on his right shoulder as Fanny slid into the front passenger seat. "Oh, Bucky," Nell said, "it means, so much to me. To have you. For my friend."

Arbuckle started the car. "Well, Mrs. Farley," he

said, clearing his throat, "it's nice to see you. Feeling better."

"Do you love me, Bucky?" she said.

"Now Nell," Josephine said, "we're all very fond of you, and that is why we're here. Of course Bucky loves you. Now do try to stop getting yourself so upset."

Nell leaned forward as the car moved down the drive. "Is Ken, all, right?" she said to Arbuckle. "You, see him. Every day. I wish, I wish, I could."

"He's fine, Mrs. Farley," Arbuckle said. "He's down in Plympton today, on a road job."

She sat back against the cushion. "He doesn't, though. Wish. He could see me. Kenny does not love me. Kenny's, through. With me." She resumed crying, silently.

3

Estelle Stoddard feared that some of the male customers of Wayne's World-Class Haircutters at 200 Federal Street in Boston might get the wrong impression. She was careful to explain to each occupant of her chair that she had permission to work the first two weeks of September for Wayne, filling in for Toby during his vacation. Martin Sands was one of those patrons.

"See, I'm on vacation too," she said, shampooing his blond hair at the sink. "My regular job's at Salon Dorothy, out on Route One down in Westwood? And Dorothy gives us each two weeks' vacation, and she says we got to take it. Because Dorothy, Dorothy Franklin, this is, she don't want the time piling up. Like people saving it up, you know? So all of a sudden, one of the girls, she's taking a month or six weeks. Because that always screws up the schedule, you know? All her regular women get mad. So, two weeks it is, 'less you're getting married, in which case you can take three, one for free.

"Well," Estelle said, "happens I don't want, I don't want the vacation. Not this year at least, and maybe not the next, because me and Steve ain't saved enough. See what we want's a Camaro and Jimmy — he wants the truck, naturally, and I want a Z28 with a T-roof, and then we need furniture, too."

"For the car or the GMC truck?" Sands said, rising as she lifted the chair from reclining to sitting position and draped the towel over his hair.

"For what?" she said, rubbing his head.

"I was wondering," he said, his chin pressed against his chest as she rubbed. "I was trying to imagine how you'd get a dinette set, or a Hide-A-Bed, say, into a Chevy Camaro."

She gave the back of his head a playful slap. "Oh, a freshie," she said, "a regular comedian, huh?" She pulled the towel off and grinned at him.

"You've got a lovely smile," he said. "I can see why Steve'd want to put a Hide-A-Bed in his Jimmy."

She pushed him on the left shoulder, causing the chair to revolve. "Turn around and face the mirror. I'm already taken, and I see that ring pretty good."

"It's not gold," he said, "it's bronze. My left ring finger's arthritic, and I'm hoping for a cure."

"You should go up to Sainte Anne de Beaupré," Estelle said. "Up there in Quebec. My great-aunt went there one year and climbed all the stairs on her knees, and she had a miracle."

"It cured her arthritis?" Sands said.

"No," Estelle said, combing his wet hair, "her alky husband, Joe, stopped drinking. Well, what he did was die, but the way he treated her, you know, that was just as good."

Sands laughed.

"How's Toby usually do you?" she said. "You tell him what you want?"

"Sure," Sands said, "and he listens very closely, and then he ignores me and does whatever he pleases. And he's right to do that. I'm a lawyer. I don't know anything about cutting hair. I wouldn't let Toby tell me how to try a case, and I don't expect him to listen to me, I start telling him how to cut hair."

She tilted her head and squinted at him in the mirror. She put her hands on his jaw and moved his head from profile to profile. "Well," she said, "you like it, you know, full? Or, you like it short? Or sort of in-between?"

"Sort of in-between sounds safest," he said. "Gimme in-between."

"I think: sort of full," she said. "You got kind of a narrow face. Makes you look, you know, like you're foxy."

"I *am* foxy," he said. "I'm very foxy. I told you I'm a lawyer."

"Well," she said, "okay, but I wouldn't think you'd want to *look* that way. You should look cute and innocent, right? Like you don't know what's going on. Wouldn't that be better, I made you look like that?"

"Where did Toby go?" he said.

"I don't know," she said. "You'll have to ask Wayne that. Why, am I making you nervous?"

"Uh uh," he said. "I just want Toby to stay there, wherever it was that he went. All these years I've been coming to Toby, Toby never came up with that. Do it your way. It sounds good."

"*O-kay*," she said, reaching for scissors and a comb, "let's see what we can do."

"So, you're on vacation," he said.

"Yeah," she said, "and me and Steve want these things. We're kind of grabby, really, and so I went to Dorothy and I said: 'Look, I know it's my vacation, and I know you got your rules. But I was wondering, all right? If it would be all right with you. Because this guy I know,' this's Wayne, 'I know from styling school we both went to out in Vegas, and they had this competition, he's got this shop in Boston and he could use a substitute for one his guys that's off. And I wouldn't take no customers from here or anything, but I wondered it'd be all right, I worked for him two weeks.' See, it's not like me and Steve don't go out or anything. We don't have kids, nights when he's off, well, we're out partying. So it's not like we really need to go somewhere, in order to have fun, or that we never have any. Now Dorothy doesn't understand that, but she was real nice about it and she said it was okay. She said: 'That's the kind of mistake you make when you're young, honey, and that's the time to make it. While you've got the energy. 'Cause someday you will be my age, and anybody says you then: "Why not work your vacation," you will bust him one, right in the chops, no matter how much dough.'" She stood back and inspected her work. She nodded. "This's gonna look *good*," she said. "This's gonna look *very* nice, I think." She resumed cutting.

"So," he said, "but why tell me all this?"

"Because," she said, "for all I know, you got a wife. Well, I mean, I *know* you got a wife, or else you'n your boyfriend're married, 'cause you're wearing that ring. Except you don't look like that kind, which I work with a lot of them. So, I figure your wife's a woman. And all I know, she's one my regulars, although that's not very likely, since I known most of them long enough I know what their husbands do and even what they look like. But still, it's possible. So, just in case your wife's one my regulars at Dorothy's, I just want you and her to know I'm just temporary here, because I need the money, and if she was in there this week or next, looking for me, do her hair, well, I haven't quit and I will be back, and she shouldn't worry, all right?"

"You worry like this about all your regulars?" he said.

"Sure," she said. "Tips 're better, you take an interest. I told you: I'm money-hungry. I listen to any sad story. I bet, I bet I know 'way more about divorces'n you do, for example. And I'm not even a lawyer."

"I'll bet you do," he said. "I'm a criminal lawyer. I don't know anything at all about divorces, except I hear they're unpleasant."

"Oh, they're that, all right," she said. "I bet you I heard, oh probably a hundred divorces, and they're all terrible. Every single one of them. Lying and cheating and running around, telling dirty stories on them?"

"These're the husbands, of course," he said.

"And the wives, too," she said equably. "I had some of the nicest ladies you'd ever hope to meet, and they turn into Dracula right before your eyes. Or

39

some kind of hooker or something. Some lady you've been doing for years, and she's always been so nice? Ice cream wouldn't melt in her mouth? So, one week she comes in and she just found out her husband's, you know, with his secretary, and she's really down-in-the-mouth, don't know what she's gonna do. And then maybe two or three weeks later, she comes back for the full treatment 'cause *one* of her new boyfriends—you get what I'm saying here? In less'n a month she's picked up three guys, and boy, is she having fun? And she's going New York for the weekend.

"I'm telling you, it's awful," Estelle said, "I said to Steve, you know? I said: 'Steve, I'm telling you, you got any doubt whatsoever in that busy brain of yours we can't make a go of this, well, let's not get married then. I mean: Like just forget it. We can still live together, and share everything, and the day ever comes when either one of us wants to mess around, well, fine and dandy, bye-bye. But we get married, boy, that's it. We are staying married. I'm not gonna stand around and watch you turn into a shit, and you're not going to do that either, if that happens to me. All right?' And he said: 'All right.' and I hope we are.

"My sister, Shan," she said.

" 'Shan'?" he said.

"S,h,a,r,o,n, wise guy," she said, slapping him on the right shoulder. "Keep in mind I'm the one with the scissors here, all right? You wanna lose an ear?"

"No," he said.

"We call her Shan," Estelle said. "Shan's hadda rough time, no question about it. Her and this guy

40

Timmy went together about a hundred years, and he's gonna marry her. And this and that, and blah, blah, blah. Well, he didn't. Shan's two years younger'n me, but we look a lot alike. People sometimes think we're twins, not just sisters, you know? You see what I'm trying to tell you?"

"Shan is stacked," Sands said.

"Exactly," she said, patting him on the left shoulder. "You really are smart, aren't you. Must be a good lawyer. And Timmy, well, Timmy . . ."

". . . didn't see any reason to marry Shan as long as she was putting out for him without all that bother," Sands said.

"That's *right*," Estelle trilled. "Well, Shan didn't like that a bit, 'cause Shan wants to have babies. Just can't wait to have babies. Isn't like me at all. What I want is Hawaii, that and a Z28. But Stelle is Stelle and Shan is Shan, and that's how the world goes round. So Shan dumps Timmy and goes out, Shan starts cruising around. And now she's going this guy that says he wants to marry her, and this's what I'm saying. I said: 'Shan,' I go, 'he's 'way too old. This guy's too old for you. I'm telling you, I'm telling you, you get hooked up with this guy and you will get your babies and then he'll take off on you.' And she won't listen."

"How old's too old?" Sands said.

"Well," she said, "it all depends, you know? On the couple, I mean. Now take me and Steve, for example." She stepped back and eyed her work critically. "Steve is thirty, all right? Never been married, thirty years old, handsome as handsome can be. And he's got a good job, too, when he works, managing bars and like that."

"He can't hold a job?" Sands said.

"Oh," she said, "it isn't that. He could, but until me and him started making plans, and this was over two years ago, he never wanted to. See, Steve's like me, a lot of ways. Steve wants his own good times. So what he'd do was work a while, save his dough and so forth, and he'd quit. Always gave notice, never left nobody mad—except one, and he was right—and take off and go some place. He's been Egypt, all over Africa, Australia, Rio, all those places. Spent a year in Europe alone. 'Joined the Navy, see the world,' he said, 'all I ever saw was this end the Med, the other end the Med, then back the first end and start all over.' See he was in the Sixth Fleet, on the *Kitty Hawk,* and this was when they, well, I guess they're always having trouble in the Middle East. So now he's seeing all the stuff he missed, or was, anyway, till we got serious.

"So, Steve is thirty," she said, "and me, I'm twenty-four. And I don't think that's too much. Too big an age difference. But when Steve was dating Shan there . . ."

"Wait a minute," Sands said, "Steve was dating Shan?"

"Just a little while," she said. "After Shan broke up with Timmy, she started dating Steve. And I said: 'Shan,' this was almost three years ago and she wasn't even twenty-one, I said: 'Shan, this guy's too - old. You're not even twenty-one, and he is twenty-seven. I mean, this guy's been around, and you're still just a kid.' And she goes: 'Yeah, maybe you're right,' 'Well, of course I'm right,' I said. 'Naturally

I'm right.' "

"And then you started dating him," Sands said. "That must've gone over big."

"Well," Estelle said, "not right away. I mean, I waited almost three months, I finally asked him out. And she don't know that, Shan don't, because I said he asked me out.

"So anyway," she said, "I don't think that's too much in our case, because I happen to be very mature, but it was in her and his. So what's she doing now? Now she's dating this guy and he's forty-one years old. You beat that? Now she's twenty-three, and she's seeing this guy that's eighteen years older'n her."

"What's he do?" Sands said as she trimmed the back of his neck. "Has he got a steady job?"

"Well, I guess so," Estelle said. "I mean, she's only been going with him a few months, but he's been working all that time. He's a driver, you know? A whaddayacallit?"

"A chauffeur?" Sands said.

"That's it," she said. "Bucky's a chauffeur."

"Well," Sands said, "it doesn't sound like a job with a lot of future in it, but those guys make pretty good money, I understand, tips and everything. And they own their own limos, those that do, there's a regular bonanza in this new drunk-driving law. People hiring limos to take them everywhere that drinks're served."

"He don't own anything," she said. "He works a guy, full-time. He's his driver, you know? This very rich guy that he works for, he owns the limo, and about nine hundred other cars too, I guess, and he's the type of guy, jeez, would I like to marry him."

"Rich, huh?" Sands said. "He's probably got a clubfoot and a harelip."

"I wouldn't care," she said.

"He probably can't get it up," Sands said.

"Even better," she said. "I could marry him then, and Steve wouldn't mind, and Steve could work for me. He could be *my* driver, and Bucky could be the guy's, and everybody would be happy. Happy and friendly and rich."

"Wouldn't work," Sands said.

"You're probably right," she said. "Steve can be a little touchy. If he knows what's going on." She jerked her head toward the mirror. "Whaddaya think?" she said.

He inspected his hair. "I dunno," he said. "You gonna blowdry it? I can't tell what it looks like till I've seen it dry."

"Cheesh," she said, reaching for the dryer, "aren't you the demanding one. You remind me of Mrs. Kilbride, one my regulars? 'I don't *know,* Stelle. It's not *dry.'* " She fluffed his hair with her fingers while the hot air blew on it. "Anyway," she said, "we're, I'm meeting him tonight, this guy. Me and Steve, and him and Shan. And we're all going down Providence, the Civic Center? Julio Iglesias. That Shan thinks is just super, and I can take or leave alone. And this guy's got one, his boss's cars, a Cadillac, I think, and we're gonna have dinner, the whole nine yards, and I'm going to check him out, and see he's right for Shan."

"You think she'll listen to you?" Sands said, as she brushed his hair into place. "You decide he's a clinker, after what happened the last time when she listened to you, you think she'll pay attention?"

She laughed. "Probably not," she said. She stepped back. "Very nice, I do say so," she said. "Your wife's gonna love it. I could fall for you myself. You want some spray on that, keep it nice till you get home?"

"Yeah," he said. "Nothing smelly, though. Don't want the people in the office calling me a fancy boy."

She applied spray from a pressurized canister. She patted the hairdo in place.

"Too bad I'm just temp here," she said. "Give me about two more shots with you, you'd be on TV." She took a whisk from a hook under the counter and brushed the clippings off his shoulders. She unsnapped the apron at the back of his neck and removed it deftly to his left, spilling the clippings onto the floor.

He stood up. "It does look good," he said. He turned to face her, tightening his tie at his collar. "And I'm sorry you're just temp, too. I'd love to know how the checkout turns out. Toby's nowhere near as entertaining." He reached into his pocket and took out a twenty. "Does it have to be a haircut?"

"You pay at the front," she said, eyeing the bill.

"I know that," he said, "this's the tip." He handed the money to her.

Her eyes twinkled. "Steve works lots of nights," she said. "I hate to have dinner alone."

4

The Civic Center cavern for the Iglesias concert had been set up in a U shape with the stage at the westerly end, bathed in phosphoric blue light. Early arrivals straggled down the steep stairs to the seats tiered along the sides and rear and small groups of people gathered among the chairs set up on the floor.

In the dining room next to the bar on the third level at the westerly end of the building, Sharon and Estelle Stoddard ate baked stuffed shrimp and drank Almadén Chablis while Steven Cole and Eugene Arbuckle consumed filet mignon and beer. Sharon wore a short strapless white dress with sequins on the bodice; she had a white sweater with seed pearls draped over her shoulders against the air conditioning. She smiled and patted Arbuckle's hand: "This's really nice, you know, Gene? This's really nice."

Arbuckle wore a dark grey twill suit and a black dress shirt with a narrow red silk necktie. In the center of the tie there was an embroidered silver laurel wreath. "Thank the boss, you ever meet him," he said, shrugging, sawing away at his meat. "He's the guy that does it—not me. Makes a call here, makes a call there—first thing you know, it's done."

"That's the whole secret, things," Cole said. He wore a dark maroon brocade dinner jacket with black satin shawl lapels, and a blue ruffled formal shirt with a clip-on black bow tie. "Everybody's always running around all over the place, 'Hey, do this,' and 'Hey, do that,' and: 'How come nobody listens to me, I wanna park my car?' When all you got to do is make your mind up, what you're doing, make some calls? It's done. I'd get people, when I was managing down Hyannis, that last summer there? You'd get these crazy people, and I mean, this's Saturday night, right? And the whole joint's ready, bust right through the walls, we had this dynamite group, this banjo band, that really packed them in. And these people'd come up to me, you know? People that I knew, either from Natick, or maybe from Delia's, back when I was in Boston, or maybe someplace else, and they're waving twenties at me. And they're mad as hell when I won't let them in. Hear them peeling rubber inna parking lot, they're so mad they go away. And, I hadda say that to them, you know? 'Hey, all right? Don't gimme that shit, I don't remember you. I remember you all right. You're a good customer. I'd like to let you in. You, you're the type of person that we like to have in here. But we got the fire laws, you know? We're at capacity. Hell, we're over it. And all you hadda do, you know, you don't need to duke me here. All you hadda do was call me, onna phone this after, say what time you're coming in. And I would've been right here to meet you, saved you a nice place. But no, you didn't do that. You didn't think of that. You didn't think of coming here, till you finished dinner. And now you just show up, you know, and lay this guilt trip on me. Throw your weight around—"Hey, no prob, I c'n get us in. Friend of mine's the boss." Wave the sawbucks in my face, think that makes it right. It don't. I'll do the best I can for you, but do me a favor next time, call, all right? Just call.' And you know what they do, the next time?"

"They don't call," Arbuckle said.

"You got it, pal," Cole said, putting a large piece of steak in his mouth. He continued to talk while he chewed, interspersing wet noises among his words. "Next week, two weeks later, same thing all over again. Really frosts your balls. Because there ain't no need for it, just no need for it at all."

"Yeah," Estelle said, "but still, like Gene says, you know, you still, got to know someone." She wore a tight white ribbed sweater with a shawl collar, and tight red leather pants. She had three heavy gold chains around her neck. "It don't do any good, you just call up out of the blue, and say: 'Hey, fit me in.' We get that, Dorothy's. We get that all the time. Someone we never heard of, just calls up out of the blue, and it's always Friday, lunchtime, or Saturday, before, our very busiest times the week, and she says: 'Just a wash and set, maybe a little trim. We just got this invitation, and I got to look my best.' Well, I mean, all right? We don't even know this person. 'Who gives a shit, lady? Who're you, that you come in and screw our schedule up? I mean, we got things we got to do, and things we said we'd do, and we can't just be saying: "Hey, forget people we know." You got to wait your turn, lady. Go get a Toni home-perm kit. Try not set yourself on fire.' "

"Well, that's what I'm saying," Arbuckle said, pushing the plate away from him. "Don't want anybody getting the impression, you know, *I* could set this up. All I did was say the boss, found out his schedule was, I said: 'There any chance, you're going to be away, I could use the green Cad, you know? Take my girl, a fancy date?' And he says: 'Sure. You got in mind?' And I tell him, you know, Julio down here, 'and she really wants to see him.' 'No problem,' he says. 'You take me and Jennifer the airport, the afternoon, I don't expect to see you till Thursday. Anything else I can do?' And he, he was the one that thought the rest of the stuff.

"See," Arbuckle said, "he comes here a lot. Well, not like every week, or anything like that, but we've been here before. They had the NCAA basketball thing in here, few years back, and he's a big Providence man, account he went there and all, and they're playing Seton Hall. So we got the big car and he's got about four his pals and I drive them down, all right? He comes here all the time. Knows all the people around. And he says: 'You know, Bucky,' which is what he calls me, 'Bucky,' he says: 'You know, Bucky, you're gonna need, I think, a little touch here and there, make it a really nice evening.' And I say: 'Hey, Boss, no need of that.' 'Cause I don't want, abuse it, you know? Car would've been enough. And he says: 'No,' and he won't listen to me. He says: 'Hey, I know what you went through with her,' this's his wife I'm talking about now, I hadda take her out to western Mass., there, the other day, and he says: 'You didn't say nothing, but I know that's hard for you. So, lemme make it up to you a little bit, all right?' "

"What's with the wife?" Cole said. "She some kind of bitch? You got to put up with one of those, some cunt riding you? Thinks because you work, her husband, she can order you around? I had one of those once. Quit because of her. Went and told him: 'Look, all right? I don't take this shit. I manage the club. That's what I do. I don't take her car the brake shop. I don't drive the dog the vet. I don't drop the kids off parties, and I don't do no yard work, either.' And he says: 'She says you do, you do.' And I say: 'I say I don't, and I don't. Good-bye.' And that was the end of that. Left him right inna fuckin' lurch, and this was the Fourth of July. Biggest night of the year onna Cape, and left the fuckin' guy high and dry. Spend most that summer in Greece. You got to stand up for your rights."

"Steve," Sharon said, "just, just stay out of it, all right? Eugene, some times he has to drive the wife someplace. Just leave things alone."

"I was just asking," Cole said.

"Well," Sharon said, "so, just don't ask, all right? Just mind your own damned business."

"It's all right, Sharon," Arbuckle said. To Cole he said: "She's sick. She's not sick all the time—least she doesn't act like she's sick all the time. I guess, probably you wanted, get technical about it, I mean, a doctor would say she was sick. But when I see her, most of the time, she seems okay to me. She just ain't, she's not right, okay? And she can be kind of a handful."

"She nuts?" Cole said. "Or a drunk? I can't get over these rich guys. Make all that money, and the first thing that happens is their wives go haywire. Absolutely haywire. And it's not the guys' fault. It's like they're allergic to money or something. I seen it happen a lot."

"*Steve,*" Estelle said, "leave it *alone*. It's just something Eugene has to do."

"It's okay, Estelle," Arbuckle said. "I thought the same thing myself. It's a very sad situation, and I don't care how you slice it. Nice woman, three nice kids, hardworking husband, successful, and she can't enjoy none of it. Tried to kill herself, I guess, six or seven times. Time before last, she got out the hospital and we're taking her a place, she's very quiet inna back, and we're going along and everything, and all of a sudden she says to one these two women that take care of her—her 'watchdogs' she calls them, when she's feeling mean; when she's not, then they're her 'friends'—she says: 'Sooner or later, Josephine, you'll have to go to sleep, and when you do, you vicious bitch, I'm going to kill myself. And this time I'm going to make it.' And Jo taps me onna shoulder and says: 'U-turn, Bucky. We're taking her right back.' Because you say you're gonna kill yourself, well, then they can put you in, get a court order and all, no matter what you say. And so, back we went, and back she went. Screaming and crying and yelling? Hollering she's gonna take the wheel away from me and kill us all at the next bridge? Fanny hadda turn around and slap her a few times — got her face cut doing that. Very sad situation. I don't know what it is.

"But anyway," he said, "every so often, something happens, and it's time to move her again. And it happened, and I went and I checked the place out, and it was okay, so he did it. And, I think he takes it harder'n I do — that part the job, I mean. I mean, it's not like it isn't *hard* for me, because it is. Even though, this time, she's not out her mind or anything. She knows what's happening to her. You get a long ride like that, and it was over a hundred ten miles, she's right there inna back seat with one of the women, takes care of her, and naturally she's going to talk to you. It sounds like, the first time I hadda do it, I thought: 'Well, she feels sorry for herself, and she wants me, feel sorry for her, too.' And I did. And I was mad at myself, you know? I said to myself: 'You jerk. It's not your fault, and she's got you acting like it is. What happened to her, I mean. Whoever's fault it was. If it was anybody's. But then I thought: 'Hey, that's not so bad. You should feel sorry for her. She wants you to, well, why not? It happened to you, something like that, wouldn't you want someone, least feel sorry? It's a rough situation.' So, that made it easier. Not easy, but easier.

"Well," Arbuckle said, "he knows that. And he understands it. So things like this're what he does, when I have to do it. Sort of a reward. Because he says: 'You're staying with the car, like you did the fights, Sinatra, well, that's one kind of thing. But you're gonna want to go in, I think, this young lady of yours. And that means, well, you got to park.'

And parking's a bitch around here if you got any plans to get out, after the concert is over. So he calls up a guy, and that's how we get inside the gate like that. Preferred VI-fuckin'-P. And he says: 'Now you're gonna want some dinner.' See, I drive him down here, I drop him off and whoever he's got with him, and they come up here and they eat. And I just put the car someplace. maybe eight, ten blocks away, and I go in Winkler's there, have a steak, a little beer, food's really very good, and he picks up the tab. And then I walk back and pick up the car and I'm waiting outside, they come out. But I can't do that, tonight, so he arranges that. Then he says, all right? He says: 'Now, the best thing to do's have dinner right inna hall, so you're there when the concert's ready to start. Lemme make you a reservation.'

"Now, this is where I got to be careful," Arbuckle said. "Because I know how he always is, see? So I say to him: 'Now, Boss, no fast deals here. I asked you the car. I didn't ask you, lemme be you, one night down there. So, I'm paying for this. Me and the people I'm with.' And he says: 'Yeah, yeah, of course. Can I send you a bottle of wine? You maybe let me do that for you, Buck?' So I said all right, but afterwards, inna bar, all right? And that's going to be our champagne."

The women exchanged pleased smiles. "He's a very nice guy," Estelle said.

"Lots of people do that," Cole said. "That's a very popular thing to do. Lots of the people that I know, for example, they will call me up when these friends of theirs're coming in but they can't, themselves. Going to be out of town or something. And they'll say:

'Steve, no check, all right? Just tell 'em it's my treat, and I get back, I'll come in and I'll settle up with you.' And I say: 'Look, Mister Whoever-it-is, I'd really like to oblige. But that really screws everything all up, you know? We got this open check, we can't settle up that night, maybe before you get back the waitress decides she quits'—we get a bid turnover, the help in the clubs, people always taking off on you just when you least expect it. 'And the busboys, rely on their tips? They already got them all spent.' See, they don't understand, the customers, the mechanics the business. They think it's just catch-as-catch-can. 'So,' I tell them, 'I know what you're asking, but it's just a big pain in the ass. So whyncha do this, all right? Just a suggestion, you know, but it makes things lots easier. Lemme just send them over, couple Moëts and Chandons. Be sure they'll like it—everybody likes champagne. Cost you twenny-five a bottle, tip and everything, and I'll cover it, my pocket, and you come in, you settle up.' And they love it, they really go for that. Which I do, too, because I get it, the house price, and the guy always hits me sixty, so I make about thirty-five bucks. It's a very popular thing."

Estelle sighed. "It really must be nice," she said, "to be rich like that."

"Oh," Cole said, "these're not the rich guys, Stelle. These're just the good steady customers, you know? Working stiffs, like you and me. Only, their work pays a little better'n ours, naturally, so they can do things like that. But the really rich guys, not we get that many of them, but the few we got, they run accounts. Or we got their credit cards on file, and

55

when *they* call up, with something like that, we just say: 'Sure, Mister Moneybags, whatever you say.' And then when the party's over, we add it up, twenny percent the tip, few bucks the captain and me, just like they were actually there themselves, and signing the check. And we just put it through. Like any other charge. I bet half the time, I don't think they even look at it. It's just a convenience for them, you know? Business expense. Whatever it costs, it's all right. Not that we're clipping them or anything, even though it'd be pretty easy, add on some stuff or something, but I bet they don't even check."

"That's the kind of rich I mean," Estelle said. "Rich-rich. So you don't even care what it costs, you know? You don't even bother to ask."

"The boss's like that," Arbuckle said. "He took me to Paris with him?"

"Oh yeah?" Cole said. "I been there. When was that, that you were?"

"Two years ago," Arbuckle said. "That was two years ago."

"We must've been there about the same time," Cole said. "I probably bumped into you, the Arch of Triumph or something. You get over, the Left Bank at all? *Reeve Goshe?*"

"I was working," Arbuckle said. "I didn't get to see that much. That's why he took me there. 'Cause he wanted me, to work."

"That's too bad," Cole said. "It's really pretty there. I think Paris's the prettiest city I ever saw. I'd like to live there some time. I was there three weeks, almost. How long were you there?"

"I was there in October," Arbuckle said.

"Oh," Cole said. "Well, it wouldn't've been the same time then, that we both were there. I was there in April. April in Paris." He looked fondly at Estelle. "That was my last trip, 'fore I started seeing Stelle. Since then, go noplace." He covered her left hand with his right. "Too happy at home."

Sharon scowled. "What did he have you doing in Paris, Eugene," she said. "Just drive him around and stuff?"

"Yeah, well, mostly," Arbuckle said. "See, him and Jennifer, Jennifer's big on this art stuff. Always going around, museums and stuff. That's where I took them, that's where they were going this afternoon. Santa Fe. There's this big exhibition or something, I guess, down in Santa Fe, and they're going there first, and then they're, there're these friends of theirs that live in Santa Barbara or something, and they're meeting them, this guy's got a stretch Rolls, and they're going with them to LA because there's this big new museum there. And then Thursday they're coming home. But the Paris thing, what she wanted to do was get out in the country and see where the painters actually painted their stuff. Normandy, Brittany, Provence, Burgundy—all of them places. And, he didn't want to drive. So that was my job, why he took me. We went all over the place. She's snapping pictures and saying: 'Oh, look at that. Ken, just look at this.' And he's in the back there, reading his book, and saying: 'Uh huh, very nice.' See, he was at D-Day, or right after, at least, and all this country she's looking at, and taking pictures of, well, him and his buddies marched through it, you know? Or rode, I guess. He was

Third Armored. Tanks? And all he wants to see's where he was when the Germans're shooting at him, and that's why he's reading the books and looking the maps all the time. So it was kind of funny, but it was a real nice trip. I enjoyed myself. Learned a lot, too, the same time. Those guys had it rough—I don't care what they say."

"It must've been nice," she said. "Stay in a hotel, have wine—I bet the food was good."

"It was all right," he said. "They got this sauce they put all over everything. Which I could go without. And the wine, well, the only time I could have any was at night, after I got them back the hotel and I was off, okay? I mean, the boss's all right. I'd've wanted a couple beers with lunch, he wouldn't've said anything. But I, I mean, I wasn't used to this car. What he did, before we went over, he bought this Mercedes sedan, all right? The big one? Almost six-liter jobbie? And picked it up over there. Well, this's a powerful car, and I'm not used to it, or to the roads, you know? So I thought: 'Well, Jesus Christ, Buck, be careful. You crack up a sixty-thousand-dollar piece machinery, the boss's liable, be mad. So I didn't have nothing to drink, I had that buggy inna barn at night. And who wants to, you know, drink much alone? I liked the beer pretty good, though. Kronenbourg? Very nice beer. Alsatian."

"Where'd you all stay?" Cole said. "Everybody says: 'Oh, Paris—too expensive.' But I had this place that was very reasonable, up near the Opera, there? Nine bucks a night, and breakfast included."

"Well," Arbuckle said, "we stayed different places, naturally. Because we were going around. Like I said. These big castles on the rivers, châteaus and that stuff. But in Paris they stayed the Plaza, the Plaza-Athénée? And I had a room in a place the other side the Champs-Élysées, right near the garage for the car. It was pretty nice. It was really all right. I like to get up early in the morning, and they don't. So I would do that. Get up early, give the car a quick wash'n wipe, then go down the street this little coffee, pastry shop. And have croissants and coffee and read the American paper. Then when I knew they be getting up, go back to my room, shave and get dressed, go over and pick them up. I liked that trip a lot. Better'n I realized at the time."

"Still, it must've been tough," Cole said, "big car like that, those narrow streets and traffic. And all those crazy Frenchmen driving."

"No worse'n Boston with the big car," Arbuckle said. "Besides, you know, the places we went, there weren't that many big cars. All little cars. Jennifer told me: The French hide their money. Because apparently what they do, they figure your tax bills on what they see you got. So all the rich people're driving around in these tiny little beat-up things that look like your dog wouldn't drive them, and then out in the country they got their Porsches and their BMWs and all their real good stuff." He laughed. "You know the funniest thing?" he said. "You know how you can tell from someone's car in Paris if he's really rich? So rich they could care less about taxes and that shit? You know what those guys drive? It was Jennifer, first noticed this. She says the boss: 'Hey, look at that,' she says. It's the Givenchy store, all right? Where an arm and a leg's the bargain price, and stuff usually costs a lot more? And here's these two Sixty-eight Mustangs and about a Sixty-one, -two, white Corvette, parked out front. Spotless. Absolutely perfect. 'Mint' is what I'm saying. Cherry. Off the showroom floor. And he tells her, the boss does: Those the cars that the *real* rich people drive in Paris. *Those*'re the status symbols. The big Mercedes, the Turbo Porsches, Ferrari Testarossa? Nothin'. You want to show Paris, you have got class, what you want's a black Fifty-seven T-bird with a red interior. Isn't that something? And Jennifer says: 'Ooh, I want one.' And he says: 'No, no place for Buck to drive, and I am on vacation.' I think, I think you took a prime Edsel over there, they'd make you new king in a week."

Musicians began to file onto the stage under the blue lights, finishing conversations and straggling to their seats. The keyboard players warmed up their amplifiers with great groaning swoons and riffs that billowed through the cavern. About two-thirds of those with tickets in the orchestra had taken their seats on the floor, and in the higher dimness of the tiers the narrow aisles had begun to fill.

"We'd better," Arbuckle said, "I think we'd better start thinking about getting our check here, we don't want to miss the show, we come all the way down here to see." He reached for his wallet.

"You got the binoculars, Shan?" Estelle said.

Sharon patted her handbag next to her on the floor. "Right in my bag, Stelle," she said.

Cole took his billfold from his inside jacket pocket. "Gene," he said, "me and Stelle, we discussed this, and we'd like it if you and Shan'd let us take care, the dinner."

"Hey, no," Sharon said. "This's a double date. Me and Gene're paying our way, just like you and Stelle. You guys've got your future plans, and we both understand that. Now don't be a big pain, Steven. Just don't be a big pain."

"Yeah," Cole said, "but the tickets and all. And the parking and gas, and so forth."

"I didn't pay the tickets," Arbuckle said. "I tried to, the boss gave them to me, and he said: 'No. Forget it. You had that ride out the Berkshires and back. Hell, you had *two* rides, and you hadda stay that place. Now this's my treat, all right? And no arguments, okay?' And the same with the parking. I'll hit the guy a fin, the way out, if he's still around. But I don't pay the gas, the oil, the tires, anything. So, let's just split the tab, all right? Let's just split the tab." He beckoned to the waitress. The waitress looked away toward the maître d', caught his eye and nodded toward their table.

The maître d' approached and rested his hands on the backs of the women's chairs. "Everything satisfactory, Mister Arbuckle?" he said. "Ladies? Sir?"

"Oh, véry nice," Arbuckle said. "I was just trying, get the check, 'fore the concert starts."

The maître d' straightened up and smiled. "It's been taken care of, sir," he said. "Mister Farley hopes you all enjoy the concert, and wishes me to tell you ladies and you, sir, that Mister Arbuckle has earned this night, every bit of it, and you should consider yourself his guests."

5

Arbuckle wheeled the Cadillac smoothly out of the ess-curves of Route 95 through Pawtucket and accelerated to sixty-two miles an hour as he crossed the State line into Attleboro, Massachusetts. "Now, this's more like it," Cole said from the left rear seat, his arm around Estelle's shoulders. His voice was thick and he had trouble enunciating sibilants. "Nice car like this, plenty of power, not meant to just loaf along. I was beginning to wonder, you know, we'd get home in time enough to do some things tonight." He drew Estelle more tightly to him. She resisted slightly. "And Jesus, doesn't this leather smell great? Love the smell of new cars."

"It's not new," Arbuckle said. "It's three years old. That's the cleaner and preservative I use. Boss, some his friends, smoke cigars, but the boss don't like his car the next day, smells like old stale cigars. So every time, whichever one he happens to use, except the Jag—that's his own personal car and I keep my hands off it — but all the other ones, I go over them right the next day."

"Jeez," Estelle said, "this guy, does he appreciate you, Gene? I mean, all you do for him? You'd make some man a fine wife."

"Well, I don't know," Arbuckle said. "You tell me. You like that champagne we had two bottles of, tonight? The meal, the concert, the rest of the shit? I would say he does. Four hundred a week, room and board, all the health insurance, the expenses? Not bad. Yeah, I'd say he appreciates, yeah."

"I thought to God," Sharon said, snuggling up next to Arbuckle, "I thought to God I'd die when that attendant in the lot wouldn't take the five."

"I know it," Arbuckle said. " 'Appreciate it, sir, but Mister Farley's taken care of it.' Had this feeling, I was really smart, what I'd do is die tonight, and then I get up the Pearly Gates, all ready to start explaining, 'Well, I know all the bad things I did, God, but I got an explanation.' And God if I get there tonight'll say: 'Never mind, son, it's all taken care of. Mister Farley just hung up.' He's an amazing guy."

"Is he the reason, Gene," Cole said, "why this bucket won't go any faster?"

"Steve," Estelle said, "leave Eugene alone. He's the one who's driving. Honest to God." She sat up straight and moved to the right side of the car. "I don't see why the hell you hadda put that gin in your champagne. There wasn't any reason to do that. You know how you get."

"Hey," Cole said, "because we were talking about Paris, there. Those're French Seventy-fives. And anyway, I was just asking. Thought maybe this amazing guy's got a governor on this thing." He put his forearms on the bolster of the front seat and peered at the speedometer. "We're only going sixty," he said. "Can't it do eighty, at least? I got to go in early tomorrow, set up for Saturday night. I'd like to get in tonight, if I can, that's all right with you, Gene."

"Oh, Steve," Estelle said, "you fucking asshole."

He wheeled on the seat. He grinned. He chucked her under the chin. "What did you say, baby?" he said delightedly. "Did 'oo use bad ranguage? Did 'ums, did'ums, huh?"

She jerked her chin out of his hand. "What I said in three words," she said, "is that when you've had too much to drink, you're a fucking asshole."

"Inna first place," he said, "I didn't have too much. I can drink a bottle champagne myself, easy. No trouble at all, and gin don't affect me, the slightest. I was in Paris, used to drink them alla time. And inna second place, I'm not driving—shouldn't I drink if I want? Old Gene here was a Boy Scout, enough for all of us. All I'm saying now is, let's go a little faster so you and I can fuck." She glared at him. He turned back to face the front. " 'S matter, Gene? Mister *Farley* got a governor on this thing, so his gofer don't get *stopped?*"

Sharon clenched Arbuckle's right forearm tightly and let her breath out loudly. "Leave him *alone,* Steve," Estelle said softly. "He knows what he's doing, and you're too sloshed to care."

"Yeah, Steve," Arbuckle said gently. "Just sit back and enjoy the ride, all right?" The headlights illuminated the pines lining the highway on both sides.

"The only governor that's ever been on this chariot's a guy who used to be. One of the boss's friends. And when Governor Tierney, boss still calls him that, when he was with us one day, he, well, naturally he knows a lot of State cops from when he was in office, and he told me. And he told me, dunno if it's true but I'm acting like it is, that the limit's fifty-five but you're okay at sixty-two. They won't bother you unless you're weaving in and out. So maybe it's not true, but I've been doing sixty-two for quite a while now with no tickets, and no moving-violation surcharges on Mister Farley's insurance, so I plan to keep it up."

"Oh, big fuckin' deal," Cole said, "you drove a governor around. I know a governor, too. You ever hear of Governor Joe D'Ambrose? Used to see him all the time. I was working over Delia's, there, and he came in, oh, he come in every two, three nights or so. Very nice guy, too. Always had the same table. 'Howya doin', Steve,' and everything. He wanted me, go to work for him. He was always, you know, offering me jobs."

Sharon turned in the front seat to stare at Steve. "That's interesting, Steve," she said. "That was when you were going with me. I never heard nothing 'bout that."

"Well," Cole said, "I mean, I didn't necessarily tell you everything that happened, when some guys came in the place."

"Oh, bullshit, Steve," Estelle said. "You're just making all that up. What'd he, he's a lawyer now, right? What's he want you to do, huh? Throw loud drunks out of his office? Make sure the waitresses're splitting tips with the busboys? Get the liquor delivered on time? What could you've done for him?"

"Well," Cole said, "we never actually got down to that, because I was happy, Delia's. But we got to be pretty good friends. He would've gave me a job, his office, if I had've asked him. If I'd've took him up on it. He wasn't kidding me."

"Well," Arbuckle said, "see? that's what I mean. The guy who told me, 'sixty-two,' he's a former governor. So I tend to listen, he thinks. After all, I'm a guy who depends on his license to eat, and it's like the boss always says: 'There's a law against just about everything these days, and you're gonna have to break some of them. But that means you pick your spots, and know which ones you can break, and how much you get away with.' So that is what I do."

Cole sat back against the cushion. "Yeah," he said, " 'depend on your license to eat.' You know what you depend on your license to eat? Shit, is what. You eat shit for this guy Farley. That is what you do. You'd lick his ass for him." He giggled loudly. "How *old*'re you, *Eugene?*" he said. "How fuckin' *old*'re you?"

Arbuckle glanced into the rearview mirror. "I'm forty-one," he said mildly. "Why you ask?"

"Oh, I don't know," Cole said. "I was just wondering. Because all I could think of is that you're acting like a pimply-faced kid, a sixteen-year-old, out on a date in his daddy's car. A *good* little boy. His daddy is proud. He knows he can trust his nice boy." He lunged forward to rest his forearms on the front seat bolster again. "Doesn't it make you feel stupid?

Doesn't it make you feel dumb? 'No, no, just one glass of champagne for the driver. Gives me a headache, anyway.' I mean, aren't you a little *old* for this gig? Being afraid of your boss? Haven't you got any balls?"

Estelle groaned. "Steve," she said, "please shut up now, all right? You've done what you wanted: you've ruined the evening. Now just sit back and enjoy what you've done. Let the rest of us have peace and quiet."

"I don't mind," Arbuckle said, glancing into the rearview again, holding the Cadillac steady at sixty-two. A black Audi Quattro slid by on the left, moving at the 100-mph range of its driving lights. "I know I'm cautious, maybe too much so. I used to think I was bulletproof, too, but then a few things happened to me, and now I don't anymore. And I don't know about Sharon, but my evening's still perfectly fine." They passed a rest area among the trees on the right. Headlights came on in the turnout and another car pulled out about two hundred yards behind them, accelerating until the gap was closed to half of that.

"Fine," Cole repeated, "oh, yeah, very fine. Absolutely aces-up. Top-notch, old bean, top notch. Fuckin' greaser up there sings a whole buncha songs with words no one can understand. . . ."

"It was Spanish, Steve," Sharon said. "Julio is Spanish. That's his native tongue."

"Yeah, 'native tongue,' " Cole said. "How about his native *cock?* That's all you two broads looked at, you and your binoculars. You think I couldn't see where you're pointing them, and laughing? You were

68

looking at his crotch. He could've been singing in *Chinese,* for Christ sake, difference it made to you."

"He did have quite a lot there, didn't he, Shan?" Estelle said thoughtfully. "Whaddaya figure, about seven or so inches, he gets a good boner on?"

Sharon turned in the passenger seat and rested her left forearm on the bolster. "I couldn't tell," she said. "You remember that other guy? Back a few years ago? He used to wear the tight pants too, and then I read somewhere he stuffed them, with an extra pair of socks."

"Oh, no," Estelle said, "no, that much I know. That was the real tool we were looking at tonight. When he sang 'All the Girls'? I think he was getting a little excited himself. You could see it moving a little there, under the fabric."

"Yeah," Sharon said meditatively. "I wonder he wears boxers or jockeys?"

"Or maybe nothing at all," Estelle said. "Just everything hanging nice and loose in there, all ready for action."

"You two shut up," Cole said. "You two just shut up. You're disgusting me."

"Make a deal with you, Steve-oh," Sharon said, "we'll shut up if you will."

"I'll talk all I want," he said. "I'll say anything I want." He belched.

"Too bad our seats weren't a little closer," Estelle said. She leaned forward and patted Arbuckle on the shoulder. "Not that they weren't great seats, Gene, you know? Because they were, great seats. But if they'd been down in the center, on the floor?"

"Yeah," Sharon said, "I *thought* about that. Were

69

you thinking about that, too, when they were running up and throwing their panties up there on the stage?"

"Uh huh," Estelle said. "Only thing I couldn't figure out, though, was whether they were taking them off at their seats, and running up, or if they brought extras in their bags or something. 'Cause I didn't see anybody doing that, you know? Taking them off first."

"They could've taken them off in the Ladies'," Sharon said. "Just go home in their panty hose."

"Fuck you," Cole said. "Fuck both of you."

About two miles south of the northern terminus of 95, the black Audi sat on the right shoulder of the highway, illuminated by the blue lights of a State Police cruiser. A tall cop was handing papers through the window to the Audi driver, a blonde woman who had tear stains on her face. The headlights in the Cadillac's rearview remained steady, a hundred yards back.

"Well, Steve, you already have," Sharon said. "Fucked both of us, I mean. There's no need to get grouchy about it."

"But you're not gonna tonight, Stevie baby," Estelle said grimly. "Not after the way you've behaved. You can just stagger on in to the old commode, and beat it till it's limp."

"You bitch," Cole said. He lunged at her. She fell back against the rear pillar of the roof and shoved the heel of her left hand against his windpipe. He fell back, gagging.

"Don't throw up in this car, Steve," Arbuckle said. "I'll put up with a lot from a friend of Estelle's, but cleaning up vomit is out."

Cole coughed repeatedly and tried to speak. He managed a hoarse croak. Arbuckle took the southbound turnoff onto Route 128, the rumble strips in the roadway sending mild vibrations through the car. The headlights in the rearview stayed one hundred yards back.

"You could hurt me sometime, doing that," Cole said hoarsely.

"You don't seem to understand, Steve," Estelle said. "That's *why* I do that. Because I *want* to hurt you. You don't get like this very often, I know. It's only the second time with me, and . . . how many with you, Shan?"

"Twice also," she said.

"You're a nice guy, Steve," Estelle said, "when you're sober. When you're behaving yourself. We both love you then, but in different ways, and we're glad to have you around. But every so often, you get like this, and then you are not so much fun. You're very nasty, in fact, and you make a girl have to wonder if she really wants to stay with you, you're going to act like this. I mean, do I really want to spend the rest of my life with a guy that ninety percent of the time's a real prince, but every so often's a *shit?*"

"You should listen to her, Steve," Sharon said. "I tried lots of times to tell you, and you wouldn't listen to me. I used to talk to Stelle, when you were still my problem, and she told me then, I tell her now, the exact same thing: You just can't let yourself drink too much. You just can't do it, Steve. 'Cause you become a different person, not the one we like. You

71

remember that night, you tore my blouse, down the Gurnet Inn? 'Show 'em those nipples, baby?' And in front of all those people, I hadda kick you in the balls? I didn't like doing that, Steve. Not at all. It wasn't no fun for me. It was *embarrassing,* go home like that, having Mom ask me what happened."

The headlights remained in place a hundred yards behind the Cadillac as Arbuckle signaled for the southbound exit ramp at South Shore Plaza in Braintree.

"I'm sorry," Cole said hoarsely. He reached his right hand toward Estelle. She slapped it away. "Nothing doing," she said. "No feelies tonight. No nothing tonight. You're being punished, my friend."

He slapped her across the face. She came out of her relaxed position and jumped on him, her nails clawing for his face. Arbuckle took the exit ramp smoothly and continued on to the right turn at the Sheraton Tara Hotel. The car behind him followed. Arbuckle pulled into the parking lot on the easterly side and stopped at the white 1980 Trans Am parked against the fence. The trailing car pulled into the parking lot of the office building across the drive and stopped next to an arclight standard. It was a Massachusetts State Police cruiser. Arbuckle glanced into the rearview. He shut the engine off and opened the driver's side door. He stepped to the left rear door and opened it. Cole's head, his face bloodied, lolled out. Arbuckle grasped him under the arms and hauled him out from under Estelle. She tried to scramble after him. Arbuckle pushed her back. He stood Cole up. "Just stay in there and get yourself dressed, Stelle," he said. "Who's got the keys to that

72

wreck?" Cole stood with his brocade jacket unbuttoned and his ruffled shirt out of his pants, weaving in place in Arbuckle's grasp and making grunting sounds. Twice he reached out feebly and shoved Arbuckle on the shoulder.

"He has," Estelle said. "Dunno which pocket. Usually in his right front."

"Well," Arbuckle said, "I'm not gonna frisk the silly bastard." He released Cole. Cole lurched, but recovered his balance and stood blinking in the harsh white light. "Steve, you dope," Arbuckle said, "you in there? Gimme the goddamned keys. Stelle's gonna drive you home. I assume she's gonna drive you. I would leave you here for dog meat, or better yet, I'd *let* you drive. Alone." He grabbed Cole by the left shoulder and turned him so that he faced the police cruiser across the way. "You know how far you'll get before that big old cop jumps you? Maybe through one set of lights, you don't hit nothing. Then he'll take you to the can, which is where you ought to be."

Cole said nothing. He licked blood from his lips and snuffled.

"Come on," Arbuckle said, "gimme the fuckin' car keys. I haven't got all night."

"Fuck you," Cole said. He took two unsteady steps. He swung a looping right at Arbuckle, missed, nearly lost his balance and then recovered It. He fished in his left front pants pocket and pulled out a set of keys. "See?" he said triumphantly, waving them at Arbuckle. "Fooled you, silly bastard. Fuckin' asshole. Daddy's boy." He raised his voice to a roar. "Stelle," he said, "get out here. Get your pussy out here now. Goin' home for hot wet poon-

73

tang. Come on, babe, good times roll." He began to sing.

Estelle emerged from the back seat with her sweater neatly in place and her gold chains carefully arranged. "Hit him," she said softly to Arbuckle.

"You're sure," he said. "I'm taking your word, he's not always like this. I don't want another enemy. Especially one that's dating my girlfriend's favorite sister."

"I'm sure," she said. "It's the only way, make him listen to reason, he gets like this. I'd do it myself, but it's a four-mile drive and the most I can knock him out for's about two. 'Less I got something to use. I hit with a stick of firewood one night, down in Duxbury, and thought I finally killed him. Hadda leave him in the car that night. Coldcock him."

"Okay," Arbuckle said. "Mister Cole," he said, "can you walk over to your car?"

Cole interrupted his song. "Car?" he said. "Sure. Walk to my car. Stelle, there you are. Come on, let's go home. Fuck our brains out inna moonlight. Do it inna road. Do all them real good things."

She took him by the elbow and escorted him unsteadily to the right rear fender of the Trans Am. She turned him and he rested his buttocks on it. He resumed his singing. She brushed imaginary lint from her hands. She stepped back. "Okay," she said to Arbuckle. "Whack him so he falls off towards the door. He's out of commission, then I'll take the keys, unlock the door, we'll shovel him in and that's it."

"I'm right-handed," Arbuckle said. "That's calling for a left."

"He's got a glass jaw," she said. "Can't take a

74

punch. Belt him."

Arbuckle shook his head. He cocked his left hand and clenched his fist. He reconsidered. He dropped his left hand and clenched his right fist. He brought the fist back over his left shoulder and then backhanded Cole with it under his right jaw. Cole's head snapped back, then forward. He began to collapse gradually toward the ground. Estelle wrenched the car keys out of his left hand. Arbuckle held him weak-kneed but semi-upright under the armpits. She opened the passenger door and grabbed Cole by the shoulders of his jacket. Pulling and dragging they loaded him onto his left side into the passenger seat and shut the door.

"Whew," she said. "Heavy bastard. Mean drunks should all be flyweights—that's what I think. Thanks a lot, Bucky, all right? Sorry Rocky here fucked up the evening."

"Safe home," he said. "Oughta do something though, 'bout the rust, those rocker panels."

She unlocked the driver's side door. "Huh," she said, "tonight what I'd do's take it down to the crusher, him in it, and never see either one them again."

Arbuckle got back into the Cadillac and waited until Estelle had started the Trans Am and started out of the parking lot. Then he started the Cadillac, turned around, and headed onto the driveway. The State Police cruiser's lights came on and the driver stuck his left hand out the window, making a STOP signal. Arbuckle drove the Cadillac across the drive and pulled up next to the cruiser. He could not see the trooper's face in the darkened car. He said: "Yes sir?"

"Everything under control, sir?" the cop said.

"Yes sir," Arbuckle said.

"Way it looked to me, sir," the cop said. "Have a pleasant evening."

6

At 6:40 in the evening, Phil Morse chose an isolated parking place for his metallic blue Acura coupe on the middle level of the garage underneath the LaFayette Mall and removed a black vinyl attaché case from the trunk. He went to Winter Place. He walked down to the second set of doors on his right and entered the Locke Ober Café. There were three men and a solitary woman seated at the bar; two of the men and the woman had newspapers. The man in the middle sipped thoughtfully from a Manhattan and stared frowning into the reflection of himself in the mirror behind the bar.

Morse placed the case next to the chair second from the door, leaving two vacant between himself and the woman. He pulled out the first chair and sat down. The bartender placed a cocktail napkin in front of him. "You'll be having dinner, sir?" he said.

"No," Morse said, "just killing a little time."

"Because you can check your case," the bartender

said.

"It's all right," Morse said. "I'll keep it."

"Fine, sir," the bartender said. "What can I get you?"

"Coca-Cola," Morse said. "With a squeeze?"

"Coming right up," the bartender said.

At 7:35, Morse paid for two servings of Coca-Cola, got down from the bar chair, picked up his case, and left the café. The woman, glancing irritably at her watch, remained. The men had been replaced by small groups of jovial men and several couples. Morse turned right on Winter Place and took a left on Winter Street. He turned left on Tremont Street and walked down two and one-half blocks to the GENUINE New York Style Deli. As he approached the restaurant, he paused and changed the setting of the three-digit lock on the case from "6-6-1" to "7-8-9." He pushed down on the clasp-release button. Inside the case a machine beeped.

At the back of the restaurant there was a glass-shrouded service area where large pieces of roast beef and corned beef sat in deep aluminum pans, surrounded by dishes of steamed sauerkraut and frankfurts. There were three men in white uniforms behind the counter, serving customers who pushed their brown plastic trays along a three-rail chromium rack.

Buster Feeley was sitting with another man in the last booth on the right, moving his hams on the red vinyl seat and looking displeased in the harsh white light. He had one-third of a corned beef sandwich on rye before him, and half a bottle of Miller Real

Draft. There were two Miller empties to his left. He stood up as much as possible behind the white Formica table and offered his hand. His suit was brown flannel, and it buckled at the lapels over his yellow shirt. "Yer late," he said.

Morse slid into the opposite bench. He put the attaché case next to him. "Sorry," he said. "I hadda meeting. Ran late. Didn't have the number here."

Feeley resumed his seat. He gestured with his right hand. " 'S here's Jim Dacey," he said. He picked up the remains of the sandwich. "Guy that I told you about. Asked you to meet here, six-fuckin'-thirty. I'm supposed to be down Florian Hall, right this very minute, buying the beers for the new cops, all right? The boss's gonna be pissed off at me for this. I'm already pissed off at you."

"Hey," Morse said, "I already apologized. I said I got hung up and there was nothing I could do."

"Yeah," Feeley said. "Well that oughta fix it up just fine with Sonny, don't you think: 'Sorry, Yer Honor—Mister Morse had a little problem, so I stiffed the new cops, okay? They won't mind, next time you run. They know how busy we all are.' He'll tell me: Next time I need something, I can go piss up a rope."

"You're not making the clock run backwards, you know," Morse said, "you're sitting there ranking on me. Why don't you do what you came here to do? Introduce this gentleman and then get your ass out of here."

"I'm staying the fuck where I am," Feeley said. "I started this thing, which I now see's a piss-poor idea

79

from the start, and I'm gonna goddamn finish it. Dacey? Morse. Morse? Dacey."

"Mister Dacey," Morse said. He extended his hand. Dacey was about forty. He was approximately six feet tall and he weighed about one hundred and seventy pounds. He had black hair and his blue eyes were clear. He wore a muted plaid blazer, grey flannel slacks, and a button-down yellow oxford-cloth shirt with a wool challis tie. Most of a Miller Real Draft was in the glass before him. "Sorry to keep you waiting. It was unavoidable."

"No harm done," Dacey said, exhibiting immaculate teeth and shaking hands. "Just appreciate you seeing me. At all."

"Hey," Morse said, "any friend of Buster's, right? You can see how close we are. Got to be a friend of mine. Can't say I'm too clear, what you wanna see me *for,* but life's an endless discovery, right? Me and Admiral Byrd."

"Get you a drink?" Dacey said.

Morse held up his left hand. "Long's there's no hooch in it," he said. "My family's part Indian or something. 'Jewish Comanches' we call it—none of us can handle the stuff. They got any seltzer, this so-called New York Deli?"

Dacey laughed. He started to get out of the booth. "Probably not," he said. "Soft drink, they don't? Coke, or some ginger?"

Morse shrugged. "Or coffee, black coffee, or tea. Or: just nothing. I'm doing all right." Dacey got up from the booth and headed for the counter.

"Where the hell you been?" Feeley said, leaning

forward. "I told you this guy was important. You're over a whole hour late. Whaddaya think, I do this for fun? You think I use my contacts like this, I'm doing it for laughs? I'm tryin', do you a favor. You and your asshole boss. You guys never used to act like this, Sonny was still getting mentioned, he might run for governor. You wanna be careful, you know, you two just write him off. He's still got a lot of weight in this town, and you never know what might happen, couple years or so."

"What the hell're you talking about, Buster?" Morse said.

Feeley leaned back. "Oh," he said, "playing dumb? You know what I'm talking about. I told you onna phone. There's the potential here, make some money. I told you all of that. This guy's in a position, well, I could see a finder's fee, and Sonny likes rich guys from out the city—that he don't know that many of. These guys, this guy's a selectman in Cardiff. You know what they all got in Cardiff? Money. Nothing but money. Which means they got good *taste*—they can afford to. You wanna sell poles, the light company? Forget it in Cardiff—all buried. All the power lines and bone lines, all underground. They don't think overhead power lines look pretty. One them might fall down on top one of their fuckin' Volvos or something. Pipes're probably fucking platinum. Last for fucking ever. Electricity and phones? In Cardiff all that shit it looks like comes from God. *They* all come from God. You know what their fucking zoning is? Since Nineteen-sixty-one, all right? Strictly residential. The Cardiff Depot's *it*. For industry, I

81

mean. No more of that shit. Nothing now but four hundred K houses, on at least two-acre lots."

"So what?" Morse said. "I'm not inna market for a house, and if I was, I couldn't afford it. Why am I meeting this guy?"

"They want cable," Feeley said. "They want cable fucking TV. They're not getting the opera, often as they like. They wanna be able see Congress, every goddamned day. And they want the fucking *cable* fucking *buried,* in the ground. In the platinum pipes with the phone lines. For this they need a guy to dig up the goddamned streets. Paved with gold. You imagine how much dough these guys're whipping off the people with the cables? They're the ones, get to decide. Who gets the goddamned franchise."

"So why talk to me?" Morse said. "I'm just a guy works construction. I don't know nothing, TV."

"Because they're *greedy,* all right?" Feeley said. "They want more. They figure, you know, they tell the guy that gets the franchise who he hires to dig the trench, and you got, easy, forty miles of trenches to be dug, he's gonna take the hint and do it. Hire the guy they recommend. They're very particular, their ditches there in Cardiff. They like 'em dug with nice neat edges, filled in right and paved. Everything nice and neat, just like it was before."

"You had too much beer, I think," Morse said.

"The hell're you talking about?" Feeley said, as Dacey came back. "Just what the hell're you talking about?"

Dacey put a tall Coca-Cola glass of soda water in front of Morse. He grinned. He sat down. "Seltzer it ain't," he said. "Club soda it is. Mister Feeley here brief you a little more?"

Morse drank some of the soda and nodded. "Wasn't what I expected, though," he said.

"What exactly did you expect?" Dacey said.

"Well," Morse said, "I was under the impression, my boss, that I was coming here to meet you tonight to see whether we'd be interested in bidding on some excavating work."

"That's what you are," Dacey said. "That's why I drove in tonight. Mayor Donovan, I know Sonny from my daughter's school. She's a sophomore at Assumption Academy, and his daughter's in my daughter's class. Has been for a couple years. So they have these Parents' Days and so forth, and naturally the parents of classmates tend to sort of congregate with each other. And I got to know him."

"I only met him a couple times," Morse said. "Seemed like a very nice guy."

"Sonny's the salt the earth," Feeley said.

"And we got to talking," Dacey said. "This's last month, they had a tea to start the year and Sonny Donovan was there. And I know he had his hands full with this cable thing in town, and jeez, us hicks in the sticks're up to our ears with this thing. Absolute babes in the woods. So I said to him: Is he, is there any part the city where they're burying the cable? And he says: 'Yeah, all over the place.' Beacon Hill and so forth. And I said: 'Well, cripes, who does that kind of work?' And he tells me various companies that the cable people get, 'And they do a lousy job,' he said. 'Beacon Hill, the other day, some asshole with a backhoe hit an Edison main line and knocked out everyone's power. Took 'em almost a day, get the juice back on. See, that's where we made our mistake. We should've insisted, we keep the right to choose the subcontractors. Get somebody who knows how to do things right, that's dependent on keeping *us* happy. 'Stead of just letting these cable guys just go and cheap it out, hire the cheapest outfit they can find. Who then tinplates the job and get all my citizens pissed off. They don't just call the Edison when their lights go out and their street's dug up for days. They know how to find me, right off, and I can tell you, friend, they do. You're a sap if you let that happen. You want those folks directly responsible to you.'

"And I asked him," Dacey said, "well, if he could do that, if he'd thought of it at the time or he could do it now, who'd he get? And he said: 'Arrow.' And I said, keep in mind that all I am's a salesman. You want to know something about the bond market? Metal futures? Commodities Index? That I can help you with. But this selectman thing's just something I do. It's really just public service, and it's that way for the other four people on the board, too. We don't know anything about this stuff. We're all in over our heads. Want to do what's best for the town, but at the same time we really don't know what that is. And Sonny said: 'Look, get ahold of this guy,' meaning Mister Feeley, 'and he'll put you in touch the right people. Let him walk you through this thing.' So that's what I did."

"Well, look," Morse said, "naturally we're glad,

Mister Farley and Mister Daniels, we're all glad Arrow's being considered here. And we'd certainly like to see some specs or something, give us some detailed information, what the job entails. But one the things you've got to keep in mind here is that the reason Mayor Donovan recommends us is that we do good work. And we can do good work because we pace ourselves. It's very seldom, there're very few people we've done work for, that can look you in the eye and say: 'They didn't have the right equipment.' Or: enough of it. Or we didn't have the manpower. Because we always do. We're very careful all the time, make sure that we can do a job, and do the job right, before we take it on. Hell, 'fore we even bid."

"I can get you that," Dacey said. "That's no problem at all."

"Okay," Morse said. He removed a wallet from his right inside jacket pocket and took a business card from it. "This's where you can get in touch with me," he said. "You ship me the specs and any plans you've got, and either I'll get back to you or Mister Daniels will, and we'll come out and look at it. And we'll tell you if we think we can handle it, the time frame and everything. Because I got to warn you: you're pretty far away from our normal area, and we could find we've got some problems tying up equipment on a job that's a good forty, fifty miles from our central plant. You talk about flatbedding that stuff around, it costs. You may find you don't want to pay the extra we'd have to charge over what somebody closer to you, maybe just as good, could do the same job for."

Dacey took the card. He put it in his pocket. He glanced at Feeley. He looked back at Morse. "Well, this's good," he said. "Now, uh, I'm, as I say, kind of new at this. Okay?"

"Mister Dacey," Morse said, "every job is new. To everyone involved. The day you start thinking you know all the answers, that's the day you start getting into trouble."

"These major projects," Dacey said, "can have substantial impact on the local economy. As I understand it, at least."

"No question about it," Morse said. "You start this thing, you might as well tell your police chief his men're going to have all the overtime they can handle, probably for the next year or so."

"And you pay that, of course," Dacey said.

"It's easier for everyone, we do," Morse said. "We open our books to your auditors, naturally. But if it goes the long way around—we hire the cops; we submit vouchers to the town; town has to act on them and then bill us for the charges; we pay the town and the town pays the cops—it can take six, eight weeks to get a guy his check for doing extra work. And that's too long. You get a lot of people mad at you, you do that, and then you're halfway through the job and they won't work for you until they get their dough. Which puts you at a standstill. So it's better, we just pay them. Settle up every two weeks or so. Keep everybody happy."

"And your insurance and bonding," Dacey said.

"We're fully covered on every job," Morse said.

"Where," Dacey said, "how do you secure that

protection?"

"It depends on the job," Morse said. "We used to buy as much coverage we possibly could right in the place we were working. 'Cause that meant we're putting back into the community some of what we're taking out. Because what the hell, right? The rates're pretty much standard, no matter where you buy the coverage. But these new laws you got now, you know? They can be a real pain in the butt. Back years ago we could buy a bond through a selectman's brother-in-law, ran an insurance agency. But now that's a conflict — it's illegal, family member benefits from a contract his relative let out. And a lot of people don't know that. So we have to be extra careful."

"What about," Dacey said, "I'd imagine a company with your cash-flow situation probably's in the money market quite a lot."

"Well, we have to be," Morse said. "You got your progress payments coming in as you go along, and you're financing the next stage on the proceeds, the last one. So you're going to spread it out, and the way you do that's invest in short-term securities and then cash 'em out as you go along."

"Do you use any one firm for that?" Dacey said.

"We use lots of different ones," Morse said. "What we do's ask our general counsel whether this particular thing looks okay to him. And if he says it does, that we do. It's like the insurance commissions, you know? There's a lot of commission overhead on this kind of thing, but it's almost all the same, no matter who you're paying. Just an example here, all right?

You're talking, say, a twenty-mill job. Well, our experience is we're gonna pay out probably somewhere between forty and sixty, maybe seventy-five thousand, just to keep things balanced, the books, in the course of your average year.

"Does it matter to us who we pay that? No, as long as the rates're the same and the brokers give us good service. But does it matter to them, besides of course they like getting the money? Well, it could, and that could make it matter to us, if somebody decided we got the deal because we got somebody in our pocket by promising commissions. It could matter in terms of some people going to jail, and there is no job and no commission on the earth that's worth that kind of trade."

"Well, that's good to hear," Dacey said. Feeley looked stunned. He wet his lips and drank some beer. "It speaks well for your company that you're so careful about this."

"Well," Morse said, grasping the attaché case and sliding out of the booth, "as you already know, I'm running late. But I'll expect to hear from you, then?"

"I'll be in touch," Dacey said, extending his right hand. "Very nice to've met you."

"Yeah," Feeley said, "thanks a lot for coming by."

Dacey and Feeley without talking watched Morse leave the GENUINE and head south on Tremont.

"Whaddaya think?" Feeley said, finishing his beer.

"I think that's one smart bastard," Dacey said. "You go fishing for that gentleman, you'd better carry a harpoon, and you better hit him your best shot, your first one."

"You don't think," Feeley said wistfully, "you don't think maybe, when you play the tapes back, it's gonna sound, you know? Different?"

Dacey snickered. "In the first place," he said, "it would not. It never sounds 'different,' meaning 'better,' when you don't think you hooked him and then you play it back. It sounds worse. And in the second place, there aren't any tapes."

"Well, of course there's *tapes,*" Feeley said. "I got all this crap strapped to me. You got all that crap strapped to you. We got enough equipment, the two of us, send messages to Mars. The truck's right down the street. They got enough tape in that truck to wrap around the world."

"That's right," Dacey said, "but I'll bet you a chocolate soda, Buster, there's nothing on those tapes."

"Because he was too cute," Feeley said.

"Because the tapes are blank," Dacey said.

"They worked, it was working all right we came in," Feeley said. "Didn't you tell me that? You had the earplug there, and they said it was coming in fine? I heard you tell me that."

"It was coming in fine, and going out fine, before he came in here with his briefcase," Dacey said.

"I don't get it," Feeley said.

"I was trying," Dacey said, "all the time he was sitting there with the briefcase on the seat—how many people you know put their briefcase on the seat beside them, they sit down?"

"I dunno," Feeley said. "I never thought about it."

"Very few," Dacey said. "They stow it on the floor. But he didn't. He wanted, right up beside him. Because that way if we're miked below the waist, it'll block transmission there. And if we're wired above the waist, it will also get them there."

"I don't follow," Feeley said.

"That's an antisurveillance kit he had there," Dacey said. "It's got a jammer in it, so you can't transmit when it's around. That holy little speech at the end was just in case something got through — whipped cream on the sundae."

"You're shittin' me," Feeley said. "How can that be legal? You got, you got your warrant thing there. You're a federal cop. And you're telling me this guy can just go around with a wonderful box and stop you from doing, you do? How can he do that? Why didn't you, how come you didn't just reach over there and say: 'Well, I'll take this item, Mister Morse, you don't mind too much'?"

Dacey shrugged. "In the first place," he said, "the warrant didn't say I could search him — it says I can bug him, is all. In the second place, I don't know for sure what's in there, so I couldn't just grab it. And in the third place, until he knows, and we can prove he knew, that he's obstructing me, he's got a right to assume that anyone who bugs him's not a cop, and is breaking the law. Which means he can defend himself, his privacy against illegal bugging."

"Jesus," Feeley said.

Dacey laughed. "No," he said. "A 'Jewish Comanche' — that was what he said."

Three days later Asst. US Atty. William S. Pratt

sent a memorandum down the hall of the US Attorney's office in the federal courthouse in Boston. It went to Deputy US Atty. David M. Curley. It reported the failure of electronic surveillance measures to secure evidence incriminating Philip Morse in an ongoing scheme of bribery and extortion. Pratt recommended that the investigation be abandoned. Curley wrote his response on the bottom half of the second page: "No. You know how Harry feels about this. Harry thinks Sonny Donovan's bad. He thinks we can prove it. He thinks Farley's the way. Okay, so Morse wasn't. Think of something else, because here in Dodge City, we do what Harry Dodge wants done."

7

The headquarters of the Arrow Construction Company occupied slightly more than three sandy acres surrounded by pines on the easterly side of Route 4 north of Waterford, Massachusetts. A ten-foot chain-link fence topped with three strands of barbed wire surrounded three large green heavy equipment barns, a two-story wooden frame office building, and six thirty-foot piles of loam, sand, crushed stone, salted sand, firewood and used bricks. There was a thirty-foot motorized gate opening onto the highway.

Late in the morning, Victor Champa drove through the gate and parked his blue Buick Skyhawk between a black Jaguar XJ6 and a green Oldsmobile Cutlass Ciera under the picture window at the front of the office and emerged into a light drizzle with his shoulders hunched. He wore a grey tweed jacket and grey polyester pants. He hurried to the door and entered.

There was a counter faced with maple-grained Formica and topped with white Formica to his left. Behind the counter there were two grey steel desks where two women worked over piles of fan-folded computer printouts alternately striped pale green and white. Both of them wore eyeglasses with spangled elaborate frames and black neck-cords. Each of them had a tightly permed hairdo; the one to his left had chosen a rose tint, and the one to his right a blue. He went to the counter and placed his hands on it.

The woman to his left raised her right hand with the forefinger extended. "With you in a minute," she said. She traced her left forefinger down the sprocket-holed margin of the sheet in front of her, found an entry, and punched it into a computer keyboard that translated it into green light on a screen in front of her. She nodded in satisfaction. She stood up, rubbing the palms of her hands down the seams of her wool skirt. She came to the counter. "Can I help you?" she said.

"Uh," he said, "Mister Farley?"

"I'm sorry," she said pleasantly, "Mister Farley's out on the job today. Him and Mister Daniels both. Could I maybe help you with something? Or, Mister Morse's here, out in the back someplace."

The man jerked his head toward the parking area outside. "I, ah," he said, "I understood Mister Farley, that the Jag was one his cars."

The woman's eyes narrowed behind the eyeglasses. She removed them and let them drop against her chest. She stepped back from the counter. "Who're you?" she said in a low voice.

"That doesn't matter," he said. "I just got, I got to see Mister Farley."

She nodded. "You've got something you want to give him, I bet," she said. He allowed his discomfort to show on his face. "Uh huh," she said, "it never fails. That bitch gets out, the next thing we know, we got one of you guys in here, pretending he doesn't know what's going on and acting like a jerk." She rested the heels of her hands on the counter and lowered her shoulders. She stared at him. "Lemme tell you something, Mister, all right? Just lemme tell you something. And lemme *finish* telling you, before you start to talk.

"You're gonna tell me this's your first time here, and all you're doing's following orders. And you're gonna gimme the name of some lawyer, I never heard of, my life. And you're gonna tell me how that explains, how come you're raising this fuss. And then later on, Mister Farley comes back, after you are long gone. And Mister Farley explodes, all over me, because what you're doing is wrong."

The man started to speak. "Lemme finish," she said. "I didn't interrupt your work. You interrupted mine. You don't like the speech, well, get the hell out of here — fine. But you want some advice here, might help you later, you will listen to me.

"For your information, Mrs. Farley does this every time she gets out. Gets out the hospital. Mrs. Farley's a nice woman, when she's okay. But she hasn't really been right now for over twenty years. So she has to go to the hospital, so they can keep an eye on her. What she does, when she gets out, there's nothing on her mind. Which used to be because of the electroshock, or drugs, or whatever they happened to use to get her back, an even keel. What it is now, I don't know. So it takes her a week, maybe two, maybe three, start getting her act back together. But she's got the time, Lord knows, with nothing else to do, and sooner or later she remembers, what her situation is and then what it used to be. She liked 'used to be' better, which is reasonable, but she thinks she can get it back, which is not.

"That's when she goes back, when she calls the *last* lawyer that had guys like you driving us crazy when he first came on the case. Until we taught him, and you guys, how to handle this. But the last lawyer's had enough. By now the stars're out of his eyes. He knows by the time she gets back to him he isn't gonna get rich, fighting Mister Farley—in fact he's gonna probably have to sue Mrs. Farley himself, he ever expects to get paid. And get back the fees he paid constables, too, to butt their way into our work. So he says, no, he won't start again, and she has to find somebody else. And she does. There's always another clown out there that didn't get the word, and he takes the case, and he gets all sweaty, and he writes out a paper for you. And here we go again.

"Now I don't know who you're working for," she said. "If you told me his name, I most likely wouldn't recognize it anyway. But I'm telling you, and you tell him for me, I don't care how good he can bark, the two of you got the wrong tree. The way you handle this, the way you save everybody lots of grief and your boss there some money, is by calling up Jack Corey, all right? You gotta piecea paper?"

He shook his head and then looked puzzled. He reached into his pocket. She reached for a memo pad on the counter. "Never mind," she said, "I'll write it down myself. That's John Corey, and he's a lawyer, and his office's in Boston but he's also got one down the office complex in the mall. Which is south of here." She printed the name on the pad. "And this's his phone number here, and this's the number in Boston. And what you do, or your boss does, instead of going through all this foolishness with summonses, what you do is call Jack up and give him the latest news. Which is naturally that Nellie Farley's out again, as Mister Farley of course knew, and she's hired a new lawyer to make his life miserable, and the case is on for hearing again. And give him the date and the time, or his secretary if he's not in, and that's all you have to do."

She tore the paper off the pad and proffered it to the man. "Okay?" she said brightly. "Makes sense now, don't you think? Saves everybody all this grief, and gets the same result."

The man recoiled from the paper. "It's not that," he said. "It's not, I don't know what you're talking about."

"You don't," she said flatly. "Okay, my friend, then you tell me: What are *you* talking about?"

"Well, for starters," the man said, "I don't know anything about this Mrs. Farley business. Nobody said anything to me about no Mrs. Farley. What I am looking for, I am looking for Mister Farley himself. Or . . . whadda you do here?"

She sighed. "My name is Edith Keller. And what

do I do here? Well, as you can see, when I'm not standing around yakking with strangers, I run the place, all right?"

"What's your title?" he said. "You got a title, maybe?"

She nodded. "Sure," she said. "Not that it's got anything to do with anything, but I'm clerk, the corporation. Also: treasurer."

"Right," he said, taking two white papers folded twice in half from his inside jacket pocket, "you'll do." He separated them and handed one of them to her. He put the second one down on the counter and took a pen from his pocket. "You are hereby subpoenaed as the Keeper of the Records, Arrow Construction Company, Route Four, Waterford, District of Massachusetts, to appear before the federal grand jury at Boston on October the third at ten o'clock, and to bring with you all records and documents called for by this subpoena." He frowned and wrote her name, and the place and time at the foot of the copy he retained. He refolded it and put it in his pocket. He clasped his hands on the counter. He smiled. "Any questions, Ma'am?" he said.

"What the hell is this about?" she said, scanning the paper.

"You now know as much as I do," he said. "All I know's that I'm a Deputy United States Marshal, and I was ordered to serve that subpoena on either Mister Kenneth Farley or the Keeper of the Records of the Arrow Construction Company, and that's what I have done."

"But what's it about?" she said.

"It's about the United States against John Doe,"

he said. "The federal grand jury, well, the US Attorney, wants to take a look at your records. You got any questions, Mister Farley's got any questions, I suggest you call Assistant US Attorney William Pratt. His name's at the bottom, the page, and so's his private extension." He tugged gently at the paper and pointed out the name and the number. "See? And I'm sure Mister Pratt'll be more'n happy, answer all your questions." He stepped back. "Nice talking to you, Ma'am," he said. "Hope you all have a very nice day."

A steady drizzle fell from a flat grey sky above the Berkshires. Fanny Clancy waited with her suitcase in the solarium of The Foothills Inn, her tan raincoat spread over one of the green wicker chairs facing the iron fountain. The owner, a slim man in his middle forties with a narrow grey mustache, came in from the foyer, clearing his throat. He took one of the chairs on the opposite side of the fountain. He stared at Fanny.

"Yes?" she said, drawling it out.

"Miss Demers says Mrs. Farley's still sleeping," he said. "And that she doesn't want to leave her alone. So she asks you to wait until Mrs. Farley wakes up and gets dressed. And then they will come down."

"Thank you," Clancy said.

He gazed at her. "As usual, we've prepared lunches for the three of you," he said. "Club sandwiches. I hope that's satisfactory. And mineral water, of course."

"Entirely," she said.

"As a matter of what I hope is forgivable curiosity," he said, "how long do you and Miss Demers expect Mrs. Farley to be a guest here?"

"It's hard to say," Fanny said. "The last time she needed a rest of any duration, in a place such as this, it was about, a little over four months."

"I see," he said.

"Does that present a problem?" she said. "You don't seem overcrowded."

"Oh, no, no," he said. "Not at the present time. But depending on when we get snow, of course." He laughed sardonically. "Assuming this isn't one of those years in which we get no snow, the inn begins to fill up to capacity on a regular basis, and we need every one of our rooms."

"For what?" Fanny said.

"Well," he said, "for our regulars, the ones who come back every year."

"What do they give you for those rooms?" Fanny said. "I assume it's money, isn't it?"

"Well, yes, of course," he said. "And goodwill, of course. At least we hope. If they have a good time here, we hope they'll tell their friends. Who may even, for some eccentric reason," — he grimaced — "choose to visit at another season of the year. When we're nowhere near as crowded."

"It's my understanding, Mister Sherburne," Fanny said, "that money is what you're being paid for the suite that Mrs. Farley occupies, along with Miss Demers and me."

"Well, ah, yes," he said, "that's correct."

"Money's money," she said. "What difference does it make whether the money comes from some skiers who've never been here before, and may never come again—or proselytize their friends to come, either—or from Mrs. Farley?"

"Well," he said, clearing his throat, "there's, ah, the matter of the bar. Most of our guests are reasonably temperate in their drinking habits, but in the winter we do serve *glug* and other beverages like that, and we do make a certain profit on it."

"I should imagine," Fanny said.

"Now," he said, "the incident the other night . . . well, it was most unfortunate. I don't know if you've heard."

"Oh," she said grimly, "I've heard, all right."

"Well," he said, "what I mean to say is that we can't have that happening during the holidays, and the school vacations, and that sort of thing. A lot of families come here, people with young children. We can't have that sort of display. She was reeling around the lobby here, announcing that the parrot's the devil and he's a spy for her husband and his lawyers. And I'm coming naked into her room late at night and getting into bed with her and trying to rape her. Now, fortunately it was well after the other guests had retired, and since all three of them're quite hard of hearing, I doubt that any of them heard her." He paused. "Although I did get a couple of rather strange looks the next day from The Reader."

" 'The Reader'?" Fanny said.

He chuckled. "We call Mrs. Whitlock 'The Reader,' he said. "She always has a book with her. She's a remarkably slow reader, but she plugs away at it. I'm not sure she can see, as a matter of fact. I think it may be that she's vain, too vain to admit that her eyesight is gone. So she brings a book with her everywhere. But her hearing, well, she doesn't shout as loud as the other ladies, when she wants something, so she may have heard."

"Yes," Fanny said.

"Well," he said, "you see what I mean. Naturally we're very appreciative of having Mrs. Farley, and yourself and Miss Demers, as guests. But we're concerned about the possibility that Mrs. Farley may, well . . . We worried she might do that again when the skiers are here."

"She was able to do it," Fanny said, "because you failed to keep part of your bargain. Which was to make sure that the bar was locked up."

"And you, well, Miss Demers," he said, "failed to keep part of yours. Which was to keep her in her room at night. Miss Demers told me she was asleep."

"It was after three in the morning," Fanny said. "I imagine you were, yourself."

"Yes," he said, "I was."

"And the reason Mrs. Farley was able to leave the room," Fanny said, "was that you had foolishly provided her with a key the day before."

"I gave her no key," he said.

"No, you didn't *give* her one," Fanny said, "but you left the duplicate on the hook behind the desk, and you left the desk unattended, and the woman can read numerals, you know.

"Then," Fanny said, "once she was able to get out of the room, she was able to investigate the security measures you had taken to keep her out of the bar. And she found that by turning the doorknob, she could get in. And that by taking the key next to the cash register, she could open the liquor cabinets. Mrs. Farley is ill, Mister Sherburne, but Mrs. Farley isn't stupid. You're taking seventy-five dollars a week to keep her out of that liquor supply, and you didn't do your damned job. Now you're complaining about the results? I should think you might well apologize, instead."

He frowned. He leaned forward. "Miss Clancy," he said, "let me be frank. Mrs. Farley's ill, I know. Ordinarily she's no trouble, but she is noticeably ill, visibly disabled. She doesn't, she isn't, well, *normal*. She isn't *right*. The people who come here to ski come here to have fun. And we have to make sure they do have fun, or they won't come here anymore. Some day Mrs. Farley will leave, and if we don't still have our regular customers, we'll go out of business. We can't get the reputation of being a rest camp or a halfway house for the mentally disturbed. It'll ruin us."

"Miss Demers," Fanny said, "is a registered nurse. She was formerly on the staff of a large hospital in New York. She remains in close contact with her former colleagues."

He looked puzzled. "Yes?" he said. "Was she a psychiatric nurse?"

"Intensive care," Fanny said. "Miss Demers, soon after she arrived, saw a man taking the sun in the back, beside the pool."

"I see," Sherburne said.

"He looked sick, she thought," Fanny said, "and when she tried to speak to him, he ran away. To your quarters. But she has very good eyesight, and she hadn't seen him before, and she wondered why that was. So the next time she spoke to one of her former colleagues, she mentioned the strange occurrence, and described what she had seen. And received what she thought was the probable explanation both for his appearance and his — your — wish that he not mingle with the guests."

"I see," Sherburne said.

"Now," Fanny said, "make no mistake here. This is your establishment and you can do anything you wish. If you want Mrs. Farley to leave, then other arrangements, though with some difficulty, will have to be made. But isn't it a bit contradictory to say that you're afraid she'll drive other guests away, when your obvious compassion for this other gentleman creates a more extreme danger?" She paused. "After all," she said, "we both *know* what she has is not a contagious disease. Frighteningly common, perhaps, but not contagious. And we don't know that about your friend's case. Do we, now?"

He pursed his lips. "I see your point," he said. He stood up. "I'll have the lock changed on the suite," he said. "I'll give you and Miss Demers each one, and I'll lock the extra key in the safe. And I'll change the lock on the bar cabinet and guard that key as well."

She nodded. "Very good," she said.

"Will you," he said, "do you think you and Miss Demers can devise some way of keeping Mrs. Farley in her room in the evening during the busy season, when the bar just has to be open?"

"We will do our very best, Mister Sherburne," Fanny said. "We will all do our very best."

8

In the Bay Tower Room on the top floor of 28 State Street in Boston, its view of the harbor to the east blocked by the newer high-rise at 60 State, Martin Sands over champagne cocktails complimented Estelle Stoddard on her appearance. "It's a classic look," he said. "I've often wondered why women allow themselves to be hornswoggled by a bunch of designers. Just because it was eight, twelve years ago when women generally started wearing trousers to social occasions, now you seldom see a woman wearing a simple black pants suit with a silk blouse and stock. Because they can't sell them to people who already have them. But it still looks good. It still looks good. That outfit, Stelle, has class."

She smiled and looked down at her ivory stock. She looked up. "Thanks," she said shyly. "I got to tell you, though, I wasn't sure. You asked me here, I almost said to you, what should I wear, a place like this?"

"If you had," he said, "and I'd've thought of it, that's exactly the kind of thing I would've suggested. Why didn't you ask? It would've been all right."

"Oh, I was embarrassed," she said. "I didn't think of it, you called up, and then I didn't know if I should call you back, the office."

"Why not?" he said.

"Oh, come on," she said. "How's your arthritis? Any better now?"

He laughed. "Okay, okay," he said. "Let's get that tedious business out of the way right now. My wife lives in Beverly in the house that her parents bought when they decided they liked horses more'n Symphony. She has now reached approximately the same age they were when they moved out of town, and she's reached the same decision. Personally, I rank horses and Symphony at about the same level: I don't care if I never see another one.

"What I do care about," he said, "is enjoying to the fullest what I've worked very hard to get. And've been very lucky to get, too. When I first leased my place at Ninety Beacon, I had to strain to make the rent. But I made it. When the building went condo, I had to hock everything I owned, and sell my Mercedes that I'd worked very hard to get, in order to make the down payment. But either I had faith that I would make it, or else I was too stupid to consider the possibility that I might not, and as things turned out, I did make it. Which left me, after several years of brutally hard work, night and day and day and night, with a quiet, beautiful third-floor, four-bedroom place overlooking the Public Garden, with a parking place out in the back and a

106

new Mercedes to put in it. So I looked around like God, and I saw that it was good, and, always needing a new goal to strive for, considered what was next. Why, marriage, of course. What I needed now was a wife suitable to the station I'd achieved in life."

"Bet you had your pick," she said.

"Let me put it this way," he said. "I did. It sounds like bragging, but it isn't. This is a man's town, when it comes to that particular area of enterprise. The prosperous, single, unattached heterosexual men are vastly outnumbered by the number of eligible ladies. Or, to put it another way, less flattering to me: I had no excuse. I was in no hurry. I had an agreeable social life, so I wasn't lonely. I certainly didn't need her money, although I must confess I was glad that she did have it—that seemed to eliminate the possibility she was after me for mine. She's a very beautiful woman, well educated, accomplished, good taste, and she was more than adequate in bed. But so were a number of other women I knew around that time, and I didn't propose marriage to them. The only way I can account for it is that I'd already decided the time had arrived. And I talked myself into it. Logic said we should get married. And she does have lovely eyes.

"Logic," he said, as the waiter served vichyssoise, "is a lousy basis for a marriage." To the waiter he said: "We'll have the Sancerre served with this, please." The waiter nodded. "We thought we liked the same things. That was what we told ourselves, at least. I liked going to Symphony Hall and the ballet with her, which I'd never been in the habit of doing myself. She liked going skiing up at Bolton Valley

107

with me and two of my partners and their wives, which of course she'd never done before—she'd always gone to Chamonix. I liked sailing with her father and her mother out of Boca Grande on their Bermuda Forty in the winter, and out of Edgartown in the summer; it was quite a change from blowing down to Greenwich for lunch in Billy Olson's Cigarette at sixty miles an hour, and then blowing back at sixty for cocktails and dinner at Falmouth, but I did like it. For a while.

"The trouble was," he said, "the trouble was that it was all such *damned, hard, work.* We were always putting each other on our mettle. Judith bore the speedboat with exceptionally good grace, and regaled many a dinner party with the story of leaping along from wave to wave with those twin Mercs wide open. I enjoyed nodding politely to senior partners of stuffier law firms, who refused to hire me out of law school, when we recognized each other at museum openings. We were performing, you see? Always performing. I performed all day in court, when I still went there a lot, and she performed good works. Then: evening comes; we hurry home, quick drink, and change, and out. It was exhausting.

"We didn't realize it, I guess," he said, "until we'd been together long enough to get into multiple repetitions of the new activities. The first three or four visits to Bolton went fine, but then she began to make excuses, and I wound up going alone. Two trips to Greenwich with Billy were quite enough to meet her needs. Once I'd learned the rudiments of sailing a sloop close-hauled in a variable breeze, I began to long for something with a bit more git. I

108

don't like playing doubles when I play tennis, and I especially don't like having a sixty-eight-year-old left-handed woman — Judith's mother — as my partner when I do it. Nor do I like taking it easy on my opponent's weak backhand just because he happens to be my father-in-law. That's not the way I'm built.

"So," he said, "we had a whirl of it for two years. Then we kept up appearances for four. Then Judith's father was diagnosed with leukemia, and he lingered, and they brought him home from the Deaconess to die, and he lingered some more. There was plenty of help in the household, but Judith felt — or said she felt — that she should stay in Beverly to give her mother emotional support. And with a certain hidden relief, I agreed with her.

"It took the old man almost a year and a half to die. He'd go into remission, then have a relapse, then go into remission again. And in the meantime Judith was whiling away the days riding her horse in the springtime, working on her short irons, getting her putting touch back, taking the train into town for suitable occasions, generally living again exactly the life that'd suited her so well before she married me. She and her mother're pals. I should've known more was involved than just the simple statement she made, before we were married: 'Judith's like a sister to me. Just like a younger sister.' And I was trying cases, working late, having a few with the boys, making excuses for her rejection of weekend invitations I accepted for myself, without even bothering to tell her."

"And you started fooling around," Estelle said.

"I *resumed* fooling around," Sands said. "I don't

know for sure, but I assume that she did, too. It was nothing personal, as odd as that may sound. I didn't see any reason to bring it up to her, while her old man was still alive, and after he died, and she didn't come back, well, I couldn't think of one then. I still can't. What's the point? I don't dislike the woman. I don't think she's mad at me. She's still good company, and I think that I am, too. If she needs an escort for some function in town, and it's not one that'll have me grinding my teeth the whole time that I'm there, I go. And if it's one of the things that'd put a stone to sleep, I plead too much work and she goes with someone else. Now and then, not very often, something comes up, that I have to do, where her presence would be nice, and I invite her, and she comes. We don't fight, we don't argue, and we don't embarrass each other. A good many partners in other law firms'd give their souls for such harmony."

"So," Estelle said, "you're telling me that it's okay, your seeing me and stuff."

"I don't know if it's okay," he said. "I sort of hope it'll prove to be a little better'n that. But it's not going to get you in scandalous trouble, that's what you mean, if we are seen together. Besides, I keep a pretty low profile. My clients do colorful things, sometimes—lots of times, in fact, when they choose not to listen to me. And sometimes they get caught, which leads to publicity. But publicity for them, not me; I stay well in the background because that's the way I like it. And the money's better there."

"Because," she said, toying with the flatware as the waiter removed soup plates, "I, look, all right? I'm not gonna sit here and tell you, you know, because you wouldn't believe it anyway, that I never went out with married guys before. Okay?"

"Okay," he said solemnly.

"Because I did," she said. "The first time I did, well, maybe I didn't know it. For sure, I mean. But I knew something was up, and I still did it anyway. And it was fun, too, until finally my mother started giving me, whole load, and I couldn't take it anymore so I broke up with him. Which I didn't want to do. He was a very nice guy. Worked the telephone company and treated me like an absolute *queen*. But Ma, jeez: 'He's spending money on you, Stelle, he should be spending on his family.' Noise, noise, noise. So, and I didn't do it again until I had my own place, away from all that static.

"But still," she said, "you're different. This's something new to me. 'S why I went to Dorothy yesterday, after you called, and I was panicked. Well, not panicked, maybe, but I didn't know what to do. And I said to her: 'He's taking me this place that I never even heard of. What do I do? What do I wear? How do people look?'

He reached over and touched her hand. "No need of that," he said. "This's not supposed to be a pressure-cooker situation, where you have to get prepared. This's just supposed to be a nice evening out."

"Yeah," she said, as the waiter served quails in a brown sauce, "but it's a nice evening out on your turf. You know this place, the people in it. I don't. Or I didn't till I got here. I don't know what I'm in for, when I'm talking, Dorothy. And she's the one, not me, that said: 'The black suit. Wear the suit.' And this's hers, you like so much—this is Dottie

Franklin's suit, and Dottie Franklin's blouse. The only things that I got on, really belong to me, 're the shoes, the underwear and stuff—the rest is Dorothy's. She even did my hair. She said: 'Stelle, what you need here's a good shot of confidence. Tomorrow,' meaning today, 'you bring all your stuff to work. And after we close up, all right? I'll do your hair for you. Then we'll go to my place and you can shower there, get dressed and everything, and then I will comb you out.' Which is why I left the message, new address to pick me up."

The waiter brought a bottle of Fleurie and poured the wine into their glasses. She laughed. "Dottie almost flipped when that limousine drove up. How come you did that?"

He grinned. "I had a three-thirty conference with a long-winded client up in Burlington, Vermont," he said. "The guy thinks just because he sends his Lear-jet for me, he can talk as long as he wants. And maybe he's right—I don't dare ask. So I knew I'd be back to shower and shave, but probably not in time to drive out to Randolph to get you. So, the limo seemed like a logical choice, and that was what I did."

Estelle laughed. "Dorothy was really floored," she said. " 'Jesus Christ, kid,' she goes, 'I'd've known this was involved, I'd've bopped you onna head and put the suit on, take your place.' "

He smiled. "I've never met Dottie," he said, "but I'd bet I'd've noticed the difference."

"Yeah," Estelle said, "but you might not've minded. Dottie's pushing fifty, I'd say, but Dottie stays in shape. Unless her husband bothered you, the idea of him."

"He would've," Sands said. "Husbands in general strike me as undesirable traits in my female companions. As do steady boyfriends, as far as that goes. I made an exception in your case."

"No, you didn't," she said.

"Well," he said, "what about Steverino? The guy who's hot for the truck? Doesn't he qualify?"

"He did," she said, deftly separating a drumstick from the clean carcass of her second quail. She looked up at Sands, carving his second quail. "Okay to pick these up?" she said.

"I would," he said, taking a drink of wine. "And I will, soon's I get to that point. Tell me what happened to Steve."

She gnawed contentedly at the quail but swallowed each bite before speaking. "Well," she said, "I threw the bum out. Dumped him, is what I did." She bit and chewed. "My mother used to call him 'a pill.' When he was seeing Shan. And she was right, goddamnit. It's bad enough when parents nag you, but it's pure hell when they're right. But I finally ditched him. That is over with."

"Not on my account, I hope," Sands said.

"Well," she said, swallowing and dabbing her lips with her napkin, "not entirely, no. But you had something to do with it. Not that I'm counting on you, or anything, but I sort of had it in the back of my mind, you know? Sort of my ace in the hole. While I was kicking him out, I'm thinking all the time: 'Here you meet this classy guy,' 'cause I could tell that much, 'that wants to take you out and maybe have some fun. And here you're living with

113

this prick that's like a cherry bomb.' Because I never knew, I was never sure, when that bastard'd get shit-faced and start doing stupid things. You remember I told you, the Iglesias concert?"

"You said something about a concert, I recall," he said. "Big date of some kind."

"Yeah," she said. She told him about the fight. "Now," she said, "that was more'n bad enough. My mother always told us that a hitter's like skin disease. There isn't any way to cure either one of them. 'You get it once, you'll get it again, and that's all there is to it, kids.' So, that was twice for me, and he did it twice to Shan, and I figure, maybe, two oughta be the limit.

"But I hadn't decided," she said. "I hadn't really made up my mind, you know? And that was Friday night, it happened. So I shut him off Saturday, not that it matters, he gets home so late and worn out. And I shut him off Sunday, and Monday I went to work. And I'm thinking: 'How many people're getting punished here? Steve's a bad boy, he's getting no nooky, but what the hell is it I did? I'm a good girl, and I get no nooky? Something is definitely wrong."

"Then you call up," she said. "Now, before that, before you call, all I got from you's what I've had from lots of guys—basically some flirting. There's a certain number, there's a *lot*, of guys that like to do that, and don't want nothing more. And that's all right. It's kind of fun. Don't do any harm, and that's the last you see of them, but still, everyone feels good. You called? That made you a little different. Now I know you're interested, and I start to think about that. But so far, as far's I've gone till then, I'm

114

just, you know, *thinking*. I have not made no decisions.

"I go home that night, he's supposed to be working. But there he is, on the couch. And he's sitting there in his Members Only jacket, cost me sixty bucks, his birthday, and he's watching the TV. And I say: 'Excuse me, Steve, don't mind me asking, you come into some money or something? Win the lottery?' Because this is the guy, keep in mind, that wants a truck that's gonna cost, sixteen grand, he's finished. And I'm paying the apartment, I buy most the food.

"And he says: 'No.' And I say: "No"? No what? What're you doing home?' And he says: 'I hadda go the doctor.' And I say: 'What for, you hadda go the doctor? You miss your period or something? What'd the rabbit say?' Because that's another thing about Steve, that rots my ass sometimes. He won't take no responsibility for that. *I'm* the one that always has, has to make sure the birth control. Once, *once* I asked the guy, he's going down the drugstore, 'Hey, Steve, some gel, my diaphragm, okay? I ain't got too much left.' And he wouldn't do it. He acted like I was asking him, grab-ass the druggist or something. 'Well, Jesus Christ,' I said, 'if it don't embarrass me, go in there, ask for birth control, the hell's it bother you so much? 'S because of you, I need it. We're not the only people, you know, that they're stocking that stuff for. Lots of people like to fuck. It's not like it's a secret, we're the only ones that know.' But, nothing doing. 'All right,' I said, 'get rubbers then. You bought plenty of rubbers, your time. Couldn't've made you feel funny then, buying condoms, go out

115

on a date.' Which I really hoped he wouldn't. I don't like those things."

"Really?" Sands said. "Why is that?"

She glanced around to see whether anyone was eavesdropping. Satisfied that no one was, she lowered her voice anyway. "Because *I* want it," she said, "all right? That's part of it for me. First I feel myself, coming. Then I feel, well, you. If you're him. The man's got one of those sheaths on, I feel like I've been gypped. I don't like thinking about what that stuff can do afterwards, inside me—Shan had two abortions, one of them when she's with Steve, and she told me all about them; I don't want to go through that. But at the same time, it's funny, you know? When I'm doing it, I want to *do* it. All of it. Complete. I know this AIDS thing, brrr," she said. "I know it's taking chances if the guy don't use a condom. What is it they're telling us? You screw somebody tonight, you're also screwing everyone that person's screwed the past seven years? Bedrooms're getting crowded. But I still don't like those rubbers. I don't like them at all."

Sands removed a drumstick from his second quail. He picked up and inspected it. "Interesting," he said. "I had a vasectomy."

She winced. "The operation?" she said. "That thing where they, ah . . ."

"Uh huh," he said, "where they take a knife and lift up your balls and you're scared to death they'll miss. Actually it's a very simple operation and there's little pain involved. But thinking about it's not much fun, and the visible aftereffects are very unpleasant indeed."

116

"What happens?" she said.

"Most of the equipment," he said, "most of my equipment, at least, turned black. Like it was gangrenous, and in a few days it'd fall off. Fact of the matter is the tissue's just reacting the way any tissue does when it's bruised—it changes colors until the damage heals. But try telling that to a single man, watching his balls turn black, and then purple and green."

"Why'd you do it?" she said. "Why'd you do it, then?"

"Basically," he said, "basically because I probably agreed with both you and Steve. I don't like condoms either. I don't like making, or having my partner have to make, trips to the drugstore beforehand. All that planning ahead is depressing. The kind of sybaritic life I lead has its hold on me, and doesn't leave enough room to raise children properly. Which, since I had to spend most of my adolescence and my early adult years making up for the fact that *I* wasn't raised properly, is not something I want to do half-baked—and therefore I refuse to do it at all. So, I want lots of fun, and no kids? Operation made good sense. Good sense at least for me."

"But that doesn't," she said, "that doesn't do anything, the AIDS thing. Does it?"

He sighed. "Not that I've heard about," he said. "Sort of makes you wonder, doesn't it? Society finally catches up to the facts of life and everybody's game. Then medicine offers this simple procedure that insures the male's not in season. Whoop-pee, throw the code out. Screw the Puritans. Bedtime, boys and girls—and boys and boys, too, girls and

117

girls. So then what happens? 'Oh, we forgot to mention: You do it and you die.' " He snickered. "Don't have to go to the drugstore now, kids. Now all you have to do's have a lab tech in attendance, take a blood test from each player, 'fore the games begin."

She looked worried. "What does that mean?" she said.

He smiled and patted her right hand. "Not to worry," he said. "We'll take the proper measures even though we don't like them, and see how things go from there."

She relaxed. "Go the doctor, you mean," she said.

"Something like that," he said. "Was that why Steve went, took the day off, see if he had AIDS?"

" 'My jaw's dislocated,' he said," she said. "Well, I hadn't noticed that. I mean, I didn't have a lot to say the son of a bitch all weekend, few times he was there, and I didn't see him try to eat, but it could've been. Bucky's not a very big guy, but he can throw a punch. 'The doctor says I got a mild dislocation, the jaw. They did X rays. They think they got it back in the socket, but they aren't sure. I got to go back in a week, for more tests. See if it's back where it should be.'

" 'This took all day?' I say. 'You couldn't find all this stuff out, still get yourself to work?'

" 'I hadda go down the lawyer's, then,' he says, and that's when it begins to dawn on me: I dunno what I'm gonna hear, the rest that he's got to say. But already I know: I'm not gonna like it. Not gonna like it at all. 'The lawyer,' I say. 'What lawyer is this? Since when has Steve Cole got a lawyer? You hanging around with one of them bums, comes in when

118

the courthouse closes and he don't leave till you do? I wouldn't trust those drunks to tell me about my cat.'

" 'No,' he says, 'the guy on TV. One that's always on TV saying "You may have a case"? Well, I went to see him. Well, not him, one of his people. And I told this kid what happened, and he says I have got a case.'

" 'A case of what?' I say. 'Measles? Budweiser? Stupidity? What kind of case have you got?'

" 'Assault and battery,' he says. You beat that? 'Assault and battery.' 'How,' I say, 'tell me, how've you got a case. Bucky hit you, okay, I agree he did. But I *told* Bucky, hit you, 'cause I didn't want to die. And hitting you's the only way, it was the only way I had to make sure, that you wouldn't drive. So what'-re you gonna do? Sic the police on *me?*'

"And he says: 'No,' " she said. "He says this lawyer, if the kid was a lawyer, this kid told him: Go down the police station, Braintree, file a formal criminal complaint. 'Which, by the time I finish doing that,' he says, 'it's too late to bother, going to work, so I called in sick.'

" 'I don't get it,' I say, which I really didn't. 'Why's this lawyer telling you, file a police complaint? Lawyers work for money, least the ones I heard of do.' And he tells me, 'fore he can sue Bucky for hitting him, he's got to make out the complaint. So he did that, and the next day, this'd be yesterday, he's supposed to go back the lawyer's office and sign something else, to sue Bucky. For money. Which explains why the lawyer said that.

"And that's when I decided," she said. "Right

119

there, that very minute, on the spot. 'That creases it, Stevie,' I said. 'Get your shit out the medicine cabinet, your clothes out the drawers, your stuff from the closet, and your ass out the door.' And he looks at me, the big ape, like he was surprised. 'What?' he says. 'You heard me,' I say. 'You heard what I said. You get your butt out of here and don't come back. Or call. Just vanish, all right? Like Ty-D-Bol and all that other stuff you got so much in common with. I've had it with you, lard-ass, and if Bucky asks me, or even if he don't, I'm going to court for him against you.' " She grinned sheepishly. "And that's how I got rid of Steve."

"He didn't make a ruckus?" Sands said.

"Nah," she said, "he was sober. When he's sober, Steve's all right, maybe even chicken. A big pussycat. You can order him around some, and he'll do what you say. It's when he's drinking courage, you know? Booze makes him feel big. And, funny thing, club guy like that, he can't hold it at all. But he left. And he hasn't been back. So that's where I stand now."

Sands raised his eyebrows and dropped his napkin on the table as the waiter arrived to clear away. "Well," he said, "good news for me. And for whatever it's worth, as little as I know, it sounds like the right decision."

"Yeah," she said, "but there is one other thing."

"Oh?" he said.

"Yeah," she said. "I realize, I know it don't sound like I feel this way, but I'm, I'm really sick about Bucky. I mean, I got him into this. This's my fault. He did it because I told him to."

"Yeah," Sands said, "fine and dandy. But we're

not supposed to go around socking drunks on the jaw just because pretty girls ask us to. 'Damsel in distress' and all that chivalry notwithstanding—law doesn't always recognize such things."

"I called him up," she said. "I got his number from Shan and I called him. To apologize. And he's really all upset. Not at me, I mean, although I guess he should be. At all of this. See, he didn't know what Steve is doing until I went and told him. I guess nobody got in touch with him yet. So, I not only got him into this, I'm the one who told him he's in it. And all he was trying to do, that night, was show everyone else a good time." She sighed and shook her head as the waiter brought coffee and fresh raspberries in cream. "I feel awful about this," she said. "I just feel so bad. It's such a lousy thing, to have something happen like this."

"Well," Sands said, "it's not the end of the world, you know. Simple A and B case. Might get a fine, if he's convicted, and that's by no means assured. Decent lawyer, all this publicity about drunk drivers, might even get him off."

"You think?" she said wistfully, her eyes full.

"Well," he said, "I wouldn't bet on it. But it's possible, certainly. Very doable."

"Would you talk to him?" she said. "For me, I mean?"

He put his left hand over his mouth. He shut his eyes briefly.

"Well," he said, "I'll say one thing for me: I never seem to learn."

121

9

Assistant US Atty. William S. Pratt observed his custom of ending the workday with a 5:45 visit to the Chief of the Criminal Division in the large office at the southeast corner of the eleventh floor of the courthouse. David Curley's desk was flanked by an American flag and a banner bearing the seal of the US Department of Justice. He was in shirtsleeves, talking on the phone. Curley wore broadcloth shirts that billowed at the sleeves and chest; they had high starched collars that he pinned in gold above silk repp-stripe ties, and French cuffs that he secured with initialed gold cuff links. He had what he called "a library" of brightly colored suspenders; this day's were emerald green, picking up the stripe in his navy and green tie. He twisted the left end of his walrus mustache as he listened on the phone.

He said: "Well, no, of course I'm not sure. But it's the likeliest thing. The symptoms sound the same. Look, the Benadryl worked, the last time he had it, so we might's well try it again." He paused. "Well, I don't mind if you do that, if that's what you think, but from what you're telling me, the suddenness he came down with it—I mean, he was all right this morning, I left. But you want to take him to Gates tonight, by all means, go ahead. Perfectly all right with me." He paused. "Maybe it is," he said, "but I still think it's just like what he had before, and that was an allergy, and Benadryl handled it, so I think it will again. Try it tonight, and see how it goes, and then, he's not better tomorrow, keep him home and take him the doctor. That's how I'd handle it." He paused again. "Yeah," he said. "Me too. Now, I got somebody with me. I'll be home the seven-twenty-one. That is, if they're running on time. No, I won't forget cigarettes." He hung up. He grinned at Pratt. "Ain't love grand," he said.

"Kid sick?" Pratt said.

"No more'n kids always are," Curley said. "I dunno what we expect. Every day we ship the little urchins out the door and into buses, where they inhale the germs of friends and foes until they get to school. Where they spend all day inhaling germs that other kids brought in on other buses, before they get back on their own buses for a second dose of those germs. And keep something else in mind, too: Kids're devious. They are perfectly willing to use deceit in order to achieve their goals, a major and continuing one of which is to stay home from school. I'm not saying they fabricate their diseases; that would be extra crude. No, what they do is magnify any ailment that they get, in hopes of raising it to the status of disease, so that they can get a free day off, that doesn't count against vacation." He chuckled. "Those that show talent at it grow up to become court clerks, and the truly gifted ones get jobs in Washington."

"We still having trouble with Sterling?" Pratt said. "I dunno—he's that hot to get that Dunn case indicted, maybe I shouldn't've declined on it."

"Oh, cut it out," Curley said. "Don't take everything to heart so. You were right on that file. I read it over, keep in mind, and I could not *believe* Tax signed off on it. It's a regular definition of a scut case. They're so hot to try it? The IRS's so goddamned proud their handiwork on that one, they want to see it tried? Fine, then leave them find a way to indict it and try it. Themselves. And leave them lose it, too. I don't care how big a hair they got across their ass for the guy, or how eager Sterling is to bear any burden, pay any price, or kiss any ass that's presented, in order to insure his orderly progression to the D.C. District bench: a shit case is a shit case is a shit case."

He leaned back in his leather chair and clasped his hands behind his head. "I was starting out, all right? The Department's version of the First Marine Division, almost twenty years ago. And they shipped me out to Chicago. And I'm there. And they give me this sack fulla shit, and say: 'See what's in this.' This was nothing in it. The subjects were a couple of certified maggots, of course, but the evidence to nail them just wasn't there. I spent four months on the goddamned thing, and there wasn't a triable case. So I go into the trial chief, and I say to him: 'Look, I can't make a case out of this.' And he looks at me, and he says: 'Son, ever occur to you, someone down at Justice spent a long time drawing up forms? Like Form Nine-oh-one? "Request for Authority, Decline Prosecution"? Why you think he did that? Because we get a lot of cats and dogs, and we can't win the bastards. So, Nine-oh-one the bastard.' And that is what I did. That is what you did, and it was exactly the right thing. Put it out of your mind. Scroll up something else on your screen, and entertain me some."

"Hard day?" Pratt said.

"Ah, the boss," Curley said. "I sympathize with him, really. All his life he's been aiming for that slot that Sterling's got, maybe without knowing it, but aiming nonetheless. And now as soon's that indecisive turkey gets out of Tenth and Constitution, if he ever clears the Senate, the boss gets what he wants. Except look at the Department he's getting it in. What an irony, huh? All your life you plot and scheme to get to be The Chief, of all the Criminals? And then, when you're finally on the brink of it and you're salivating so much Pavlov's work is obsolete, what are you looking at? *Wilkommen, Herr Dodge, und sieg heil!'* " He shot his right arm out in the Fascist salute. "My father used to watch *The Life of Riley,* and that's all I can think of when Harry starts talkin', and shaking his poor head and moaning: Chester A. Riley: 'What a *revoltin'* development this is.' "

"Here's another one," Pratt said, scaling a document onto Curley's desk.

"Ah," Curley said, " *'US* v. *John Doe.* Motion to Quash.' Some day we got to capture this guy Doe

126

and shoot him, all the trouble he gets into. Which John Doe is this one? This the John Doe who runs guns? Robs banks? Runs the damned Mafia? Defrauds the government? Or this the John Doe who runs dope?"

"This's the John Doe who bribes politicians, kicks back on contracts and stuff," Pratt said. "Just by way of no harm I slapped a paper on Arrow Construction, *duces tecum,* all of that good stuff. Like you memoed me, try something else, Dacey's wire didn't turn out so good."

"Buster Feeley's a piece of shit," Curley said.

"Well yeah," Pratt said, "but Harry's in love with him. And also in hate with him. And he thinks Buster knows things. And so we go with stuff we shouldn't go with. And we get in the shit."

"We should just take him in, no deal, and kick his ass into the cooler for shaking down vendors," Curley said.

"That's what I said," Pratt said. "Harry don't like it, you recall. Harry says Buster's more valuable, setting up guys to make Sonny."

"He's done a great job of it, so far," Curley said. "Problem we got, Buster setting guys up, is that they're all smarter'n Buster. You average the IQs, him and the agent's, you come out to about one-eighty. Of which the agent's one-twenty and Buster is sixty. He didn't have the muscle, he'd be eating in soup kitchens. Getting his clothes out of bins. I don't understand it. One breath, Harry's telling you Sonny's smarter'n serpents. And the next breath, he's telling you, Sonny tells all to Buster. Well, the two of them don't mesh. The only thing that Buster ever did was what Sonny told him, and Sonny told him nothing more'n what he needed, know. And Buster's got his dick in his zipper now. So he's scrambling. And if you think Sonny told him things before, he sure fuckin' *God* doesn't now."

"So," Pratt said, "thus the *duces tecum*. Anything's better'n Buster."

" 'Books and records, the past hundred years, plus your Wassermann tests and tattoos'?" Curley said.

"That's the one," Pratt said. "And, can you believe it? They say it's 'overly broad.' 'Unduly burdensome.' "

"The nerve of these civilians," Curley said. "Now I suppose they've got some antique notion . . . yup, there it is, right down here at the end: these disrespectful persons think they've got a right to a *hearing* on the matter." He scaled the paper back to Pratt. "Memo me tomorrow," he said, "reminding to call the Bureau, saddle up a flying squad their very best and brightest. Evidence's too strong to ignore any longer. Some clandestine group's running around out there, spiriting copies the Constitution, Bill of Rights, into impressionable hands. Maybe Magna Carta, too. I want those provocateurs tracked down and clapped in irons. And none of this *habeas corpus* shit, either; transportation to Australia, in the next available hull." He nodded toward the document. "You got any problems with this?"

Pratt shrugged. "Same problem I've had all along with it," he said. "I know Harry's hot for it. He cornered me the hall last Monday, I'm coming from the head, and asked me how it's going. I did not have much to say. 'Well, jeez, Boss,' I said, 'not so good, you want the honest truth.' 'What's the matter, Prattsie,' he said, 'you going pussy on me? Made your mind up His former Excellency, Kenny, His Honor, pure as the driven snow?'

"Well," Pratt said, "I didn't take it personally or anything. I know Harry was Marines and it's a permanent condition—same as hives or shingles: it comes out, he's under stress. And, like I told him, I said: 'No, I have not decided that. I'm just having trouble proving it.' Proving that he's right. 'Well, then *do* something, goddamnit,' he said. 'The goddamned Demmies've been running things in this State for the past thirty goddamned years. The only time we ever get a crack at those bastards is when we win the White House, someone like us gets this job. Now, we know they're playing footsie with each other, and the papers know we know, and they're sitting back, just waiting, see how good we are. So let's show them. Let's go out and prove it.' And stomped off to take a leak.

"And I went back to my office," Pratt said, "and I *did* something. I sent out that paper, and all it really does, it demonstrates just what I said to him. I'm groping, Dave. I'm making it up as I go along, and I'm not making much headway."

Curley studied him. He made a sucking noise with his tongue against his teeth. "Worries me, hear you talk like that," he said.

"Why?" Pratt said. "Because Harry's got his tail in a crack with the media, we don't make Kenny Farley? At the very least?"

"No," Curley said, "but close. Because *you* think that Harry'll have his nuts squeezed in the press, we

129

don't at least make Farley. Therefore there's a danger that you might try to take Farley out on a case that's less'n prime. You can't get away with a magic act, this one, one of your bumblebee jobs that can't possibly fly, and you bring it in to conviction. We whack Farley, he's not gonna have some overworked court-appointed snot-nosed kid his table. Or some rump-sprung buffalo, wife cuts his hair, an off-the-rack suit Farley found in a second-floor office, over a drugstore in Chelsea. He's gonna have howitzers in Brooks's blue serge, with squads of lackeys running ammo in shifts, and they'll sit back just out of range, and shell you till they blow you out."

"I know that," Pratt said.

"I *know* you know it," Curley said. "I just don't want you forgetting it. Much as we love Harry, great a guy as Harry is, and as much as it'd luster his record and soothe his digestion, nailing Farley for his sendoff down to Washington, anything less'n an ironclad case's not going to be enough. What'd you hope for? Why'd you want the records? You don't think Kenny Farley'd be dumb enough to write in 'Kickbacks' in his own account books, do you? Cripes, even if we weren't on the earth, he wouldn't dare do it because of Daniels. Jim Daniels ever has to admit what we suspect is the truth, we may never get to try Kenny—Jim'll call an emergency meeting of Opus Dei, have his partner crucified."

Pratt laughed. "But that doesn't change anything, does it?" Curley said. "You still got to fight this motion to quash, because you brought the god-damned thing knowing it was useless, or most likely useless at least, and now you're stuck with it. Can't let them ram it up your ass—might give them confidence. And then you're gonna win it, naturally, because Judge Kennerly's got the garbage session next week and the last time he quashed a subpoena no one alive remembers."

"That's the way I read it," Pratt said.

"That's just the beginning, your reading," Curley said. "Which I don't envy you. I was Farley's lawyer, I'd photocopy every piece of paper I could find, including toilet tissue, used, and put into one of Arrow's dump trucks and unload it all on your head. I'd fuckin' bury you, 's what I'd do, and figure I gained two, three years, wait for the next administration. Which may be friendlier."

"Yeah," Pratt said. "I just hope, when Harry's gone, and Ronnie naps full-time, I just hope that you and I aren't legally dead around this town."

"Well," Curley said, "it's a risk. No question about that. Only way I can think of reducing it's either to get Farley, and get him good, so no one can holler 'Vendetta.' Or else go as far as we can till we're satisfied we can't, and then, as honorable men, let the whole thing go to sleep." He paused. "Unless you can think of some other way, other'n the ones we've tried, to put the hooks in him."

Pratt stirred in his chair. "A couple of things've crossed my mind," he said.

"You ready to talk about them?" Curley said. "Or are they such egregiously shocking violations of due process and elementary fairness that you hesitate to mention them, even to the calloused likes of me?"

"One of them might be a little borderline, at best," Pratt said.

Curley exhaled loudly. "This's how Klaus Barbie got in trouble, I bet," he said. "One his eager young *Oberleutnants* came prancing in his office in Lyons one bright spring day and said: 'Hey, Klaus. *Herr Kommandant*. Whatever. Let's round up all the Jews in town and ship them east for vacation.' And Klaus was on his way to lunch, wasn't even listening, and just said: 'Go ahead.' So, go ahead. But I am listening."

"Farley's separated from his wife," Pratt said. "Now I realize you can't always project your own experience onto someone else's life and say: 'This is what's going on.' But my ex-wife was really mean. Hell, she not only told everybody what I did—she lied on me. She 'made things up, I'd never done. Never even dreamed of." He hesitated. "Actually, some of them sounded pretty interesting. Wished I'd thought of them."

"So you want to take a shot at Farley's wife," Curley said.

"I was thinking about it," Pratt said. "Not for evidence, exactly. Not to testify in court, or even the grand jury. Just for leads, you know? It's been about four years, they haven't lived together, but still, there's a year's slack in Limitations there, and she might very well know something we could then go out, track down."

"And be ready to give it to us," Curley said, "to get revenge on him."

"Something like that," Pratt said.

"No," Curley said.

"I ask why?" Pratt said.

"You know where she's been living," Curley said,

132

"she hasn't been living with him?"

Pratt looked uncomfortable. "I know she's been sick," he said.

" *'Sick?'* " Curley said. "She's NCM, is what she's been. *Non compos* fuckin' *mentis*. In the booby hatch."

"Well," Pratt said, "but not all the time. On and off, I know that, but she's not in the booby hatch now. Vic Champa, served the paper, the woman in the Arrow office told him she was out. So I had the Bureau check. And she's staying at The Foothills Inn, up near the Vermont border."

"You had the Bureau check," Curley said. "You wanna bet how much sweat the Bureau hadda put into that check? I bet *she* called *them*. They had the pink slip right onna desk when you called. She's been calling them for years. Also the State cops, the IRS and the CIA, I bet. The first thing those people do when they get out is run for a phone and call the Bureau to turn in the family members, put them in the last time. They all do that."

"Dave," Pratt said, "this is a private place. A hotel, not a hospital, some kind of asylum or something."

"Yeah," Curley said, "and you know what that private place is?"

"You know about it?" Pratt said. "I never heard of it."

"Not specifically, I don't," Curley said, "but I still know what it is. Or I bet I do, at least. Dollars to doughnuts it's an old firetrap that started downhill when the Interstates went through, too far away, and hasn't had a decent season since. And some pair of

133

romantics, probably nice young couple from Weehawken, always wanted, run a hotel, bought it cheap, on the cuff, and now're living hand-to-mouth, boarding rich unfortunates. You ever had any mental illness, your family?"

"I had a couple funny aunts," Pratt said. "Nothing serious, but they weren't good for much. Kept cats, you know? Hundreds of cats. And acted like they were broke. They didn't bother anyone, and no one bothered them."

"Where'd *you* keep *them?*" Curley said.

"They had their own place," Pratt said. "My grand-uncle and grand-aunt died and left them their place up in Maine, and Bessie and Alice just lived in it. Lived out the rest of their lives heaped in catshit. Probably inherited a couple hundred thou apiece, back in the late Thirties. Seldom touched a dime of it. Trustee down here paid taxes, paid their grocery bills and that stuff. Kept them as well as they'd let him, and then he buried them. Trusts went to Bowdoin and Harvard, goddamnit — couple, three million dollars. Should've visited them more often. Never mind the smell. Blocked my nose and gone to call. Always got along with Bessie. Alice didn't like me, though — downright hostile to me. Probably thought I was after their money."

"You haven't had any mental illness in your family," Curley said. "What you're talking about's 'feeble-minded.' 'Odd.' What I'm talking about's *'crazy.'* Mania depression. Paranoid schizophrenia. Hallucinations. Dangerous behavior — homicidal, suicidal — take your pick: that stuff.

"Reason I'm well versed," he said, "is Geraldine's

father is like that. Until he was about fifty-two or-three, he was perfectly all right. Seemed to be at least. Maybe he was roiling and boiling inside all along, but as long as he was young enough, could keep it in control. Or there's the other theory: that what precipitated it in him was the booze finally got to him — Dick's in sales management, or was when he could operate — he's retired early, now — and he used to be on the road all the time, drinking it up with his boys.

"Whatever it was that brought it on," Curley said, "it turned a glad-handing hail-fellow into an engine of fucking destruction. And suddenly, too. One day he's fine, just doing his job, playing some golf and some practical jokes, pressing the flesh, making speeches. Then, whammo, overnight it seemed like, he comes back from Denver and the Coast and it's like Johnny Carson became Tamerlane, some witch waved a magic wand. Beating the shit out of Cathleen, whacking Geraldine's sister around, next time he sees me he's drunk as a goat and he's gonna put out both my eyes. I tell you, it was really something. I was still in law school, fitting in my running, squash three days a week and like as not on weekends, just to keep the flab at bay, and there I am, solid one-ninety, and he's going to take me out. You know something? I think he might've done it, there hadn't been three other people in the room, he went for me. Couldn't've weighed more'n one-fifty-five, not in the best kind of shape, but when he got the wind up him, boy, it was like grappling with a fucking buck lion. Jesus was he strong. Till I went best three falls with him, I thought straitjackets were

135

funny. Pathetic. Antiques left over from a bygone age when people feared the mentally ill and locked them away in the attic, or retained exorcists. Lemme tell you something: when I saw the struggle the EMTs had, fitting him that wardrobe, then I understood — I learned some respect.

"Since that eventful day," Curley said, "and this's fourteen years ago, old Dick's been in and out the rubber roundhouse more times'n Santa's come. Which by the way has become a sure bet, he'll be in when Santa's expected. He also flips in springtime, and he's had bad summers, too, but the time we braced ourselves each year was when the colored lights went up. If it was a good year, he was home, he got through Thanksgiving. If it was a bad year, the little boys and girls were really taking chances when they rang the bell for Trick-or-Treat at Eighty Ridley Road. Either way, I don't think Dick saw a Super Bowl at home after the Jets beat the Colts, sixteen-seven, back in Sixty-nine. And the reason that score sticks in my mind is because Gerry and I had about twenty people up to our pad to watch the game, one those cheery law-school gatherings where everyone chips in, a keg, and dines lavishly on pasta and meat sauce with cheap red wine, and I didn't get my share. Because halfway through the third quarter we got a Mayday from Shrewsbury, and I heard the last part the game on the car radio on the Pike. Seems right after halftime Dick'd suddenly realized that the angels, or the Pentagon top brass, or the National Security Council — maybe even all three — were giving him secret commands voice-over the play-by-play, something about how his next-door neighbor was a Communist spy who must be liquidated, pronto, and he was looking for his fowling piece."

Pratt laughed.

"I know it," Curley said. "It *is* funny, when you tell it. But it's *not* funny, when you live it. Then it's pure unshirted Hell. They make you so fucking mad you'd like to kill them, just to end the siege. And then the doctors remind you the poor fella's sick, and they'll try to help him again, which means that the docs've still got those lease payments on the BMWs to think about, so don't count on seeing him soon. And you're just seething with anger, so much so you wonder if maybe you're headed the brink on your own, and I'm telling you, friend, then it ain't funny. It isn't funny at all."

"I know," Pratt said. "I mean: I understand. It just goes on and on."

"Oh, he's slowed down some," Curley said. "He's getting older, after all—he'll be sixty-six, next year. Losing his stamina. He's done a lot of damage, himself. He can't get better from that. *Anyway*," he said, and coughed, "that is what I mean. A long time ago, Harry opened this case, and shipped the file over to me. And I knew what it was about.

"It said: 'Kenneth Farley, Vincent Donovan, et al.,' on the tab, but what it meant was that Harry had a hero, back when he was twenty-four. Or maybe twenty-five. And his hero was Brendan Rooney, erstwhile Boston city councilman, friend of those who had no friends, and guardian of virtue. And Harry was in law school, then, or just fresh out of it. And he thought Brendan Rooney was the Lone Ranger on stilts. As in fact did Brendan Rooney."

"Rooney," Pratt said. "He the same pet right-winger, they got over the Kennedy School?"

"The very same," Curley said. "The hell you do in Boston, you're an Irish politician, you can't get yourself elected and you really need a job? You take the Red Line 'cross the river, and you teach the up-and-comers how to do, you couldn't do."

"Rooney' a fuckin' liberal by Harry's standards," Pratt said. "I heard people say a lot about Harry, but that's one I never heard."

"Harry's a liberal when it suits him," Curley said. "And it suits him when he thinks that making liberal noises might get him what he wants. Don't let him buffalo you into thinking Harry Dodge has principles. Harry's a real piece of work, and Harry's never dull, but when he nicks himself, his razor, what he bleeds is ambition. And when Harry says he's hungry, don't think he wants a sandwich — what he wants is power.

"Now, when Harry sent that file to me, it was pretty enigmatic on the subject of the wife. But when you've had my experience, you *know*, what those cryptic entries mean. So I went in to see Harry. And I said: 'Harry, you know I'm as grateful as hell to you, saving me the clutches of the trolls in Washington. I know you didn't have to ask for me to be assigned here,' which I happen to know a fact that he didn't do, didn't ask for me. Harry had no prosecuting experience, zero, and the only way they'd give him the job was if he took some guy in like me and at least pretended to take my advice. But I don't say that to Harry. And I said: 'I didn't love you anyway,

138

I would for doing that. But I got tell you, Harry, there're things that I won't do. Not even for you, Harry, will I do some things. 'Cause if I did them, when you're riled up, you would thank me for a while, but then when everything calmed down, well, you would love me less. Because I'd done something you're ashamed of, and I should be protecting you.' And he said, he was in the Chesty Puller mode that day — 'On to the Chinese border! On to the fucking Yalu! — What the fuck you mean?' And I said: 'You know what I mean, Harry. I'll go after this bastard hammer and tongs. I think he's a wrong one, too. But the wife's off limits, Harry. Posted. Immune. Clear? I know how easy it is to ignite manic-depressives, and I know what happens to their kin when they get paranoid, and schizoid, and they try to kill themselves. Keep in mind what we do here: "Justice," it is called. Sabotage is not included, and it won't be on my watch.' And he sits there growling at me, 'Um, shit, fuck, piss, shit.' And I said: 'Good. We understand each other. Now I'm going home.' "

Curley stood up and stretched. "Ahhh," he said, "and that's what I going to do now, too, okay? Get on old Eighty-one-eighty-one that takes me out to the hinterlands, where even government employees can afford four tiny bedchambers, a mudroom and garage. Unless there's more on your mind. But we're leaving the wife alone, Billy, my boy. We're not going to set off a bonfire for Farley, right in his own marriage bed."

Pratt stood up. "How about," he said, "how about other people, he might've talked to, or been present, when he did some dirty deal? Okay to roust his friends, the people work for him?"

"Find 'em, grill 'em, serve 'em up," Curley said. "Get some use from all those papers, you're so hot to grab. No man's a hero to his valet. Haul his loyal yeomen in here, his vassals and his serfs. Interrogate their asses off. Put the screws to them. But forget about old Buster. They got pin-setting machines now, in the bowling alleys—Buster's obsolete. Bust him if you got him, on what you got him on, but take no more of his help. Or leave him out there on the hillside—and hope for a cold night."

10

Agnes Lloyd at 53 had very little to do for Kenneth Farley, but was so well compensated for doing it that she did not feel she could look elsewhere for more stimulating work. Nevertheless, she was bored. On Thursday afternoons, when the St. Vincent de Paul Society of Homemakers in Marshfield gave her sister, Nancy, eight hours' respite from her emphysematic husband, Agnes complained about it. They usually went to lunch at The Green Tree in Duxbury. They almost always chose the same meal, and ate every bit of it. Agnes said she was overweight because she didn't have enough to do: "I don't get any exercise." Nancy said she was too heavy because she was cooped up at home with her husband all week "with nothing to do but eat."

"I've asked him and asked him," Agnes would say, "pleaded with him, really, to fire that expensive cleaning service. Let *me* take care of the house. Give me something to *do*. And he won't do it. 'It's too much for you, Agnes,' he says. 'It's a twelve-room house, and I'm not going to have you breaking your back like some slavey when there's no need of it.' He wants me to stay just because I feel needed, but that's the whole trouble — I don't."

"Well Nancy said, "but what if she gets better, well enough to come home? He'll need you around then, keep an eye on her."

"No he won't," Agnes said. "He's got Fanny and Jo for that. And besides, that's not the kind of care I'm experienced with. I didn't know what to do those times before, when she got sick at home. I was no real help at all, except to comfort the kids. I wouldn't know what to do now, either, even though they're gone.

"Besides," she said, "everyone may still say they expect her to get better, but all these years? All these years we've been saying that? And she hasn't?"

"She's out now, I thought you said," Nancy said.

"Oh, she's out, yes," Agnes said. "Out of the hospital, that is. But he's got her hidden away in a hotel out west someplace. 'She's not well enough to come home,' he says, which is his way of saying that having her at home'd put a crimp in his style. Make his love life difficult."

"Agnes," Nancy said, "now you know they don't get along. They're getting a divorce, aren't they? I wouldn't want to live in the same house with someone I was getting a divorce from. And he's got the apartment in Boston."

"Oh, I know, I know," Agnes said. "But I still feel sorry for her, out there almost all by herself. I know he's done everything they say you're supposed to do, someone gets sick like that. And it wasn't deliberate. But I think lots of the things that he's done, supposedly to help her, I think lots of them've made her worse. Even if he didn't mean them.

"At least she sounds worse to me," Agnes said. "Jo came by the other day to pick up some books that Nell asked for, and Jo said she's not in good shape. She's back and forth, this way and that, one day pretty good, the next day down in the dumps and having those hallucinations. Jo said there's a parrot in the sunroom, and some days Nell believes the parrot never talks to her because it's Mister Farley's lawyer, watching on her. 'Nell thinks it doesn't talk to her because he'll give himself away. Or it can't talk because it's a robot that can only take pictures of her and record what she says. But I asked the owner,' Jo said, 'and he said: "Some parrots don't talk. I happened to wind up with one of those. He came with the building. God knows how old he is, but I've been here eleven years, and I've never heard him talk. I doubt he's going to start now." But Nell won't accept it, when she's low. You can't convince Nell when she's like that. Can't reason with her. Never could. It's just like those times when she was home, and she knew that the people in the boats out on the water were spying on her with binoculars. "No, Nell, they're not. They're just people out on their boats. Having fun. Like you and Ken'll be doing again, soon as you feel better." "Yes they *are*, Jo, they *are*. They're more of Ken's spies. You're in cahoots with Ken *too*. Don't try to trick *me*, Tricky Trixie. I'm smarter than you think. I'm onto the whole bunch of you, and some day, when you least expect it, I'm going to escape from you *all*." So,' Jo said, 'she isn't doing at all well. It's very discouraging.'

"So, no, it's not for Nell," Agnes said, "not in case Nell does come home. I know what he's doing. What Patti Ann calls 'keeping me on ice' until new Farleys come along, and I can start again. He thinks he's being so crafty, but he's so obvious. My goodness, when Patti Ann was six, she could see right through him, and I guess I learned it from her. 'Daddy thinks he's so tricky,' she'd say, and she was just a little girl then, but smart, smart as a whip. 'If you want Daddy to do something, really want him to, all you have to do is think of a way so he thinks it's his idea and it will be a nice surprise.' And then, when she was about twelve, at the most thirteen, I remember her saying to me once when she was home from school: 'Next year Bobby goes. And then three more years and Lizzie. What will you do then? Take care of Mum or something? Will that be enough for you?' One of the things I like so much about Patti Ann is that she thinks about other people. Not many kids that grew up with the advantages she had have that attitude. She's a very feeling person."

"Just like her father," Nancy said, working methodically through her order of clam chowder, prime rib *au jus,* baked potato, salad with blue cheese dressing, and two very dry Rob Roys, before cream puffs with vanilla ice cream and hot fudge sauce, and coffee. "And just like you, Agnes, far as that goes. I don't give the mother much credit for the way those kids grew up. Heck, she wasn't there enough. Whatever good qualities they have, to go with their good looks, their nice manners, how they act — most of that's your doing."

"She couldn't help it," Agnes said. "Nell's a good-hearted person. When Mister Farley interviewed me, all those years ago, when Bobby wasn't thriving, he made it very clear to me it wasn't his wife's fault. 'She hasn't been well,' he said. 'I don't want anyone getting the idea I'm hiring someone to help out with things because she's not capable. She is, and she will be again, when she's recovered. And I have to be honest with you: This may be only a year's job, a two years' job, whatever. She gets back on her feet again, if she decides she wants to take the whole thing over, well, it won't have anything to do with you, and it won't change the way we'll feel about you.'

"That was twenty-one years ago," Agnes said. "Of course she didn't get better. She got much worse, in fact." She paused. She shook her head. "All those doctors," she said, "all those thousands and thousands of dollars for hospitals and doctors. Hundreds of thousands of dollars by this time — must be, after all these years. And not one of them's been able to help her. Not in the long run, anyway."

She looked wistful. "I'll always think," she said, "I'll always think that if they'd sincerely kept their faith, if they'd had that to fall back on and support them, maybe she *still* would've gotten sick, but she might've gotten over it. And what do the doctors do for her that her priest couldn't? Oh, the medicine, of course, but aside from that, all the doctors do is listen. And a priest would've done that, done it happily, for free. And maybe given her enough hope and

145

sympathy, enough comfort, so that she'd've been able to help herself a bit more. Find some resources in herself to draw upon. If she'd truly believed that God was with her. That's why we've got so many, many sick people like her around today, I think, and I don't care what faith you're talking about, either. So much sickness around. People've lost their trust in God. They've just abandoned the things that kept them safe, in harmony with God.

"Look at all these sex diseases now, those young men dying in what should be the prime of their lives. Isn't that part of the price of it? Of people losing their faith? When we were growing up, I'll bet there were young men and women with the same weaknesses that these people have today, the same shameful desires of the flesh, the same sinful cravings and all. But in our time, people kept their faith, and controlled themselves—didn't do the things that the Church forbids. And all of us were better off.

"I interfered as much as I felt it was my place to do so," she said. "I told Mister Farley. I said: 'She seems so *lonely*. Trapped inside herself. So *desperate*.' That first night she left the house naked and the police picked her up. And she told them her husband'd made her into a prostitute and'd told her to offer herself to any man who wanted her? I told him after that. I said: 'Mister Farley, that's not your wife. That's not the woman I've seen since I've been here, when she's been better. She has no respect for herself when she's like that. She thinks no one else does, either. But God not only *respects* her—He loves her. And if you could just find a sympathetic priest who could convince her of that truth, I'm sure she'd begin

146

to get better.'

"And he just looked at me with this heartbreaking expression on his face and said: 'Agnes, if only you were right. And maybe if I were Jim, instead of me, maybe I would try that approach. But the doctors say she's ill. Just like she had a broken leg, only hers is a broken mind. That's why they call them "breakdowns." No priest is going to be able to help her, any more than a priest could fix her leg. Maybe the doctors can't either, but no priest can do the job.' " She sighed again. "I wanted to say to him: 'Mister Farley, it's not the priest who answers your prayers — it's *Jesus*. Jesus loves us all. All the priest does is direct your feet on the path to *Him*. When she says the spirits are moving the furniture at night, when she says the devil is tempting her, well, that's exactly what the Bible tells us — that Satan prowls the world like a beast seeking whom he may devour.' I wanted to say: 'Mister Farley, think about it: Before you married her, her name was Ellen Anne McNamee. But now it's Ellen McNamee Farley — eighteen letters — Six-Six-Six. Satan's number. The number of the beast. Did you ever think about that? That maybe he's possessed her? That that's why she acts like this? And does these hateful things?' But I didn't. I'd said enough. It wasn't my place."

"Probably a good thing you didn't," Nancy said. "What'd you want him to do? Have her exorcised? Besides, I remember the movie, if the devil's got you, the furniture really does fly around. Yours never did. She was just nuts. You'd said that stuff to Mister Farley, he probably would've had you locked up with her, next time around, he heard that kind of non-

147

sense from you."

"You've always had that mocking side to you," Agnes said, "that skeptical, disrespectful attitude. *I* hate it when you take that worldly attitude of yours. Nancy Ann Lloyd Armes—eighteen letters: Walter Jay Dean Armes—eighteen letters. Six. Six. Six. Has it ever occurred to you that Walter's self-destructiveness may be the proof that the devil really is in him?"

"Bullshit," Nancy said. "Just, plain, bullshit. I hate it when you get to harping on religion like this. *That's* what brings out the part of me that *you* hate. Talk about something else, please."

Agnes shook her head sadly. "Well, anyway," she said, "I told him then, when he hired me, and any number of times since, when it seemed like she might be pulling out of it to stay: I said: 'Mister Farley, now I don't want you worrying about this, because I know you're a very busy man and you've got a lot of things on your mind that have nothing to do with running this house. But I remember how my mother was, she was sick so long and I took over—she resented it. Sick as she was, flat on her back, helpless, she resented it. And I know how I would feel if I was your wife and some other woman, I saw some other woman running my house all the time. I know I can get another job. It won't be as good as this one, I'm sure, and I don't think I'll ever become as close to another family again as I have to yours, but if Mrs. Farley wants it, and you do, well, I remember my promise.' And I did, too. I would've kept it."

"It would've broken your heart, Agnes," Nancy said. The waitress brought the dessert and she dug into it. "Not that he ever would've let you, leave them like that. I don't think the kids would either. But if they had, it would've broken your heart, and you know it. What would you've done? Gone to the archdiocese, and put your name in as a rectory housekeeper? Spent the rest of your life doing wash for some smelly old priest, and answering phone calls from people who don't know what time Midnight Mass is? It would've killed you, Agnes—it simply would've killed you. You never, never could've done it."

"Well, luckily for me," Agnes said, "I never had to. And that's what I mean. It's *so* boring for me now. I've got nothing to do, except my own things in the laundry. At least when Lizzie was still at Milton, coming home on weekends with her friends, I could cook for them, make cookies, drive them around to parties. And Bobby, before Bobby got his girlfriend there, when he came home from Providence he had just piles of laundry. Can you imagine that? This lovely little slip of a thing actually does his dirty clothes? She's studying herself, and she finds time for that?"

"She's smart," Nancy said. "You told me that yourself. How she butters you up and asks for your advice, what he likes and doesn't. Her parents sent her to school to find a good husband, and Bobby sure qualifies for that."

"He's not ready, though," Agnes said wistfully. "He's only twenty-four. In lots of ways he's still a kid, a handsome one, but still, a kid."

"To you, he's a kid," Nancy said, scooping up the last of the fudge sauce. "To you he'll always be the puny little boy that started school a year late, and then got kept back a year, because he was sick all the time. Because that's the way you saw him, when you 'adopted' him. But to her, he's a catch, a very good catch, with his future all mapped out. And if she plays her cards right, her future as well."

"That's what Patti Ann said," Agnes said, stirring her lemoned tea absently. "The last time she was home from Colorado, she told me she'd broken up with Sandy. Broken their engagement. 'It was probably the distance,' I said. I was trying to comfort her, or thought I was, at least. 'I don't think so,' she said. 'Oh, that was part of it, of course, Sandy being at Cornell. But it would've happened later if it hadn't happened now. It's your fault, and Dad's, the way you both raised me. I don't think I'm a libber, but maybe I am. I'm used to making my own decisions, and then having people like you help me make them come true. Sandy doesn't like that. Sandy wants to make the decisions, and have me help him see them through. I think I'm spoiled.' "

"Of course she's spoiled," Nancy said. "Spoiled in a nice way, but spoiled just the same. She's going to be a real handful for the man who marries her. Unless he's got a very strong personality, she'll run right over him. It wouldn't surprise me in the slightest, and I've said this many times, if Patti Ann didn't turn out to be the one in the family that takes over her father's business. She's much more like him than Bobby is." She paused. "I remember when Walter first got sick," she said. "When you started including me when you had to drive them to movies and so forth, and the pizza afterwards."

150

"We had such fun," Agnes said. "We all had such fun. Remember the night we went to see *Lady and the Tramp,* how Lizzie was crying all through the movie until Tramp found Lady again? I thought she'd never stop."

"And so did Patti Ann," Nancy said. "Kept sticking her elbow in the poor child's ribs and saying: 'Stop it, Lizzie, stop it. It's just a silly movie. Don't be such a little *shit.'* "

"That was Charles," Agnes said. "He taught her all those words. I well remember trying to break her of that habit, and finally, I was at my wits' end, I went to see Mister Farley. And I said to him: 'Mister Farley, I hope you know, there's not a prejudice bone in my body, and I know Charles works hard for you. And I don't care what he did in his life before he came here to work for you' — although I did care, of course, convicted rapist in the house with me and three young children, until I finally convinced Mister Farley it would be better if the chauffeur slept over the garage, but I didn't dare say so — 'everyone deserves a second chance. But he's teaching the kids, at least they're picking up, a bad vocabulary, and I don't care what kind of language you and your men may use on the job, I don't want it used in this house. I don't think it's wholesome for them, for young children, talking like roustabout bums. And you don't think so, either, because you don't talk like that around us, and I don't think Charles should, either.' And I know he spoke to him about it, and Charles did control his tongue. Or tried to, anyway. But it didn't do much good, by then. The damage was done. You can't unhash hash."

"But that's what I mean," Nancy said. "Can you picture Bobby, with his music and his art? Can you picture him telling people what to do? In that little soft voice of his? The men would laugh at him."

"His father doesn't think that," Agnes said. "I know he expects that Bobby will take over, after him."

"He may *say* he expects that," Nancy said. "I doubt very much he does. Bobby Farley never could've built up what his father did from scratch. The boy's not tough enough."

"Yes," Agnes said, "but it's not the same thing now, now that it's been built. Bobby would have lots of help, his father didn't have. Edith Keller in the office? Mister Farley's told me many times she was his breakthrough hire. 'Until I got Edith,' he's said many times, 'until I got Edith it's a wonder I didn't go myself, the penitentiary. Or the bankruptcy court at least. Place was a complete shambles. Didn't know what we'd bought, what we'd sold, or what we had on hand. Didn't know whether we'd collected what people owed us, paid people what we owed them, withheld the taxes or paid the withholding—whole place was a total mess. And she straightened it out. And Phil Morse: now there I was really lucky. I suppose if I'd thought about it, would've said: "Look out. Guy who goes to college, graduates from law school but won't take the bar exam? Admits he's alcoholic, and he's twenty-six years old? This bird's got one wing broken, at least, and he probably can't fly. You gonna hire a guy like that, manage your business for you?" If I'd've thought twice, I never would've done it. But I didn't have time, think twice, not in those days. I needed a guy could read contracts, figure out taxes and codes. I needed a guy that could deal with the unions, and meet with the bigshots, I can't. And I wanted, I wanted a guy I could trust, someone that after I trained him would stay, repay my start-up expense. And look at the guy now, will you, all right? Twelve years later, and he's the best hire I could've made. Sober as a judge. Seventy thousand a year he is making, better'n most of his classmates. Confident, sure of himself and his work, he's better at some things'n I am, and better than Jim at the rest.' "

"I bet he talks the same way about you," Nancy said. The waitress returned with the check for Agnes, who looked inquiringly at her sister. "Well," Nancy said, "I might have just a little drop of port. Do you still have ruby port?" The waitress said she thought so. Agnes ordered another pot of tea. The waitress went away.

"You know, Nancy," she said, "you can do anything you want. God knows you're old enough."

"Yes, I am," Nancy said, "and yes, I can, and do. One day a week, I can do anything I want, and each week I am older. Six days a week I spend waiting hand and foot on a helpless man who ruined his own health, knows it and tries to blame me. Once every two weeks, Jeanne sends me twenty dollars from Houston, with a short note that doesn't say much of anything about the grandchildren I never see, and who don't thank you for presents, and she always ends it with: 'Buy something nice for Dad.'

"Like what? Is there a better kind of oxygen than I'm buying for him now? Should I maybe buy him a solid-gold phlegm dish from Shreve's, have them engrave it from her? How 'bout a monogrammed bedpan, or a walker with AM-FM? And anyway, I'm the one that's doing all the work. Why should I buy something nice for him? How about if I buy something nice for me? Doing all the dirty work—she never thinks of that." She giggled. "You know what I buy with that money she sends me, to get something nice for him? I pay for the cable TV's what I do, it just about covers the bill, and I tell her he watches the sports. But he seldom does any such thing at all. He's usually too worn out to care, even to know what's on. I'm the one who watches the stuff, the movies and all of the plays. I'm fooling you, Jeanne, if you're listening. I'm spending the cash on myself."

"I know," Agnes said. "But you have to keep in mind that it's a sacrifice for her."

"It's not," Nancy said. The waitress brought the port and tea. "It's not a sacrifice at all. It's a conscience sop. She sends me twenty dollars in the mail instead of spending, herself, three or four dollars on a long-distance call, because she knows if she calls me she'll have to ask how her father is, and maybe even try to talk to him for ten minutes, the way I have to all day long, listening to him wheeze and choke and gag, and he'd probably ask her to come up and see him, and bring his grandchildren along. And she doesn't want to face that, and she doesn't want to do that, and she doesn't want to think about the fact that she's left her parents far behind her, in bad trouble—a burden she just *dropped*."

She raised the port. "So, Agnes," she said, "here's

154

mud in your eye, and I must say you've done pretty well. Better than I sure have done. All you have to do is play your cards right, bide your time, and sooner or later, Bobby will marry, or else Patti Ann will. And you can go on to the next generation, bringing up their children, too." She drank. " 'S funny," she said, "really strange, way that things finally turn out. Here we are, and when I got married, I felt sorry for you. I pitied you, Agnes, and I mean it, living your life like you did. Somebody else's family to raise, in somebody else's big house. All of the worries, responsibilities, none of the personal, you know, rewards. But now, look at me, look at you, and who would you say got it backwards? And who got it wrong? I did, is who, not you. *I* feel so trapped sometimes, something like I imagine Mrs. Farley does. Like I was tied down with ropes by my feelings. I envy you, Agnes, because of that—and please don't remind me envy's one of the seven deadly sins. I envy your freedom, you know? I know you have strong feelings, sure, about the people around you. But if Bobby turns out weak, or Patti Ann runs off and never comes home again, if Lizzie really does do what she says, that convent stuff, well, you still did the best you could. They're not your flesh and blood and it is someone else's fault."

"You don't understand," Agnes said.

"Oh, don't get offended now, Agnes," Nancy said. "I don't mean you don't care. Heck, I don't even think any of those bad things will happen. Not to the Farley kids. Not to anyone that's with Kenneth Farley, blood or kin or hired. He's too lucky, you know? Too in charge of things. His choice of a wife was the only mistake he ever made. It was a pretty big one, but it's almost as though Something was making it up to him, with all the luck he's had. And he can rub it off. He can take someone like Agnes Lloyd, from a family with no luck at all, except bad, and just by having her with him, change all her luck to good. Set her up for life."

That evening Arbuckle brought the green Cadillac home shortly after eight. He put it in the six-car garage and went up to his apartment on the second floor to wash and change. He put on his dark blue windbreaker over his white tee-shirt and jeans and walked up to the main house in the deepening chill of early October, the smell of low tide in the harbor down the bluff lingering summery in the air.

Agnes served him four sweet sausages, three scrambled eggs, hashed browned potatoes, and three cups of coffee with cream. "He didn't come back with you?" she said.

Arbuckle shook his head and swallowed what was in his mouth. "Only to the plant," he said. "He had the Jaguar down there and he said just leave him off, he was going in to town."

"Her again," Agnes said.

Arbuckle drank a quarter of his third mug of coffee. He reached into the right windbreaker pocket and fished out a bent cigarette and a wooden match. He lighted the cigarette and dropped the match onto his plate. He took the smoke deep into his lungs and held it a while. Then he let it out and said: "Ahh. Jeez, I love these things."

"They'll kill you, though," she said.

"Two a day won't, Agnes," he said. "And if two a day will, well then, I guess I am dead. Because there're days, most days in fact,when my two cigarettes are about the only thing that keeps me alive."

"You sound like him when he's on the phone with her," she said. "Three years older than Patti Ann."

Arbuckle shook his head. "Let him up, Agnes," he said. "She's a good kid. A nice person. She treats him nice. I never saw him really *with* the wife—missed too much history before and you know I like her, too. But this Jennifer is all right. Never makes demands, or anything like that."

"Why would she?" Agnes said. "What's there for her to demand? He gives her anything she wants, 'fore she even thinks of it."

"He's in love," Arbuckle said. "Ever think of that, Agnes, maybe that's the explanation? He's the same way with everybody. Me, you, everybody else. I didn't hear you complaining, that day you come home and you're going out again, and you hadda wait until I take the plates off your Country Squire, put them on your new LeBaron. He likes to make his people happy, and that's all it is with her."

"For now, at least," Agnes said. "Until the next one comes along."

"Maybe," Arbuckle said. "You been at this longer'n I have. But if a new one comes along, then he'll take care of her, too, just like with Jennifer. And you, them two nuns, and me."

"Speaking of which," she said, "did you do what I told you?"

"You mean, about the fight?" he said.

157

"No," she said. "I mean about getting you seats at the circus. Of course, about the fight. Did you tell him?"

"Ah, no," he said, frowning. "I, ah, I didn't have a chance. Didn't have a chance today."

"Eugene," she said, "you were with him from quarter of seven this morning until, what, seven-thirty tonight? He was never out of your sight? And you're telling me, you had no chance? That's what you're telling me?"

"There was somebody with him," he said. "There was somebody with him in the car almost all day. And when there wasn't, he had a whole briefcase full of stuff he was reading in the back. This thing, this problem that I got, this isn't something he needs getting in his way, he's trying, do his job. I got to wait for the right time. Right opportunity."

"If you don't tell him tomorrow," she said, "if you come back here tomorrow night and you tell me you still haven't told him, I'm going to tell him myself."

"Look," Arbuckle said, "inna first place, I got a date tomorrow night, and when I get home, it's gonna be late. And I'm not gonna be alone. So you're not gonna see me, after work tomorrow night, and I'd better not see you, either, when I do get home. Sitting in the study in the dark, so you think I can't see you, spying my private life."

"I do no such thing," she said indignantly.

"And, inna second place," he said, "you're pushing me, all right? And I, I'm not used to it. And I don't like it. So, don't do that either, all right? I'm used to handling things my own way, and that's how I'm gonna do this one. In my own way. I realize you

158

think you got my best interests, to heart, and I appreciate it. But I been on my own for a long time, and you got to get used the idea, this's my way of doing things."

"Yes," she said. "Well, that's all very nice, but that man brought that paper to me. I'm not used to having policemen showing up at the back door during the day and signing my name for complaints. I don't like doing that, Eugene. There's never been any of that kind of thing going on around this house since I have been here, and that's over twenty years ago. Cruisers in the driveway? People who work here charged with crimes, *after* they started here? And I don't like it. It scares me. What if another one comes?"

"Tell 'em I signed the Celtics and quit my job to go to camp," Arbuckle said. "I got no control over that, somebody decides he wants to put my name, a piece of paper, have a cop bring it where I live. Point the whole thing is, my girlfriend's sister got me this lawyer, and I'm seeing him Saturday, all right? Saturday morning. Find out what he has to say. And then, depending on that, then maybe I'll decide I got to bother Mister Farley with it. And also, maybe I won't. Which I would rather not, you haven't gotten the idea yet. But you got to leave me alone on this, Agnes, just like you do when I got, I got company my place. Just pretend it didn't happen, like it didn't concern you, and don't get me all confused."

11

John Corey was candid. "I don't mind telling you, Ken," he said, "I don't feel at all comfortable, us handling this thing." They sat in Corey's Waterford office, a thousand square feet of tightly partitioned space on the first floor of the executive wing of the Waterford Mall, incongruously dominated by a carved oak double door duplicating on three-quarter scale the thirty-first-floor entrance of Spencer, Lines and Corey at One Beacon Street in Boston.

"You said the same thing, Jack," Farley said, "when I asked you to handle the divorce."

"Not quite," Corey said. "What I said then was that I wasn't sure of *my*self, putting myself forward as an expert in domestic litigation, and allowed you to talk me into appearing chiefly as counsel of record. On the understanding that Sam Feldt would be in charge of strategy and tactics."

"Because I've known you for a long time," Farley said, "and you're handy when you're down here, and

I trust your judgment. And you've done well for me. No one could've done better."

"Yes," Corey said. "Well, that's all very nice to hear, when you've been practicing law for almost forty years and you still get up in the morning wondering if you've ever done anything right. But the facts of the situation are that I did nothing more than play Charlie McCarthy, or Mortimer Snerd, to Sam's Edgar Bergen in the probate court—I didn't file a paper or utter a sentence that Sam hadn't drafted in advance. And I remind you that after all his ventriloquism, and all my empty posturing, you are still not divorced. Not what I'd call a promising precedent for the notion that since we've gotten away with playing it by ear in the divorce court, we might as well now go blithely into federal court, unprepared on a criminal matter."

"Don't you have a Sam for that, that gang you've got in Boston?" Farley said.

"Frankly?" Corey said. "No. Until very recently we had no criminal capability at all. Two, three years ago we rather belatedly confronted the fact that some of our corporate clients might be facing a new sort of jeopardy under changed SEC rules and policies, if they persisted—against our advice—in their more swashbuckling mergers and acquisitions. So we had a rather acrimonious partners' meeting at which the faction against adding criminal specialists ended by compromising with the faction advocating it, with the usual unsatisfactory results. We now carry on our payroll one former Assistant DA and one former Assistant AG who seldom earn their keep, and in my estimation aren't always up to the tasks they've taken

162

on. But their total remuneration comes to less than we would've had to pay to lure some expert out of a deputy counsel's job at the SEC—which is what I wanted to do, but the bean-counting partner wouldn't hear of it—so that is what we have: two very nice young people no doubt expert at prosecuting robbers and polluters, by now more or less well versed in stock law, but not generally at home with federal criminal proceedings.

"And even if they were, Ken, that's not what I see in your case. This fellow Pratt isn't looking to throw a hitch into some plan Arrow might have to recapitalize by issuing junk bonds. And his boss, from all I've heard, is not sifting through local politics in search of what Jim'd call 'venial sins.' Harry Dodge is ambitious. His whole career's been one attempted power-grab after another. He was for Nixon when Nixon beat Humphrey, but he was too young, and too recent, and he didn't get anything. He was embittered when Nixon beat McGovern, and he still didn't get anything. But he worked hard for Bush, and people said he'd matured. And then when Reagan won, well, it was Harry's turn. But not right off. He's too changeable. He doesn't hide his appetites in a seemly fashion.

"I assume his assistants are of the same stripe. My friend Pucci at *The Commoner* says Dodge's the most shameless unelected publicity hound in the Commonwealth. 'We're helpless,' Dave says. 'After all, he's the US Attorney, and what he does is news. Even if he doesn't really think accused persons have no rights—the way what he says would make you think—if he says it, we have to print it. And play into his hands. He wants the reputation of being a ballbuster, and he's making it the old-fashioned way—he's earning it.'

"Now," Corey said, "I don't want you to go out of here thinking we've abandoned you. I took the matter up to Boston last week, and I asked Rita Bowman—she's the former AG—to take a look at it. And her immediate instinct was that this fellow Pratt's painting sashes with a mop, using far too broad a brush. So she recommended to Rob Tully— he's the former DA and very capable on his feet— that we bring a motion to quash on the ground that they're asking far too much. And that's on for hearing next week."

"So what's the problem?" Farley said.

"The problem is that at the very best, the most we've got here is a holding action," Corey said. "If we lose the motion, as is likely, someone will have to negotiate time to comply with the original terms of the subpoena. Pratt's not going to be pliable on that score, inasmuch as we will've tried to thwart him and failed. Government attorneys are at least as touchy as their counterparts in private practice. When they think they're being trifled with, they become vindictive. And keep in mind that they never have to pause and think: 'How much is more fighting going to cost?' Because their budgets and manpower are for all practical purposes unlimited. They have no overhead." Corey snickered. "Your tax dollars at work, Ken, at work harassing you. If we win, as is not likely, he'll just go back to his office and draft another set of demands, seeking less but more specifically, again basically posing the same bothersome questions he's raised with the first subpoena.

"I said to Rob: 'Is this a good idea? Isn't what we're doing with this dilatory motion, doesn't it amount to jabbing the tiger with a stick, after he's already shown he's awake and not in a very good mood? Do we really want to provoke this fellow any more than he is already?' And Rob had a rather disquieting reaction to that. He said: 'Look, John, it doesn't matter. You and your client may as well resign yourselves to the fact that this's just the opening gun in a long siege. And make some quick decisions. Either we're going to fight them every inch of the way, no matter how long it takes, and costs, or else we're going to have to sit down first with the client, see if he's got anything that Pratt'll bargain for, and then, if he has, go in and offer it to Pratt to get him off our back. Understanding that he may not take it. Won't, in fact, unless it's some big scalp.' "

"Such as Sonny Donovan's," Farley said.

"Such as Sonny Donovan's," Corey said. "Or Frank Leonetti's, or . . . who's the Commissioner, now, of Public Works?"

"Kiki Boylan," Farley said. "Wouldn't be Kiki, though. Can't even buy old Kiki a drink, let alone a dinner. His mother died, there? He was getting nervous, guys do business with the State're showing up with Mass cards and Jesuit enrollments. I said to him: 'Cripes, Kiki. Ease up a little. Ethics Commission's not gonna get their bowels in an uproar, somebody does some business your office, lights a five-dollar candle, your mother.' He still looked worried. 'Tell that to Jake McGrath,' he says. 'You still know where to find Jake, that is, now he's been paroled.'

"Well" Farley said, "it's not the same thing, of course—when Jake was Commish, one outfit had a season's box at Fenway, and they did pretty good on contracts although they got to see no games. And someone else, the Patriots, skyview suite for Jake. And then there was Rufane Construction—Celtics midcourt for old Jake—and Morningview took care the Bruins and they also did okay."

"What'd you do?" Corey said. "Just in a spirit of friendly curiosity, of course, because this was a long time ago. I'm assuming the Statute has run."

"As a matter of fact," Farley said, "we didn't do a damned thing. Time me and Jim decided, you know, only way we could beef up on the equipment was by getting plowing contracts and praying: Lots of snow, so's to keep the stuff from being idle, make our payments on it, well, by that time Jake had most of what he wanted. From guys that got there before us. I put some feelers out, and what I got back was that maybe Jake wouldn't mind the use a cottage, down Sea Island, Georgia? Or maybe Lauderdale? And I said: 'Oh, forget it. Buying one of those things for him'd set us back more'n we'd clear, we resurface the whole goddamned Turnpike.' So we went local. We leased the equipment, just like we planned, made it pay with local jobs. Which was the same thing, on a smaller scale, but more of it. I don't like to think how many dinners, how much booze and cigars we hadda buy, all those damned selectmen. And cozying up to some of those guys, boy, really makes your stomach churn. I hate to think what those TV cable companies must've had to do, get the local franchises.

"Look," Farley said, "I know what I am. I'm not a real polished guy. But Jesus Christ, some of those guys, they act like animals. You take them out of their hardware stores, their funeral homes and their drugstores? You see them doing business, or they're up there on the platform making plans and setting budgets, you'd think they're ordinary people, kind of dull but decent guys. Then you get them in a restaurant and they have a couple drinks? They act like animals. Guys that never order fruit cup, never have dessert—double lobsters, all around. And: 'Where the hell's the wine?' Eat their dinner with their hands, bother waitresses, holler at the other guests. All because they aren't paying—that is all it is. Act like kids let out of school, School for Wayward Boys, and all it takes to do it to them is a thirty-dollar dinner. That's what really gets you—not that they're so greedy, but that they are so *cheap*.

"I finally said to Jim one day: 'Hey, look, all right? Whyncha let me just be in charge keeping all our new pals happy? 'Cause I know you hate the drill.' And he was only too happy to agree. And I breathe this big sigh of relief, because you *know* what I was afraid of: it was just a matter of time before one of those fat bastards sidled up to one of us and asked could we get him a blow job, some convention, and if it happened to be Pure Jim that he picked to ask, dear God you would've heard the howling clear to Rome."

"Did you," Corey said, "maybe I shouldn't ask this, but did you ever do that? Run into that, I

167

mean?"

"You're right, Jack," Farley said, "you shouldn't ask. It was nothing very serious, but it did come up. There're three or four guys, and we're dealing on a regular basis with, oh, seventy or eighty, so it wasn't what you'd call a regular thing. But there were three, four of them that when they're planning their trips, National League of Cities and Towns, well, they figured they're gonna be off in Vegas, Denver, wherever, and their wives a million miles away, so why not a little strange gash?"

"And you did it," Corey said.

"I didn't do anything myself," Farley said. "I don't hire hookers for myself, and I don't pimp them for anybody else. But I arranged for introductions, yeah. I did do that much, they asked. The hell else could I do? Lose the goddamn contracts? How we make our lease payments then?"

"Did you pay for them?" Corey said.

"Out of my own pocket," Farley said. "For cash. American money. There's no way you could trace it."

Corey scowled. "Sordid little creatures, aren't we," he said. "Dirty squalid swine."

"Well," Farley said, "you can speak for yourself if you want. Way I looked at it, I never sneaked into some guy's place of business and said to him: 'Hey, Clarence, you wanna piece of ass, next time you're in Phoenix? All you gotta do is give me, highway maintenance.' Time they asked for that stuff, we'd had their work for years. It was just like, you know, like when I went to Paris, and you recommended places, go and eat and have a drink. Except it was pussy. Well, hell, to each his own. At least it was normal—

it wasn't little boys."

"Suppose it had been," Corey said. "Would you have done it, then?"

"No," Farley said. "Absolutely not. I was talking to Jay Cappola from Morningview? I saw him one time at a meeting, and he looks like he's gonna throw up. And he says to me: 'You know what that bastard,' and I'm not gonna give you the name, Jack, because you'd recognize it just like I did, and I haven't been able, shake hands with him since, I didn't want to have a hot bath 'fore I touched my dinner fork, 'you know what he asked me to do? He's a delegate this shindig that they're having in San Juan, and he asked me set him up with a fucking kiddie pimp.' So naturally I asked him if he did it. And he says: 'Of course I did it. That son of a bitch's the only thing standing between me and a four-million-dollar net. I don't do what he wants, he'll ask Rufane. And Rufane'll do it. And I got two dozen good men on my payroll I might as well pink-slip tomorrow 'cause I got no work for them. You would've done it too.' And I said: 'No, I would not've. That I would not do.' But I didn't, you know, piss on him. I knew how he felt. It's a hell of a choice, between doing something like that and maybe going out of business. Guys, guys're just different, how far they're prepared to go. Women, yes, I will do that, guy asks me respectful. I may not have any respect for *him* after that, and he'd better not get the idea, the future, he's gonna give me a hard time. Because I've got something on him, and he knows I have. He's a fool in fact, give me that ace, but if he wants to do it, well, figure that's his business. For us? Part of the job."

"How little we know," Corey said. "How little we dream of, in our daily lives, what's going on all around us."

Farley laughed. "Hey," he said, "you don't know the half of it. The sex things, shit — the reason they stand out in your mind's because they're unusual. What really drives you nuts is the normal stuff. That comes down, an avalanche. You know what we dread? We're getting started with the plowing, road repairs, then the sewers, water pipes, we had about eight towns, one city, we did snow removal for. This is right after the war, three, four years after the war. And we were still pretty small. And we didn't know too much. Making some dough, sure, but small, learning our way around. So they kept us real busy, making sure they stayed happy. But we did it. We fed them, and they were satisfied. Eighteen years we're doing this, and doing pretty good, and then disaster hits."

"What happened?" Corey said.

"Nineteen-sixty-seven happened," Farley said grimly. "The Red Sox win the fucking pennant. Playing in the Series. And all of a sudden you couldn't make a call out on our line, so many guys're calling in. I don't even want to think about how much we paid to scalpers, get those guys into games. It seemed like hundreds of them. Out of the woodwork they're coming. You got no idea how many kids've got leukemia, how many fathers, councilmen, been Red Sox fans for years, and now they're dying prostate cancer, never live another Series and we got to get them in. I thought Jim was gonna lose his mind.

170

Jim hates sports, you probably know this—his idea of games is two good wakes and up all night, Perpetual Adoration of the Holy Eucharist. Could not understand why all these guys're so upset. 'For a ballgame?' he keeps saying. 'All this for a game?' So I told him: 'Jim,' I said, 'do something useful, next time you're in church. Pray against the Red Sox, all right? All the local teams. Keep the Celtics out the finals, no Cup for the Bruins. We got all this pull with pols, it's from the work we've done. You must have some pull with God, all you've done for Him. Put the word in up there, all right? Tell Him we can't afford it, and He expects a new wing at cost on the Home for Retired Nuns, He'd better cut our overhead this damned ticket expense.' Jim didn't think that was funny, but I'd bet my watch he did it.

"So what happens?" Farley said. "Well, in the first place, fact we got those Series tickets proved we could get tickets. So now people that never bothered us before because they didn't think we had pull, now they know we have. And the Celtics've got Cowens, and they're winning every year. The Bruins've got Orr, and they're winning every year, and damned if the Patriots don't start to come around. Gives me a laugh every year, I watch the Series, Super Bowl—on TV, of course; think I waste one of those tickets on my*self?*—there's always all this gab about the thousand-dollar tickets and it proves the fans're nuts. The hell it does. Ninety percent those four-digit tickets're getting scooped up by poor bastards like me, watching home on TV while fat bastards we do business with wear funny hats and puke."

"Jim didn't pray very well, I guess," Corey said.

171

"Well," Farley said, "I dunno how hard he prayed, but he sure didn't get results. Could've been God was mad, He didn't get a dinner, tickets the Olympic Games. We took it on the chin with the Celts, practically every year. Sox give us another good licking in Seventy-five, and then again two years ago. Same year the Pats about bankrupt us, getting shellacked by the Bears. But not as bad's it used to be. We got bigger towns now; three're really cities. Same kind of handouts involved, but nowhere near as many, so that takes some the pressure off.

"Point is," he said, "I don't believe, unless I'm kidding myself, but I really don't believe they're gonna jug me, doing that. Is that a possibility, a realistic one? I get to know a politician because I do business with him, and I treat him to a ballgame — I go to jail for that? This guy Pratt and his boss — do they really think like that? Oysters on the half-shell and a baked stuffed lobster dinner, maybe with a little wine: they gonna slap the cuffs on us, we're leaving Anthony's? I mean, a lot of these guys, all right, it wasn't for the business, well, I wouldn't buy them coffee. But some of them, goddamnit, Jack, some of them are my friends. Butch Healy's down Pocasset, summers, not that far from us. I'm going down Coonamesset, Jennie likes his wife, there something wrong, I call him up, ask them to come along? Join us for a bite to eat, and I pick up the tab? Sure, after Labor Day he goes home, and he sits on the board, and every year we do the plowing, all the streets in town and the school parking lots as well. And two years ago we redid half the water mains. But the contracts're fair. The costs're fixed.

172

Morningview can't do the job right, any cheaper'n we can, unless they don't put the plows down and the town don't mind glare ice. The same as we can't low-bid Morningview in Duxbury, where they've had the jobs for years. And most likely bought as many dinners, just as many tickets, as we have for guys, our towns. So what's the beef with this thing? What the hell is wrong? Who the hell gets screwed in this? Where's the damage done?"

"It doesn't matter," Corey said. "In the first place, Rob and Rita substantially agree with you. This campaign that Dodge's on's not a trawl for little fish. Unless your entertainment expenses're way out of line, and nothing I know about your operation suggests to me they would be, nobody's going to get exercised about big dinners and fine wines. Especially when those victuals were consumed by nobodies. It comes back to the same thing we were saying before: Sonny Donovan or Frank Leonetti. The papers've been full of leaks and sly hints for months that Dodge's got one or both of them in his crosshairs. It's a regular pattern. First there's a gossip-column rumor that some mysterious gentlemen have been nosing around some small bank or public archive. Then, a few days later, there's an unconfirmed report that subpoenas have been issued in an as yet undefined investigation. By the first of the following week there's an anonymous but authoritative source quoted as identifying the subjects of the matter. The next day there's a denial by the person or persons named, saying they know nothing of such shenanigans. By the end of the week, the court papers've been served. Sunday's paper carries the subjects' denials of any wrongdoing, and expressions of confidence that this unpleasantness will enable them to clear their good names of slander and innuendo. There's usually a slap at Dodge — 'We welcome this chance to put an end to all the vicious rumors and unfounded accusations.' Tuesday morning's paper has Dodge's pious denial of any part in any of the slanderous speculation, and his firm refusal to comment in any way on any investigation, actual or fictitious, that he may have under way. Then it all quiets down until the next episode. It's been going on three years.

"In your case, so far," Corey said, "someone's either been asleep at the switch at the papers, or else Dodge and his merry men aren't confident enough yet of getting something on you to've set the hounds to barking. My guess is the latter. The question right now is therefore whether there's anything in all those documents that might eliminate their misgivings and prompt them to start getting you and Jim slurred in public. So Dodge can hold a news conference where he fields the planted question by righteously citing the legal rules prohibiting him from comment."

Farley laughed. "It's a great game, isn't it," he said.

"It would be," Corey said, "if it weren't for the jitters news like that gives the bonding companies and the banks that handle your business. Not to mention the leprosy it'll give Arrow, competing for new public work, all of which your friendly competitors will take full advantage of. You didn't answer my question: Is it possible that there's anything in any of your books and records that could lead to such a problem?"

Farley shrugged. "Possible? Sure, it's possible. I can't imagine what the hell it'd be, but five years of records? I don't keep them in my head, Jack. That's why they're kept on paper. Edith? I suppose she could've made a mistake. Put something under the wrong heading or something so it might make us look bad. But we've been audited six, eight times, the IRS, and they've never come up with anything. So it doesn't seem too likely."

"How about your payroll records," Corey said. "Will they give the government the names of any enemies of yours?"

"You mean," Farley said, "guys I hadda fire, something along that line?"

"Yeah," Corey said. "Fired, didn't get promotions they thought they deserved—things like that."

"Sure," Farley said. "We've had as many, a hundred and eighty-two guys working for us. Job ends, you lay them off in order, seniority, except you always got to make sure you keep enough minorities. But there's always some that think they got the shaft, and they of course blame it on you. And then there's guys that I fired for not showing up, and guys that Jim fired for coming in drunk, and one or two fellas we hadda let go because they were stealing from us. You believe a guy'd risk a six-hundred-buck-a-week job to swipe fifteen gallons gas? Or a clout a case of motor oil, he's taking home three-eighty? But they do it, they sure do, and then we have to fire them. Which they don't like much, either. But they'd have to tell lies, make that a crime, and I assume this Dodge and them, at least they're not gonna go quite that far."

"Not knowingly," Corey said. "They get a natural-born liar who manages to con them, it could be a rough haul before we unmask him. But no, they won't intentionally build a case on a lie. The danger's more in the partial truth, where the piece of the story they get is incriminating, but the part they don't know makes you innocent. That's the kind of thing that leads to long and expensive trials, and cripples your reputation."

"So what do I do?" Farley said. "I'm fighting with shadows here."

"Ken," Corey said, "I want your permission to go outside the firm with this case. I want to have a specialist go over what we know, and whatever else he thinks of that what we know implies, in his superior expertise. And if he's of the opinion that the situation's grave enough to warrant his expense, which will be a lot, I'll want you to sit down with him and let him take you in hand."

"That serious, huh?" Farley said.

"That serious," Corey said. "I've known you and liked you a very long time. I don't want you going to jail."

"What's this guy's name?" Farley said.

"James Saxon," Corey said. "Classmate of my son Ted's, in law school. His firm is in Washington, but that's no handicap for him—he travels all over the place."

"Funny name," Farley said. "Sounds like the old theater or something—the one on Tremont Street? What is he, one of them Jews? That all changed their names? That where he got that name from?"

"Yes," Corey said. "Or, his grandfather did. That bother you?"

Farley shifted in his chair. "Bother me?" he said, grinning. "No, not at all. And Jim'll be just plain delighted. I'll tell him he changed it from Jesus or something—we're going straight to the top."

12

Nell Farley in a green turtleneck and white wool slacks sat well back in one of the green wicker chairs at the iron fountain. She had her back to the parrot cage. The turtleneck hung loosely on her torso, and the slacks were baggy on her legs. Her feet were planted firmly on the flagstones, and her hands were clenched on the arms of the chair. She stared at the man opposite her.

"No, I don't," she said. "I don't remember Doctor Wendell telling me any such thing. Doctor Wendell told me *he'd* be out to see me—*that's* what I remember. I don't see why everyone keeps trying to trick me like this. Why do you all do it? I see right through it, you know. All of you. I'm much smarter than you seem to think. But *why*, why do you do it? Does it give you pleasure? Or is it just that my husband's so powerful and wealthy, so *corrupt*, that you think you can get away with it? No matter what you do to me, he'll pay you off, and buy you off, and protect *you*, no matter what. While his own *wife,* whom he *promised,* before *God,* to *love,* and *honor,* and *obey,* languishes in this *dump,* with *guards?* And *spies?* Why are all you people *persecuting* me like this," she said in a pleading voice, her eyes filling with tears. "What did I ever do to you?"

Victor Frontenac, M.D., sat relaxed, his hands clasped loosely at his waist, his shoulders slightly hunched in his brown tweed jacket, his horn-rimmed glasses halfway down his nose. "Mrs. Farley," he said, "I know Doctor Wendell told you that, because I was there on the day that he told you. Sitting right there. In the same room."

"Doctor Wendell told me," she said, taking a deep breath, *"don't* you tell me what Doctor Wendell told me. *I* know what Doctor Wendell told me. *I, know.* Doctor Wendell told me he was coming to see me, *himself."* She shouted the last word. The parrot, shielded behind the tall plants, shrieked.

The doctor jumped. "Good God, what on earth," he said.

She smiled knowingly. "Oh, don't play dumb, Doctor," she said. "Don't pretend that you don't *know.* Don't try to deceive me like that. It's too transparent, don't you see? I've told you, told all of you: I'm onto your games and your tricks. All of your sneaky baloney."

"A parrot or something?" the doctor said. "Cockatoo, cockatiel — talking bird?"

She leaned forward, bending at the waist and resting her forearms on her legs. "Stop it, *Doctor,"* she said, "if you really are a doctor. You know what it is. It's an electronic thingamajig. It doesn't talk at all.

180

All it does is listen to what I say, and record it, and take pictures of me, on television. And I just broke it — *that's* what happened. By yelling. *My* son has stereo equipment. My son, Bobby. So I know you can break some kinds of equipment with noise too loud for it. And that's what I just did. So now your little strategy of coming in here and thinking you could trick me into saying things for it to eavesdrop on, well, it isn't going to work. Because *I've* broken the machine."

"Now, Mrs. Farley," he said, "why would I want to do that?"

"For my *husband*," she shouted. "That *bastard*. For my husband to use against me in court, so he can divorce me by saying I'm *crazy*." She shook her head. "Oh, no," she said, "I'm, not, *crazy*."

The parrot shrieked again.

The doctor jumped again. "Mrs. Farley," he said, "let me ask you something: If you broke the machine just a moment ago, why is it necessary to continue to shout? Why not now just have our conversation in a normal tone of voice?"

She shook her head, smiling tightly, and sat back in the chair again. "Uh uh, *Doctor*," she said, "that little game won't work either. I know, I *know* there's a man in a secret room behind that machine, and if it breaks, well, he just sneaks right out and *fixes it*." She shouted the last two words. "He'll be hopping this afternoon, all right — I've got him jumping now."

"Okay," 'Frontenac said, sitting back, "we'll do the best we can. Is it okay if I talk? I don't care if I'm recorded. And I'm not afraid of your husband."

She nodded and smiled. "Why should you be?"

she said. "Since you work for him."

"Mrs. Farley," the doctor said, "I don't work for your husband."

"Oh no?" she said. "Who do you think's going to pay you, then? *I'm* certainly not going to pay you for coming here to spy on me, and try to make me say things so he can persecute me more. And just ditch me. I can tell you right now, Doctor, and you can tell him for me: He's never going to get that divorce he wants so much. So he can marry his harlot. Not while I'm alive. Because I know how to stop him."

"Touché," he said. He took a deep breath. "Let me try it this way. I work with Doctor Wendell and the other staff at Hall Institute to help patients in western New England after they've been discharged and gone home."

She smiled again. "Well, you shouldn't be here harassing me, then," she said. "I may have been discharged, but I can assure you, *Doctor,* this is *not* my home. My home's more than a hundred miles away from here. This is my prison, that's what this is, this *dump.* My husband's a successful man. A wealthy man. A powerful man. Who can do anything he wants. Including put his wife in jail. Why am I in jail? I didn't do anything. He's the one who should be in jail, all the things he's done. He thinks he can do anything he wants. He's blasphemous—he thinks *he's* God. And isn't that what blasphemy is? That's the way I learned it—one form of blasphemy. He's tired of me so he's sent me away. Age and childbearing, bearing *his* children—my body's not what that lust-filled man wants. Not anymore. So: write me off. Put me away. Get rid of me, and find some, some young floozy with big tits that he likes better. Who'll suck his dirty *cock*." She shouted the last word.

"Some day, and I know this, *Doctor,* he's going to get tired of this and have me *killed*. My body will be found. But right now it *amuses* him, to torture me like this. It's his hobby. So he gets people like you, people who'll do anything he tells them to, and you do it."

She paused. She nodded, her face expressionless, her eyes dull. "Well," she said, "I know things. I know the things he's done. And I've written them down and put them in a secret place, and when that happens, when he has me killed, well, the people who should know what kind of corrupt snake he is, they'll know where to find them. And I'll have my revenge. I'll be up in Heaven, watching them take *him* off to *his* prison, and we'll see how he likes that. And I know that's where I'll be, because he's put me through twenty years of Hell."

"How will these people know where these papers are?" Frontenac said.

She shook her head, again forming that small smile. "Because I'm going to tell them, Doctor," she said. "That's how they will know."

"How do you plan to tell them?" the doctor said.

She beamed. "Well," she said, "if I thought you could stop me if you knew, I wouldn't tell you. But since you can't . . ." She crouched forward again. "At certain times," she said, "not all the time, but at certain times, I am telepathic. And there're officers of the FBI who also are, and they work closely with people like me. And I've communicated with them.

Opened the channels, you see? And, I haven't told them anything yet. I'm saving that for a while. But, when I'm ready, well, you'd better watch out, Kenneth Farley, because the fur is going to fly. And it's going to be *your* fur, not that mink you bought your harlot."

"I see," the doctor said.

"And nobody can stop me," she said.

Frontenac cleared his throat. "Well," he said, "I, ah, how are you feeling generally, then?"

She stretched, raising her hands, arching her back, moving her head from side to side with her eyes closed. She relaxed. She opened her eyes and smiled. She crossed her legs and sat back in the chair. She clasped her hands loosely on her stomach. "I feel good, Doctor," she said pleasantly. "There aren't very many people here, but those who are, are nice. In the morning I have oatmeal with half cream, half milk, and a piece of toast and coffee. Then if it's nice, I go for a walk. The woods are lovely here, and there are lots of trails through them where you can walk without getting briars or burrs stuck on your clothes. It's very quiet in the woods, except for the birds. There are cardinals and bobwhites and bluejays and sparrows, and I've seen *three* eagles since I've come here. Such a beautiful sight. So majestic. Isn't it wonderful how they've come back, since we've stopped using DDT? How stupid that was, to use that poison. The poor things couldn't breed. They got the DDT from the fish they ate, and it made their eggs too fragile. It shows you what concerned citizens can do, if they band together. They can save the wild creatures, and they repay us with the wonder that they give."

"Yes," Frontenac said.

"On the other side of the woods where I usually walk," she said, "there's a big meadow. With tall grass. And I sometimes walk through it. There are pheasants in it, hiding, and they burst from it like thunder when I come too near. I saw a blacksnake on a rock in the sun a week ago. He didn't even move when I approached. I think he's getting sluggish. The nights are cold now, and soon he'll have to go down in his hole to sleep the winter away. Don't you think?"

"Yes, I do," Frontenac said.

"I think that would be a nice way to spend the winter," she said thoughtfully. "Sleeping peacefully in the dark, under the cold snow. And then the snow melted, and it started to get warmer, you could feel spring, and up you'd wake, ready to mate and then enjoy the summer." She paused and smiled. "There's a family of raccoons down by the brook," she said. "A mother and three little ones. I sat on a rock not far from the snake — neither of us were afraid — and I watched the raccoons walk along the brook. I think she was teaching them how to fish. She was really quite large, and they were, oh, so cunning." She paused again. "I wonder where the male raccoons are, when the little ones are learning things like that. Probably off with the boys, having fun."

"Playing cards or something," the doctor said.

She laughed. "Or bowling," she said. "Maybe having a few beers and talking about sports."

He grinned at her. "What do you usually do after your morning walk?"

"Why," she said, "I do different things. Sometimes, if I know it's going to be a nice day, the night before, I have Mister Sherburne pack my lunch for me, and I take it with me to eat on my walk. It's a simple lunch—sometimes a ham sandwich, roast beef. I tried tuna fish once but it got too soggy, so I told him I didn't want any more of that. Same with chicken salad. Anything with mayonnaise. And an apple or a pear. For dessert. I bring a cup with me and drink cold water from the brook. Mister Sherburne assured me it's quite safe.

"Then sometimes," she said, "I come back here for lunch and have it in the dining room. I used to think, when my children were still little, before they started school, how much I would miss having them around me for company at lunch. But then they went away, the last one did, and I found it was really quite nice, to make myself a sandwich with a cold glass of milk, and take it into the living room and watch the noon news. Or maybe read the paper that I never had time for in the morning. And it's still nice. I go into the kitchen here and get the box with my name on it, and I get some milk or tonic from the refrigerator, and I take it into the dining room and enjoy it. After that, I may get my book from my room and come in here and read." She paused. "I'm certainly glad I quit smoking."

"Yes," he said. "What book are you reading just now?"

"One of my very favorites," she said. "That's what I'm doing now. Not reading the new bestsellers, or any trash like that, but reading again some of the books I've enjoyed most in my life. Books I haven't

186

read since I was in college, some of them, and that was nearly forty years ago." She mused. "It doesn't seem that long, but I guess it is." She coughed. "It's been nearly fifteen years since my twenty-fifth reunion, but I still remember, that was one of the things we all said, the one thing we still had in common. How we wished we had the time to go back and read again the books we shared in school, the books we shared with our children, reading them to sleep. Life passes so *quickly*. The wink of an eye."

"Which one are you reading now?" he said.

She frowned. She pursed her lips. "I," she said, "two weeks ago I read *Charlotte's Web*. By E. B. White. How Bobby and Lizzie loved that story, when I read it to them." She hesitated. "Patricia Ann didn't as much, though. Maybe she was too young to understand it. At three. I waited until her brother and sister were five and six before I read it to them."

"It's a lovely story," he said. "But which book are you reading now?"

She looked at him anxiously. She laughed nervously. "I don't remember," she said. "Must be it isn't one of my favorites after all."

"Well," he said, "not to worry. We all forget certain things. Like my license plate number, for example. If you asked me the number on the license plate of my own car, I'd have to take out my wallet and look at the registration card before I could give it to you."

She sucked on her lower lip. She shook her head twice. "It isn't that," she said. "I really worry about it. My memory's so unreliable. Of course I so seldom talk to anybody, since I've come here to rest. Have a real conversation, I mean. I say things like 'Good morning, Mister Sherburne,' and 'Good evening, Mister Sherburne,' and I thank the lovely little girls who serve me my oatmeal in the morning and my supper at night." She smiled. "I must say, Doctor Frontenac," she said, "the food here isn't the best. It's packaged oatmeal, and you can't do much to that, but even though I never was, really, a *good* cook, I did better than the cook does here with supper. He overcooks the meat, and doesn't cook the potatoes enough. Supper really isn't very good. I've thought even of going in to the cook, or asking Mister Sherburne if they'd mind if I prepared my own supper." She paused. "But I haven't done it. I was afraid they'd be insulted.

"Anyway," she said, "I think, you know, that the walks I take alone and the reading, by myself, and how I spend my day without really talking to anyone, I think that may be why I have trouble remembering some things. I'm all the company I have, and naturally I don't ask myself many questions, so when someone does ask me a question, I don't know the answer. It makes me sad."

"Well," Frontenac said, "what about Miss Clancy, Miss Demers? You could talk to them. Don't they go with you on your walks, sit with you when you read?"

She frowned. "I don't know what to make of those two women," she said. "I don't know them well enough to talk to them. This is a very quiet place here. Not many guests. Mister Sherburne can't be making very much money, keeping it open for four or five guests like he does. I don't know why, though, those two women keep leaving and then coming back. I don't know what they're doing here. I'm afraid to strike up a friendship with people like that. So *mysterious*. One's here, and then after a few days, she leaves, and the other one comes. And she stays for a few days, and leaves, and the first one comes back. I think they may be doing something that's against the law. Lots of people do. I say hello to them—I have no intention of being rude, not to anyone—but not much more than that." She hesitated. "There's a younger man who lives with Mister Sherburne," she said. "He's here all the time. I don't know what he does." She laughed. "I don't think he does anything, really. Not much of anything. I've seen him three or four times when I've been roaming around, and I've thought of trying to strike up a conversation with him, but he always runs away." She worked her facial muscles. "I think he's sick. He doesn't look well. It could be he's got something contagious and he doesn't want to give it to anyone else. Some people are thoughtful like that."

"How are you sleeping?" the doctor said. "Have you been sleeping well?"

"Pretty well," she said. "I sleep better if the day was nice, because I've had my walk. Gotten my exercise. I've been that way ever since Salve Regina. In college, if I took a walk around Newport in the afternoon after classes, before I went to study in the library, I slept much better that night. I might walk down to The Breakers and back, not really paying much attention to all the old mansions—just using the time to think, plan how I was going to tackle my next term paper. And it cleared my mind as well.

And it's the same way now. If it's been a miserable, rainy, cold day, so I couldn't go out, I toss and turn sometimes."

"When were you at Salve Regina?" Frontenac said. "I take it you have pleasant memories of those years."

"I graduated in Nineteen-fifty-two," she said. "I was a member of the Class of Fifty-one, but I took a year off."

"To travel?" he said.

"Oh," she said, "no. No, I've never been out of the country." She laughed. "I've scarcely been out of New England. Oh, New York for a weekend. Ken took me to Montreal once—there was a convention there. I'm a homebody, I guess. I have everything I need, right here." She looked around the solarium with satisfaction. "Really, why go to all the trouble of packing, and then getting in the car, and going to the airport, and getting on the plane, and then getting off the plane and going to the hotel, pay money to sleep in a strange bed. And people are watching you when you do that, you know. If you go into a restaurant and the menu's in French, well, I can read French, and when I was in college I could speak it fairly well—I got an A in Conversational, so I couldn't've been too bad. But it's been so long since I've used it. I wouldn't dare to try now. If I tried to ask a waiter for something in French, he would laugh at me, I think." She gasped.

"Something the matter?" Frontenac said. "Are you all right?"

She shook her head, holding back tears. "No, no," she said. "I just had a thought. That when my husband, my husband Ken, when he was alive, we could just go into any restaurant, and he would order for me. Ken spoke French very well. He learned it, well, he had two years of it in college before he was drafted. In World War Two. And then he was in France for a long time before he was wounded." She gazed sadly at the doctor. "My late husband was a brave man," she said. "He made his mistakes, but nobody can say that a man who won two Silver Stars and a Bronze Star and a Distinguished Service Medal with Oak Leaf Cluster—along with the Purple Heart, of course—nobody can ever say that Kenneth Farley wasn't a brave man."

"How did he die?" the doctor said.

She took a deep breath. "Oh," she said, "I don't know. The usual thing, I suppose, for men who work as hard as Ken always did. That was one of the things that attracted me to him in the first place. My roommate at Salve was dating a Providence senior, Sonny Donovan, and his best friend was Ken Farley, who'd graduated the year before and was starting his own business. Construction. And Beth fixed us up, and I fell in love. Not right off. He was so much more sophisticated than I was. I suppose I was a little bit intimidated by him. But he was solid, you could see that. He was ambitious and he worked hard, and he was determined to make something of himself. And even 'way back then, so long ago, you could see he was going to succeed." She smiled. "I guess in a way he succeeded with me," she said. "He was just as determined to marry me as he was to make his business succeed, and after a while, well, I just gave in. Ken was a strong, strong man. And a good one, too. There wasn't a better husband and father on the face of the earth than Ken Farley."

She smiled and looked down at the floor. "Some nights, some of those nights when I just *can't* seem to get to sleep, I just say to myself: 'Well now, Nell Farley, you just think happy thoughts and soon you'll be having happy dreams.' That's what my mother used to tell me, when I was a little girl. Only she of course said: 'Nell McNamee.' And I, I think of those wonderful years that Ken and I had, when the children were growing up. I used to tell the children, to have happy dreams. And I think they did. The business was going well, and making money, and by the time Patti Ann was ten or eleven, well, we had a wonderful life. New, big house—we had a sailboat and our own dock, on our own land. And on the weekends we'd take it out. I always made the children wear lifejackets, though, and I wouldn't let Ken have anything to drink until we all were safely back. And those were wonderful days, taking care of them, bringing them up, teaching them things. Reading to them." She looked up and smiled. "Those were wonderful years, Doctor, wonderful years, and when I think about them they make me happy, and I drift right off to sleep."

"Do you have any medication that you take regularly?" Frontenac said.

She shook her head. "No," she said firmly. She drew her legs up into the chair and shifted her weight to her left buttock and thigh. "No, the happy memories are fine. Besides, I don't believe in taking medicine unless it's absolutely necessary. I don't even take aspirin unless I have a really bad headache. I've always been that way. My mother taught me that people depend too much on medicine to cure things they don't even have, and once you start doing that, why, it's nothing but pills, all the time. And you can get in trouble that way. Look at Betty Ford. And all those people in show business who've had to go to her for help, now that she's recovered." She reflected. "I'd like to do that some day, I think. I've been thinking of doing that. That once I've had my rest and so forth, gotten really back on my feet, I'd like to do something that would really help people. People in trouble. Maybe counseling, maybe volunteer work with some agency that helps the homeless. Or crippled children. Or children with cancer. I could do that, and I think I really will. I've never really been involved with any public issues. Ken always was, of course—politics, mostly. He had to be. But I have to face the fact that he's gone now, and pull myself together, and think how I can serve as Christ did. That's what I have to do."

"You had trouble coming to terms with his death," the doctor said.

She covered her face with her hands. She sobbed. "Oh, Doctor," she said, "it was awful for me." She uncovered her face. It was wet with tears. She shook her head twice. "Just awful," she said. "Here was this wonderful man, cut down in his prime. Only fifty-one years old. And there I was, a widow, and I was only forty-six years old. It'd always been at the back of my mind, that he was older, and that some day I'd be a widow and I wouldn't have him anymore. And I'd have to get along. But so *soon*." She shook her head. "I went all to pieces," she said. "I admit it. If it hadn't've been for Patti Ann and her husband, Sandy, I don't think I could've made it. Sandy's a wonderful young man. Tall, strong, handsome. He's a physicist. A brilliant physicist. Has his Ph.D. From Cornell. He was wonderful to me. Sandy and Patti Ann—they're the reason I'm alive today. I never would've made it without them."

"You were fortunate to have a family to support you," Frontenac said.

"The wake," she said, "why do we have wakes? Four hours a day for two days, him lying there in the coffin, people coming into the funeral home to pay their respects, and you know they want to help, but it just, it's just *terrible*. All it does is make you feel worse. All they're doing is reminding you he's dead, and he'll never kiss you again, Lizzie won't have her father to walk her down the aisle, like Patti Ann did. And Bobby, well, he's got to take over his father's share of the business long before he's really had a chance to have any fun. I collapsed when Jim Daniels came in. Jim was Ken's partner. He was there at the funeral home both days, all afternoon and then back in the evening, just stayed with us all the time. He didn't really want to be chief honorary pallbearer, but I insisted that Ken really would've wanted it. So he was all in his uniform, you know—he's a Fourth Degree Knight, and a Knight of Malta as well. And then the soldiers—not the American Legion but real soldiers—at the cemetery, the firing squad, and 'Taps,' and when they handed me the folded flag from Ken's coffin, I just broke down.

"I haven't been the same since," she said. "It was a terrible, terrible blow to me."

"But you're feeling better, now?" he said.

She pursed her lips and nodded, twice. "Yes," she said, "very much. I made the right decision, coming here to rest. It's only been a year after all, since Ken died, and I need the time to be by myself, rest, relax, read. And I'm going to make it, I know."

"I'm sure you are," he said.

She stared at him, her eyes glittering. She smiled. "Oh, *Doctor*," she said, "I *know* I am. I know there are people out there who hope I won't. But I will. I promise you, I will. I'm going to get even with all those people who've hurt me, who've tormented me. Those bastards. Those goddamned fucking bastards." She nodded. *"Yes,* I'm going to," she said. "They can laugh at me all they want, make fun of me behind my back and say: 'There's Nell Farley, poor old hag. Husband ran off with a whore and left her to dry in the sun.' But I'll show them what I'm made of. I can hold my head up high. And you tell your Doctor Wendell that, too, him and all the other informers and the spies that my all-powerful husband thinks he can pay to destroy me: They're not going to do it. I'm *strong*. I'm going to *win*." She shouted the last word.

The parrot shrieked. The doctor started in his chair. "Uh *huh*," she said, "your machine's broken again, *Doctor*. How do you like *that?* What do you think of me *now, Doctor?"*

He stood up. "Well, Mrs. Farley," he said, "I've enjoyed our conversation, and I'm sorry to have to leave. But I do have another patient to see, so I have to run along."

She sat gathered and small in the green wicker

chair, her knees up under her chin. She smiled. "I'll bet you have to *run,* Doctor," she said. "This isn't what you hoped to find at all, is it? What that bastard and all his, his soldiers, what they were hoping to hear. When you report to them. That Nell Farley's strong, and she's going to win." She dropped her voice to a whispering hiss. "Well, you go ahead and *run,* because his plan isn't going to work. And I am going to win."

Josephine Demers was reading a newspaper in the foyer when Frontenac emerged from the solarium. She lowered it and looked at him inquiringly. He jerked his head toward the entrance. She got up and followed him out into the cool, sunny day. They stood on the columned porch.

"You must have your hands full, alone," he said.

"I do," she said.

"I'm going to suggest to Mister Farley, through Doctor Wendell, that he should hire another person, so that she's always got two people with her. One for days, one for nights."

"Good," Josephine said. "If I don't get a full night's sleep pretty soon, I'm going to go crazy myself."

"Will he do it?" Frontenac said.

"Anything," Josephine said. "Mister Farley's a rare gem."

Frontenac sighed. "I know it's silly, even to ask," he said, "but I have to report to Earl Wendell, and I want the report complete. She says she takes long walks and eats alone. Is that by any chance true?"

Demers laughed. "She doesn't leave the building," she said. "Fanny and I've both tried to persuade her

196

to go out. We've told her about all the wildlife and everything that's supposed to be around here—so the guidebook says, anyway. Eagles, raccoons. Mister Farley told us, when she had that period a few years ago, when it seemed for over a year she'd make it? And they tried to reconcile? He said she was fanatical about the environment. And wildlife. Embarrassed him, even, in public, about what his company does. So we thought that might interest her. But she won't budge. In the morning we bring up some oatmeal to the suite, and she eats a little of it. In her robe. Then she goes back to bed and sleeps, until around noon. Then she gets up, and we bring up her lunch, and she picks at it. In her robe. Then she sits at the window and just stares out of it. Almost catatonic. When she isn't raving, I mean. She's burying her husband again."

"She told me," Frontenac said.

"She tell you how her son's in prison in Rhode Island for dealing drugs?" Josephine said.

"She left that one out," Frontenac said.

"How her youngest daughter's pregnant, and won't name the father?"

Frontenac whistled.

"Is she committable, Doctor?" Josephine said.

Frontenac shook his head. "Nothing she said would warrant me filling out a paper saying she's suicidal. Nor homicidal, either. Hallucinating a living person's funeral, taking place several years ago, is not a display of homicidal intentions."

"Look," Josephine said, "I really appreciate what you said you're going to do. Get another nurse. But this woman's not doing well. She should be in a hospital."

He shrugged. "What can I tell you," he said. "The law's the law. Suicidal or homicidal. Danger to herself or to others. She isn't. She's severely disturbed, but she's not committable. Not under the law."

"Fuck that goddamned law," Josephine said through clenched teeth.

"I know that," Frontenac said. "It's really frustrating. Is there any way you can, have you tried to persuade her to commit herself? Voluntarily?"

Josephine laughed harshly. "Sure," she said, "and we've also tried to persuade the sun not to set. Are you, are you kidding? 'I'm perfectly fine.' "

"She says she takes no medication," Frontenac said. "I assume that's untrue as well."

"So do I," Josephine said. "When we give it to her we watch her like hawks, make sure she doesn't spit it out. I don't think she could hold it in her mouth as long as we watch her, without it dissolving into her system. But you never know with these birds—they have abilities we lack."

He nodded. "So she told me," he said. He started toward his Saab Turbo. "I'll increase the dosage on my way home," he said. "Miss Clancy can pick it up tomorrow, on her way in. Feel free to call me, if that doesn't work. Or if she makes any threats to inflict harm on herself. *Then* I'll sign a paper."

"She won't," Josephine said. "She knows what triggers involuntary commitment. She knows more about it than we do. Why the hell are crazy people always so fiendishly *smart?*"

"They aren't, necessarily," he said, in the drive. "It's just that being crazy's all they have to do. All they have on their minds. So they can concentrate on being crazy, and they do it very well. When they're as sick as she is. Besides, this isn't an art, or science, you know, this psychiatric stuff. It's a theology — I think."

"Yes," she said in the cool air, "a pagan theology. And all the gods are dead."

13

The sky was darkening to evening when Kenneth Farley emerged from the back seat of the green Cadillac at the Arrow plant. "No," he said to Arbuckle " u go on your date. I'm perfectly all right.
I Monday morning. The usual time."
rse stood in the doorway of the plant.
d to Farley to follow him. They went into the yard, where a disabled grader sat, its flat on the spindly axles. Morse propped foot on the right front wheel and cupped his hands. "It was a setup," he said.

"Shit," Farley said.

"Guy had FBI written all over him," Morse said. "It's amazing. Half of Somerville's in prison for giving bribes and payoffs. You can't pick up a newspaper without seeing where another simple bastard bit the dust, talking to an agent. And then taking money from him. Or paying it to him. Don't they think people can read? Only a crazy man'd pay off a stranger these days. And another thing I can't figure: Why's Buster doing this?"

"They got him for something," Farley said. "It probably wasn't too hard, either. My guess is he was probably hustling guys that do business with the City Purchasing Department—small shit, you know? Just like Buster is, himself. A buck a case on toilet paper for the schools, another premium on pencils by the gross. Buster's grabbed everything but the third rail in the subway, in his time. And he'd take that, too, or try to, he knew a way to sell it."

"Not with us," Morse said. "They got Buster for nothing with us. That time with Buster, was a long time ago. They haven't got Buster for that."

"No," Farley said, "but they know about it. This guy Dodge, Sonny tells me, very large with Brendan Rooney. Took it hard when Sonny finessed him with Mooney. 'You'd think that a guy,' Sonny said, 'you'd think that a guy that grew up in this town, and knew the political game, you'd think he wouldn't hold a grudge like that. A straw in the primary? Hell, was mild. Just a little insurance policy. He sh been around the old days, when they vote ies and the most popular guy, City Hall, was Veterans' Benefits guy that kept the lists, the ones that died. But Harry Dodge did get a grudge, and it's still eating him.' And that's why, now they got Buster for something else, they're doing everything they can to use him to get me. Figuring I'll get them Sonny."

"That'll teach you," Morse said, "helping a friend out like that."

Farley chuckled. "Well," he said, "I wasn't thinking straight, back then, when Sonny not only talked me into making that little contribution, but delivering it to Buster. I had other things on my mind. But now I am. I'd do business now with Jesse James, 'fore I'd do business again with Buster. Maybe after all these years, you know, Buster now hates me, too. Thinks maybe he should've gotten some, that envelope. Old age can make you greedy: 'Hey, some of that should've been for me.' But he never got around to doing anything about it. Until they started sweating him. You had the magic briefcase?"

"Uh huh," Morse said. "That's the best four grand you ever spent. I sat there, and I had it on, and I'm looking that guy right in the eye, and I can see he knows, and he can see I know he knows, and there ain't tap-shit he can do about it. It was all I could do, keep from laughing. I even gave him a little lecture about conflict-of-interest law."

"I wish I could've been there," Farley said. "I would've like to've seen that."

"You would've given it away," Morse said. "You'd've gotten the big shit-eating grin on your face, and given the whole thing away."

"Probably," Farley said.

"I wonder," Morse said, "I wonder they're still hitching the machinery on, with adhesive tape. Yank all the hair off Buster's body, they take all the stuff back."

"I hope so," Farley said. "I'd love to be there. Hear him yelp. How'd you leave it?"

Morse smiled. "Told the G-man, I needed specs. Blueprints, and maps, and that shit. He's never seen

Cardiff, his life. There's about as much chance of him coming up with that stuff as there is Bucky hitting the lottery. It was all I could do, keep a straight face. What I wanted to say was: 'Hey, all right? Think up a ruse I'll believe. Gimme a little credit here, okay?' Buster gives me this big song-and-dance, how I'm late and everything? I wanted to say: 'Hey, there's a reason. This turkey hauls me in, the grand jury, he's not gonna tell them, first, I came galloping up the minute he called, offering him a bribe.' But I didn't." He sighed. "I'm too nice."

Farley laughed. "Where do these guys come from?" he said.

"The moon, I think," Morse said. "Wouldn't you think they'd have enough on their minds, enough to do, just catching the bad guys already out there? Instead of working like bastards to make more bad guys out of people behaving themselves?"

"Well, yeah," Farley said. "But Sonny's tempting. To them. And he's also kind of recent in the good-guys line. Far as I know, he hasn't taken anything major in the past three, four years. Hasn't from me, at least. Hasn't even asked me. Since that Texas Ranger Dodge came in, making noise from Day One about how Sonny could start packing, kissing his family good-bye, he's been purer'n Ivory soap. But Dodge doesn't know he's reformed. Or else he still thinks he can nail him for something he did before he went straight. He's a serious man, Harry Dodge. Sonny's convinced that he's nuts. 'He's one of those fuckin' Marines,' he told me, 'that never got over the thing. You and I get up every morning and get dressed and go to work. Harry Dodge gets up and

204

hits the beach from an LST, got the rifle at high port. He doesn't just want to do his job, and then do something else, pays better, way most of those guys do. He wants to conquer the fuckin' world, and if that means he has to rip off all my arms and legs, or anybody else's, well, that's what he will do.'

"Sonny says: 'You know, if it wasn't, what this guy can do to me, wasn't for that, it'd be kind of funny. I mean, what'd I, we, ever do to him personally? Sit on his hat? Fuck his wife? Run over his dog? I never even heard the guy's name, until he got this job. I was talking to Frank about this, you know? Because Dodge's just as hot for him, and I said: "The hell is it, Francis? The Leonettis and the Donovans? One of our women give his daddy the clap? What is it with this guy?" And Frank said: "Trophies, Sonny, trophies. He wants us all stuffed and mounted, to hang on his office wall. So everyone'll see what a big, strong man he is. What'd the lions ever do to the hunters, huh? Out there munching antelopes? Not a hell of a lot. But they're still big game, aren't they? And that is what we are." And I think he's probably right.' "

"Sort of makes your skin crawl, doesn't it," Morse said. "Guy gets all that power, do whatever he wants with, and this is what he decides. Setting traps for people. Son of a bitch. Nothing but a schoolyard bully—that is all he is."

"Yeah," Farley said, "but you got to remember something, all right? We look at it different from him. Those things we used to do, you know, we just looked around and everybody else was doing them, and we said: 'Well, that's the way the things get

205

done. And we will do it, too.' And time went along, and we just assumed because we always did it that way, and nothing bad happened, it must be okay. And then the other people said: 'Hey, no, it's not okay. Don't do that stuff anymore, or you're going to the cooler.' So we hadda stop. Or at least cut back a little, and do it in different ways, and be lots smarter.

"Maybe in the long run," Farley said, "maybe inna long run, this way'll turn out better. I heard stories, you know, guys go back a lot further'n I do, the fuckin' pols used to just grab you by the ankles and hold you upside down and shake you till all the loose change and your billfold fell out of your pockets. Guys're practically killing each other to get in a position where they awarded contracts. Jobs that didn't pay *any*thing, and they're fighting each other like goddamned tigers to get them. Because that meant they were gonna get rich. For what? For working? For building something themselves? Nah. Guys that do the building're lucky they see eight percent on their investment, but guys that don't have any their money tied up're making one hundred percent clear profit, without doing any work. I used to do it. I admit it. You know I used to do it. And I still do, what I have to, but I'm damned careful about how I do it, and I don't have to do it anywhere near as much. Which is fine by me, because I hated doing it. Letting those bastards stick me up. I wished I had my tank back. Christ you know what it cost me? And never mind: money. I hadda make a choice between going out of business and then, after Nell found out, watching her go right down the toilet,"

206

"You think," Morse said, "you still think it made her nuts?"

"Nah," Farley said. "I think, I think she was nuts all along. What the docs've told me, everything, I think what happened was that as long's she could believe I was between her and the world, which scares her, she could deal with being nuts. And what'd I know? I didn't know she was fragile, like glass. I didn't even think about the possibility. She was my wife. She took care the house, I took care of the business. She didn't want to go anywhere? So what? Lots of people, don't like to travel. It can be a big pain in the ass. She had those moods of hers? Lots of women have moods, their period or something. But then, you know, she finds out, and that's it: I am going to jail. I'm not gonna be around for a while, to protect her from the world. And she decided, I'm not doing these things because I have to; I am doing them because I *want* to go to jail, on purpose. To get away from her. All of a sudden she's found out I hate her. That's why I'm paying the money to these guys I don't even like. Which is a crazy thing to think, but like I say, she's crazy. Which up till then, I never dreamed."

" 'You take the victim as you find him,' " Morse said.

"What?" Farley said.

"It's a law thing," Morse said. "You run over an eighty-year-old derelict with your car, no living relatives, and kill him. It's not gonna cost you anywhere near as much, you hit a thirty-year-old brain surgeon with four kids and a wife and the only injury he suffers is the loss of his right hand. You didn't pick your victim right, and so it's gonna cost you. Sounds kind of mean, but that is the law. And the law's fuckin' life—so they say."

14

Martin Sands in his second-floor condominium office at the corner of Beacon and Park streets waved aside Arbuckle's thanks for the Saturday-morning appointment. "In the first place," he said, "once the summer really ends, weekends on the Cape are not all that attractive. This year the summer really ended sometime around the middle of August, so I've been here most weekends. And it isn't winter yet—nothing to ski on. Fall and spring, I'm in here most weekends. It's quiet and the phone doesn't ring, and that gets me out earlier, week-nights.

"In the second place, Mister Arbuckle," he said, "and I want to be very clear on this with you, I haven't agreed to represent you, and I doubt very much that I will. Estelle asked me to *talk* to you, which I take to mean: Listen to what you have to say, and tell you how I think you should proceed. I don't know if she told you, but at least the way she described the fix you seem to be in, it's not the kind of case I handle. Not that kind at all."

"I can raise some money," Arbuckle said.

"That's not what I mean," Sands said. "I work on annual retainers from clients who pay me a premium in advance to be available whenever they need me. Day, night, weekdays or weekends—doesn't make any difference, I am always on call. In fairness to them, having taken their money, I can't put myself in a situation where I'm tied up in court and can't leave when one of their calls comes in."

"Oh," Arbuckle said.

"So," Sands said, picking up a yellow pad, "on that understanding, let me get some facts. Full name?"

"Eugene Rudolph Arbuckle," Arbuckle said.

"Place and date of birth?"

"Charlotte, Vermont," Arbuckle said, "February eight, Nineteen-forty-five."

"Mother's maiden name?"

"Julia Arbuckle," Arbuckle said.

"No," Sands said briskly, "not her married name—her maiden name."

"She wasn't married," Arbuckle said. "I never knew my father's name. She may've, but she said she didn't, and I wasn't much interested, finding him anyway, so I never pushed her on it."

"Oh," Sands said. "Sorry."

"Hey," Arbuckle said, "it happens. She was just a kid herself. Got sick of the farm, ran off to the city—she thought Portsmouth was City. She was a pushover, too. Some sailor from the base knocked her up. She didn't have no money and she didn't have no job, so she came back home and had me. What else could she've done? Did the same thing myself, seventeen years later, and I probably would've gotten knocked up too, except I was a boy."

"Education?"

"GED," Arbuckle said. "Graduate equivalence. I went tenth grade at home, and then soon's I turned seventeen, my junior year, I cut out and joined the Navy. Finished my diploma inna service. I had, I think I got about two, three credits, college, from some courses I was taking. Rhode Island extension, you know? It was boring out at sea. I kind of had this notion, when I finally retired, maybe I would like to teach. High school, you know? Industrial arts, shop, whatever they happen to call it. Because that was basically what I was doing, most the time—teaching kids how to do things with their hands and their brains. And I liked it. I liked doing that. But it never amounted to anything. I never got very far. I was just reading stuff."

"Married?" Sands said. "Children?"

"Never," Arbuckle said. "Married, I mean. I don't think I got any kids, but then my father probably doesn't either, at least if I'm the only one involved. I suppose I could. It's possible. But none I know about."

"Religion?"

"Nah," Arbuckle said. "I was raised Catholic, but they treated my mother like shit, and I haven't paid any attention to it, a long time."

"Military?" Sands said. "I know you were Navy, but what branch? Or section? Whatever they call it."

"Submarines," Arbuckle said. "I put in for it because you got extra pay. Food's better too. They sent me sub school down at Groton. It was pretty good."

"How long were you in?" Sands said.

"Uh, lessee," Arbuckle said, "I joined February, Sixty-two, and I got out September, Seventy-eight. Little over sixteen years."

"Rank at discharge?" Sands said.

"You want the actual classification, or you want what I was?" Arbuckle said.

"Whatever," Sands said.

"Ordinary seaman," Arbuckle said bitterly. "That's not what the Navy calls it now, but that is what it is."

"Yeah?" Sands said. "I take it you had some disciplinary problems?"

"I was satisfied," Arbuckle said. "Had as many as *I* wanted at least. Like the guy that hadda shoot his dog? And his friend says to him: 'Oh, was he mad?' And the dog guy says: 'Well, I don't think he *liked* it.' I got fuckin' screwed, is what I got."

"Does this have any bearing on this fight that Stelle described?" Sands said.

"Well," Arbuckle said, "I don't know. It might. In fact, yeah, I'm afraid it does. That's why I'm so, you know, why I'm so worried about this. Because I think it does."

Sands nodded. "Better tell me about it, then."

"Yeah," Arbuckle said. "Well, I made Chief, all right? Chief Petty Officer. My third hitch, I made it, little more'n eight years in. Which is unusual in

212

peacetime. I was, I was gonna say I was pretty good, but I was better'n that. I knew my job and I knew how to make guys, get things done. I was twenty-five years old, all right? Twenty-five years old, and I had something none of those shitkickers back home'd ever see. I'd been all over the place, and I had a secure job that paid me good and no place that I could spend it, and all I had to do was stay in, man, and I was set for life. I wanted, I'd be able to retire when I was thirty-seven, I felt like it, and if I didn't want to, well, I wouldn't have to, either. I liked everything about it. Well, not everything—there're times when anybody'd just like to get away from what he's doing for a while, and just go do something else. But mostly I liked it, and mostly I got along good with the guys that shipped with me.

"But there was this one fuckin' prick," he said. "Now I know there's a fuckin' prick on almost every ship, but it's different when you get a guy like that on a sub. The goddamned thing's over four hundred feet long, and you'd think that a hundred and sixty guys could live on it together for ten weeks a time 'thout getting into scraps. But you'd be wrong. Because it's awful goddamned hard to avoid somebody, when you're all cramped in together and you're submerged most the time. This was on the *George Washington,* and the *GW's* got the exact same mission's all the other Poseidon class, which is to put out to sea and dive deep, and make the fuckin' Russkies wonder where the hell you are. When the only thing they know for sure's that you're in range of Moscow with those birds you're

213

carrying. Which means that if somebody wants to bother you, man, really wants to ride your ass, he's not gonna have too much trouble, finding you to do it.

"Guy's name was Lee Ford," Arbuckle said. "Warrant Officer Lee Ford. Transferred over from the *Andrew Jackson,* we put in, King's Bay. And for exactly the same reason, too—he couldn't get along on that ship, so they switched him onto ours. That's the Navy guy's way of dealing with a problem on his ship—put the problem on somebody else's ship.

"Now one the things you learn to do," Arbuckle said, "one the things you learn when you got men under you, is make allowances their faults and weaknesses, and try to give them jobs that they can do just the same. You know what I mean? Like what you do. I could no more do what you do'n I could be an opera singer. But I would bet I can do things, that you'd never figure out. Machinery, for example. I look at a manual once, that is all I need to do, and if somebody lost the goddamned manual, well, I'll give it a try anyway, and the chances are, it's fixed. And I can do something else, too, which is show somebody else who can't figure it out by himself how to fix it if it breaks. And maybe even in some cases, how to catch it 'fore it breaks, so it doesn't even happen. So I was good at my job. If I didn't have the best sonar crews, the best radar crews, working under me, well, I'd like to meet the guys that say that theirs were better.

"I got on my crew this one kid, and he was a sorry shit. He wasn't mean or anything, and he was

214

willing as hell. But it must've taken me three weeks to find a use for him, and at the same time I am busting ass the other guys who razz him. See, he was small, and if he wasn't one of them albinos, he was close enough, and naturally the first thing that everybody thinks is that he's queer, and somehow he beat the tests. I dunno if they're admitting it, now, but when I was in the Navy, fags were not a bit welcome. And especially on submarines. That's all you need is two of them, bumfucking in the wardroom, giving blow jobs in the shower. You could poison a whole crew.

"Well, I didn't know if this kid, his name was Todd Cornelius, I didn't know one way the other, he was all right or not, somehow beat the fuckin' system and slipped through. And I didn't care, either. Any healthy man, you put him out to sea and sink him for ten weeks at a time, he's gonna get a certain number of erections that he's got no place to put. Either he lopes his pony, or he starches his sheets—that's all the Navy allows. He gets back on shore leave, it's his choice in this world, what he goes out to find. He plays by those rules, way I look at it, rest of it's none of my business.

"Well," Arbuckle said, "when Ford come on the vessel, it was after Cornie's first cruise. And I took a certain amount of pride in what I'd done with the kid. I paired him with this big black guy, Homer Harrison, and the two of them made a good team. Homer was the kind of guy that didn't say a damned thing, unless he really had something to say. Like today maybe you sit down to breakfast

215

with Homer, and say you've been reading a book they just showed a movie of, and you've still got it on your mind. And you say: 'Jeez, this Wambaugh guy. That *New Centurions* movie there was nowhere near as good, the fuckin' book itself.' And Homer sits there, chewing, and somebody else says: 'Pass the salt,' and you do, and that's the end of it. Three, four days go by. You get up in the morning, or whatever's morning for you, way the hell under the ocean, and you get your food and your coffee and you sit down at the table and say: 'Somebody pass the salt?' And Homer passes it and says: 'I see what you mean.' And you naturally say: 'What?' Because what you meant was you wanted the salt, and of course he saw that's what you meant 'cause he handed it to you. And Homer says: 'The book's lots better. If I was Joseph Wambaugh, I would be pissed off.' You see what I mean? The guy's not stupid. You made that statement first, he didn't know if he agreed with it because he'd seen the movie but he didn't read the book. So, before he makes a comment, he goes and reads the book. And that was the way he was with everything, and that included Cornie. He was satisfied Cornie was doing the job, the two of them could get along, well, that took care of that.

"Now, Ford can't leave this alone," Arbuckle said. "I couldn't tell you how many times I hadda get between him and Todd and Homer, the son of a bitch's doing his best, get 'em both riled up. And I finally, it's getting close the end this particular cruise, this was the middle of August, back in Seventy-eight, and I finally went the Exec and said:

'Look, I hate to do this. I never done this before.'
And I never had, either. Not once'd I ever gone to
the braid and said, Look, this man's got to go. 'But
if there's anything you can do,' I said, 'get this
prick Ford transferred, I wish to God you'd do it.
He's interfering with my men. He's making problems for me.' And the Exec was a good guy. 'I
know,' he said. 'Skip's filing a report. We'll see what
we can do.'

"Well," Arbuckle said, "that made me feel better.
Felt as though all I hadda do was get through the
last week or so of the cruise, the brass's on my side
and that usually means the guy's gone. So I'm sort
of off my guard, you know? I don't expect anything'll happen, and as a matter of fact, nothing
did. And we put in to recharge the reactor rods at
Quonset Point-Groton, and we naturally all get
shore leave.

"Now, you got to understand," Arbuckle said.
"Normally when a sub comes in, the crew all scat-
ters. The Blue Crew, say, brings her in, and the
Gold Crew takes her out. Only ones that stick together're the young guys away from home the first
time. Because you're sick of each other, you know?
Lookin' up each other's assholes on the job all the
time, last thing you want's more of the same, you're
on the loose.

"Now at the time I am dating this woman that I
met through a buddy of mine on the *Washington*.
He was in sub school with me, and they were married for a while, and it didn't work out so they got
a divorce. And she moved back to where she grew
up, which was up on Cape Cod, down in Falmouth,

and when I come in I would get on the bus, change at Providence and go up and see her. And I did that. We always got along good. And one day she says to me, Well, whyn't we go see the National Seashore, the surf out at Coast Guard Beach. She had this Jeep, and we went. And we had a nice day, like we usually did, and it starts to get cool, we think: dinner. And we decide we're gonna eat this fairly nice place over Wellfleet, I don't know if it's still there, that they call the Old Blue Kettle. It's a house they converted into a restaurant, and the seafood's really good. Funny, huh, I love seafood? Spend all my time on the job with the fish, get off work and I eat them.

"Well," Arbuckle said, "it's small, and we don't have a reservation, so they tell us it's probably gonna be an hour, hour and a half's wait, and if we want to stay would we like to have drinks on the patio. And that sounded good, so we're out there on this terrace, there's this view of the marshes, and we're sitting under this umbrella maybe on our second, third, and who shows up but Ford. He's with this other guy in one of those trucks that sits up high on the big tires, and what they've been doing is fishing—got all their tackle in racks on the roof. And they've also been drinking. So I try to ignore them, pretend I don't see him, because I am having a nice day and the last thing I need is Lee Ford.

"For a while it works," Arbuckle said. "The sun's going down and the light's not too good, and he's a couple, three tables away, him and his pal having their drinks, laughing and talking too loud. And the lady comes over and says our table's ready, and we get up and go in.

"We almost finished dinner," Arbuckle said. "If we hadn't've ordered dessert, if Gina'd only hadn't had to have her damned Indian pudding, everything would've been all right. But she did, and before she gets it, Ford and his buddy come in for their table, right opposite the booth we are in. And he spots me. 'Arbuckle,' he says, 'you fuckin' faggot, the hell're you doin' with *her?*' And he's got this huge ration of shit that he starts giving Gina, and this is in a nice place. He's in a nice restaurant, nice people trying to eat, and here's this loudmouth asshole calling me a homo and a queer, and telling Gina, everyone can hear him, she shouldn't go to bed with me 'cause I spent my last three months getting blow jobs from a fairy, name of Todd Cornelius. Who was blowing this big black guy when he wasn't sucking me.

"I don't like getting in fights," Arbuckle said. "I used to like getting in fights when I was young, because I learned some Tae Kwon Do from a guy used to be on the *Boone,* and I thought nobody could beat me. I was in about three, and they didn't last long, and then I come up against a guy that knew more martial arts'n I did, and it seemed like that lasted forever. Since which my idea's been that if you want to have a fight, well, good, and I hope you like it, but I myself personally will be over the other side the room there, playing the pinball machine and maybe having a few beers, and when you're finished fighting, well, you still feel up to it, feel free to rejoin me.

"So I do the best I can, ignore the guy," Arbuckle

said, "and what I am hoping is the management the Old Blue Kettle either's got a billyclub or knows some reliable cops. I mean, this kind of thing, it can't be too good for their business, right? And after what I suppose is no more than three or four minutes, seems like a week, he shows no signs of shutting up and I still haven't said a word, pretty soon these two young gentlemen about the same size the Budweiser Clydesdales come out the kitchen in their aprons, and the hostess comes over Ford's table and says she's sorry but they have to leave, they're disturbing other customers. And Ford doesn't want to do that. He says it's his duty as a US serviceman to warn defenseless women when they're hanging out with dirty perverts and queers, which he knows for a fact I am one. Oh, he's having a *good* time. But after a while they get him to leave, and I think I can start to relax.

"I tell Gina the story," Arbuckle said, "not that she believed what Ford'd said, and she finishes her dessert and we decide, you know, after we've been through all that, we deserve some brandy and some more coffee as well. And the hostess is very nice — no charge for the brandy, and she wants me to know she appreciates it, I didn't give him any his guff back, or make things worse'n they were.

"So we're feeling mellow," Arbuckle said, "and now it's about maybe nine-thirty, ten, we pay the bill and we leave. And the minute we get back out on the terrace, Ford is waiting for me and he jumps out the cab and comes after me. Him and his side-kick may've gotten thrown out, but they didn't go anywhere. They've been sitting in that goddamned

220

truck emptying their beer cooler and waiting for me to come out. And he's gonna jump me, and that's really what I mean—like a flying mare or something, that the goddamned wrestlers do?

"I chopped him high," Arbuckle said. "At the same time, I kicked him low. This takes his feet out from under him so he falls forward faster'n he would've if I hadn't chopped him, too, so the result is he hits the terrace—bricks, I think it was—with his head back and his chin down. And he doesn't move.

"At first I'm pretty pleased," Arbuckle said. "Been a long time since I practiced, and it wasn't like I'd been ready for the son of a bitch, and I did it all on instinct. But then he still doesn't move, and I think: 'Oh oh, we got trouble here.' And I feel for a pulse and there ain't none. And I say to the people, that run the Blue Kettle: 'Better get the cops here, and an ambulance.'

"Now that is two bad surprises I had already that night, and I still got one more to come. The town cops do come, and they bring a medic, and he's got no better luck finding pulses'n I had. The lousy bastard is dead. And the next thing I find out is that the goddamned land the restaurant's on's part the National Seashore, so I'm not gonna be charged by the Wellfleet cops—they're getting the Park Rangers in.

"Now what I technically got convicted of," Arbuckle said, "was Crime on a Government Reservation. What I got charged with was voluntary manslaughter under Massachusetts law, but they didn't turn me over, civilian authorities, for trial. I got court-martial, and instead of drawing a real lawyer, I got a legal officer, which is usually one of the bigger jerks among the junior-grade lieutenants that thinks when his ROTC hitch ends, he might, just might, go to law school. Or if that don't work out, maybe furnace repair. The prosecutor was a real lawyer, though, and he was also a real prick. He was a Lieutenant Commander, Judge Advocate General's, and I guess he must've been bucking for promotion and decided I'm his ticket. He came after me like I was a lamb chop and he was a wolf, and my guy didn't protect me. Going in, you know, what do I know? I thought it was self-defense. But the guy that's prosecuting says the reason Ford attacked me was all the fights we had on ship, and I sucked him into going for me when I knew he was drunk. Like I planned it, or something, went all the way out to the end of the Cape with my girlfriend to get in a fight. How the hell did I know Ford was gonna be there, stiff and loud? That part never got explained. My guy did nothing for me. He may've been stupid; he may've been scared—either way, didn't much matter.

"I got seven to ten in the Portsmouth brig," Arbuckle said. "Which was the end of it with Gina—married another guy. Not that I blamed her. And there I am, back where I started from, more'n one sense the word, only now there're bars on my window. Killing my shipmate, bad blood between us—they pulled out all of the stops."

"But you served your time," Sands said.

"I did," Arbuckle said. "I did over four years. I got out of the jailhouse four months later'n I

222

would've retired on full pay and allowances if I'd've made twenty years. Except of course they forfeited those, and all my retirement stuff, too. I went in the Navy busted broke and young, and I came out old and busted broke, a Dishonorable Discharge."

"So you're worried," Sands said, "and naturally enough, that if they try this case of you hitting this guy Cole, the fact you've killed a man with your hands will be brought up and used against you."

"No," Arbuckle said. "Well, yes. Yes, I am worried, that. But that's not the principal thing—that's just a smaller thing. See, I got out, four years. And the terms of my release, I not only hadda have a job, I also had to agree, report probation every month for the rest the complete sentence. So they can make sure I'm not drinking—which Cole of course can say I was, the night I laid him out—and not getting into fights. Which obviously I was, even if it was short. And if I am, doing those things, back inna brig I go. I get convicted on this thing with Cole, I'm afraid they're gonna yank me back to Portsmouth, with six more years to serve."

"I see," Sands said. "That does raise the stakes some, doesn't it?"

"Look," Arbuckle said, "just between you and me, all right?"

"This's all in confidence," Sands said. "I can't tell anyone unless you order me to. What you've said, I mean."

"Okay," Arbuckle said. "Thing is, I lied to them. I lied to them when I got out. It was the only way. The way I got out, I didn't have a prayer of getting out unless I did something they could enter in my record and say: 'See? This guy's reformed. He's showing remorse, and this's how we can tell.' Whether it's true or not, they got to have something, and if there isn't anything you can give them, well, you got to make something up. So I became a drunk."

"In the lockup?" Sands said. "That must've taken a certain amount of ingenuity."

"Well," Arbuckle said, "not really, no. I don't mean, I was getting something to drink in the can. What I mean is I went to them and said I seen the light, and the reason I got violent was because I couldn't handle booze. And I wanted to start going, AA. Because otherwise they were liable, say to me, you know: 'Well, if you get violent when you drink, this's the best place inna world for you. No cocktail hour here.' But if I was showing them, I'd never drink again, well, then they could all smile at each other and say: 'What a good job we done with this murderous bum, and to prove it we're letting him out.' And they did. Which was how I met Phil Morse, guy that got me my first job with Mister Farley. He's some kind of honcho, the New England AA, and he used to travel around, the meetings, make sure everybody's still got the Higher Power in mind, all that good shit, take off his coat and say: 'Hi, I'm Phil, and I'm an alcoholic.' And we all'd say: 'Hi, Phil,' and then he'd tell us all over again how he became a lush 'fore he's old enough to vote, and if he can stay sober with AA, certainly all us miserable specimens society can do it too. I think he gets his cookies, doing that, but what hell, huh? He's still a nice guy. And it worked out fine. He sent a letter in, saying how sincere I was, and he got Mister Farley, hire me to work in the shop, and I did that a couple years. And then his old driver on his day off in Boston got nailed on a crummy marijuana charge, and that's how I got my job. The job I got right now. Mister Farley gives second chances—no thirds."

"I see," Sands said.

"Which job, now that I got it, I really don't want to lose," Arbuckle said. "At least not for belting some cheap little piece of shit that beats up women when he's drunk. He's telling me, he's in Paris? I'm thinking: 'How the hell come the cycles didn't get him?' You ever seen those things, those motorcycles that the guys ride down the boulevards, got tanks and suckers on them and they suck up all the dog-shit? My boss's girl, she named them: 'Motorized, heavy-duty, super-duper pooper-scoopers.' Cole should've gotten sucked up.

"Instead," he said, "I'm the one getting sucked up. My age, my experience, I'm not likely get a new job good as this one, and I'll never find one better. Mister Farley never lets anybody go, 'less they force him to. I'm making twenty-one a year, and in lots of ways it's like on the submarines, you know? I got places to spend it now, but I never have the time to go them. I live free, room and board, and if I want a car, I got my choice, except for the black Jag. I can hang onto this, I got money in the bank, and when I get to the age where I can't work anymore, can't see the white lines on the road or something, well, Social Security, plus I get a pension from Arrow, because that's where I get paid. I could be

225

pretty well-off. Almost as good as I could've been, right? If I'd've stayed in the Navy."

"You're really concerned about your security, then," Sands said. "That's your primary concern."

"Hey," Arbuckle said, "I never had none. Well, for a while I did, the Navy—thought I did at least. But then they took that away from me. I was growing up, I never had none. Naturally I am. And I got something going with Stelle's sister there, she's a little young for me but she don't seem to mind. I mean, why's all this shit have to happen? Why I need this Cole? Minding my own business, taking care my job, and now all of a sudden back the shit is in the fan. I think it really sucks."

Sands raised his eyebrows. "Well," he said, "this isn't what you want to hear, but it's the best that I can do. I don't know what to tell you. If it weren't for your parole situation it'd be a simple case. Go in and try it, and maybe you win it—the criminal case, I mean. Cole might persist in the civil case, where he wouldn't have to prove the thing beyond a reasonable doubt. But it's not very likely. On the other hand, if you lost the criminal case, well, the most a judge'd give you'd be a suspended sentence, and maybe a small fine. You could even plead the thing, perhaps get even less. Your problem is that if you do that, you're liable be back in the brig. That's where the knot's in this rope."

"So what do I do?" Arbuckle said.

Sands grimaced. "Look," he said, "this doesn't mean I'm taking your case. Not all of it, at least. But my own present feeling is that I don't know enough about the actual situation even to advise you on whom to see next. Which is what I'd planned to do.

"Now it happens I've got some business in the federal court on next week," he said. "Nothing to do with you. But while I'm over there, I'll drop by the Probation Office and see if I can get a reading from them on what might happen here. I can't believe the Navy'd want you back inside, not after all this time, and not on a scut case like this. If that's so then either I or one of my associates can go down to Quincy with you and treat this A and B with all the rich contempt it deserves. And that will end the matter."

"You really think?" Arbuckle said.

"I really hope," Sands said.

15

James Saxon's build and appearance defeated the intentions of the people who designed and altered the clothes his wife chose for him at Britches in Georgetown. When she completed her selections and managed at last to bring him in to have them conformed to his physique, novice tailors blanched and retreated from the fitting rooms to confer with senior personnel, who told them sadly neither Amy Saxon nor her husband would hear of custom work.

At nine on Sunday morning he looked out of place in the sitting room of his suite at the southwest corner of the tenth floor of the Ritz-Carlton in Boston, the fabric of his black-and-white glen-plaid trousers bagging around his short, bowed legs, the pure cotton of his fresh white oxford-cloth button-down shirt mussed and rumpled over his long barrel-chested torso after less than an hour of wear, the thirty-dollar red silk ancient madder tie pulled down from his opened collar and skewed away toward his breast pocket. His thick wrists, black with hair, protruded too far from his cuffs. His heavy black beard had survived his morning shave by lurking safely just beneath the surface of his skin. He appeared to have groomed his black forelock and done what he could with the fringe of hair around his uneven bald scalp, but his habit of passing his right hand over his head had made the hair stick out again. He chewed at his fleshy lower lip.

After Kenneth Farley and James Daniels introduced themselves and Daniels removed his coat — it was sunny in Boston, with only a mild hint of chilliness, but Daniels had arrived in an electric blue hooded down parka, worn over a weighty grey tweed jacket and bulky grey flannel pants — Saxon wordlessly assigned them flanking wing chairs and sat down on the couch facing them across the coffee table, like a boxer waiting for the bell to ring. "I think Jack Corey's given me a pretty thorough briefing," he said, "so if you gentlemen don't object, I think we can save some time here if I just assume that, and start asking you questions based on the assumption that I have a working knowledge of the problem."

"The quicker the better," Daniels said. "The traffic starts to really build up out there by eleven-thirty."

Saxon grinned. "Remarkable," he said. "Schroeder's going to pick you to shreds today, and you're

230

actually driving out there to see the humiliation?"

Daniels did not smile. "You think," he said.

"Well," Saxon said, "the spread's what, four points, four and a half? The Pats haven't been the same since Dawson went down two years ago. They still forget the running game, or at least where they put it when John Hannah hung it up. Redskins're hot, you know. Partner of mine took the points and the Pats—RFK season-ticket holder, but no loyalty at all when it comes to making bets—and I told Gus it was big mistake. 'Skins by nine, at least; that's what I would say.' "

"Is that what you bet?" Daniels said.

"I don't bet," Saxon said. "I used to play the game—not pro, just Ivy League—and I know how uncontrollable it is. My taste is for sure things. Now the way I get it, neither one of you nor your company itself is the US Attorney's actual objective. Jack's interpretation is that the prosecutors see you merely as a means to an end, which end is a viable case against either Sonny Donovan or Frank Leonetti. You share that view?"

"I know very little about it," Daniels said, showing some resentment. "I've never had more than nominal contact with either one of them. You'll have to depend on Kenneth for that."

"Ken?" Saxon said.

"Seems like the only possible explanation," Farley said. "Far as I know, all of our dealings with government officials have been totally open and aboveboard, and none of them've been with either

231

Sonny or Frank. Or agencies under Sonny. Contract awards, I mean. We've done some major work on projects in the city that got under way since Sonny was elected, but all of them've been subs—demolition work or site preparation that we did for prime contractors. Sonny and his people had no direct say in giving us those subcontracts. And Frank of course is out of office. But even when he was in, we did very little State work. If he does succeed in knocking Paul Finnerty off next time, repaying Finnerty's favor, I'll be personally pleased, because Frank's a friend of mine. But I'd doubt very much the amount of State work we'd end up doing would be much greater than we had, his first administration. Which, in relation to our total business, was very, very small."

"So what's the connection, then?" Saxon said. "I talked to some friends of mine in Justice, career types that I call my moles, holdovers from Johnson's days, and they tell me Dodge ain't dumb. Ambitious, maybe, but not dumb. They also tell me his deputy there, this guy David Curley? They say he's very smart, very shrewd, will not go off half cocked."

"That's not the name of the prosecutor on the subpoena," Daniels said impatiently. "Pratt or something. I never heard of that guy until Ken showed me the paper."

"He's the point man," Saxon said. "I don't have a book on him, either, but the basis what I do know, Dodge and Curley must figure him for their

232

varsity. That's the way those offices work. The top guys make a preliminary, seat-of-the-pants decision that something naughty's going on. Then they designate someone they at least think's one of their better warriors to dig into the facts and see if they're right. The office's well run, and there's every reason to think this one generally is, the guy they pick is seasoned. Has at least three, maybe five years' experience. Knows how it feels to lose a case that shouldn't've been brought, and doesn't like the feeling. If this guy Pratt's ramrodding the grand jury on this, at least they think that Pratt's got good judgment, and is smart, and'll either find it if it's there, or has the balls to tell them flat-out if it isn't.

"So," Saxon said, "first question I've got for you is the same question they had for Pratt: Is it there? And if so, what is it?"

"It's there," Daniels said grimly.

"Oh, come on, Jim," Farley said irritably. He shifted his gaze to Saxon. "You should know that Jim's a pessimist. We've never gone in on a job where he thought we'd win the bid. We've never won a bid that he didn't immediately say was sure to end up losing us some huge amount of money. We've never had an incentive clause that he thought we could meet. When we've tied up suppliers—steel, asphalt and cement, say—Jim's always been absolutely certain the market'd glut and the bottom'd fall out the price before we took delivery. When we've come to the conclusion that the market was shaky and we'd be better off on a buy-as-you-go basis, Jim's always come in the next day predicting the market's about to soar."

"And several times I've been right," Daniels said.

"*Some*times he's been right," Farley said. "Once in Seventy-three, I think it was, and then there was a job we had six, eight years ago, when we had to pay more for clean fill than we would've if we'd bought ahead. Otherwise, for coming up on forty years I've been partners with this guy, and every year, we close the books, we made another profit, and I sit there and look at the numbers and say: 'Well, there's no question about it. The Tooth Fairy's sneaking into banks at night, making deposits, our account.' It's the only explanation how we've done so well, making what, you listen Jim, was one bad choice after another. Oh, and another thing: it's always *after* we've made the decision, Phil and me and Jim, just the three of us around the table, and we've acted on it, that Jim's feet start to get cold. Never *before* we've committed ourselves. Always afterwards."

"I admit it," Daniels said. "I've always let you and Phil talk me into too many things, against my better judgment. I give in to preserve peace in the operation, and then driving myself home, I start to think again, and I'm awake all night as a result, convinced my arguments were sounder and I should not have given in. You two'd listened to me more, or I'd stuck to my guns, those profits'd be a lot bigger, mark my words on that."

234

"Which is why you should get a driver," Farley said. "That way you could concentrate on business, get through some that paperwork you're always complaining about backed up on your desk, and you wouldn't have time to be picking away at decisions already made."

"Kenneth permits himself the luxury of a driver," Daniels said primly. "There's another area where we haven't always agreed: Just exactly how many frills and luxuries we can stand, our overhead, before we spend ourselves bankrupt before we ever see a dime."

"Jim is also cheap," Farley said, "in case you hadn't noticed."

"I believe in a dollar's worth of value for a dollar spent," Daniels said. "I don't think a company our size is in a position to provide a retinue of butlers and stableboys for the people who happen to be running it. Maybe Bechtel could justify those kinds of perks for George Shultz, but they were building dams in Africa, and God only knows where else, and we're resurfacing secondary roads for small towns and flat-broke cities. Go around living like pashas on what we gross in a year? Supporting a bunch of hangers-on with criminal records, and nuns thrown out, their orders? Makes no sense at all."

"Of course," Farley said, "if the nuns're still wearing their habits, and haven't renounced their vows, then Jim thinks it's perfectly all right, give them dough for gratis, at least far as we're concerned."

"The company, Mister Saxon," Daniels said, "the company so far as I know has never given the nuns a dime."

"The Cardinal, then," Farley said.

"Or the Cardinal, either," Daniels said.

"All right," Farley said, "I'll say it a different way. The company's done one shitload of work, tying up manpower, wearing out equipment, building stuff for the Church that nets us not one dime. I call that 'making gifts.'"

"And I call it keeping men at work who'd otherwise be idle and would have to be laid off, at some immediate hardship to themselves and also at the risk to us that we would lose good people we'd find it hard to replace. Not to mention that the only thing that ruins equipment faster than hard use is rust and idle neglect. We may not have made profits expanding the school for special children, but we kept our organization intact, without out-of-pocket costs to us, until regular work resumed. Regular work that in some cases we got because of our reputation for helping out the Church."

"Some day," Farley said, "some day I would like to see a list of the jobs we got, and the money we made, because you play kissy-face the Cardinal so much. You've been saying that for years, and for years you've been promising me that list, and I've still never seen it. You wanna drive around in a Ford and give the difference, the Jaguar, the

Bishop? Fine by me, but don't then come around looking like a bloodhound and tell me you're depriving yourself for my benefit's much as yours."

"Mister Saxon, I tithe," Daniels said. "It seems to me my wife and I have a perfect right to decide how to distribute my fair share of the company profits, and I want to stress that. Ken's always got some crack to make about what a sucker I am. He overlooks the fact that what we choose to give away is *our* income. Not a drain on undistributed profits of the corporation. Not a personal indulgence charged off to company overhead. Maybe if I felt the same way Kenneth does, maybe if I made my contributions out of corporate gross income, maybe then he'd have a point. And maybe then Patricia and I could afford to go gallivanting around all over Europe, with our own driver, staying at the best hotels and eating high off the hog, drinking expensive wines. As fancy Ken here does."

"My poor old father," Farley said, "my poor old father told me: 'Never trust an Irishman who doesn't drink.' I should've listened to him."

"Let me ask you guys something," Saxon said. "Because we seem to be getting just a little far afield here. Who owns the stock in Arrow?"

"We do," they said together. Daniels said: "Fifty-fifty. Been that way since the beginning, back when Kenneth seemed to be quite sane, and I thought I could trust him."

"No public offerings?" Saxon said. "No little

237

stock trusts for your kids that seemed like taxwise good ideas when you set them up, and now you've got some wise-ass trustee screaming: 'Dissipated profits'?"

"I don't approve of children anticipating unearned income before they've ever worked," Daniels said stiffly. "I think it discourages initiative. We had an attorney in Corey's office, back in the early Seventies, and he was bound and determined we should do something like that. And Ken of course sided with him, which was natural enough since Ken was of course watching his marriage disintegrate, and had problems different than mine."

"Jim disapproves of my choice of companions," Farley said. "My wife's been ill for years. Mentally. Jim believes the proper response to that situation is celibacy for the innocent partner. I disagree with him."

" 'Innocent,' " Daniels said. "I don't think anyone who flouts his marriage vows is in a very good position to suggest he's innocent."

"Oh-*kay,*" Saxon said. "But the point is that the two of you own Arrow Construction, the lock, the stock and the barrel. So there's no way the US Attorney can substitute the government for some disgruntled third-party stockholder claiming fraudulent diversion of profits. Regardless of which of you spent them, or what they were spent on."

"Correct," Daniels said. "Whatever differences we may have on the proper running of the business, they're between us and us alone." Farley nodded. "And so far, at least," Daniels said, "they haven't been serious enough to force a breakup of the company. Knock on wood." He rapped on the coffee table.

"More superstition," Farley said.

"Which brings us back to the political stuff," Saxon said. "Assuming for the moment that you're right, and the US Attorney's cool-headed enough to reach the same conclusion: that whatever connections you may have had with Donovan or Leonetti, there was no illegal impropriety that resulted in any unlawful contract award. No kickbacks, no bribes, no extortion."

"I'd think he'd almost have to reach that conclusion," Farley said. "I don't think he's got any choice. There haven't *been* any kickbacks, any of that stuff. I meant what I said, James, when I said we've been totally honest and aboveboard. For one thing, nothing I ever saw said to me that you could make money off of something like that, unless you were prepared to skim so much off your fixed costs—which in our line of work is materials; labor you can't skim—that the project'd fall apart the first time the wind shifted north. And when that happens, word gets around fast. You might make a killing on bad concrete once, but as soon's that stuff starts to crack, word gets around like lightning and your good name is crap. So even if you do get away with it, once, maybe even twice, in the long run you're gonna ruin your busi-

239

ness, and then you're out of luck."

"I agree with that," Daniels said. "One thing Kenneth and I've never argued about, and it's a good thing because it's been the foundation of our business, is that you don't skimp on materials and you don't do slapdash work. I was in the Seabees, the Pacific, World War Two, and I know Kenneth had the same experience with Third Armored: Neither one of us's ever even considered trying to do work without maintaining the equipment. And neither one of us's ever hesitated one instant when maybe weather or something else set back a project and maybe presented the temptation to make up the time by doing an inferior job. That's how you lose goodwill."

"All right, then," Saxon said, "is there anything in all those records they've asked for, anything that might *look* like you did something that you say you've never done?"

"I don't follow," Daniels said.

"Is there anything in your records that a man could hang his hat on, whether because he didn't like you or he just made a mistake, that he could point to and say: 'This proves Farley and Daniels've been doing naughty things'?"

"No," Farley said.

"Yes," Daniels said, "and the reason that there is, Kenneth, is because you wouldn't listen to me. And I didn't dig in my heels and say that if you went ahead, I'd leave the company."

"What might this be?" Saxon said.

240

Daniels stood up. "Since I had no part in it," he said, "even though my name's involved, I'm going to let Kenneth tell you about it. All by himself, since he's the architect." He grabbed his parka from the closet in the entry. "I am going to the football game," he said, shrugging into the coat. "Not only am I going, but when I pick up Monsignor Clayton I'm going to instruct him, Mister Saxon, to pray against the Redskins. But I will ask him as well, to put in a good word for you." He went out and shut the door.

Farley sighed and shook his head. "There," he said, "goes a solid-gold man. Best friend I ever had. Without him I'm a working stiff, hitting time clocks toward retirement. With him I've become rich, like I never would've dreamed of. If only I could stand the guy. If only I could stand him."

16

"He does seem a little rigid," Saxon said.

"He doesn't bend at all," Farley said. "That's what makes him such a great friend to have. And such a godsend when it comes to doing business. Once he's made up his mind about somebody, that's the end of it. He never changes it. He decides you're his friend? You're his friend for life. He decides you're a bad guy? Same thing. He either trusts you or he doesn't. He will always be polite. He will never curse you out, and he will not bad-mouth you, but he won't trust you, ever. And you're stuck with that.

"What was he talking about there," Farley said, "what I did, he didn't like? Jim is the kind of guy that you have to protect. He really enjoys, eating the steak, but he doesn't want to know what that steak used to be, or what they hadda do to the animal that grew it for him. And he doesn't want you to tell him. And I know this. It wasn't like I was trying to hide things from him. It was just that I knew him, and I also knew some things were necessary, that he wouldn't like. Routine things. Dirty, maybe, but routine. So I did them, and the contracts came in, and he liked the contracts the same way he likes the sirloins: medium-well, because that's another thing about Jim—he never likes anything too much. You know how I know exactly how many times Jim's laid his wife? I do—I know because they got six kids, so they have fucked six times."

Saxon laughed. "Sure," Farley said, "but there's reassurance there, working with the guy like that. You always, he's predictable, you know? It's like the guys on the flying trapeze, you're in our line of work. It's not important if the guy that's supposed to catch you happens to believe that Calvin Coolidge was our greatest president. What's important is whether he's there to grab you, you come flying through the air. Jim's always where he's supposed to be. And you know that he will be. You can depend on Jim.

"Now," Farley said, "the way it worked out, I'd go and look at the job. And then I'd go to Jim. And I'd say: 'Massage these numbers.' Before we bid on it. And say I thought, well, eighty men for seven months, two big Cats, two small graders and the trucks, and however many tons of the gravel and the asphalt that it looked like it'd take. And a couple days later, Jim's figured out that unless the time's a factor, more'n usual, I mean, we can do it, thirty-two weeks, sixty guys and one Cat, and that'll let us piggyback it with a small job down in Sandwich that we need twelve guys for, only six days with the grader. Which means we make a lower bid, and also make more money. Combination's hard to beat.

"Thing of it is," Farley said, "since I was the up-front nigger, scouted out the jobs and scoped out the possibilities, I was also the guy that people came to when they put the touch on. Because they knew me. They didn't know Jim. And I naturally didn't like it, because when we were green, Jim and me, we honestly didn't know how much money it costs to make money. So I went to Jack Corey, and I'll be honest with you about this, what I wanted him to do was tell me what they're asking me's illegal. So I could go back, see? And say: 'Hey, I'm a law-abiding guy. And you're telling me, you're asking me, finance your campaign because you gave me a contract.' And Jack Corey was no help at all. Because the law, this was before the law changed. And he said, no, there wasn't any violation, I lay out five hundred bucks for a table of ten at a fifty-a-plate dinner that I'm not gonna go to, and wouldn't send my friends to, either. I said: 'Whaddaya mean?' He said: 'Hey, look, you're cheap. Jim's even cheaper, and that's all right—I am cheap myself. But that's all the answer you've got to give them, you don't make the donations: "No, I won't go. I'm too cheap." And that's gonna clobber you, word gets around. I'd pay the money, and weep.'

"So I did," Farley said. "I got used to it. You can get used to anything, you live through it all. You got friends in high places? They want to stay there? You want them to stay there, 'cause that's why they're friends. They're the ones, give you the money."

"So you gave *them* money," Saxon said.

"Of course I did," Farley said. "Sonny Donovan's a nice guy. I mean that. There's a lot of stuff in the papers, he's no Einstein or something, and I got to admit, I knew him in college, he stuck out more onna basketball court'n he did in history, math. But he's good-hearted, you know? I helped to bankroll him, the School Committee, and then for City Council. Then he wants to be Rep, and I help him there, too, and State Senate—those campaigns cost more. Well, we're doing pretty good by then, Jim and me, and I figure: The hell, why not do it? He's doing good, we're doing good, can't have too many friends."

"And your partner knew about this," Saxon said.

"As much as he wanted to," Farley said. "Not

very much. Jim and his wife, well, they're funny. They think donations, and they make a lot of them, donations're for God's work. They got a bright line they draw, between the Maryknoll Fathers, the Jesuit Missions and some guy that's running for office. And my wife was worse. It got so I dreaded, go home, we landed a new job. I knew I was letting myself in for a whole week of ragtime, the impact onna wetlands or the fucking water table. It got so she was embarrassing me. We're down there on the Cape, laying out the site lines, and she's up the State House, all her hysterical buddies, hollering about all the damage we're doing to the aquifers. The reporters loved it, naturally. I'm down there, doing my job, and she's up there, telling them I'm raping the earth. I took quite a lot of shit from Frank, the guys his cabinet. Then Frank's wife comes out for ERA, which Frank did not feature at all, and he took quite some shit from me.

"And that's what I'm getting at, you see?" Farley said. "I didn't, I wasn't handing out the dough to Frank, or to Sonny, because I had any particular interest, their policies and stuff. Sonny I knew from school. Frank was his classmate in law school. I like them, all right? They're nice guys. It's the same with Dale Christian, the congressman from Plymouth? I like Dale personally. She's a tough, good-hearted person. I took wholesale loads of shit, my friends the VFW, 'her lists come out the papers and my name's on for donations. Because she was very anti-Vietnam, and they thought: 'Well, Communist.' Close to it, anyway. And I said: 'Hey, I don't care what she says. I don't care what she thinks. What I care is, she *does* think. And she's smart, and honest, too. I'd rather have a smart person that doesn't steal sitting there in Congress'n a dope that's got his fingers in the cookie jar and's stupid, but says what I want to hear.'

"And that was the way I felt then, and the way I feel today. I don't know anything about running the Commonwealth. Or the city of Boston, either. I don't know anything about foreign policy—I haven't got one, and I don't have time to make one. There's somebody I like, I'll give them money. They live in my district, I'll vote for them, too. I'm right, they'll take care the jobs they get, and I'll take care of mine.

"Nell," he said. "Nell always took things too seriously. I called up Dale one night, get her to vote against the Japanese, some trade bill that was gonna hammer us on steel costs, if we couldn't buy foreign, you know? Because they were killing whales. I said: 'Nell, forget it. The Japs eat whales. You got this same bug up your ass a year ago, the Eskimos killing seals. Well, that's how they make their living. Next summer, I suppose, you'll be telling me the lobsters've got souls, and we can't boil them anymore. The Im-

248

maculate Heart of Mary or something. Bullshit. When you gonna learn that most people in this world don't give a mortal shit what you think, their eating habits?' I think it was about three weeks, she didn't speak to me. I didn't mind that much. It was kind of a relief."

"Yeah," Saxon said, "but all that aside, you're telling me that any contributions you've made've been innocent in purpose, and also in effect. At least for the last five, six years."

Farley showed discomfort. "Well," he said, "yeah. I was never, you know, out after anything for us. Like I say, I didn't particularly *like* doing it, spending dough, that particular item, but I can't do without it, so: 'Gimme the check.' "

"And you followed the advice of counsel when you did that," Saxon said.

"Yeah," Farley said. "Yeah, always did that."

"You're full of shit, I think," Saxon said. "You know how dangerous this is? You know what kind of risks you're taking, you run this charade on *me?* Lemme tell you something, all right? I dunno this guy Pratt, wouldn't know him if he bit me on the leg. But I know guys who know his boss—his real boss, not Harry Dodge. This guy that Pratt works for's named David Curley, and he looks like your standard-issue, split-level, suburban jerk. And he plays that role to the hilt. He did it when he was OCRS, down at Justice, and he's doing it now because those guys don't change. He *wants* you to think he's in the wrong line of work, that what he should be doing's running a camera store in some small town with white shutters on the stores and regular commuter trains to New York. Being president, the Rotary, and coaching the damned Little League. Maybe having a discreet affair with the librarian, if he really goes hog-wild.

"Well," Saxon said, "that's camouflage. That fucking Curley's got springs in his sleeves and more cards in his deck than you ever saw, my friend. You want aces? He has got them, all of them, and they pop up when he needs them. He'll never tackle you unless he knows he can flatten you, Harry Dodge or not. But if he comes at you, well, you've got a big problem. And if you don't believe me, I can give you names of some Italians that're doing time today because they misjudged David Curley. And that problem will get bigger if you keep blowing smoke at me."

"There could be a few minor problems," Farley said.

"Expand," Saxon said.

"Well," Farley said, "in, ah, in Eighty-four, Frank Leonetti's running, reelection. And his attorney general, you know, he got kind of restless. Not going, wait his turn. So Frank's taking this pounding in the primary, and I don't know how much you know, Massachusetts politics, but . . ."

"Mister Farley," Saxon said, "I've been active in

250

the Democratic Party since I graduated from Saint Peter's Prep in Newark in Nineteen-sixty. I spent the next four years at Harvard College, then three more at Harvard Law. I worked in RFK's Sixty-four New York Senate campaign in the summer between college and law school. I was an honor intern in Katzenbach's Justice. I worked for RFK's Sixty-eight campaign. You want to tell me about Massachusetts politics? What's next on your agenda today? Going to wash a fish?"

"Yeah," Farley said. "Well, I guess not. Anyway, Frank's AG mutinied, and he's gonna knock him off, the primary. And Frank gets desperate for money. So he comes to me, and I said: 'Jeez, lemme talk to Jack and see how we can do this.' And Jack tells me, the limit, one person can give. What—a grand in the primary, 'nother grand in the general. So we figure it out. Nell is a person, I am a person, and then there's the kids, and they're persons, and the people that work for me, right? They're also persons as well. So Nell pisses and moans, she don't like Frank's attitude about medical insurance or something, but she signs the fucking check, and so'd everybody else.

"Well," Farley said, "Frank loses the general. Not by much, but he lost it. And he calls up all his friends for this breakfast, and the gist of it is that he loses his house if he don't come up with big money. Because he borrowed against it to run, and borrowed too much, and can't pay. He was

251

really embarrassed."

"Well, he should've been," Saxon said. "Never understand these guys, hock their families' whole future without a second thought, get their clothes stolen from them on a goddamned ego trip, and then come around all sheepish and say: 'Hey guys, bail me out.' And: 'Bend the law to do it.' Just because they've been assholes, everybody they know has to be, too. Infuckincredible."

"Yeah," Farley said, "but I still like the guy. So I go back again, and I do the thing with the wife, and the kids, and the people that work for me, and I even used the sister, this governess we had ever since the kids were little? Agnes, Agnes Lloyd. Except Nancy, the sister, I give her a five-hundred bonus for giving a thousand to Frank—which I also give her, of course—and she oughta run for office herself. She kept the grand and sent Frank the five hundred. And old Jim, of course, well, he had an attack, 'Ten thousand dollars? From me?' He used to think that was the price, become a Knight of Malta. But he did it, kicking and screaming."

Saxon cleared his throat. "These people that you signed up," he said. "Outside of members of your family, but the ones that worked for you? Did they know what was going on?"

"Sure they knew," Farley said. "I hadda tell them. I explained the situation. I said: 'Look, I know you don't make the kind of money, you're

252

running around all the time heaving thousand-dollar checks at bigshot politicians. But you know your Christmas bonus? Well, it's gonna be a little larger, and I'd appreciate it, you could see your way clear, do this little favor for me.' "

"How much bigger?" Saxon said.

"It was," Farley said, "it was, we never had no profit-sharing, any formal kind of way. We did good, then you did good. Your salary stays the same, but we all get rich together or we all go down the dumper. So what I did, that year, like if Agnes Lloyd was probably gonna get twenty-one hundred, her bonus, well, she got forty-six hundred, which was her regular bonus plus the thousand for Nancy and five hundred for Nancy, and I expected them to give Frank two checks for a grand apiece."

"And you didn't," Saxon said, "you didn't force any of these people to participate."

"Force?" Farley said. "What's to force? These're my family, my friends."

"No browbeating," Saxon said. "No: 'Do this or you're fired.' "

"Nope," Farley said. "My wife, her big kick then was The Bomb. And I hadda, in order, get Nell to do it, I hadda give a thousand bucks, Physicians for Survival or some other goddamned thing. But she did it. Jeez, does she love nutbags. It figures, I suppose."

"Did you do this with Donovan, too?" Saxon

said.

."Not as much," Farley said. "Prolly, seven, make that ten—could be I've given Sonny twelve grand in the years you're mentioning."

"Using the same people as straws," Saxon said.

"Yeah," Farley said. "Some of them. Not Agnes, and not her thieving sister, but all my kids, my driver, and the women, take care of Nell."

Saxon sighed. "Well," he said, "technically, Curley has got you. You do business with State and local governments. You've been at least circumventing campaign laws, and money has been changing hands. That's a federal violation, on paper if no more. Any of these people liable to talk?"

"To hurt me, you mean?" Farley said.

"Yup," Saxon said, "that's exactly what I mean."

Farley groaned. "Only Nell," he said.

"There's that much animosity?" Saxon said.

"Not 'animosity,'" Farley said. "More like rage or something. She gets crazy, she'll say anything. Our youngest daughter's pregnant. Our oldest is a whore. Our son's a little fag. You get home from work at night, Agnes gets messages wrong so I turn on the machine, and I get home, and here's all this dirty garbage Nell's put on the tape. And I know what I'm gonna find. My daughter upstairs in her room, crying her eyes out, because of course she answered the call while it was being recorded, and she's already heard all that hateful stuff. I took the tape the hospital, and I played it for the docs. And I said: 'Look, all right? One crazy person's enough, for one family. Don't let her drive the kids nuts. Keep her away from the phone.' And they did. After that. After the damage was done." He paused. "It's really strange," he said. "Nell sounds just like a cobra, she starts doing that. She hisses. Like some killer in the movies, that really likes his work? She sick? Of course. But that doesn't stop the pain. And then after she comes out of it, after they finally get her off the booze, back on her medicine, eating real food, well, then she doesn't remember. All the bad things she did. The people she did them to, though— we remember. Forgive her? Maybe. But it gets harder'n harder It's like who the hell ever intended, get shitfaced and run his car into some guy and his family? Nobody. But is the guy with the family still dead, and his wife and kids all crippled? Yup. Doesn't matter what you meant— what matters's what you did."

"And if she was in one of those episodes," Saxon said, "and someone invited her to do harm to you?"

"She would do it," Farley said.

"Ahh," Saxon said.

"Would they do that?" Farley said. "They gotta know she's crazy. Anyone can see it. Would they believe what she said?"

"They might," Saxon said. "If they were hot enough for you, yeah, maybe they might do that."

"Jesus Christ," Farley said. "You know, you know what this woman's done? The first time that the cops came, they were all set to arrest me. I was violent, see? She was upstairs, the door's barricaded, but she could hear me, the first floor. She hadda whisper on the phone. I was inna kitchen, getting a carving knife. I was sharpening it on the can opener. I was breaking the furniture. She heard me smash the piano. What the hell did the cops know? They put on their flak jackets, would've sent a SWAT team if they'd had one, and they broke the back door down. Scared the shit out of Agnes and the kids. And where the hell was I? In Dallas, a convention, I had two more days to go. But did the cops believe her? Sure they did, at least that time. I'd've been there, smoking a cigar, having a drink, they would've taken me the can.

"Now," he said, "you're telling me, these federal guys might do that? I must be getting old. This used to be America. What a rotten bunch of pricks."

"Don't kid yourself," Saxon said. "They are a rotten bunch of pricks. But they're no worse'n the rotten bunch of pricks that Bobby's men, and Ike's appointments, FDR's and Truman's, all of those guys were. They all did the same damned thing. Suited them to crucify someone because the public'd like it, well, the next sound you hear'll be the carpenters at work. War is the extension of diplomacy by other means? Justice is quite often the extension of politics by prosecution."

"Well," Farley said, "guess all I can do now's hope she keeps a good grip on her marbles, this whole shitty thing blows over."

"That," Saxon said, "and that nobody else in your little entourage gets cold feet and lets you down."

"Never happen," Farley said. "My people are loyal."

"Right," Saxon said. "That's what Jesus thought. 'Have a piece of bread, Judas. 'Nother cup of wine? Nothing like a little supper with your friends all by your side.' "

17

The conference room off the US Attorney's office was paneled in dark mahogany above the shelves filled with buckram-bound volumes of Supreme Court decisions and a maroon leather-bound set of the United States Code Annotated. Dodge sat at the easterly end of the long table, with Curley and Pratt and Asst. US Atty. Donald Murphy to his right. Dodge smoked a long slim cigar with a white plastic holder he had gnawed into a deformed tip that enabled him to shift it abruptly from one corner of his mouth to the other without touching it with his fingers.

"If it wasn't for this happy horseshit," he said affably, "I could be on my way to the island right now. But no, I've got to sit here on my ass like a friggin' mushroom, because Brownie as usual can't get *his* in gear to come up here on time and discuss something we all know the outcome of anyway. Why're we doing this? You wanna tell me that? Is there any question in anybody's mind here what we're going to say when that scumbag's case comes up? No, there is not—of course there isn't. The only thing that's gonna save Matthew Macmillan from having us say 'Thirty' is the fact that Matthew just didn't happen to screw us personally." He laughed, plain evidence of two purposes accomplished at once: the expression of amusement and the rearrangement of sinus mucus. "His fucking father," Dodge said. "I hope he's enjoying this. That son of a bitch. When he was with Sonny, nothing he liked better'n giving some poor bastard a good fucking going-over if they didn't do what Sonny said. Miserable bastard. I had a guy, liquor license? And yeah, he was serving minors. And yeah, he did try to pay off the cop, a cop he was already paying for the extra detail time, keep the rough trade out. And I called up Sonny's office, right? And they shift me, to Macmillan. And he listens to me, okay? Very polite and all. And I get through what's on my mind, and he says: 'Just by way of no harm, Mister Dodge, are you the same Harry Dodge that was with Rooney, last election?' And I say: 'Yeah.' And he says: 'That's what I thought,' and he starts this great big song-and-dance about how the laws're plain, and they have to be enforced. Well, they're gonna be, this time. Against his fuckin' kid.

"My learned predecessor called me, Tuesday," Dodge said. "I should say: 'My learned predecessor's *secretary* called me Tuesday,' and when she was fully satisfied that I was personally ready to receive counsel from the great man, she connected us. I tugged my forelock and wrung my cap in my hands, naturally. Not every day that the master calls the serfs. Harry Dodge gets a personal call from Joseph Kiely? Got to show proper respect when that happens, or the next thing you know word's getting around over coffee at the Somerset Club that you're a 'rather rough cob.' And: 'Quite stable, you think? Entirely sound? Heard some bothersome things. Rows a rather choppy oar. Rather vulgar chap.' Fuckers. All those years they treated this place like their private property—some kind of finishing-school seminary for their bright young polished men. And then the day finally came when they didn't control it anymore. And *still* they've got the fucking gall to think they can dictate how the joint is run. No wonder the Bolsheviks killed all the Romanoffs. That's the only thing to do, an aristocracy like that, once their days're over: Take the bastards out in the courtyard and shoot 'em."

"What'd he want?" Curley said. "Little plea for leniency, behalf his prodigal?"

"Hah," Dodge said, "fat chance. You don't know these guys. Way Kiely and them look at it, larcenous Matthew got his crack at the goodies by

261

perverting their *noblesse oblige*. Here they'd extended the olive branch of opportunity to one the lower orders, their version of Exeter's scholarship bounty to some ghetto kid, and the ungrateful wretch betrayed 'em. Leniency, my ass—Kiely wanted me to know 'that all of us who worked with Matthew are appalled by his duplicity, and hope you will see fit to punish it severely.' He didn't say it, but he intimated he'd also taken the precaution of calling Judge Aloisi, just in case he might need some bucking up before the sentencing. Which, if he *had* come out and said it, I would've been all over him like a bad case of psoriasis, meddling in my office and making improper calls to chambers four years after he got the heave-ho. But he didn't, so I didn't. Besides, him and Aloisi're thicker'n my mother's chicken gravy. Aloisi's Joe's tame ghinny, guy he always mentions if someone says he's a bigot, and Henry's so damned grateful he'll do anything Joe says. He thinks Joe's voice comes from Heaven. So, I don't care if Joe's got no business, telling Henry what to do. Anything that puts a little extra backbone under that robe I got to think's a good idea."

"I'd feel more comfortable, myself," Pratt said, "Macmillan'd drawn some other judge."

"Ahh," Curley said, "Henry's all right. He's a little wishy-washy sometimes, but his heart's in the right place."

"Yeah," Pratt said, "but he was never one of

us. He doesn't know how it feels, you get one of our commissions and then you have to prosecute a guy that pissed all over it. I'd like to see Matthew grovel in before Judge Baker and snivel up to him that he didn't mean no harm. I'd like to see Andy Baker's life flashing before him in that instant — scholarship kid at BC and Suffolk, one mad scramble: make a living in a two-bit private practice over a bowling alley in Somerville, before he finally catches a break and makes AUSA. Andy Baker could tell all those Pro-Life agitators when life begins, all right — his began the day Herbert Brownell signed his commission as a federal persecutor. And now he's a federal judge. I'd like to see Matthew's mouthpiece tell old Andy that it's just a minor boyish prank, you know, an Assistant US Attorney takes bribes from a drug smuggler to tip him off, the FBI is doing. Andy'd really go for that, all those times Matt stood there for the government and recommended hanging for some pusher with two ounces, and there's speedboats coming in untouched to his guy's dock at night. Yes, I certainly would. Andy'd have him on the rack, and I'd take a vacation day to watch. Hell, I'd crank the goddamned wheel."

"They oughta," Murphy said, "they oughta play *The Nutcracker*, Bill, you come into the room."

"Fuck 'em," Pratt said. "I represent the people of the United States of America, and we've got certain laws. You break 'em? We nail you. Simple as that. And this son of a bitch not only swore he'd uphold them—he took money to help others break 'em. In he goes, and bye-bye, and I hope he rots in there."

"You took this one pretty personal, didn't you?" Dodge said. "I like that in a guy."

"Yeah, I took it personal," Pratt said. "That son of a bitch made fools out of a lot of good people, including me, for quite a long fucking time. DEA installs a bug, Carson's line goes dead. FBI puts up the cameras, infrared sees nothing because Carson moves away. Hot tip on a shipment coming in, all our guys crouching in the weeds? It's like Moonlight Bay out there. Not a sign of anything—the whole thing was compromised. You got any idea how many good cops and agents got the fish-eye from their people before Carson finally got bagged, and squealed? And then it turns out, it's not a bent cop; it's a former AUSA on the take, ratting on his friends that made him look good in court. You got any idea how those guys feel now, waiting to see what we do to this guy of ours that croaked them? I'm telling you, if I didn't personally have a real raging hard-on for this bastard, I'd do a damned good job pretending, just for agency morale."

"Whaddaya looking for?" Dodge said. "Consecutive lifes on and after?"

"It was in the statute, he would be," Curley said. "I finally got him wrapped in a wet sheet in my office Tuesday, got him down to ten on the first count, five on and after each the other two."

"Plus Marion," Pratt said. "You agreed to Marion. This guy, whatever he gets, we're recommending Marion. I want this son of a bitch to do hard time. I thought there was something tougher somewhere else — Alcatraz or Devil's Island — that's what I would want. No fucking golf course for this turd."

"Well," Curley said, "we can recommend Illinois, but it's still gonna be the Marshals and the Bureau Prisons that decide where he ends up. And I can tell you right now, Billy, if there's any guests at Marion still there on time he got them, Prisons will not put him there. They get anxiety attacks if they pick up even odors that some inmate might get shanked."

"Ask for it anyway," Dodge said. "Least we can throw a good scare into him. Where the fuck is Brown?"

"We had a funny summer," Curley said. "Stayed cold late and got cold early. They're cold-blooded animals down there, you know. They're probably all still shedding their skins. You know how they get when they're shedding — very slow. That's what they're doing now, just moving around in slow motion, rubbing off their old scales."

"Yeah," Dodge said. "I ever get to Washington, that's one thing I'm gonna do. Get the head Probation bozo out of his little nest and stick a railroad flare up his ass, get those guys to do some *work*."

"You ever get to Washington, Harry," Curley

said, "the only guy you'll want to see's the one that helps you make out the retirement applications. You're gonna be so old, they won't meet you at the airport with a limo—they'll send one of those transporters with a little elevator that just hoists your wheelchair in. When your calls start coming in, your secretary won't say she'll see if you're in—she'll say she has to check and see if you've got a pulse."

"Yeah," Dodge said, "well, that's all right. I'm still almost three years younger'n you. I admit forty's two years behind my timetable, and maybe I'm not gonna be AG, the whole damned Republic, but I'm still on my course and steady. Fun you two're gonna have's when neither one the Senators agrees, submit your name. 'Curley?' they'll say. 'Who the fuck is Curley?' They'll have one of their guys call me up. 'Nah,' I'll say at first, 'I never heard of him.' And the guy'll say: 'Isn't this that fucking pencil-pusher you rescued from a life of shame at Justice? Guy that's pestering our pals there, Sonny Donovan and them?' And I'll say: 'Oh yeah. I forgot. Chubby guy? Funny-looking mustache? Now I remember him. He was never around much. Don't know what he did.' And the Senators'll say: 'Oh sure, we're gonna pass this guy, make *him* US Attorney. Next thing we know, he's after us. Right—that's just what we need.' And then they'll cut some kind of cute little deal with the White House so Mother Teresa succeeds me, and the next thing you know,

266

you'll be making the novenas. And Brother Pratt here'll be feeding ham sandwiches the beggars, over the Arch Street Shrine, 'stead of sitting in your chair."

"What I think we should do, Dave, after he's gone," Pratt said, "assuming he does ever leave, but what we should do is empanel a special, see what's in the Dodge closets. Wouldn't that go good?"

"Shh," Curley said. "I told you to keep that quiet until he's at least left town."

"Which, speaking of which," Dodge said, "is probably what Brownie's done." He was reaching for the intercom buzzer when it went off. He picked up the phone and said: "Yeah. Well, then send the bastard in, Elaine. He was due here yesterday."

Ted Brown apologized for his tardiness. "This new guy," he said, "I'm telling you: Since Joe Gillespie retired it's been a Mexican carnival. I don't know how the hell they stood him down in Miami. The guy's a total zero. Every morning he wakes up, and it's a brand-new world. Comes in here, most of us've been doing our jobs for twenty years or so, and it's like nobody ever got probation before, and nobody supervised them. Nobody ever did a pre-sentencing report before. None of us've ever seen a real, live, criminal. Nobody ever caught a guy lying to him — hell, nobody ever even *suspected* that a guy would lie to him. He's giving us all these instructions, how we can tell when somebody's father or his mother or his wife, or his damned girlfriend, isn't telling us the truth. You know something? This's gonna really amaze you: 'Keep in mind when you interview the family and the friends of the accused, they have every motive to put his behavior in the best possible light, and if necessary they'll omit relevant details that shed a bad light on his history.' "

"No," Curley said.

Brown nodded. "It's true," he said. "It must be true. I just heard it myself from Mark Hoskins, and since Washington went to all the trouble of bringing him up here—instead of giving the job to somebody like Ernie, who only earned it, after all—it must be he's onto something. He's a real expert."

"I never would've dreamed it," Dodge said. "You mean these guys . . ."

Brown nodded. "That's it," he said. "A guy that's been convicted of trying to smuggle in a whole boatload of cocaine or heroin or something may actually lie about it to the US Probation Service."

"Well," Pratt said, "I never. Sure changes your ideas about human nature, now, doesn't it?"

"Beats 'em all to shit," Brown said. "And then, after he gets through telling us the sun comes up in the east, Marty Sands shows up, and I have to spend another half an hour listening to him."

"Speaking of boatloads of cocaine," Curley

said. "You violating one of Marty's big importers? Been a while since we caught one fresh. Not that we ever caught that many — Marty's boys're hard to catch."

Brown laughed. "David, David," he said, "that's why they pay him all that dough — because when they do get caught, they do chapters, not sentences. It'll be another eight years at least 'fore any of Marty's clients even comes up for parole. I'll be retired and Hoskins'll be top dog in Washington before Sands's boys start to get out."

"So what'd he want?" Dodge said. "I've known Marty ever since law school, and I've never known him be the kind of guy that just drops in for a chat. What'd he have on his mind?"

"Funny case for him," Brown said. "Sounds like real chicken shit. I said to him: 'For God's sake, Marty, you? An A and B in Quincy District Court? Business falling off? You're not gonna finance many of those trips to London doing dogs and cats like that.'"

"London?" Dodge said. "What kind of scam's he got working in London? They bringing in hash from there, now?"

"He goes there to gamble," Curley said. "He's a big roulette bug. Picked up the habit from his client there, Cassidy? 'Member Tommy Cassidy? Got grabbed coming through Customs with an ounce of pure in his wig? Marty belongs a couple private clubs over there. You got to be a member, go in and run your elbows up against the sheiks and oil men. And the high-priced hookers, too. I said to him: 'Marty, why London? You can lose your shirt just as fast, Atlantic City, and it's a helluva lot closer.' Said he doesn't *like* Atlantic City, doesn't like Las Vegas, either. Concorde doesn't fly there. 'No class. Riffraff all over the place. People in madras shirts and black socks, with leather sandals. Never spend your money in a place where the customers think Don Rickles is hot stuff.' Marty is refined."

"So what's he doing, Quincy District?" Dodge said. "And more to the point, why's he talking to federal Probation about a case he's got down there?"

"Guy's *on* federal," Brown said. "Marty wanted to know if we'd violate him here, he gets convicted there."

"Will you?" Pratt said.

"Tell you the same thing I told Marty," Brown said. " 'I dunno. It all depends. His supervising officer gets the papers, normal course, he'll look at them and then decide, the circumstances warrant.' He wasn't satisfied with that. Kept pressing me, hard answer. I couldn't give him one. How the hell do I know? Not many of our people still get into fights in bars. Or after evenings in them. Our customers're way beyond that, time they come to us. They get in fights, there's guns involved, except one guy doesn't have one and he dies — he doesn't file a cop complaint."

"Who is this toad?" Dodge said. "Who is this

270

guy that Marty's got, big dollars for a fight? We interested, this character, he's already been through here?"

"I doubt it," Brown said. "Got his ticket punched for killing a guy in a fistfight he had in the Navy. Did a little more'n four up in Portsmouth. Got let out and we inherited him when he got a job down here. I didn't run his sheet, but from what Marty told me he's an ordinary Joe. Just's got a hot temper, and a solid punch, and it runs away with him. So they got a mutual friend, which in Marty's case probably means a bimbo with legs that go all the way up, and he's doing this case as a favor."

"Which means some great blow jobs," Dodge said.

"Well," Pratt said, "at least they're not taxable. Yet. Can't blame a guy in his bracket, using barter when he can."

"You didn't recognize the guy?" Dodge said. "Name didn't ring a bell?"

"Nope," Brown said. "Like I say, a regular jamoke. 'Eugene Arbuckle' is the name that Marty gave me. Meant nothing to me."

"Does to me," Pratt said. "If it's the same one, at least."

"The same one as what?" Dodge said.

"The same one that's on Farley's payroll," Pratt said. "I give Rob Tully credit. He lost that motion Wednesday, that was the end of that. No attempt to stall around. I got two big boxes of stuff

271

yesterday, and another box today. Haven't been through it all yet, but I did scan the payroll records. There's a Eugene Arbuckle, Eugene *Rudolph* Arbuckle, that works for Arrow — Farley. Don't know what he does, but he works for him."

"He do anything else?" Curley said.

"I got that intern, Morrissey?" Pratt said. "Found him dozing in the library last night, asked him if he wanted, do something useful. Said he wouldn't mind. I put him cross-checking Arrow's personnel against Sonny Donovan's list of loyal supporters. Also Leonetti's roster, faithful contributors. He's really digging into it. Said he's coming in this weekend. I should know on Monday if he's matched up anything. I really like that kid. Doesn't throw a lot of attitude on you, you ask him to do something."

"Yeah," Dodge said. "That's what we need in this kind of operation: good haters. Soon's I get down on the Potomac there, that's what I'm gonna institute right off, matter policy. 'Effective immediately, screw all this bullshit about what grades they got in law school or whether their mothers and fathers knew the President out west. Gimme a whole buncha people with rats in their bellies and fire in their eyes, and then we'll kick some ass.' "

"Policy," Brown said. "What you'll be making mostly is plans, get out of town. Before the posse comes. Followed by the lynch mob. Time Sterling's finally out of there, Demmies'll be back in with their power lawnmowers at Sixteen Hundred Pennsylvania, and your ass'll be grass. Tops on their hit parade."

"Dream on," Dodge said. "Senator Arnold? I know what he's doing, his goddamned committee. He's holding up my nomination until he gets some fresh meat. It's the same old con—'We got the Senate, and you got the White House? Fine. You do what we want, or we don't do what you want.' Fucking hypocrites. It's all principle with them. For the evening news, at least. What you got on this turd Macmillan I didn't read last night on a lavatory wall? Anything should prevent us, cutting his balls off?"

"Well," Brown said, "he says he's innocent, and all his family and his friends, they agree with him."

" 'It's all a horrible mistake,' " Murphy said.

"That's the gist of it," Brown said. He distributed copies of a seven-page memorandum on blue stock. "He's a poor trusting lad, and it's all a terrible misunderstanding. He thought Carson gave him the thirty-five-foot cabin cruiser and dough, the Cadillac, because he admired what Matt'd done in his career in public service. His father's especially firm on that, and his mother, well, I felt sorry for her."

"How about wifey?" Pratt said. "She have the usual sob story?"

Brown chuckled. "I give him about as much

273

time as it takes him to unpack his comb and hairbrush in the slammer before she starts divorce proceedings. Silent as a grave, when I went to see her. I finally said: 'Look, Mrs. Macmillan, I know this isn't easy. But the law says I have to talk to you. It's my job, you know.' And she said: 'I know that. But it doesn't say *I* have to talk to *you*. He got himself into this fix, without my help or advice. He can get himself out the same way, if there is a way.' And that was all she wrote."

"Good," Pratt said, leafing through the report. "Maybe she didn't tell the truth, but at least she didn't lie. Very seldom that I side with the wife in such matters, but this time, ladies and gents, I am with her all the way. More of these women had the guts to come forward with the shit their husbands're up to, or at least tell the truth if we ask, make our jobs around here one hell of a lot easier."

Curley looked up from his copy of the Macmillan report. "No," he said.

"No?" Dodge said. " 'No' what?"

"I was talking to him," Curley said, nodding toward Pratt. "He knows what I'm talking about. It was No when we talked last week, and it's still No today, and it will be No tomorrow and on Groundhog Day as well."

Pratt shook his head. "You know, Dave," he said, "you're the guy that ordered the omelet. Sooner or later you're gonna have to let me, you know, break an egg or two."

"I don't know what this is about," Murphy said.

Curley stared at him. "Things go right, Don," he said, "you will. And you'll be sorry when you do."

18

Earl Wendell, M.D., Ph.D., arrived promptly for his 11:00 A.M. appointment in John Corey's Boston office on the thirty-first floor of One Boston Place. He introduced the woman with him as Atty. Gilda Bostock. She was thirty-one; she carried a thin brown attaché case and she wore a grim smile. "Nice to meet you, at long last," she said. "You're a very hard man to track down."

"Oh, not at all," Corey said, offering them the red leather upholstered barrel chairs positioned in front of his desk. "I'm in Waterford Monday and Tuesday, here on Wednesdays and Thursdays, and back down there on Fridays. Regular as clockwork."

"Yes," she said. "Well, all I know is that whenever I called one place, you were in the other one, and then when I called that one, you had always left."

"I'm semi-retired, Ms. Bostock," Corey said. "I conduct my practice to suit me and me alone. For personal reasons I limit that practice to a small number of the firm's clients whom I've represented for years. This reduces my contact with strangers, which is as I prefer it. It's very seldom that one of my clients presents me with a matter unfamiliar to me, and therefore most unusual when I receive a call, or calls, from a lawyer whose name rings no bell. To be perfectly candid with you, I'm afraid I therefore erroneously inferred from your refusal to describe your business to either of my secretaries that you were soliciting contributions or committee service from me, for some ceremonial occasion. I wish neither to make such sacrifices, nor to explain to anyone else, usually quite persistent, my reasons for refusing. So I did not return your calls."

"Really," she said.

"Well," he said, "you must forgive me, but when you've been a member of the bar as long as I have, you will be more than amply aware that many of our colleagues seem to devote vast amounts of their waking hours to the planning and production of public spectacles meant to distinguish one occasion or another. Most of them are quite shrewd. They decline to specify their business when asked by secretaries, lest their intended victims not return their calls and in turn be subjected to their blandishments.

"So," he said, "when someone like you with

legitimate business imitates their reticence, I'm afraid I must ask you to excuse my mistaken deduction—that you wish me to address a gathering of fifteen mystified strangers in a Grange Hall in Granby, next Fourth of July, on the subject of our noble Constitution. And the Bill of Rights, of course. In exchange for a ham-and-bean supper, the ham with raisin sauce. I play golf at Great Eastern, the Fourth of July. I don't play it well, but I like it. While it is true that constitutional lore and law have been an avocation of mine for decades, it is not true that I eagerly welcome invitations to share the fruits of my scholarship. I do it for my own pleasure, and for mine alone. When I sniff such an invitation in the offing, I act on my deductions—or, more accurately, fail to act. If you don't like the results you get, you retain the option either to describe your business, or to become peevish when I don't return your calls."

"In other words, Mister Corey," she said, "you don't care what I think."

"Not until I know first what it's about," he said, "and second, that it concerns one of my clients. No. Should I?"

"John," Wendell said, "I did have to move a couple patients around to make this meeting possible. Could we move along, do you think?"

"By all means," Corey said.

"Ms. Bostock is Mrs. Farley's new lawyer," Wendell said.

Corey bowed toward Bostock. "My profound sympathies," he said.

"For whatever it's worth, Mister Corey," she said, "I don't find your labored attempts at humor very funny. Ellen Farley happens to be not only my client but a mature woman who has suffered very much. She deserves better than she's gotten from the assortment of men who've surrounded her during her illnesses and pounced on her personal turmoil, and I mean to see that she gets it."

"Oh, you'll see, all right," Corey said.

"What will I see?" Bostock said. "If you're telling me she's had numerous breakdowns, and relapses, I'm well aware of them, and they don't change a thing. She's still my client, and I intend to represent her as vigorously as I possibly can."

"No doubt," Corey said.

"In keeping with that," Bostock said, "the reason I began calling you last week was to register her—our—protest at your attempt to arrange a private conference between you and her physician. Doctor Wendell quite properly told her, when he visited her at Foothills after you had called, that you'd asked him for an update on her condition. She was quite reasonably concerned. She called me to inquire whether it was desirable for her doctor to be talking to you, when you represent her husband in the divorce proceedings. I said: 'Not without one of us there, at least one of us present, and probably not even then.' Well, she evidently likes you, Mister Corey. She said you've always been entirely courteous to her on the stand and otherwise during the long pendency of this matter, and looking at it from your point of view she didn't think you'd try to get into any areas of sensitive doctor-patient confidences. So that was when I started calling you. To introduce myself, and go over the ground rules here."

"The 'ground rules,' " Corey said. He looked at Wendell. He returned his gaze to Bostock. "Ms. Bostock," he said, "whatever you may imagine, this is not a croquet match. I don't know whether you've had the leisure to review the docket entries in this case at Waterford. In the Probate Court. They're quite extensive. They span a period of nearly seven years. Have you ever read *Bleak House?*"

"In high school," she said. "Not since then, I'm afraid. I found it very dull."

"You must have been a perceptive student," Corey said. "It is extremely dull. To read, I mean. To live? It is interminable. And excruciating.

"Those of us who have had the misfortune to become professionally involved in *Farley v. Farley* know that at first hand. With the exceptions of Mister Farley and his wife, and their poor children, of course, I am the senior participant. Clerks have come and gone. Bailiffs have died or retired. Guardians *ad litem* have been appointed and reported, and gone on their merry ways. And still *Farley v. Farley* drags on undecided, the deciduous trees in the springtime bursting forth in bud, in summer in full leaf, and in autumn, gold and crimson. Then those leaves tumble to the earth, where snows of winter fall upon them, and soon again the voice of the peepers is heard in the land and the buds shoot forth once more, nature renewing herself after winter's long sleep, the hedgehog and the honey bear awakening from slumber. To find what before them in Waterford Probate Court, did they care to inquire? Why, *Farley versus Farley,* as immutable and unchanged as Holy Writ. Do you know why, with the exceptions of the parties, I am the senior pharisee in this long dispute? Would you care to hazard a guess? No, perhaps not—very wise of you. I am senior because I represent Mister Farley, a treasured friend and client, and since Kenneth Farley trusts me to endure this torment with him, well, then I will endure. And why are you, at least by my perhaps imperfect count, the ninth most recently shanghaied into this legal wonderland?"

He leaned forward on his right elbow. He slapped his right hand on the desk. "Because you are a *nincompoop,* and you know *nothing.*"

"Now, Jack," Wendell said.

" 'Now Jack' nothing," Corey said. "I will tell this young woman the truth, whether you like it or not. For all I know there have been others, other lawyers for Nell Farley, but to my own personal knowledge, she has had eight lawyers before. Eight, Ms. Bostock, count 'em: eight.

Every one of them as full of beans and truculence as you can ever manage. At first. At first each of them is going to hammer out a settlement here, get this thing over with, and I get all kinds of dire warnings of my client's impending penury.

"I know what to expect next," Corey said. "Next will be the new lawyer's representation to Judge Wells that so much time has elapsed since discovery was completed, depositions must be reopened, and new financial statements filed. Have you ever appeared before Judge Wells, Ms. Bostock?"

"No," she said, "I haven't. My practice is primarily in Middlesex and Essex."

"I thought not," Corey said. "You retain that certain assurance of the courtroom lawyer who has not yet come up nose to nose against irrefutable proof that at least one of our governors, much revered now in retirement, appointed to the bench of the Probate Court a pedigreed moron. *Knowing he was doing it*. That governor intentionally, with malice aforethought, willfully appointed a man to the bench who couldn't get his pajamas on without a co-pilot. Do you know when Judge Wells passed the bar?"

"No," she said, "I don't. Does it matter?"

"No," Corey said, "it doesn't. Not in the damned slightest. What matters is that this honored jurist passed the bar on his sixteenth attempt. *Sixteenth*. How would you like to have a licensed electrician fooling around with your wir-

283

ing and switches, knowing he flunked the license exam fifteen times before he passed? How would you like to meet a truck driver on your way back home tonight, who passed his trailer-driving test on his sixteenth attempt?"

"I see what you mean," she said.

"I will not bore you, Madam," Corey said, "with the colorful inventory of reasons that Judge Wells has accepted as adequate justification for your predecessors as Mrs. Farley's counsel to withdraw from the case. For one thing, my memory's not what it used to be, and I sometimes get details wrong. For another thing, the details don't matter anyway. She doesn't pay them — that's been a popular averment, among those seeking to retire. Several have gone so far's to sue. I think two of them have won — worthless judgments, of course, with her off in Gagaland. The others've generally contented themselves with sums from Mister Farley sufficient to cover their out-of-pocket costs on those depositions and those hearing transcripts that you're gearing up to order." He smirked. "I urge you, Ms. Bostock, to look up what I say. It's all in the record. Chapter and damned verse.

"Now," he said, "the reason I called Earl, and the reason for the conference you're here to monitor, is quite plainly and simply to enable me, and consequently Earl, to make some sort of educated guesses about what's likely to happen next. Our experience — well, mine, at least, and therefore most likely his—is that Nell will be back in the courthouse pretty soon. Making those in her world, at least, forget the Celtics and the Red Sox, and the Patriots as well. All I'm looking for's a reading, and you by all appearances here've given me a strong inkling that nothing's changed at all."

Bostock shifted in her chair and clenched her facial muscles. "My client remains determined to dissolve the marriage according to the terms of the libel," she said. "She expects a fair division of property, joint custody of minor children, support and alimony adequate to maintain her in the style to which she's accustomed."

"Well, now," Corey said, "that really adds a lot to the store of human knowledge. The last time I heard something as incisively applicable to the human condition, it was a Pepsi-Cola commercial. 'Six full ounces, that's a lot; gives full energy and that's what counts.' Let me be candid again, Ms. Bostock: Shit."

"I won't take this," Bostock said. "I won't have opposing counsel swearing at me."

"Then leave," Corey said. "I didn't ask you here in the first place, and I'm 'way past the age where I care what impression I make on greedy young lawyers looking to tally big fees that'll get them out of Leverett Square and into the hotshot big time. Earl, give me a reading: Is Nell close enough to fifty-two cards in the deck right now so she's in a position to end this nuisance, once and for goddamned all?"

"Some days she is," Wendell said, "and some days she hasn't been. We have a liaising physician in Springfield — Doctor Victor Frontenac. He's seen her at the Institute and is familiar with her case. He got a call from one of her attendants, living with her at the inn. Clancy, I think's her name. She was very concerned about Mrs. Farley's condition since her discharge. Said she appeared to be going downhill. Doctor Frontenac drove up to see her. He found her severely disoriented. She was hallucinating and going through rapid mood swings. The other of her attendants, a Miss Demers, told him she was severely agoraphobic, would not leave her room, had no appetite for food and showed signs of incipient catatonia. But she was not committable.

"He increased the dosage of her medication. He reported to me. He recommended that I, as her principal attending physician, make the time to examine her myself." He paused. "I confess I did not welcome that recommendation. But I was able to hitch a ride on a State helicopter a week later, and I did see her. The change in her medication appeared to have helped her. She was still physically frail, but she appeared to have a grasp of reality. She knew where she was. Where formerly she had told Doctor Frontenac that she did not know Miss Clancy or Miss Demers, she now expressed gratitude for their long care of her. She was lucid about her marriage and she recalled

286

accurately—as she did not for Doctor Frontenac—
details of her children's lives. She did not repeat
what she told him—that her husband is dead—
and she did not tell me, at least, that he has her
under surveillance." He drew a breath. "In short,"
he said, "she displayed no symptoms of paranoia
or schizophrenia. She was slightly depressed, but
in the circumstances I consider that appropriate
behavior. I would say that, at least when I saw
her, she was rational and calm.

"I can't say how long this will last," Wendell
said. "Her history shows a pattern of recurrence.
She seems to develop a tolerance for any medication—regardless of what it is. There are limits
beyond which we dare not increase dosage. Usually—well, in the past, it has taken three to six
months for that tolerance to recur. I hesitate to
predict what will happen in this instance, primarily because of her physical condition. Which concerns me. She's dangerously close to anemia.
She's, in other words, weak. That means she may
either *not* come to tolerate the medication, which
would be a blessing for her mental equilibrium,
or in the alternative, develop a tolerance more
rapidly. And collapse.

"Right now, though," he said, "or at least when
I saw her at the end of last week, she was rational. She knows the marriage's over. She's talking about reconstructing her life. There's very
little of the rampant hostility that there's been
toward Kenneth in the past. She isn't lashing out.

She seems to want it resolved. The legal proceedings, I mean."

"You see, Ms. Bostock?" Corey said. "What my good friend Earl has just told me, if you understand the codes encrypting this controversy, is that there's every probability that the carousel's resumed turning, and we're all going for another ride. The operative message in his statement is encapsulated in the words 'right now. As in: 'right now she's got a good grasp on reality.' The paradox enfolding the riddle of this case is that progress toward its resolution is feasible only when Mrs. Farley has that grasp. But her exercise of that grasp seems to exhaust her. When she perceives that progress appears to be under way toward the dissolution of the bond, she becomes panicky. She resorts to the devices that loosen her grasp on reality. She ceases her medication. She drinks. She becomes secretive with Earl. She commits bizarre if harmless acts. She acts out suicide scenarios. She has to be recommitted. And we are all back to Square One, with nothing changed except the pages ripped from this year's calendar."

He took a deep breath. "My client believes that she behaves like that in part to prevent him from getting the divorce. Earl and the several — many — doctors who've preceded him in her therapy take some mild exception to that opinion, and I must admit I was initially skeptical of it myself. But the years have dragged on, and as Doctor Wendell has observed, the pattern hasn't changed. The fact

288

of the matter is that her incompetence has been a major factor preventing resolution of this matter. And she knows it. So, since she doesn't really want the divorce to occur, her madness is a refuge for her. A tactic, if you will.

"Our lives are finite," Corey said. "All things, happy or sad, must sooner or later come to an end. Now, I have a proposal. I intended to present it to Earl and ask him to put it before Mrs. Farley's current counsel. Your visit today, Ms. Bostock, saves me asking him that favor. The last time Mrs. Farley's composure deserted her, the precipitating incident appeared to have been her acquisition of Mister Farley's seventh set of depositions. The transcripts represented that his financial situation had changed in no material respect since his sixth such ordeal. Which of course reflected only the most minuscule improvement over those described in his fifth."

"You wanted Doctor Wendell to talk me into withholding new transcripts from my client," Bostock said. "Naturally I could never agree to do that. She's the one who has the detailed personal knowledge of his business, at least until recently. Not only would it be unethical for me to keep my client in the dark—it would be impractical and stupid."

"The code of ethics, Ms. Bostock," Corey said, "adjures you to act always in the best interests of your client. I do not hesitate for an instant to suggest that those interests at the very least include the preservation of whatever precarious equilibrium her latest stay in the hospital has permitted her to achieve. And I believe Doctor Wendell will endorse that point of view."

"She's had a very difficult time, Gilda," Wendell said. "It's gone on for a long time. There's a limit to what her body can stand, never mind her psyche. These episodes she has have cumulative physiological effects. She comes out of them, but she's weaker after each recovery than she was before relapse. We have a real danger here, if this goes on long enough, that whether she can permanently regain her ability to function mentally will become academic. We really don't want to find ourselves in the position of mourners for a person whose ability to survive physically happened to fall even a little bit short of her recovery from mental illness."

"You're saying I should do what he says," Bostock said.

"No," Wendell said. "I'm a physician, not an attorney. I don't expect you to tell me how to do my job, and I have no intention of instructing you in yours. All I'm saying is that Jack Corey's known Ellen Farley much longer than I have. I'm her fifth or sixth therapist. Some of my predecessors were discharged—she lost confidence in them. And some of them resigned from the case, despairing of being able to help her. I know how they felt. Hers is easily one of the most intractable, stubborn, obstinate cases I have seen in my thirty-three years of practice.

"But," he said, "when I took her case over, my immediate predecessor among other things told me that Jack Corey is a truthful man who could put a lot of things in perspective for me, if I'd listen. I took that advice, and I've never been disappointed. I realize this is an adversary situation that you're in with Jack, but I also realize the kind of antagonisms those situations create can be very harmful for my patient. They can be, and have been, triggering factors that will send her into another episode. Of course Jack doesn't want you to put his client through another round of depositions—he has something to gain. But what he says about Nell's reaction to previous rounds is indisputably true. So, while nothing's certain in the world or in psychiatry, you could do lots worse than reflect on his proposal. And maybe accept it."

"Let me say something further that may ease your mind a bit," Corey said. "I'm sure you think you're a crackerjack cross-examiner. We all do. I'm also sure you've by now reviewed all the earlier depositions, and gone over them with your client, and she's pointed out to you that none of her previous attorneys even put a dent in Mister Farley's insistent denials of secret accounts and numbered safety-deposit boxes stuffed with cash in every hideaway from the Grand Cayman Islands to Zurich. And you have formed the determination to bring those matters to light."

"It's my job to trace assets," she said.

"Of course it is," Corey said. "The point is that there are no such assets. That's why none of your estimable predecessors found them—they exist only in Mrs. Farley's fertile imagination. Look at his business, woman. Every job that Arrow undertakes has to be bonded. Arrow is a closely held corporation—a partnership, really, doing business for its owners' convenience as a corporation. When the bonding companies set the rates for Arrow's contract performance insurance, they don't stop at the company's assets and its liabilities. For all practical purposes they consider the corporation indistinguishable from its two owners. Every contract bond that he and Jim Daniels buy contains a personal guarantor's clause that binds each of them personally to completion of the job. They've been filing personal financial statements with those carriers for years. Mister Farley's statements for such purposes have been *Xeroxes* of the ones he's filed in court, in this damned divorce. When, that is, he didn't photocopy one of the court statements to the insurer because it was more recent. Do you think those companies don't evaluate those statements? Do you think Mister Farley wouldn't like to get the lower rates that they'd give him, if he did have all those hidden millions piling up in offshore banks? Do you seriously think your investigative powers are superior to those of Aetna Life and Casualty? This man has been doing business under gimlet-eyed scrutiny for almost forty years. If your client still insists that he's hoodwinked eight previous lawyers, the IRS and all these private companies for all of those decades, and you choose to believe her, I respectfully suggest that both of you ponder the probability that anyone so supremely guileful could probably outsmart you."

"You have a point," Bostock said.

"More than that," Corey said, "I have a proposition. Take a week to study his last deposition and the supporting documents. Take two weeks, if you wish. Copy them to any financial reporting service you choose. Commission a confidential, detailed field investigation of Kenneth Farley's assets and his liabilities. Dun and Bradstreet would be my choice, but that's up to you. When the report comes, there will be a bill for services rendered. Send the bill, not the report, to me. My client will pay it. If there is one material variation between what our materials tell you, and what your investigators say, give us a chance to explain it—even top sleuths make mistakes. If we can't explain it, notice him for depositions, and we all can brace ourselves for Mrs. Farley's next attack. The worst you can possibly get out of this approach is far better preparation for that deposition, paid for by my client, than you or Mrs. Farley could possibly afford on your own. The best we can all get out of it is that one of the speed-bumps impeding progress toward resolution of this matter will have been removed."

"Also true," Bostock said. "Yes, I will do that. You should have returned my calls."

"I now wish I had," Corey said. "In exchange for that—not a condition but a hope—you will exercise your best efforts generally to bring this tiresome matter to an orderly and swift conclusion."

"That could cover a lot of ground," Bostock said.

"Earl?" Corey said.

Wendell cleared his throat. "Gilda," he said, "we've got a real problem here that neither you nor Jack nor I—or God knows, Ellen Farley—has any control over. What he said about Judge Wells is true. The man's incompetent. I alone have testified in this matter no less than four times. I don't have time for it. Judge Wells doesn't have the brain for it. He will not issue a decision. His method is to delay and delay and delay, until the people involved either resolve it themselves, or die, or forget about it. He obviously can't handle something of the magnitude of this case, and because he can't, he won't. If Ellen and Kenneth are ever going to get divorced, they or their lawyers will have to confront Judge Wells with *fait accompli*. Everything tied up in ribbons and bows, nothing left to decide. Then he will sign it, as his decree, and then the case will be over. Whether that will expedite her eventual recovery, I do not know. But it will be one less obstacle looming in the reality that she retreats from into illness.

"Three years ago," he said, "even two years ago, I would not have taken this position—the one I'm taking now. But she's had four serious episodes since then. I don't want my patient to die. And to Jack and his client's credit, I don't think they want that, either. If she can get this behind her, I think my prospects of easing her back into a satisfactory lifestyle will be better. Not by any means certain, but better. Whereas if it's not resolved pretty soon, well then, things can only get worse. Sooner or later she's got to trust someone enough to pick up a ballpoint pen and sign her name to an agreement, and start getting on with her life. You're the newest nominee. I have big hopes for you."

"They may be misplaced," Bostock said.

"I don't follow," Wendell said. "She just hired you. How could she possibly have come to mistrust you so soon?"

"Oh," Bostock said, "she doesn't mistrust me. That's not what I mean, not at all. What I mean is that she trusts someone else. I may need his help to do this."

"Who exactly is this?" Wendell said. "She's never mentioned him to me."

"Eugene Arbuckle," Bostock said. " 'Bucky Arbuckle's my friend.' The way she said it, I took it to mean: 'my lover.' "

Corey coughed. "Miss Bostock," he said, "Eugene Arbuckle is Mister Farley's driver. And

295

factotum. The suggestion that he's Mrs. Farley's lover is the sheerest nonsense."

"That's your opinion," Bostock said. "My client's is quite different."

"Miss Bostock," Wendell said, "your client is disturbed. My patient is disturbed. That's what Mister Corey has been telling you."

19

On Wednesday of the third week of November, Sen. Elias Arnold, D., Md., chairman of the Senate Committee on the Judiciary, through his spokesman issued a statement to the press. He refused to make further comment.

"After extensive hearings and deliberations, the Committee has voted to send to the floor the President's nomination of Marvin Sterling to the bench of the United States District Court for the District of Columbia, with the recommendation that it be approved by the Senate as a whole.

"I reluctantly joined the majority voting in favor of this action because I believe that while Mr. Sterling is certainly qualified, academically and professionally, to serve as a member of the federal judiciary, I was and remain disturbed by his views on civil liberties. Mr. Sterling to a degree has allayed some of those fears. He has testified that his published remarks on court-ordered busing to relieve *de facto* segregation in public schools were taken out of context. He has told the Committee that in most instances he opposes liberalization of so-called 'Stop and Frisk' laws. While he admits his personal commitment to the prevention of abortion is deep, 'and uncompromising,' he has assured the Committee that he will be able to separate it from his duties as a member of the court, and will faithfully follow existing law in all respects on the point. I take him at his word.

"I remain nevertheless concerned that the White House persists in sending to the Senate only those nominees for the federal judiciary who appear to reflect ideologically the views of the party in power. Without question, the President is entitled to nominate those attorneys who share his opinions, but the issue remains: Shall such opinions, such strict insistence upon ideological orthodoxy, control whether the ablest are nominated? Or: Are those whose views are different, but abilities no less unimpeachable, to be disqualified from serving?

"Senatorial tradition honors the presidential prerogative to select judges whose views correspond to those of the Chief Executive. But there is a point at which that prerogative must yield to the interests of the nation as a whole, and the principle of ordered liberty. This Administration is dangerously close to that point."

On the third Friday in November, the Senate confirmed Sterling's appointment. The President signed his commission the following Monday.

On the day before Thanksgiving, the Atty. General of the United States announced the nomination of US Atty. Harold Dodge of Massachusetts as Assistant Attorney General and head of the Criminal Division of the Department of Justice.

On the Tuesday following Thanksgiving, informed sources reported that the White House would not oppose a Senate bill appropriating $8.9 million dollars for measures to alleviate traffic congestion, improve solid-waste disposal and reduce water pollution in the Chesapeake Bay area.

On the Thursday following Thanksgiving, the Senate Judiciary Committee heard one hour and fourteen minutes of testimony from Harold Dodge. He said that he favored "vigorous pursuit and prosecution of white-collar criminals." He promised "aggressive enforcement of federal statutes prohibiting importation and interstate trafficking in narcotics." He said he would enforce laws protecting the exercise of civil liberties "without fear or favor." He concurred with Senator Arnold's "perception that the health of the nation as a whole depends upon rigorous enforcement of those laws which the Congress has seen fit to enact for the protection of consumers." He said that "the integrity of American business is critical to the economy, and must be vigilantly guarded by energetic enforcement of laws governing the sale of, and trade in, securities, and the banking business." That same day, the Committee unanimously recommended to the full Senate that Harold Dodge be confirmed as an Assistant Attorney General of the United States. On the following Monday, the President signed his commission.

On the third Monday in December, the judges of the United States District Court for the District of Massachusetts voted unanimously to name Deputy US Atty. David Curley Acting US Attorney, "until his successor shall be nominated and confirmed." Curley issued a press release praising his predecessor and promising "the same vigorous and aggressive stance toward corruption in public office that Harold Dodge instituted during his tenure in this office." The press release noted the promotion of Asst. US Atty. William Pratt to Acting Chief of the Criminal Division of the US Attorney's office in Boston, replacing Curley.

"Now look," Pratt said, flanked by the flags in the office at the southeast corner of the eleventh floor, "I can't do it anymore. Not on day-to-day. Dave's expecting me to do for him what he did for Harry, and I watched him a lot. It ran him ragged, 's what it did, and even though I don't have that goddamned train ride that he says he likes so much, and I live by myself, I'm still not

300

going to have the time to ramrod a corruption case myself. So you're just going to have to resign yourself, that you're gonna have to take over completely. At least until the time for trial, if that day ever comes. I'll help you as much as I can, but it won't be that much."

Donald Murphy looked dour. "It's not that, Billy," he said. "It isn't: I'm ducking work. Or that I don't want to do it. It's just that I'm up against a brick wall here. I mean: What the hell do I do? I got all those records. I've been through them. I've gone over Morrissey's memo. There's only one thing I can see, and that's, four years ago Farley upped everybody's bonus. All his non-union people. And the thing that's interesting is that every single one of them seems to've gotten about a grand more'n they did the year before."

"That's not a coincidence," Pratt said. "That was the year Frank Leonetti had the fucking deficit. They all give a grand to Leonetti?"

"Yup," Murphy said.

"Then there it is," Pratt said. He slapped the desk. "You've got the fucking hook."

"And also," Murphy said, "there it *isn't*. It's not against the law for Farley to give his people extra cash at Christmas. And it's not against the law for them to give to Leonetti."

"It is if the only explanation for their spontaneous, 'independent' decisions is that friend Farley hammered them into it, under threat of losing

301

their jobs," Pratt said. "That's extortion, and conspiracy to violate State laws, and most likely they mailed their checks, which makes it mail fraud. And if anybody picked up a phone in the course of this little gambit, it's wire fraud, too.

"Now, lemme tell you something," he said. "I don't want to sound like our former glorious leader here. Harry got the bit in his teeth on this case, and he wasn't gonna rest until he had Donovan's scalp in his fucking top drawer. Next to Leonetti's. You want my personal view? He lost his perspective on this one."

"Oh?" Murphy said. "Did he keep it on any of the other cases? I must've been out of the office, the days he talked about those."

"You don't have to work here, you know," Pratt said. "I'm sure a bright young guy like yourself gets many flattering offers from major Boston firms that just didn't happen to notice him, he was grinding his guts out for twenty a year in a three-man office in Whitman: Going out to every Republican pig-fuck and banjo roast within fifty miles his desk, tryin' get his damned name known."

"I know, I know," Murphy said.

"It's not I don't sympathize with you," Pratt said. "Keep in mind I was pushing that rock up the hill long before you came in the door. And I had the same reservations about it that you seem to be having right now.

"But," he said, "Harry, God bless him, made

302

sure the word got out. He thought it was good business — 'Keep the bastards worrying.' Drop a little hint here, little innuendo there, keep your mouth shut and give 'em the cat-canary smile when somebody asks the right question, and depend on the gossips to take care of the rest. And he did that. There isn't one savvy guy in the State House, one even moderately smart reporter, who doesn't know this office's got a thing under way for Frank and Sonny.

"Dave's Acting," Pratt said. "He hasn't been confirmed. The people he needs to get him through the Senate promoted Harry because they liked what he was doing. And they did some things to make sure he got through with no damage. Don't kid yourself — things like Harry did're important in politics. They keep the opposition off balance. They're if Leonetti and Sonny're sweating day and night about what this office's got up its sleeve, they're not building organizations and raising money that'll make 'em even harder, one our guys to beat. So, to keep those folks behind him, Dave needs to make sure they think that Harry's little campaign's still proceeding at full steam. We can't do anything that might make it look like Curley's going in the tank here, scuttling investigations that Harry sold to them. They get that idea in their heads, Dave goes in looking damp, they'll let him die on the vine. Or, they'll nominate somebody else. Which is where my ass is suddenly exposed, because that'll put

Dave back at this desk, and me back at my old desk. And you, brother Murphy, back at yours. Handling the smaller drug busts, and the mail frauds where the victims got clipped ten bucks apiece. You won't find your name in the papers, you go back to that routine."

"Yeah," Murphy said.

"Now," Pratt said, "I'm not saying, come hell or high water, you got to indict this thing. You say we haven't got enough yet? I agree with you. But the very least you've got to do, *we've* got to do, is keep the thing alive until Dave gets confirmed. Then, we all agree the stuff's not there, *then* he can start whispering to people we just didn't have enough." He paused. "If," he said, *"if* we really don't. We can't fudge this thing, Don. Harry's down the Potomac, but Harry's got big ears, sharp eyes, and a nose like a fucking bloodhound. He gets the notion we bagged this thing, we're gonna get more shit outta Washington'n the Deer Island sludge-plant dumps in the harbor in your average month. I don't want to do the dogpaddle in a lot of shit. Especially when I know there's lots more where the first batch came from. And it won't stop, Don. It'll go on as long as those people're in power, which may not be long on the calendar, but'll seem like three-to-five."

"I realize that," Murphy said.

"So," Pratt said, "keeping an open mind and all that crap, you've got to stick your foot in the firewall and check out every single one those

304

people that papered up those contributions to Leonetti. We do that, and we come up empty, well, then Harry will believe it. He will hate it, but he'll believe it. He will say: 'Well, I know those guys. I appointed them. I believe them.' And that'll end the thing. But Harry's gotta believe it, and that means we got to stretch. And what I would do, I was you, I would start with the driver there, Arbuckle."

"Why him?" Murphy said. "I was thinking, you know, I really got to do this, the logical place to start's with the wife. She's got to have a beef with hubby, and if she can put him in the shit with us, maybe he's not quite so feisty, comes to property settlement time. So she gets to gain something, too."

"Several reasons," Pratt said. "First one's that Dave won't stand for it. He's got this soft spot his heart for the boobies. The wife's so far gone she makes the March Hare look sober. You've seen those Bureau reports—the calls she's made to them? You really want a principal witness, you want someone as far gone as that? She's liable, get up there on the stand and say the angels talk to her."

"Yeah," Murphy said, "but if she knows things, and we could prove them . . ."

"Uh uh," Pratt said. "Only as a last resort. No, Arbuckle's your guy, the guy that you got to begin. Because we've got a hammer on him. He's federal probation, and he's got a beef down the

Quincy District Court. So what you do's go in there next Wednesday, the case's scheduled for trial, and you ask for a conference the judge, the DA—and Arbuckle's mouthpiece, of course—and all you tell 'em is that Mister Arbuckle's a candidate to finish his federal vacation, he gets convicted, the State. So you're down there to observe. And I will bet you coffee and a sweet roll the first thing Marty Sands does is ask continuance. 'To confer with my client, Your Honor.' And the judge'll give it to him, because Norfolk's way overcrowded, House Correction is—if there's some way he can try a jail case to conviction without sending the poor bum to live with the sheriff for a while, he will grab for it.

"Then the next thing that'll happen," Pratt said, "is that Sands'll sidle up to you in the corridor and ask if maybe you two should talk. And you will tell Marty you're always eager to have a chat, but what you'd really like's for him to talk his client about those campaign contributions, and maybe, he's got something solid to say, sit down a little interview with the FBI. And if that checks out, entertain the grand jury for a day or so."

Murphy sighed. *"Oh-*kay," he said, standing up. "I guess we gotta do it, we might as well go *do* it."

"Hey," Pratt said, "we're covering Curley's ass. And why're we covering Dave's? Because that means we're covering ours. I dunno about you, chum, but I figure life doesn't end when the Administration changes and the new flock of AUSAs comes in. Maybe you don't care, but I want Kiely and the other guys in high places to look with fondness on what I did for Harry, and Dave after him. You're playing with my career here too, you know, and even if you want to be casual, your own, I'd appreciate it if you didn't fuck mine up—and Dave's—any more'n's absolutely, strictly necessary. You can tell your bathroom mirror what you think, old Harry. But for better or for worse, my friend, the ball's in your court now, and you'd better hit it square."

20

"It's very simple," Sands said to Arbuckle in his office. "It's very fuckin' simple. They think they've got your nuts in a vise, and they're turning the ratchet. Until they've had a chance to hoover your brains, your case isn't gonna get tried. If they don't like what you tell them, or if you don't tell them anything, they're gonna sit back like a bunch of hungry vultures and wait for Franziani to nail you. Which he won't do if the evidence isn't there, but it is, and he will. And then they'll jump on you. Nothing complicated about it all. You cooperate with them, Ken Farley gets to sit on the frypan. You don't cooperate? Fine. Then *you* sit on the griddle."

"The hell do they want?" Arbuckle said. "I dunno anything about the guy's business. All's I do is drive the guy around. That is what I do. I get up in the morning and I eat my goddamned breakfast, and then I drive the guy around till lunch. We have lunch. Then I drive him around some more. Until dinner. Then I either drive him home, or he drives himself someplace else, and I go home by myself. It's nothing, you know? I just do what I do. Then the next day comes and I do it again. I don't know anything."

"You don't talk?" Sands said. "The two of you don't talk, with all this driving around?"

"Sure we do," Arbuckle said. "We talk about lots of things. Unless he's got a stack of papers that he's reading in the back, like he generally does. But when he doesn't, yeah, we talk. We talk about the ballclubs. We talk about the President. We talk about the weather. Yesterday, I'm taking him down the job, turned out we both happened to tune in this rerun, *Bonanza,* and I forgot the show, and so'd he, that we'd both seen it before, and we were saying how good it was, and what a shame it is there's no good westerns anymore. Not even in the movies. And that's what we talked about. This prosecutor—he want me to tell him what Mister Farley thinks about *Bonanza? Wagon Train?* I can do that, all right: He likes them. He wishes they were still around. So do I. That against the law? Because that's all the kind of stuff I know."

"Listen, Gene," Sands said, "because this's taking time I ain't got. What Murphy wants is what you know about the money you gave to the governor. The former governor. That's what he wants from you."

"Well," Arbuckle said, "I know I gave it to him, if that's what you mean. He means. The boss asked me, I'd do it, if my bonus was bigger, and I said: 'Sure.' Christ, after what he's done for me? I'd rub shit in my hair if he asked me. I wouldn't have no choice. But I got a right to do that, haven't I? Haven't I got a right, give a guy some money if that's what I want to do? Does the reason, is that what makes it against the law? Don't sound right to me."

"Lemme put it another way," Sands said. "Are you willing to tell the FBI, and then the grand jury, and *then* a trial jury, that Ken Farley forced you to do it? That he made it clear that you would lose your job if you didn't give that money?"

"No," Arbuckle said. "He didn't. Mister Farley's, he's not the kind of guy that does that kind of thing. For one thing, he doesn't have to. Anybody, works for him, anyone with any sense — of course you'd do something if he asked you to. Not because you're afraid of him — because he's good to you. He wouldn't ask you to do anything if he thought it was wrong. He's not that type of guy."

"Then you're going to have to stand trial down in Quincy, there," Sands said.

Arbuckle shrugged. "Then I got to stand trial,

I guess," he said.

"And if you get convicted," Sands said, "of which there is more than an even chance, they're going to violate you. The Feds are gonna revoke your parole, and you're going back to Portsmouth. And you're going to have a choice between finishing your sentence, or telling them what they want to hear about Kenneth Farley and the money for Frank Leonetti."

Arbuckle did not say anything.

"You understand what I'm telling you?" Sands said. "You get my meaning here? Either you give them the gun hand on Farley, or you go back in the slammer."

"I," Arbuckle said. He cleared his throat. "Mister Sands," he said, "I know, I realize you're just doing this for me because of Stelle—that she's the one that made you do it. And I'm still willing, in fact I wish you'd let me pay you. For your time and everything. Because you told me, you told me how you don't do this kind of work, and I know I'm taking up your time. But what you're saying to me, you know? I can't lie about Mister Farley. And I *can't* go back to jail. It damned near killed me, when I was in before. Is there, you know, somebody else that could maybe help me with this?"

"*Shit,*" Sands said. "I knew when I got into this, I shouldn't be getting into this. Every instinct that I had, it contradicted."

"Hey," Arbuckle said, "wait a minute here.

You're not the only lawyer on the earth, you know. You guys're like wharf rats. There's more of you'n we need. You want outta this? Fine. Say so. I'll find another one. I told you I'd pay you. I'm not broke. And I sure don't want another lawyer like I had before—doesn't like the idea, my case."

"I didn't say that," Sands said. "All I'm saying is that I don't have time for this. These games those guys're playing."

"So don't play them," Arbuckle said. "I'll get somebody else."

"Easy for you to say," Sands said.

"Easy for me to do, too," Arbuckle said. "I never saw a lawyer yet, turned down a case from a guy who could pay. Which I can do, as I told you."

"That's not what I mean," Sands said.

"No," Arbuckle said, "I do know that. What you mean's that Stelle's on your back alla time, make sure you're doing the right thing by me. And that's nice of her, and nice of you, too. But I don't need that. I had that lawyer once, didn't want my case, or know what to do with it, and that got me a lot of time to think about lawyers that don't want your case. So this time I think I'd like one that does. Really does. You can tell her, you want, I released you—all right? I said: 'Look, Marty, this's more grief'n I thought was involved, and I'd rather get a guy that's got the time to handle it.' And I will tell Sharon, same thing. So, it'll mesh. No problem, your love life. No problem with mine. Everything—nice and easy."

"You don't understand," Sands said. "What I said was that I regret the fact, I got involved in this. But I *did* get involved in it, and now I *am* involved in it, and I don't *want* to get out. I'm an old trial lawyer. It's been years since I've tried a case, and I miss it. This guy Murphy's throwing rocks at *my client*. My natural instinct's to throw rocks back at him. Stelle's got nothing to do with it. *You've* got nothing to do with it. This is strictly a case of a rock fight. Him against me.

"The trouble is," he said, "*I* lose the rock fight, *you* go to jail. You prepared to do that?"

"Not particularly," Arbuckle said. "I already told you that. Whaddaya think my chances are?"

"Pretty goddamned good," Sands said. "Of losing it, I mean. Judge Franziani's not renowned for his tendencies to instruct juries about mitigating circumstances. He'll tell them if they decide you hit this turkey, and he wasn't fighting you, first, they should find you guilty. And they most likely will. Then the Feds'll hook you, and that's the end of that."

"Great," Arbuckle said.

"You know Leonetti?" Sands said. "You ever meet the guy?"

"I met him," Arbuckle said. "He was in the car a couple times. Him and Mister Farley were going to this dinner thing. I was driving them. He

314

seemed like a nice enough guy."

"You gave him the money," Sands said.

"I guess so," Arbuckle said. "I had the check made out to him. His committee, at least. Mister Farley gave me extra, and he asked me to do that, and that is what I did. All I know's that I mailed it."

"Did you object to doing that?" Sands said.

"No," Arbuckle said. "If Mister Farley asked me to kill somebody, I might and I might not. But anything else he asked me to do, I would do it. Without asking. Jeez, he scraped me off the pavement. Guy saved my life. He asks me to do something? I figure a way that I can do it, I will do it."

"Yeah," Sands said.

"Well," Arbuckle said, "I will."

"I realize that," Sands said. He cleared his throat. "You got to realize what this guy Murphy wants."

"I know what he wants," Arbuckle said. "He wants me to sink the boss."

"That's about it," Sands said.

"And if I don't," Arbuckle said, "he is going to sink me."

"Uh huh," Sands said. "That's the size of it."

Arbuckle breathed in deeply. "Then I guess I'm going back in the can," he said. "What he wants I will not do."

"You could do another six years," Sands said.

"Mister Sands," Arbuckle said, "I could do an-

315

other *twenny* years. And I would, too. I'll die in there, I have to. Mister Farley never asked me to do nothing that I wouldn't've done on my own, if I knew. All that man has ever done to me is give me a job, and a place to live. And make as sure's he could, I was happy all the time. I am not gonna turn around now and tell lies about the man to save my own sweet ass. The guy I killed, he deserved it. This piece of shit, Cole, that I hit — he deserved it. I never hurt anybody, didn't deserve it, and Mister Farley doesn't. So I'm not going to do it."

"Okay," Sands said. "Will you talk to the FBI, though?"

"I'll tell them the truth," Arbuckle said. "I'll tell them the exact same thing I told you."

"They're not gonna like that," Sands said. "They're not gonna like that at all."

21

Rachel Dixon sat in the parlor of Nell Farley's suite at the Foothills Inn late in the afternoon. She held her teacup in both hands and blew steam off the surface, her young face sorrowful and tired. She did not look up when Fanny Clancy returned from the bedroom.

"She'll be all right," Fanny said, patting Rachel on the shoulder. "It's not the first time she's done it, you know. You or I'd've done that, we'd been in the hospital with hypothermia. But not our dear old Nell. She's an old hand at this kind of thing. We're the novices around here, compared to her."

Rachel shook her head. She set the cup on the table. "I just feel so *guilty*," she said. "The woman could've *died*. Honest to God. The reason

I'm here is so someone's watching her all the time. I've been on these jobs before. This isn't my first time. I know how crafty they are. But my *God,* I thought I could go to the *bath*room. She's so *quick.*" She looked up at Fanny. "I didn't linger in there," she said. "I wasn't sitting there with a magazine, or the newspaper or something. She, well, she looked like she was dozing. Sitting there in her robe at the window with her head sort of back against the cushion. She hadn't talked to me much the whole afternoon. I thought she was asleep. She'd been napping most of the day, while you were resting. She'd hardly touched her dinner. She had maybe half of her sandwich at lunch—we had egg-salad sandwiches and she complained about how there was too much onion in it. Wanted me to get on Sherburne's case—no more onion in the eggs. Well, there wasn't any onion in it, but I didn't contradict her. You told me, and so'd Jo, that as long as she was passive, no matter how listless she was, leave her alone—that that's something for the doctors to deal with. So it's not like I riled her up or anything. I don't see where she got the energy. Did she eat any of her breakfast?"

"Some of the toast," Fanny said, sitting down on the couch opposite Rachel. Her face was crimped with fatigue. "I was surprised she didn't want more. She seemed to've been sleeping well last night, and it's not as though she'd been doing push-ups and calisthenics all day yesterday, but

318

usually after she's had a peaceful night, she'll at least drink her juice and tell me again how she misses her cigarette with her coffee." She paused. "I wonder if it wouldn't be better if she did start smoking again. Nicotine's a relaxant."

"It'd be bad for her," Rachel said.

"Oh, 'bad for her'?" Fanny said. "In the first place, what difference does it make? This's no life she's got. So she has a heart attack, or gets lung cancer—so what? What are we so anxious to prolong here, medically? And in the second place, if it helped to relax her . . . I mean after all, this's about the tenth or twentieth time she's escaped, from what I know, her history. And every time she's done it, she's been at risk of death from exposure. Or worse. If that brook'd been a pond, she could've drowned herself. If the police hadn't found her when they did? Rachel, it was three degrees out there last night—three degrees above zero. And she was in her bathrobe. A little flimsy nightgown, her slippers and her bathrobe, wandering around out there in the woods not even sane enough to know she was cold."

"That sergeant said he couldn't understand it," Rachel said, sipping from the cup. "He said, when you were in there with her, he told me he didn't understand how anyone could survive out there like that. Dressed like that."

"Huh," Fanny said. "It's a wonder she even had that on. Some of the other times she's done it, she's taken off all of her clothes before she's even gone out. I don't know—maybe I should've seen it coming, and warned you. When she makes some little change in her habits, something really trivial—which it has to be, of course, because little things are all she does—we should go on Code Blue. Because that's her way of showing that there's something building up. Yesterday morning when her breakfast came up, I took the tray in to her and she made me send the Sanka back. She wanted regular coffee, and she wanted cream and sugar. Real cream. And real sugar. Now you and I both know how she raised all kinds of hell about getting decaffeinated coffee. How many times's she lectured you about all the caffeine in your tea?"

"Dozens," Rachel said.

"Every time I drink a cup of coffee in front of her," Fanny said, "I get that disapproving look. Boy, she must've been a hellion to have for a mother, short time she functioned as one. I was a little kid, that scowl'd scare the dickens out of me.

"But yesterday morning," Fanny said, "yesterday morning she put on her pouty face and said no, she didn't want any Sanka. 'I've decided maybe I'd be more alert if I had real coffee in the mornings. I haven't been alert enough. I haven't been myself. I've always enjoyed a cup of coffee, and I think it might make me feel better. More alert.' Of course she left out that it'd also maybe make her feel like taking a nice long walk in the great outdoors, in the snow and the dark, and I'd been up all night, watching her, so I thought nothing of it." She paused. "God," she said, shaking her head, "and you know what the frightening thing is? She's in there sleeping now. Resting up. For the next adventure. And I've been up all night, and you've been up all night, and both of us're keyed up. So we probably can't sleep. And I know, I *know* that even though Jo's supposed to be sleeping, so she'll be rested enough to keep up with her if she tries to do it again, I know Jo hasn't been sleeping."

"Maybe we shouldn't've called her," Rachel said. "If we hadn't called her, she wouldn't've known."

"We had to call her," Fanny said. "That's always been part of the deal. You're too new to this case to've known it, but there's a certain kind of crazy continuity here." She smiled. "That's a good one—*all* the continuity in this thing's crazy. That's what the continuity is—craziness. But what you have to keep in mind is that when she goes 'way off the beam on your shift, she's getting into a new pattern—or going back to an old one—and I'm likely to have some real fun too, when I come on my shift. We couldn't've let Jo just walk in blind, without knowing what to expect."

"Can't they," Rachel said, "can't they recommit her now, now that she's done this? I mean, she could easily've died out there last night. If the police hadn't found her, how long could she've lasted?"

Fanny sighed. "I called Doctor Frontenac and he set up a conference call with Doctor Wendell and her lawyer. This Gilda woman?" She grimaced. "Good old Gilda. And Gilda said she'd oppose it, and both the doctors said that well, then that meant that they couldn't do anything. Along that line. I said: 'Look, this woman belongs in a hospital. She's seriously ill.' Nope, didn't matter to Gilda. Said she had to consider what another commitment'd do to her client's position in court, and she'd have to assume, no matter what we said, that it'd damage her case with her husband. So that was that—no hospital."

"I don't see how they can do it," Rachel said. "We're right here. On top of this thing. Don't they even believe us, we tell them what's going on?"

"If they're listening, they do," Fanny said. "Some of the time I don't believe they're even paying attention. Because they're *not* here. They're not on top of it. They're miles away. They don't *have* to pay attention to it. They don't *want* to pay attention to it—so they don't pay attention. Very simple. The hired help says there's a problem? 'Let the hired help take care of it.' And that's the end of it."

"I still don't see how she did it," Rachel said. "I mean, I know how she did it. She waited until she heard me go into the bathroom, and then she went through my purse and got the key. But she was so fast. She must've moved like a shot the minute I went in. Like lightning. Except: silently. She should've been a burglar. I swear — *I know* — I wasn't in there for more'n five minutes. I know, because when I went in, Johnny Carson was about halfway through his jokes, the jokes at the beginning. And I didn't want to go just then, because that's the part of the show I like best. But I had no choice. And then when I came out, there was a commercial on. And I sat down and watched it, like a fool, no idea what's going on, and then his first guest came on. It was some old lady from Fort Lauderdale, in Florida? And she's a dog trainer, and she's ninety-six years old. But very spry. And I sat there like a nitwit and watched her, and then another commercial came on, and I thought: 'Well, better go in and check on Nell.' And she was *gone*.

"At first I thought she was in, I don't know, one the closets or something. The last patient I had was an old man, and he used to do that to me. He was just senile. Used to think he was still fighting World War One. Soldier boy. I'd leave him for a minute, sitting in his chair and drooling over his newspaper, and go out to the kitchen to boil some water, and when I'd come back into the living room — gone. The first time he did it, it scared the hell out of me. I was really panicked. He was in the coat closet in the front hall. Happy as a pig in shit, he'd frightened me so much. Cackling and jumping? I didn't think he had it in him. He made it into the attic one day while I was talking to my relief, and another time, the old coal bin. Down in the cellar. Under his bed. In the broom closet—how he wedged himself in there, I will never know.

"So, that's what I thought she was doing, at first," Rachel said. "I thought: 'Oh my God, another hide-and-go-seek loony tunes.' Except there's only two closets, this place, and she wasn't in either of them. And she wasn't under the bed, and she wasn't sitting outside on the windowsill. And my key's not in my bag." She paused. "It's a good thing it snowed last night, so they could track her. That's what the sergeant said."

"And it's a good thing, too," Fanny said, "that it *stopped* snowing just before she ran out. It'd kept up a couple hours, they never could've done it."

"And the doctors say that's not suicidal?" Rachel said. "You tell them a woman pushing sixty, undernourished, disoriented—you tell them that that woman's out wandering around the countryside in her bathrobe and slippers in the winter? And they say she's not trying to kill herself? Then what the hell do they think she's doing? Just getting her exercise? How the hell can they be so *stupid?*"

Fanny stood up. "*I* could use a cup of real coffee, with real cream and real sugar," she said. "Think I'll take the Thermos down the kitchen. Get you anything."

"I think there's still some hot water in mine,"

324

Rachel said. "Probably getting cold, though—it's been there since last night. You could fill that up for me." She grinned. "And give my love to Mister Sherburne, if you see him prowling around, flapping his hands in hysterics. Boy, is he ever a help in an emergency. 'The other guests, my other guests.' My God, the hell with them. Here's this woman out traipsing all over God knows what kind of wilderness. She's gotten out of his building without anybody hearing her at all, and he's going out of his own mind worrying what'll happen to his reputation if someone finds out she was here."

Fanny smiled. "Don't be too hard on him," she said. "He's new to running an asylum. The only reason he's doing it's because he's desperate for the money. The only reason he was asked to do it's because Mister Farley's desperate for some haven, for her. And the only reason that *he's* desperate's because he has to do something with her, and he doesn't know what to do."

"I thought of something, last night," Rachel said. "When I realized she'd gotten out."

"I can imagine," Fanny said.

"I thought: 'Wait a minute. This's a tough job. Much tougher'n it sounded like, when I took the damned thing. If I quit, it hurts my references, the next job. But if she dies, well, that's the end of it.' "

"Except if she had," Fanny said, "it would've happened on your shift."

"Yeah," Rachel said. "That's what I thought of next. And that's when I ran downstairs and woke up Mister Sherburne and called the police. It's really fun, isn't it? Why'd we choose this line of work?"

"Because we're crazy, too," Fanny said. "The last case I had? Terminal obesity. Killing himself with the knife and the fork. And I said to him: 'Mister Carlson, you've got to stick to your diet. Now eat the cottage cheese.' And he said: 'Nope. Cottage cheese's fattening.' Just stunned me. And I said: 'What do you mean?' And he said: 'You ever see a thin person, eating cottage cheese? No. Just fat people. And that proves what I said.' Maybe he was right. Maybe I am right. Everybody's crazy. Just in different ways."

22

Sharon Stoddard was apologetic. "I know," she said, "I know you got to work hard all day. And Stelle told me about what Steve's trying, do. And I hate laying this on you. Asking you to come here like this."

Arbuckle sat across the table from her in Charley's Eating & Drinking Saloon in the South Shore Plaza, two cheeseburgers and two draft beers between them. "I don't mind," he said. "Do I look like I mind? You think it bothers me, meet a gorgeous kid like you after work because you call me up? Right. The hell else I do, I finish work for the day? Go home and watch TV? I was glad, I got your call back at the plant. I'd much rather eat with you." He grinned. "I wouldn't mind eating you, either."

"Yeah," she said. She blushed. "But now I don't know, you know, that's such a good idea."

"Whaddaya mean?" he said. "I like going down on you."

"I know," she said. "It's just . . . And you got, I know you got that thing that Steve's trying, do to you in court, and all that other bullshit. And I'm really sorry. If it wasn't my bright idea, double-date with Stelle like that, none of this shit would've happened."

"Well," he said, "it's not like you knew it was gonna. Like you set me up or something. Those things happen, things like that. You got to roll with the punches when they do, you know? Everyone's got problems."

"It's still, it's still something I did," she said. "I feel bad about it. Nice guy like you, getting you into trouble like this."

"Hey," he said, "cut it out. Stop putting the blame on yourself. I hadda good talk with Marty Sands. And he's going, he's going to take care of things. Protect me. And he will. The guy's really smart. And Stelle did that. I know that. Don't worry so much. It'll be all right. It's not like I don't know, you know, why they're doing it. I do. But, well, they're wrong. What they're after? It's not there. It just never happened. So it'll be all right. You got to be optimistic."

"Well," she said, and frowned, "but the fight, you did hit Steve."

"Ahh," he said, "that's just minor. That's just a little problem. And besides, Marty says he thinks

I got, I got a good chance of winning that case."

"Then what's the big problem?" she said. "Is it what Stelle said Marty told her? Something with the Feds?"

"Oh, the Feds," he said. "The Feds're just trying, make a big deal out this fight case so I'll get scared and start telling them lies about the boss. That's all. It's no real big deal."

"It sounds like a big deal to me," she said. "I knew a guy once that he was doing drugs, and pretty soon he wasn't just buying them. He was selling them, too. And this undercover guy, you know? A federal agent? He sold some meth to a Fed, and he got sent away."

"Yeah," Arbuckle said, "I know that. But in his case, what you're telling me's he did something. Where in my case, what they want me to say happened, well, it didn't. It just never happened, is all. And so they can't prove it did. The stuff just isn't there."

"Yeah," she said, "but will they believe that? I mean: Are they gonna think it is there? And you're lying to them? Because he, Marty told Stelle what those guys're doing to you, and it don't sound to me like they're the kind of people'd believe you, you told them something they didn't want to hear. Or you didn't tell them something, that they did want to hear."

"I got no control over that," he said. "All I can do is tell them the truth. And that's all I'm gonna do, too. Tell them the truth. What they're chasing me for, what they're chasing him for? It never happened. They don't believe it? They don't believe it. But they still — and I talked to Marty twice about this, and he agrees with me — they still can't prove it did. Because it didn't."

"I hope so," she said. "Because you're a nice guy."

"Oh oh," he said.

"What's the matter?" she said.

"I dunno," he said. "At least: I hope I don't know. What're you gonna tell me?"

"What do you mean?" she said.

"Every time," he said, "every time, before, that I had a woman tell me I was a nice guy, she was setting me up to get a good shot in the chops. Like this was the last time she was gonna see me, because she was with another guy, and she had me on the waiver list. That what you're getting ready to do? Ship me out?"

She grabbed his left hand and squeezed it. *"No,"* she said. "I *love* you, Gene. You're the nicest man I ever met. You treat me better'n anybody I was ever with before."

He picked up his cheeseburger. "Well," he said, "that's a relief. I was afraid this was the old dumper dinner. 'So long, it's been good ta know ya.' I was kind of worried."

She munched on a pickle and frowned. "There is something I got to tell you, though," she said.

330

He stared at her. "What is it?" he said.

"Me and Stelle," she said. "Well, you know, her and Marty Sands've got a thing?"

"Uh huh," Arbuckle said.

"Yeah," Sharon said. "Well, her and Marty, they had this talk, and a result, Stelle decided, you know . . . I dunno how to say this."

"Say what?" Arbuckle said. "Just go ahead and say it. You already said you're not gonna say what I thought, I was afraid that you were going to say. Can't hurt me worse'n that would've. Just spit it out, all right? Say what you got on your mind."

"I went," she said. "Well, Stelle went the doctor. And she had a test. And then she got the results, you know? And she was really worried."

Arbuckle grinned. "What," he said. "Did Marty knock her up? Like a couple of teen-agers screwing in a drive-in? Jeez, and here I just get through saying what a smart guy I think he is."

"Uh uh," Sharon said, looking worried. She picked up her cheeseburger, looked at it and put it back on the plate. "I can't even eat," she said. "I'm just so upset about this that I can't even eat."

"Christ," he said, "what's the matter? Tell me what's bothering you."

She nodded. She clenched her jaw. "I'll be all right," she said. "Just let me get my act together here." She took a deep breath. "Stelle called me up, she got the test. And she said, you know, that it wasn't good, and she didn't want to worry me, but maybe I should. Get tested too. And I did. I went to the doctor and I had a blood test. Where they take blood from you? And I got it. Stelle's got it, and I got it, and we probably both got it from the same damned place."

"You got what?" Arbuckle said. "*You* knocked up or something?"

"A,R,C," she said. "AIDS Related Complex. I been infected with AIDS. I got — what they call 'the antibodies.' I've, look, all right? I told you the truth. I been around. I did lots of stupid things, with a lot of stupid guys."

"Are you all right?" he said.

"Oh," she said. "Am I gonna die, you mean? Not from this. No. Not now, at least. Someday, I might. But not now. I just *got* it, is all." She hesitated. "But I can pass it on, you know? That's what the doctor told me. That I can give it to somebody else. That's what the doctor told Stelle, too. That she'd better be careful, and make sure anybody that she's with knows she's got it. Before she does anything with him." She put her elbows on the table and covered her face with her hands. "I am *so* embarrassed," she said. "And I'm so *scared*."

He stroked her right forearm. "No need to be," he said. "I've been through lots scarier things'n this. I thought you were gonna tell me you were pregnant. I wouldn't've minded. I *like* you, all right? I'm not gonna run off on you. Whatever it is that's wrong, we'll take care of it."

She shook her head. "We can't take care of this," she said. "It's permanent. It's always gonna be this way. It's that fuckin' goddamn Steve. I *know* it's him, that bastard. The only thing me and Stelle got in common, except being sisters, is Steve. And now we got this other thing, that now I probably gave *you,* and we both hadda get it from Steve. That son of a bitch. He was off in Africa, someplace, he must've fucked a monkey or something, and then he caught something. And first he went to bed with me, and gave it to me. Then 'he went to bed with her, and he gave it to her. And now we both got this goddamned dis-*ease?* That *he* gave to *us?* That *shit*. That dirty goddamned shit."

"Sharon," Arbuckle said, "I hadda, once I hadda take penicillin for about a year on account of something I caught, you know? And I didn't like it, but I got over it. Can happen to anybody. You know you're taking chances."

"Bucky," she said, "this is not like that. Like it was the clap or something."

"I realize that," he said. "I realize this is different. I'm just telling you, is all. It's not the end of the world."

"It is, though," she said. She paused. "I hadda tell, call up all the guys, you know, I did it with.

333

The past few years. Since Steve. And tell them, you know, what might've happened. And a couple of them're married now. One of them was married then, when I did it with him. One of my bosses at work. We had a goddamned one-night stand. Two years ago. After the Christmas party. We were over the hotel, and we both had our eye on each other for quite a while, ever since I started there, and he just rented a room for the night and we went to it. One lousy roll in the hay, and he just looks at me. Like all of a sudden he can't talk or something. And I didn't blame him. I know what he's thinking. 'Jesus Christ. I get drunk one night and screw this woman, and now she's telling me I'm maybe gonna *die* as a result?' How'm I going to work with this guy now? How'm I gonna take dictation and type his letters, and do all that stuff I got to do, with him knowing, and me knowing, what could happen now? I can't. I'm probably gonna have to quit my job. And jeez, all of them, all the rest of them that I at least didn't have to tell it to, face to face, you know? All of them were just, you know, *shocked*. It was awful. That fucking Steve. You shouldn't've just knocked him out. You should've, I wished you *killed* the shit. Even though he probably is gonna die anyway, this thing finishes with him. It won't be soon enough. Or slow enough, either. I really hope he suffers."

Arbuckle stroked her arm again. "Sharon, all

right?" he said. "I mean it. I really care about you. We can work this out. We'll figure something out."

She stared at him. "Bucky," she said, "Bucky, that's what I'm telling you. You see? There, this isn't something *anyone* can work out. Nobody can work it out. It's, it's permanent, you know? Like you got born without a foot or something. All you can do is learn to get around with it—that's all."

"Then we'll learn to get around," he said. "That is what we'll do."

23

Judge Michael J. Kennerly at the age of 63 suffered a fatal cerebral hemorrhage in his sleep at his home in Belmont early in the morning of the third Saturday in January. Visitors and friends of the family were invited to call between 2:00 and 4:00 and 7:00 and 9:00 P.M. on Monday and Tuesday at the Mulready Funeral Home near Davis Square in Somerville. Interment was on Wednesday, following a 10:00 A.M. Mass of the Resurrection at St. Paul's Church in Cambridge. Acting US Atty. David Curley by memorandum informed his staff that the Chief Judge had scheduled a memorial observance at the courthouse for the following Friday at 2:00 P.M., and said that he expected "all who can possibly do so to attend."

"Which, I gather," Murphy said to Pratt, in his office, "is a command performance."

"Can't fool you, can they, Donald," Pratt said.

"Yeah," Murphy said. "Well, I happen to think I oughta be excused from listening to all the bullshit I know I'm gonna have to hear about the old bastard."

" 'The old bastard'?" Pratt said. "You mean our dear, departed friend? The prosecutor in the black dress? You ever lose an important motion before Kennerly? You ever hear of an Assistant who did? No, you certainly did not. Judge Kennerly was the salt of the goddamned earth. There was a man who knew how to instruct a jury. I never actually heard the words come out of his mouth, but the melody came ringing clear: 'Ladies and gentlemen of the jury: Your job's to find this particular bastard guilty, and get this over with so I can sentence him. Now get out of here and do it.' And that was what they almost always did."

"Yeah," Murphy said, "and because the Circuit knew that, too, and all the defense people knew it, every single goddamn conviction you got in front of him went up on appeal. What was his, how often did they overturn him? What was his reversal ratio—about forty-five percent?"

"Nah," Pratt said. "More like twenty, my guess. It was still high, though. But we're still gonna miss him, Donald—unless the right things happen."

"Like what?" Murphy said.

"Like David being nominated to replace him," Pratt said.

"Oh *ho*," Murphy said.

"Well," Pratt said, "why not? The President's Republican. Both Senators're Demmies. You got your basic Mexican standoff here, and what you need's a trade. Well, who's the logical candidate? All the sitting judges already picked our David to be Acting. They all love the guy. You wouldn't have any of that backbiting and sharpshooting you get when someone gets named they don't like—they'd've thrown up all over Harry if his name'd gone in, but to have David join them? They'd turn cartwheels and handsprings clear to Washington. And who appointed him to Justice? James Earl Carter. Who brought him to Boston? Harry Dodge. Who stopped Harry, at least some of the time, from doing his mad-dog imitation? David Curley. Who nominated David to be the actual USA? Ronald Reagan. There's not a spot on the guy, Donald. He's Joan of fucking Arc."

"Yeah," Murphy said, "I guess he is. And some other people, probably, too, wouldn't mind seeing David go up."

"You learn fast, kid," Pratt said.

"Lemme ask you something," Murphy said. "Curley does go up, who succeeds him?"

Pratt grinned.

"That's what I thought," Murphy said. "And: Who succeeds you?"

"You're really bright," Pratt said. "You're gonna

339

go far in this world. Where the hell *is* Whitman, anyway?"

"Well, now," Murphy said, shifting in the chair. "And that'd mean, I got your desk, then I could make some other poor defenseless bastard take over the Farley thing."

"Easy," Pratt said. "This isn't all gonna happen right after lunchtime tomorrow. This could take several months. And in case you didn't notice, the fuckin' Statute's running, every goddamned day goes by. We don't get some action from the GJ by the end of the year, we're never going to get him."

"I realize that," Murphy said.

"I don't want us to get in a situation here where we're all sitting here with our thumbs up our ass, looking like a bunch of goddamned fools who finally made their case, and then couldn't bring the fucking thing because we waited too long and got tolled. There's too many people, know about it, thanks to our dear Harry. We goof it up like that, word'll be out all over town by nightfall that Pratt and Murphy fell on their ass, and: 'Who the hell wants to hire them?' "

"I know," Murphy said. "I know all that. But *Jesus,* this thing's so frustrating. It's like being in a blender. You just go 'round and 'round, and nobody tells you anything that you could hang a hat on, let alone a coat."

"You've talked to his driver there, Arbuckle?" Pratt said.

"No," Murphy said. "That's Monday. I've got Fielding coming over from the Bureau, and Arbuckle and Marty Sands're coming over, and he's gonna tell me, I assume, what Sands already told me he's gonna tell me. Which'll be the same damned thing that the treasurer there, the Keller woman, and her assistant, and all the other people in that office've told me. And Morse there, the general manager. That they all just worship Mister Farley, and the guy's a walking saint, and since *he* wanted to help Leonetti—*and* Sonny Donovan—*they* also wanted, help. I tell you, talking to these jokers is enough, give a man diabetes. Jesus, we've got three fucking agents working on this case? Three? I said to Dacey, he gave me his report of the Morse interview? Are we serious? We don't watch out, we're gonna get indicted ourselves, wasting the government money. I said to Dacey: 'Jesus Christ, Jim. We can't indict the guy on *this*. All we can do's propose him for sainthood, this stuff ever comes out. I show this to the grand jury, they're not gonna indict him— they'll put him up, the Nobel Prize.' And he says he knows it, but the hell's he gonna do? 'All I can do's write down what they say,' he said. 'Maybe the case isn't there.' "

"He probably doesn't *want* it to be there, either," Pratt said. "No matter you do get someone to talk, it's still gonna be a toughie to try, and you know how the Bureau feels about agents that get their names on things that didn't work.

341

'You're gonna love Galveston, Agent Dacey. We hear it's beautiful this time of year, and think what you'll save on your heating bill.' He's dragging his feet on it, just like everybody else did that Harry got into this."

"Including you, I assume," Murphy said.

"Well," Pratt said, "not entirely. I wasn't, you know, real what-you'd-call 'enthusiastic' about it. It wasn't like my favorite assignment. But when I did get a good idea, at least something I thought might just work—a long shot, but a shot—David shot *me* down."

"The wife," Murphy said.

"The wife," Pratt said. "He won't even let us *talk* to her? I still don't, you know, I don't think it's ever gonna be a stunner, one those you can't wait to take into the courtroom and just clobber the son of a bitch, front of God and all the people. But I still, you know, I think since we did get stuck with it, cripes, we oughta run down every lead we've got. What'd Sands have to say, that Arbuckle's going to say?"

Murphy exhaled audibly. "I don't know," he said. "Marty seemed like he was kind of rattled. Which I checked around and guys that know him say is not like him. This guy's rep is, well, you know him—he's been playing with the heavies for a long time, and he's made a lot of cash for a guy who's pretty young. This is not the kind player that breaks out in a cold sweat, somebody he represents has got a little problem. This is how

342

he makes his living, and a pretty good one, too—other people's little problems. But it was like he was spooked about something, you know?"

"Maybe he's started taking part of his fees in product," Pratt said. "Little that magical powder up the nostrils in the morning? Maybe he's gone for the magic, and the time he gets in here, see you, all the blow's started to wear off."

"I don't think so," Murphy said. "The guy's too smart for that. But he definitely did not look good. I finally couldn't, I couldn't help asking him if he felt all right. Wanted a glass of water or something. Because he was sitting there in my office, you know? And he was *white*. No color in his face at all. And I said to him, and I kind of like Marty even if his clients're dirty, I said: 'Jeez, kid, you don't look so good. You aren't gonna faint or anything?' And he shakes his head, you know? And he looks worried. And he tells me he just came from the doctor. 'I was having some tests,' 's what he said."

"Jesus," Pratt said, "Marty Sands think he's got cancer or something? I don't even like him that much, but I hope he hasn't got that. I don't like this shit, when people our age get that bullshit. People're supposed to be at least in their sixties, they get their name in the paper for that."

"I didn't dare ask him," Murphy said. "I just sort of said, you know: 'Well, I hope the news is good.' And we went back to Arbuckle, what his story is. And of course I also mentioned, I happened to remind Marty that I hope his client realizes we've got a guillotine on him, if he tries, dance us around. And he said Arbuckle knows that. He explained it to him. But the gist of it's that, it's the same kind of thing the other people said, far as I can see. So it's gonna be, what I expect, is that Monday's gonna come and Marty brings him in, and Fielding and I're gonna get another replay of the Blessed Farley legend. So I said: 'Well, as long's he knows the risk, the chance he'll be taking.' And he says: 'Well, I told him. I laid it out on the level. And that's what he told me.' So I told him: 'Okay, that's the way it's gonna be, then that's the way it is.' And he was getting up to leave, and he still looked like shit, and I said to him, I was trying, maybe cheer him up a little, and I know what they all say about Marty with the women. And I said to him: 'Well, you know, I hope you feel better. Don't want all your girlfriends going crazy with their passion—we'll have to call out the Guard.' And he just looked at me, you know? Like I'd kicked him in the balls. And just shook his head and says: 'Ahh, I just hadda break up with a dame. I can't even go back with my wife.' And then he went out."

"Yeah," Pratt said, pursing his lips. He shook his head. "You know," he said, "I dunno if you ever heard it, but there was a story going around town, must be three, four years ago, that Marty got—that he picked up this broad one night, well,

344

that he *thought* was a broad, in one of the hotel bars. Where he didn't go very much. And he got her all the way home before he found out her name was really, I dunno, 'Ralph.' Or something. And 'she' was a transvestite. And of course the people in the bar all knew it, she was a regular, and the minute he walked out with her, they're hysterical. And naturally the story was all over town by noon the next day, people burning up the wires—you couldn't go into a restaurant without somebody telling you about Marty and this great little chick he picked up, that told him she works for the telephone company—but forgot to mention she uses the Men's Room.

"Next time, he's in here, Harry spots him. And he puts on this long face, you know? Like he really pities Marty. And he says: 'Jeez, Marty, I heard about your problem.' And this's maybe a week after it happened, and Marty's had about enough of it, all the razzing he's been taking. And he also knows Harry's got the reputation, which he deserves, of being about as compassionate as a hungry scorpion. So Marty says: 'Yeah? You another one of those comedians, gonna tell me get new glasses? Because I heard all the jokes by now, Harry, all the fucking jokes. And I don't need one from you.' And Harry gets this hurt look on his face and says: 'No, Marty. Jeez. No, I was just gonna tell you how sorry I was.' And Marty sort of relaxes a little. And then Harry lets him have it. 'As a matter of fact, Marty,' he says,

'I think it's a sham dame.' And naturally, Harry being the well-known charmer that he is—nothing he likes better'n broadcasting it when he gets one off—the line's all over town by sundown. I'm surprised he didn't call one the gossip columnists. If he didn't, but it was too coarse for them. But which anyway revives the whole story, so that guys who didn't get around to giving Marty the leg before get reminded, stop putting it off.

"Then," Pratt said, "then somebody or other starts whispering, you know: 'Well, who really knows if Marty actually *did* make a mistake? Maybe it was on purpose. Maybe Marty's like the garden gate—swings both ways. Sure, he *says* he put the queen in a cab and shipped him out, but did he really do that? Or did he make the best, you know, a situation he really, actually wanted to be in?' "

"Oh, I would doubt that," Murphy said. "I mean, I don't know Marty that well, but: The guy's AC-DC? That I'd tend to doubt."

"Well, so would I," Pratt said. "Or I would've, at least. Guy's seen more pussies'n most vets have. But now, after what you tell me, that he looks like somebody knocked the whey out of him, and this goddamned epidemic with the AIDS thing that we had, well, you see what I'm saying."

"I'll make sure not to kiss him," Murphy said.

"Yeah," Pratt said. "And make sure that you also keep in mind that if Marty's mind seems like it's somewhere else on Monday, maybe you can flip his client a couple sidearm fastballs, get some answers Marty didn't give him when they're back in Marty's office. Maybe get the truth out him."

"And if I don't?" Murphy said. "If he sticks with Marty's lines?"

"Look," Pratt said. "That happens, you come back to me with a memo on everything you did, what everybody said, and I'll take it in to David and take another crack at him."

"The wife, you mean," Murphy said.

Pratt shrugged. "Well, he's gonna have to make the choice. He can either take the chance of having his name go in for a federal judgeship right about the same time *The Commoner* finds out we declined prosecution without interviewing all the possible witnesses — which I don't think'll appeal to him — or he can agree to it. And I think he probably will. And then we'll go and wring her out, and we'll see what we get. And then go on from there."

24

Josephine Demers served black coffee to Gilda Bostock in the otherwise empty dining room of The Foothills Inn in the middle of Thursday afternoon in the first week of February. A light snowfall added to the drifts that had accumulated outside; three large crows conducted a dispute with several bluejays in the bare trees outside. "Goodness, they're loud," Bostock said.

"I know it," Demers said. "Isn't it strange how much noisier they seem when you're not in the city or something? I'm sure there're just as many of them outside my apartment window, and make just as much racket. But I never seem to hear them there. The isolation makes you notice things more, I guess." She smiled. "They're better than listening to that damned parrot, though," she said. "Every time that bird screeches, my blood

349

just runs cold. Your client's got it trained now—whenever she gets excited, so does the bird. Fanny says the two of them in there together're enough to make you yearn for a room full of seventh-graders all loaded up on sugar. On a winter day when it's too cold for outdoor recess."

"How is she doing, generally?" Bostock said.

"Oh, not badly," Demers said. "For her, I mean. We were all apprehensive about how she'd get through Thanksgiving. And then, of course, Christmas. The more so because the owner was on pins and needles that she'd drive his other customers away. And she does at least seem to be calmer here. Most of the time, at least, when she understands where she is. Which, being the case, made us very reluctant to move her to, you know, another place. It always upsets her when she changes, when she has to adapt to new surroundings. So we had Doctor Frontenac drive up and take a look at her before each of the holidays, and he said if she stayed on the medication, he thought she'd make it through. And with the exception of a couple of her patented uprisings, that happened when there was really almost no one here, she was content to stay in her room. Her youngest daughter came up to see her both days, and her son visited on Christmas Day. She was a little out of it, Thanksgiving—didn't understand why everyone'd chosen to have turkey for dinner, when she wanted scrambled eggs. But on

Christmas she seemed fine. Not her old self, exactly, but she opened her presents with them and insisted all the rest of us have wine with our dinner, even though she couldn't. New Year's Eve was a little troublesome — she could hear all the skiers singing away in the lobby and the sunroom and the bar, and she got a little down, a little teary, because she couldn't join them. And that her husband wasn't with her, of course.

"Since then? She's been quiet. Very passive. Does generally what we suggest — we've been able to get her to go out a few times — down to the village for a change of pace at lunch, and she does seem to show a little more interest in her surroundings. She doesn't seem to be sleeping as much — whether that's good or bad, I have some trouble deciding. It's easier for us when she does sleep all the time, of course — we're not always chasing after her. But she seems in better spirits when she sticks to eight or ten hours. Not so listless."

"The reason I ask," Bostock said. "Well, there're two reasons, really. I know when I saw her at Hall Institute she was still seriously ill. But she seemed to be lucid that day, and she was very insistent that her divorce case had to be settled. Naturally I want to do, to carry out my client's wishes. But unless she's capable of understanding an agreement, I'm really not in a position to do that."

"Has Mister Farley's offer changed at all?" Demers said. "Not that I'm sure it matters—what she really wants is him back, and she's not likely to get that."

"No," Bostock said. "And it's not likely to change, either. I'm not going to tell him or his lawyer this, of course, but I frankly doubt I could get it improved much even if she were all right. It's not an extravagant settlement offer, but it's certainly fully within the parameters I'd anticipate, given what I know of the family's financial position. He'll give her the house and the furnishings, or turn over to her an amount equivalent to the appraised value of the property. He'll maintain her health insurance, continue to meet any extraordinary costs—such as you and the other two nurses, along with her doctors and hospitalization that exceed the coverage. He's offered three thousand dollars a month for her support and maintenance, and expressly stipulated that those payments will continue for the rest of her life. Which is necessary, of course, because there's no possibility that a woman her age, with her history, is likely ever to work."

"Well, that's certainly true," Demers said. "There've been days when she's been unable to feed herself."

"So I don't think," Bostock said, "that I can realistically expect to enlarge the offer very much. I've seen, as I say, the financial statements, and I took the precaution of having them researched by an auditing firm, and they're correct."

"Well, you've certainly been thorough," Demers said. "I doubt Mister Farley's ever lied about anything in his life, but no one's ever done that much before."

"I did it in hopes of easing her mind," Bostock said. "I don't want her fretting, a year or so from now, that he's managed to hide something from her, so that she becomes ill once again."

"Very sensible," Demers said. "Very sensible."

"Then there's the other matter," Bostock said. "Apparently Mister Farley's in some kind of hot water with the government. I had a call from the FBI. They want to talk to her."

Demers nodded. "I know what that's about," she said. "They interviewed me at home several weeks ago. On one of my days off—which I rather resented, I must say. A man named O'Neill. Nice enough person in real life, I suppose, but I didn't like his manner. Quite peremptory."

"Did you answer his questions?" Bostock said.

"As well as I could," Demers said. "I'd had a very rough shift out here. I was exhausted. And all *I* wanted to do was sleep. Mrs. Farley hadn't gotten out or anything, but she'd been having nightmares, and whoever happened to be with her was getting up three, four, five times a night, to stop her screaming and soothe her. Well, no sooner'n I'd gotten in the door of my place than he was ringing the bell.

"I told him I was out on my feet and I wished it could wait. He said he'd rather not. He told me what was on his mind. 'Well,' I said, 'all that happened quite a while ago.' He asked me if I had any records. I told him I don't keep a diary. I probably have the canceled checks somewhere, but I don't have the time to locate them. That what he was asking me about was of no particular importance to me at the time, and didn't make a great deal of impression on me. Mister Farley, who's been very kind to me, asked me to consider donating a substantial sum of money to one of his friends who's in politics. Two of his friends, actually. Well, he's done a lot for me, and I didn't see any real reason why I shouldn't do as he asked. So I did it. And that's what I told Mister O'Neill."

"The one who called me," Bostock said, "said his name was Fielding and he'd gotten my name from Ms. Clancy."

Demers nodded. "They interviewed her when she got home from *her* shift," she said. "In much the same condition I'd been in. And got approximately the same results. They get very stern with you, as though just their being with the government's supposed to frighten you into saying things that never happened. Fanny told me—they showed up to see her just as she was getting her things

354

from the car, and she'd been up almost continuously, she and Rachel both'd been, for the better part of a day and a half, and they just wouldn't hear of coming back another time. After she had had some rest. So just to get rid of them, she let them come in, and they talked to her for about forty-five minutes, I guess it was, and they implied at least two or three times that we'd gotten together, either ourselves or with someone else, to cook up our story. Because she of course told them basically the same thing I had. 'But that was the way it happened,' she told them. 'I can't make it to've happened some other way, and neither can Josephine. Don't you want the truth?' So she gathered that they went away somewhat disappointed. She hoped they did, at least: 'It seems to me that a person who works as hard as I do ought to have a right to come home and visit her plants once a week, without being molested by the FBI.' "

"Yes," Bostock said. "Well, the thing that bothers me about this is quite honestly the way this situation plays off against the divorce proceeding."

"Oh," Demers said. "I hadn't thought of that."

"Well, it came as something of a shock to me, too," Bostock said. "I don't care about the FBI, and except for saying Mister Farley and his counsel appear to have been candid with me, I don't much care one way or the other what happens to him. But I do care about my client, and what happens to her. If they're still married to each other, and somebody decides to haul her in to testify, I can at least argue that spousal immunity applies — that she can't testify against her husband, if he objects, and shouldn't be asked to do so. But if they're divorced by then, even though what they're looking for happened during the marriage, I'm on shakier ground."

"I don't think," Demers said, "I'm not a lawyer, of course, but I don't think she could, she'd be up to that much stress."

"And I'm afraid of that, too," Bostock said. "Along with what might happen with that reasonably generous settlement offer if Mister Farley or his lawyer finds out she's been talking to the FBI about him. Doctor Wendell told me that in his opinion, putting the marriage behind her will probably do her good. 'One less thing to worry her.' But if Mister Farley gets the idea that she's vindictively, you know, trying to hurt him? Well, two years ago I was on the very brink of an extremely favorable settlement, and my client, without telling me, had the brilliant idea of telling the IRS that her about-to-be ex was cheating on his taxes. The IRS just descended on him. And of course he was curious, what brought that about. And of course he found out, in short order. You can guess what that did to my nice little settlement offer I'd so painstakingly worked out. He withdrew it, and his lawyer told the court the reason was unanticipated tax liabilities that'd almost certainly change his net worth statement, very much for the worse. And they did, too. The two of them ended up getting hit for about a hundred thousand dollars in taxes and penalties. He was lucky he didn't get indicted.

" 'Too bad he didn't, the bastard,' she said. 'Prison's where the bastard belongs.' And I said to her: 'Okay. Now I know how much revenge is worth to you. About fifty thousand dollars. Because that would've been about your share of community property that's being sold for taxes. And I'd like you to tell me how you think your husband's going to be able to earn eighty thousand dollars a year, so he can pay you almost forty, if they get him doing time. Because I don't think he can. And where's the tuition going to come from, if he's out breaking rocks?' " She smiled. "This's not the easiest branch of the law to specialize in," she said. "Most of your clients are crazy, and after a while, I think, you start getting a little goofy yourself."

"I don't know what she might tell them," Demers said reflectively. "The FBI, I mean. It would all depend on the day when they happened to come out and see her. She might be totally serene. She might be completely silent. But she also might be somewhat manic, and tell them almost anything. Don't they know she's ill? Doesn't that matter to them?"

357

"Apparently not," Bostock said. "The one who called me, when I told him I wasn't sure she could handle an interview, he told me it's their practice, 'our invariable practice' to interview anyone and everyone who might have information. I told him I'd have to talk to her doctors, and also her nurse, and see her myself. And then get back to him."

Demers frowned. "I think you should tell him she can't," she said. "Three nights ago, maybe around ten-fifteen or so, she'd been sitting by the window all day, not talking very much. And she suddenly decided that she had to take a walk, 'just to stretch my legs a bit.' So I went with her, came down into the sunroom, and the snow was coming down, and she went around touching the leaves. And all the while she was talking. Well, not talking, really. More like murmuring. And not really to me, either. Not at all to me, in fact. I was just someone who happened to be there. And I felt like I was invading her privacy. So, there's only the one door into the place—the outer one's locked—and as long as she was in there, she would be all right. So I dragged a chair over to the doorway and sat down where she couldn't leave without my seeing her, and she just meandered around the room, almost fondling the plants. And muttering. I suppose she made, I don't know—four circuits? And it finally hit me: All by herself, she was mingling. She was at some

358

gathering. She was practicing her social skills.

"She went very slowly, going clockwise, and each time she passed me she was saying the same thing. Very softly. 'You see, I know, Francis. I know very well. My husband doesn't always tell me everything. I think he wants to protect me. Make me think it's just these lovely, harmless parties, where everyone's so nice and we're all so very charming.' And that was all I heard. All I could make out. I can't be sure who 'Francis' is, and I don't know what she thinks she knows. Maybe there isn't any 'Francis.' Maybe it's 'Frances,' a woman, instead. Maybe 'Francis' is a talking mule, and she's back at the movies again.

"The point is," Demers said, "the point is that she sometimes imprints herself. When she goes through one of her periods of hallucination, she usually forgets it. Blanks it out. But sometimes she keeps it. Substitutes what she imagined for what really occurred. Or gets so she believes that something really happened, when nothing actually did. And you can't talk her out of it. Because if you try, she goes off the handle. Flies into a rage. She's a real performer, too. She's ill, and she's frail, and she's old beyond her years, and she likes to picture herself as a helpless victim. But she conducts herself like a queen in exile, with us her handmaidens, the ladies of her chamber. There's a lot of martyr in Nell. Give her a stage to act on, and I think she will act up."

25

On the second Friday in February, Asst. US Atty. Donald Murphy waited in his office on the eleventh floor of the courthouse in Boston until the Chief of the Criminal Division had dealt with other matters that could not wait. Pratt came in at 5:47. He sat down and slumped in the chair. "Sorry to keep you," he said. "David had me sitting there for over an hour, me pretending to be a hostile senator, going over his résumé and trying to think up damaging questions so he'd have the answers ready. Which I told him there aren't any. There's nothing in his *curriculum vitae* that anyone could shoot at, no matter how much they might hate the President. But David is methodical. 'You're Arnold of Maryland, get it? You're a prick.' You maybe don't like being a

361

prick, but you are. It's the way you live. You want defense contracts now, and you're not gonna get them unless you make my life miserable first.' I got to do it again Monday, before he goes to Washington."

"It's perfectly all right," Murphy said. "Donna was very understanding. She said she'd pick up the sitter and then go to the dinner party herself, and if I love my job more'n I love her and the kids, well, fine—all I have to do's decide, and tell her, and she'll give me a divorce. No harm done at all."

"Just play the tape," Pratt said, "all right? I can't take any more temperament today. From David, I have to—I don't have to from you. They should've transcribed it and sent it over anyway, so I could take it home and read it. The hell do we have to listen to it?"

"They did transcribe it," Murphy said. "I read the transcript and asked them to copy the tape. Because I think *you* oughta hear it, just in case you think I got the wrong impression from the transcript." He reached for the tape recorder on his desk and pushed the PLAY button.

"FBI Special Agents William O'Neill and Thomas Fielding interviewed Ellen (McNamee) Farley in the parlor of her suite at The Foothills Inn commencing at two-fifteen on the afternoon of February eleventh. Also present were Gilda Bostock, Mrs. Farley's attorney, and Fanny Clancy, one of her nurses. Agent Fielding advised

Mrs. Farley of her rights. Bostock said she had advised her previously."

"What the hell is this?" Pratt said. "I thought this was a tape of the actual interview. What the hell good's this gonna do?"

Murphy pushed the STOP button. "Had them edit it," he said. "Told them all I wanted was what Mrs. Farley said. They bitched and complained, but after all, what questions they asked her, what beefs Bostock had, and what Clancy had to say—that doesn't interest us much. It was their idea, add the color play-by-play. Okay if I start it again?"

Pratt nodded.

"My husband is Kenneth Farley. We've been married for over thirty years. He's trying to divorce me even though I love him very much. I don't understand why he's acting like this. I've never understood it. I've always been a good wife to him, and we have three lovely children. Patricia Ann, Robert and Elizabeth. Patti Ann's married to a physicist. I've forgotten his name.

"My memory isn't good. I have trouble remembering the most obvious things. I think it's all the medicine I've been taking. I know the doctors know what they're doing. They've been very kind to me. If they think it's best, then it must be. But I think, whatever it's supposed to, I think it blots out your memory. I wish I didn't have to take it. It makes me feel drowsy all the time. It's all I can do to get around. I don't see how they expect me to take care of three young children when I'm feeling like this all the time. It isn't reasonable. It isn't fair. They have a son who's now two, and she's expecting again. I haven't seen them for a long time. They live in Ithaca—up near Ithaca. Bobby's thinking about entering Saint John's Seminary after he graduates from college. I don't know what Lizzie will do. She's an awful little tramp. Goes to bed with any boy who asks her. Oh, I've heard all the stories. Naturally I'm ashamed. But that's her father's fault. That's her father's influence, I know. He's been a very bad influence on her. He's a very bad influence on everybody. Look at the state I'm in. You wouldn't believe it now, but I was once an attractive woman. Now there're days when I don't even comb my hair. What's the point? I've been discarded. Cast aside. It's not fair that men should be able to treat women like this. If we had fair judges, this kind of thing wouldn't happen. I wish I could remember things.

"I don't remember when it was, but several years ago I did find out my husband was bribing politicians. He was out until all hours, night after night. At first I thought it was another woman. Doesn't every wife think that? It's the first thing that you think of, if you're a woman—and a wife and mother. He was taking all these trips all the time. Without me. I don't like to take trips. I don't like to go away from home. I'm not here because I want to. I'm here because my husband put me here, to get me out of the way. You just ask Gilda that. She'll tell you. He just wants to be rid of me, and that's why he's doing this.

"The reason I'm here is because I've been sick. I admit it. I know there've been times when I wasn't myself. But they were because—this is all because of my husband. When I found out what he was doing, buying women for these people, all those politicians, giving money to them. And I told him he had to stop. I said we were both raised good Catholics, and that what he was doing was wrong. I made a novena for him. I think. It didn't, he didn't change.

"Instead what he did was put me in this state that I am now. Do you know what he did to me? He told me he was going on business trips. Out of state. And I knew he had some whore with him. And then, when we were all asleep, he'd sneak back home and rearrange all the furniture. You can do that now, you know, with all the jet planes that they've got. They go so *fast?* Because, well, I know what his plan was. He was going to move all the furniture around and then come upstairs and kill me. While he thought I was sleeping. And then fly back to where he was with his harlot. For his alibi. So the police would think a burglar got in, and the burglar was the one that killed me. Well, I was too smart for him. I'm a light sleeper. I heard him down there, breaking things. And I called *the police*. And they came, right off. But I think they must've used their sirens or something. Maybe it was the blue lights. I think the police shouldn't use their sirens and lights when they come to catch a man like that. It just tells him that they're coming. He lived in that house. He knew how to get away. A friend of his *built* it. There's a secret passageway in it somewhere, that I don't even know about. He'd never let me see the plans. He always could get in and out without anyone seeing him. Even me. I wanted a sewing room like this one, but he said I could sew in his den. I couldn't do that. All his papers were in there. They all smelled like Edith Keller. That cheap perfume she uses. I wonder how Edith feels now, now that he's thrown *her* aside. Just soon as they reach thirty, that's the end of them. It was right after that that he dumped me. I knew what he was doing. I could tell. My husband wants me dead. But I'm not going to die. I'm never going to die. Not as long as he's alive."

"Shut it off," Pratt said. Murphy shook his head. "I hadda sit through all of this," he said, "and you're going to listen to some, too." Nell Farley's voice continued in the background.

". . . years since I've seen Sonny Donovan. I used to like him so much. But my husband cut me off from him. It was because he was bribing Sonny, and they were both ashamed. As they should've been. Sonny married my roommate. From college. He introduced me to Kenneth. We used to be such good friends. We went to the

366

movies. Once all of us went to New York when PC was playing in a tournament. A basketball tournament. That was back in the Fifties. The NIT, I think it was. The National Invitational Tournament. We all had such a good time. We stayed at the Biltmore. I don't even think it's there anymore. I haven't been in New York in I don't know how long. I always used to love to go to New York. My late husband took me there once, and we had lunch at a nice restaurant. It was called Côte Basque. And then he took me to Saks and bought me a mink jacket. We didn't have as much money then. I miss him a lot. And we went to Eddie Condon's. To hear jazz. It seems like yesterday. Back when things were good. That time we stayed at The Plaza.

"And then they started to chase women. Do you know where he found that whore he's running around with now? She was Sonny's Director of Cultural Affairs. I'll say. I don't know what she knows about culture, but she sure knows about affairs. He took her to Paris. Did you know that? He never took me to Paris. All over France they were driving. He never took me there. But because she was young, and she's pretty, well, that makes it different, I guess. She didn't have all of his children."

"Turn it off," Pratt said.

Murphy pushed the STOP button. "That mean you're satisfied, now?" he said.

Pratt sighed. He nodded. "Almost," he said.

367

"What's the deal with the chauffeur? He over?"

"Stuck to his guns," Murphy said. "I tried to do it by phone, but the judge down in Quincy said: 'Oh no, you don't. You came down here for favors, you come back to release 'em. In person. On the record.' Not putting Judge Franziani a position where he gave an AUSA a courtesy hearing, did what he said he wanted, and then undid it without him coming down and saying that he wanted it undone. So I went down there this morning and said the USA withdrew his request for continuance in the Arbuckle case."

"And who happened?" Pratt said.

"He admitted sufficient facts," Murphy said. "Judge put it down in the record he's admitted he whacked Cole, and said if he gets in the shit again within a year, he'll be sentenced on the admission. Filed the case without a finding and gave him a year's probation. Also said if he did get in the shit, he'll sentence him to one hour of community service. 'Personally,' he said, 'I think the defendant's already served the community, quite well, by hitting Mister Cole.' Plaintiff's lawyer was *bullshit*. There goes the old lawsuit."

"Marty must've been pleased," Pratt said.

"Figured he would be, too," Murphy said. "But he wasn't. I went up to him, after the thing, and I said: 'At least that's over.' And he looks at me and says: 'This one'll never be over. This one'll never end. Not while I'm alive. And Buck, here, is. And the Pointless Sisters, of course—can't

368

leave them out of this.' I dunno what he meant by that. There's more and more things I'm hearing these days, that I don't know what they mean."

"Nine-oh-one it," Pratt said, rising slowly from the chair.

"Oh, thanks very much," Murphy said. "Harry birthed this monster for David. David made you adopt it. Both of them move up and now *I'm* the guy that kills it? What do I tell the papers? I'm a country boy. I don't know how to play Harry's game."

Pratt shook his head. "I'm signing it too, remember," he said. "Before I even see the paper, I'm approving declination. And before I even see David, I know he will, too. Harry wants to have a screaming fit, down Justice, well, Harry can just go pound sand, 's what I say. We wasted enough time, and done enough damage, this little project of his. Now he's gone, and we're finished, and we're gonna fuckin' stop."

26

Snow resumed in the Berkshires late on the third Thursday in February. Paul Sherburne was jubilant. "You see? I was right, Jacob," he said to his lover. "The television was wrong. The paper was right. 'Snow will be general over the Berkshires by nightfall.' He smiled. "Those TV guys don't know anything, all their charts and maps. This'll be great for the weekend. We'll have 'em lined up for miles to get in."

"That's nice," Jacob said. He wheezed. "I'm really glad for you."

"For us," Sherburne said. "Unless little things like mortgage payments don't concern you anymore."

"Oh," Jacob said, "they won't for much longer. Nothing will. No matter what happens. With the snow."

"Jacob," Sherburne said, "when we came up here, the agreement was that we were partners. Granted that we didn't know what was going to happen. But once we found out, and then when you couldn't perform anymore, I didn't just desert you. I could've wallowed in self-pity, too. But I didn't do it."

"I'm going to die," Jacob said.

"We're *all* going to die," Sherburne said. "Sooner or later we're all going to die. Only you're going to die sooner. And then I'll be left alone, with no hope at all of companionship—not at my age, not in this place. And I wonder who'll be better off? You, with it over with? Or me, waiting for it to happen. Very interesting question, Jacob. I'm going to be alone. Stuck with a hotel that barely gets by—I could never sell it. Working my ass off all day, with no one to talk to at night, and no one to share my feelings. See what you've done now? Depressed me."

"If you're asking me to feel sorry for you," Jacob said, "I'm not. I'm in no mood for a guilt trip."

"Well, thank you very much," Sherburne said. "Here I am with a crazy woman, her keepers, and three spinsters all I've got to pay the rent, now that the holidays're over, and finally it snows just in time for a weekend. So we'll make a little money for a change. And all you want to do's insult me. The only person that you ever want to think about's yourself. I don't think I deserve this, after all I've done for you. And what you've probably done to me."

"I didn't know, Paul," Jacob said with weariness in his voice. "If I'd've known, I would've told you. It was just one lousy weekend, after we had that fight, and it was years ago. Before anybody knew."

"It doesn't matter," Sherburne said. "Next I suppose I'll get the flu, and God knows what happens then."

"The *flu?*" Jacob said. "You're worried about *the flu?*"

"Well, of course I am," Sherburne said. "You're so out of touch with things, you don't know what's going on. And you don't care, either. But if I get laid up, who's going to plan the menus? Make sure the place is kept up? Who's going to do all that? You? Hah."

"How would you get the flu?" Jacob said. "Nobody ever comes here. Who'd you get it from?"

"That's because you're so out of touch," Sherbume said. "That's exactly what I mean. About you being out of touch. Mrs. Farley's nurses. The one that left yesterday, the Dixon woman—she was coming down with it when she left. And the one that came today, the Clancy one? She said she thought she had a slight fever."

"I don't care," Jacob said.

"No, of course you don't," Sherburne said. "You don't care because you never talk to them. Any of them. But I have to. And that means *I* might get it. All their germs and all. They're in the kitchen all the time. Using the coffeepot. Never putting their dirty dishes in the washer. Knives and forks. Any of it. Very inconsiderate. And then who runs the place? While I'm flat on my back?"

"What if I get it from *you?*" Jacob said. "That could kill me, you know."

"Oh," Sherburne said.

"Yes," Jacob said. "I think you should move to one of the other rooms. I'm going to take a nap."

"I am *not* going to move out of our rooms," Sherburne said.

"Then *I* am," Jacob said. "I'm taking one of the empty rooms, and I'm staying there till you're sure you won't give me the flu."

"You can't," Sherburne said. "I'm going to need all those rooms for this weekend. If we expect to eat."

"Then you sleep on the couch," Jacob said. "I think you're very mean, to do this to me. I think you want me dead."

Sherburne had to knock three times when he brought the dinner trolley to Nell Farley's suite. She opened the door for him. Her face was radiant with makeup and her eyes were glad. She was wearing a navy blue sweater and a pleated Black Watch plaid skirt. She had on brown penny loafers. "Why, Mister *Sher*burne," she said. "How *nice* of you to bring our dinners up. I was just watching the news, and I thought, well, I'm getting hungry. It must be time to go down to the *dining* room. And *eat*."

He stared at her. "Well," he said, "Miss, ah, Clancy, she asked me to bring the dinners up. Because she wasn't feeling exactly well."

"Miss Clancy's *drunk,*" Nell said with satisfaction.

"Miss Clancy?" Sherburne said. "Miss Clancy doesn't drink. I've never seen her drink."

"Oh, she's drunk, all right," Nell said. "She's got something in that Thermos. I know a drunk when I see one, and she's as drunk as she can be. She's passed out."

He pushed the trolley through the door into the parlor. "Is she on medication?" he said. "Is she taking something that might make her sleep?"

Nell Farley laughed. "I guess so," she said. "She's been nipping at that Thermos all day. Must be something in it."

"Well," he said, "what she ordered, well, it's cream of chicken soup. And there's broccoli if you want it, and rolls and butter. And coffee and tea, of course. And custard for dessert." He hesitated. "I hate to tell you this, but the cook's ill, so I had to make it myself. And it's not one of my strengths. So it's canned. The soup, I mean. It was canned soup, I used. But I added some chicken, some pieces of chicken, and I put in some rice. So I think it's pretty good. I'm having it myself."

"I'm sure it will be very nice," Nell said. "I must say, you read my mind. Is Mister Daniels having it, too?"

"Who?" Sherburne said.

"Why, your *partner*, Kenneth," she said. *"Jimmy*. Isn't he helping you here?"

The sound of retching came from the bathroom. "Is that Miss Clancy?" he said.

"Oh," Nell said complacently, "it's either Fanny or Jo. They've both been just *miserable*, all afternoon. I don't know which one it is. First one is throwing up and then the other one is shitting. I feel so sorry for them. Have you noticed that it's snowing?"

"Yes, I have," Sherburne said.

"I love it when it snows," Nell said. "It's so tranquil here then. You can almost feel the peace descending. It's so quiet. It falls on the mountains. It falls on the sea. So quiet and deliberate. And then, when you wake up in the morning, the whole world's white. And pure. Purity's important, don't you think?"

"Yes," he said, backing toward the door.

"I'm glad to hear you say that," she said. "So

many people don't. Think purity's important. My late husband didn't. He was always, out on the town, with his fine-feathered friends, chasing one skirt or another. I bet he had his dirty cock in half the women in Boston." She smiled. "He was quite a man."

"Well," Sherburne said, "that's what I've always heard."

"It was very easy to do," she said.

"What was?" he said.

"Well," she said, "the medicine comes in capsules. So it looks like it's solid. But it isn't. It's powder. All you have to do is open up the capsules. Then you get the powder. And you can pour it into anything you want. And, if it's liquid, it dissolves. And there isn't any *taste* to it."

"Well," he said, "that must make it easier for you."

"It does," she said. "In coffee, in tea—it doesn't matter. All you have to do is pour it in. And, it works. It's wonderful."

"That's very nice," he said.

"I want to thank you very much," she said, "for bringing us this lovely soup. I'm not sure either of *them* will be able to keep it down, but I certainly will. And I *need* it. *I have to keep up my strength.* To fight my enemies. I have lots of them."

"Yes," he said, backing out of the room into the hall.

"You can close the door behind you, Mister Sherburne," she said, sitting down in one of the overstuffed green armchairs and pulling the trolley toward her. "I think I can handle everything else by myself." He shut the door. "Unfortunately," she said, as she lifted the cover from a soup bowl, "unfortunately, snow melts."

27

"It's so *still,*" Nell Farley said, letting herself out of her suite and locking the door behind her. "It's like Still River, and the Slaves of the Immaculate Heart of Mary." She walked down the hallway, weaving from side to side. The fingertips of her right hand brushed the red floral paper, and she sang softly about walking in a winter wonderland. "I know about a meadow," she said. "I know where you and I, Ken, can build a new snowman. And I know that there's a preacher, somewhere. And he will do the job if he's in town. We're going to be all right. It's all going to be fine again. You'll see. We'll have a new boat. A *big* boat, this time, and we'll name it *Guardian Angel,* and that's what it will be. Our own *Guardian Angel.* On high, with nothing to do."

379

She smiled and turned right, starting down the stairs. "Or *True Love,*" she said. "Maybe we should name it the *True Love.*"

The staircase was dim. She descended it majestically, humming. She said: "Love is eternal. Marriage is forever. Even after death, the marriage bond endures. One day when we are all with Jesus, we shall be reunited. Even though you are dead, Kenneth, still you live in Christ. I know what crimes you've committed against me. Oh, I know. I know. But you are but a sinner, and I forgive you. Seven times seven, I forgive you. And I always will. I will go in to the altar of God, to God, the joy of my youth. I will offer up my sacrifice to Him, and make us whole."

The corridor on the first floor was dimly lighted. She turned left at the foot of the stairs and walked slowly toward the foyer and the entrance to the solarium. "To You, Oh God, I lift up my soul," she said. "In You, Oh my God, I trust. Let me not be put to shame. Let not my enemies exult over me. No one who waits for You shall be put to shame. For You alone are holy. You alone are Lord. Oh dear, I don't have my mantilla. But that will be all right. Won't it? *Domine non sum dignus, ut intres sub tectum meum, sed tantum dic verbo, et sanabitur anima mea.*"

She turned right in the foyer and right again into the solarium. Snow had mounded up on the glass roof; moonlight came through the windowed walls. She walked among the wicker chairs and plants to the far end of the room, where the parrot's cage was shrouded with a green cotton cover. She yanked it off.

The bird had been sleeping. The noise awakened it. It stirred, shaking and resetting itself. It stared at her with its ferocious golden eyes. It worked its beak four times. It shook itself again. "You think I don't know," she said. The parrot said nothing. "You think I don't know what you are," she said. The parrot stared at her. "You think I don't know what you're up to," she said. The parrot continued to stare. "Well, I do," she said. *"Agnus Dei, qui tollis peccata mundi, miserere nobis."* The parrot shook itself again. "Yes," she said, "you don't know what to make, of that. *Agnus Dei, qui tollis peccata mundi, miserere nobis."* The parrot stared at her. "It means," she said: "Lamb of God, You Who take away the sins of the world, have mercy on us.' *Now* do you understand?" The parrot turned on its perch and twitched. *"Agnus Dei,"* she said, *"qui tollis peccata mundi, dona nobis pacem."* The bird opened its beak and closed it again. "Grant us *peace,"* she screamed. "Grant us goddamned fucking goddamned *peace.* Don't you understand?" The parrot screamed.

"My husband," she said, "my husband was a fine man, and then he became a crook. I discovered he was doing this. I *discovered* it. I found out what he was doing. And I said to him: 'I will not be responsible, I will not be held responsible for this illegal behavior. *I, will not, do it.*' " The parrot screamed. She stepped back from the cage. *"Benedicat vos,"* she said, making the Sign of the Cross at the bird, *"omnipotens Deus, Pater, et Filius, et Spiritus Sanctus. Amen."*

28

On the morning of the third Friday in February, John Corey advised Kenneth Farley not to drive to The Foothills Inn. "Bobby can handle it by himself," Corey said.

"I doubt it," Farley said. "If he didn't have his girlfriend around, Bobby'd still be using last year's calendar. 'Hey, why not, Dad? What difference does it make, the date? It's the day that counts. And I know what that is.' He's the nicest kid in the world, and that's a good thing, and I love him, but my God is that kid vacant."

"Well," Corey said, "maybe that's because you've sheltered him so much. Protected him all his life from all the hard decisions. Give the kid a chance. Show some confidence in him. Fanny told me he was out there within three hours after he found out. And this was in a snowstorm. When I talked to her again this morning, she said he was doing fine. He's briefed the police and he's staying right there until they find something out."

"Of course we know what they're going to find out," Farley said.

"Well," Corey said, "it's pretty difficult to muster much optimism—I agree with you there."

"Jo said she didn't even take a coat," Farley said. "Boots or anything."

"Nope," Corey said, "just the key. Skirt and sweater and the key."

"Jesus," Farley said. "I should be out there."

"Ken," Corey said, "it's just not a good idea. It's common knowledge that you two've been separated for years. You go out there now—there're TV cameras there, and people from the papers. This's out in the woods, you know. This is a big event, in a place where spring mud time's an annual celebration. You go and you're going to have to make some sort of a statement. And what kind of a statement can you make? Well, you've got two choices. You can say how distressed you are, and the family's hoping for the best—which will be taken as rank hypocrisy. Grandstanding. And hurt you, a lot, around here."

"But it's true," Farley said. "It happens to be true. I didn't want her dead—I wanted her well. Not for my sake as much as for the kids'. This whole siege has just been hell on them."

"It won't be taken that way," Corey said. "Jim called me and said you'd talked to him about doing it, and he just pleaded with me to do everything I could to stop you. 'It wouldn't be wise,' he kept saying. 'There's too many people who know. They'd resent it, and they'd take it out on him.' Either you go out there and take the hopeful position, or else you go out there and just tell people: 'Look, we used to be man and wife.' Which will sound callous and do you even more damage than the first one'd do."

"But as it is," Farley said, "with me staying away, the kid's got to carry all the burden himself. Alone. Cripes, when I called Patti Ann out West, all she said was: 'Dad, it was just a matter of time. She knew it. I knew it. You knew it. Lizzie knew it. Even Bobby knew it. She wasn't getting better. She could fool people for a few days at a time, but she couldn't sustain it for any real *length* of time. I kind of sympathize with her. I'd want to pull the plug too, if what was going on in my head was like what was going on in hers.' Patti Ann's not going to help. And Lizzie? When I talked to Lizzie after Christmas, she said it was exhausting. 'I feel like, after one afternoon with her I feel like I've been digging trenches. It's all so "pretend." "Pretend I'm fine, do you hear me? Pretend I never said any of those horrible things about you. Pretend you had

385

a happy childhood, with me, and your father didn't have to hire Agnes to take care of us. And if you don't pretend, I'll get sick again, and try to kill myself." It's all bullshit. Bullshit and threats. I can't do it anymore. If Bobby wants to play her games, well, then let Bobby play them. But not me. I'm finished. Through. I'm sick of being threatened. And then having to agree that I wasn't, so I can be threatened again.' "

"You should be pleased," Corey said. "Lizzie is therefore all right. She's survived a long, bad, time, with a lot of help from you, and she's come to terms with what she can't help but know, and that should make you feel good."

"Well, I don't," Farley said. "Fanny read the note to me. Jeez, she was blaming herself. Here's this absolutely devoted woman, dedicated, really, and she's crying to me on the phone, saying she betrayed my trust. 'Because you came down with the flu?' I said. 'Good Lord, Fanny, stop it. You can't help being sick.' And she said she didn't mean that. That she knows she's sensitive to any kind of medication—'even Contac makes me drowsy'—but she felt so awful that she took the Nyquil anyway, and just about passed out. 'And I knew Jo was sick, too,' she said. 'It was just the moment she'd been waiting for.' "

"Where the hell was the damned key, anyway?" Corey said. "How'd she get ahold of the key?"

"She drugged them," Farley said. "She apparently dumped her drugs into their coffee or something. I guess Fanny and Jo didn't want to eat very much, anyway, but she made sure they'd be flattened out. And then when she was finished she pushed the cart out into the hall. And closed the door and locked it. And since Jo seemed to feel even worse'n Fanny did, Fanny swapped shifts with her—Jo was supposed to have the night watch. 'I sat with her, and she seemed to be fine. In fact, she was better than she's been in weeks. It was the first day in a long time that she'd been active enough to do a little primping. She had a good appetite, and she was watching TV and writing on her table at the same time. She seemed cheerful and alert. More alert than I was, obviously. And then about ten-thirty, she stood up and said she thought she'd go to bed.'

"She said she sat in the parlor until about eleven-thirty, quarter of twelve. 'And I just felt so awful,' she said. She said she knew she was going to lose her dinner. 'The only reason, really, that I stayed up even that long was I didn't want to be lying down when what I knew was going to happen finally happened.' She told me she looked in on Nell twice, 'right before the weather came on, and then just before I went to bed. Right after I vomited the last time. She had the covers all pulled up around her ears—she seemed to be sleeping soundly. So I decided it was safe to go to bed, and I checked the door, and it was locked. And my purse. And the key was still there. And I went into the bathroom and took the Nyquil, and got undressed, and went into the other bedroom, and I had my purse with me. And I put it under my bed. Jo was snoring, as usual, but I felt so rotten by then I really didn't care.'

"Nell must've sneaked in there as soon as she was sure they were both asleep," Farley said. "Jesus Christ, it's impossible to watch a person every single minute. The note, the letter? 'I have been abandoned. My husband. My children. Even sometimes by my God. But I will win out over all of this, and over all of them. For God is with me now. And I know where He is. God, the Lord Jesus, fills the universe with His sweet love, and calls to those who will hear Him. I have heard that call, and I know if I go to Him, that He will receive me. I forgive, as He did, those who have tortured me. I know you did not mean it. I know you meant only to love. Too bad that you didn't know how. But Jesus does.' "

The following Sunday was clear and cold. Roger and Diana Ealer of Tiverton, R.I., left The Foothills Inn shortly after eleven o'clock for a day of cross-country skiing. Each of them secretly despised the activity, but concealed the opinion because each believed it might enable the other to lose weight, as their doctor had recommended, and both of them hated jogging. Neither of them had mastered the gliding motion taught by their instructors. They had agreed that they would not pay for any more instruction, and would do the best they could with what they'd already learned.

The snow on the shaded trail west of the inn was nicely packed and smooth, but the route was uphill and led to a plateau where the noon sun had melted the surface. Both of the Ealers labored in it, by then about three-quarters of a mile from the inn. Roger, at 214 pounds, struggled more than Diana, at 153, and lost his patience first. Panting, he shouted toward her: "Honey, I got to rest. I got to sit down and rest."

She stopped and looked back at him. Her face was red and the hair at her temples was wet with sweat. "Sissy," she said.

" 'Sissy' my ass," Roger said. "I'm thirty-nine years old, and I'm out of shape, and the air's thinner here'n at home. I'll be goddamned I'm going to have a heart attack out here in the woods because I didn't have the brains to sit down when I knew I should. I'm stopping right goddamned here. I'm going to sit down in the sun and have my goddamned lunch. You want to go on, then you go ahead and go on. It's time for my goddamned milk and cookies, or whatever shit we've got." He bent down and released his boots from the bindings. He stepped out of the

389

skis. He removed his backpack and opened it. He took out a large green plastic trash bag.

"No," she said, turning around and leaning on her poles, "not there."

"Whaddaya mean: 'Not there'?" he said, the trash bag flapping in his hands. "The hell difference does it make? I'm gonna Saranwrap my ass and sit on the snow so I probably get piles, what difference it make where I do it?"

"The sun's better over there," she said, gesturing with her right hand pole toward a large boulder that the sun had melted clean. "We can sit on that rock there, and have our lunch, and you won't get your piles from the snow."

"No," he said, "I'll get 'em from the cold rock."

"Get over here," she said, skiing toward the boulder.

"I can't ski anymore for a while," he said. "I told you, I got to rest."

"Oh, pick up your stuff and just walk," she said. "You can do that, I assume."

Their seats on the boulder faced west on the crest of a hollow filled with underbrush and dwarf pines. Two eagles circled separately high over the next range of hills. "It's beautiful here," she said.

"Yeah, it is," he said. "But it's a big pain the ass, getting here. I don't understand why everything that's supposed to be good for you has to be so much goddamned *work*. Why can't I get my exercise watching the Celtics, TV? Why the hell I have to take the kids, your mother's, pack the goddamned car, and then drive about three hours to unpack the goddamned car—so I can go out in the goddamned woods and knock myself out all day? Why should that be good for me? So when I drive back tonight, I'll be stiff and sore? This life wasn't planned right. Staying home's what should be good, for you. Not all this other shit."

"Well," she said, unwrapping her peanut butter and strawberry jam sandwich, "it wasn't planned that way. So, since it wasn't, we have to do this. You got the Diet Coke, or've I?"

"I got it," he said, digging into the backpack. "That screaming faggot at the hotel put both cans in mine. There's chivalry for you."

"You don't know that, he's a faggot," she said, raising her face to the sun. "You got no proof at all."

"No," he said, "I don't. And I've got no proof that Russia's Communist, either—but I believe it."

"You're too hard on people," she said, biting into the sandwich.

"Well," he said, "if you mean when I come to a place where I'm paying to stay, and there's a whole bunch of cops buzzing around, and the owner's a flaming queer, and then when I go out with my wife I practically have to have a heart

391

attack before I can sit down—if you think that makes me unhappy, well, you're right."

"One the guests disappeared," she said. "That's all that's going on, Roger. They're all out looking for her."

"Well, I don't like it," he said. He regarded his sandwich with distaste. "Look at this," he said. "PB and J. On whole-wheat goddamned bread. 'I'd rather have chicken or something.' 'Sorry, sir, we're all out.' You know *why* they're all out? Because they're all *out*—that's why. Looking for somebody I don't even know that got lost in the woods. Nobody went the damned store."

"Roger," she said, her face still lifted to the sun, her eyes closed, "you can't expect them just to say: 'Well, the hell with her.' They've got to look for her."

"Diana," he said, "they don't have to neglect *me* while they're looking for her. We getting a special rate this weekend, because they got other things on their minds? Like hell we are. Fucking people. *They* got a problem, they're entitled then to screw up *my* whole weekend? I called them up, reserve the room, the hell didn't the bastard tell me the whole operation's all screwed up because this woman got lost. Gimme a choice. 'You can come up and we'll cut the tab in half, or you can stay home and run up no tab at all.' Uh uh, nothing doing. I feel like I'm in ACI Cranston, all the goddamned cops around. Just like I'm in jail. Difference is, I'm not only *in* it—I am *paying* for it. Full fucking goddamned price."

She put her head down. "Rub my shoulders?" she said. "I think I'm starting to stiffen up." He put his sandwich down on the plastic bag and used both hands to massage the muscles leading from her neck into her back. "Ahh," she said. "Good." She arched her back. "That's the trouble with exercise at our age—it's all right as long as you do it, but the minute you stop, ouch." She straightened up. She waggled her head. She said: "What's that?"

"What's what?" he said.

She pointed down into the hollow. "That," she said. "Next to the little bush there. See the two big bushes and the little bush next to them? See that? In the snow?"

"It's a shoe," he said. "Somebody lost a shoe. Probably came out here last fall on a hike, and threw it away, for a blister. Some other poor bastard, out killing themself for their health."

She stood up. She peered down into the hollow. "It's more than a shoe, Roger," she said. "Go down there and look."

"I'll break my fucking leg," he said. "I'm not going down there and look, and then be on crutches the next six goddamned months. You go down and look."

I don't want to, she said. "I know what's down there. There's a body down there. I can see part

393

of a leg."

"Well then," he said, standing up, "why the hell would I want to, then? Let's go back and get the cops."

She continued to stare down into the hollow. "You said you were too tired to ski anymore. You said you had to rest."

"I'd rather ski'n look at a corpse," he said. "Besides, it's all downhill from here."

29

"Well," Sharon Stoddard said, "but was it *bad?* I mean, I know it couldn't've been *good,* but was it really *bad?*" They sat in a booth at the Regina Pizzeria in the South Shore Plaza and drank beer while they waited for pizza.

"Put it this way," Arbuckle said. "It wasn't as bad as it could've been. But it was bad, yeah—it was bad. They had, you know, the church thing, and the priest they got was this Monsignor Clayton. That Mister Daniels's always going off to watch the football with. And he's just like all the rest of them. I dunno why they do that. They get a whole church fulla people that feel lousy, 'cause funerals aren't fun, and what do they do? Well, they know you can't leave, so they stand up there and they give you even more shit'n you already got. It must give them satisfaction. He's up there and he's telling everybody, you know, pretty soon, we're all gonna be in the same kinda crate. Headed for the hole. And we'd better watch our ass. And also give double, the annual collection, and make sure we kiss their ass whenever we happen to see them. He's pretty old, but I don't think he ever knew her. I was growing up in Charlotte? The guy there was a bastard. But at least when I went to my grandmother's funeral, I was about twelve, I knew he knew who she was. And he talked about *her*. Not about us, and what a buncha goddamned shits we were. Not about the brimstone and the goddamned fire.

"Then we went to the cemetery," Arbuckle said. "And we get there, he gives us another ration of shit. Just in case we didn't pay attention, back inna church. I don't know why they do that. They get a bunch of people that have to go to a thing that nobody wants to go to—and I don't care how old the guest of honor is, nobody wants to go—and it's like they can't hold back. They got all these people there because they have to be, and: 'Boy, let 'em have it.' I wonder what good they think it does.

"But it was all right," he said. "Mister Farley stood off the side and didn't get involved. I drove him and Mister Corey. The kids rode the limo behind the hearse. Then the undertaker tells everybody, come back the house for coffee. And we all go back, and Agnes was there, and she had a caterer, you know? It was a pretty good feed. A buffet. Agnes tried her best, you know, to ruin it? Just stood there, shaking her head. Believed every word that priest bastard said. She was marking down our names, the ones're sure to go to Hell. But there was lots and lots to drink, which was the most popular thing. You ever notice how, after a funeral, people tuck into the booze? Must be the tension or something. 'Well, we got through it, and that's the end of old Nell. Now let's get a snootful, and try to relax.' I never heard so many jokes, I did right after funerals. People that never tell jokes, tell jokes after funerals."

"I never been to a funcral," Sharon said.

He stared at her. "You," he said, "how . . . You never been to a funeral?"

She nodded. "Never in my whole life," she said. "I was in high school. Two friends of mine got killed. He was driving. They'd been drinking. And they hit a tree. And he was buried, the day after her. But I couldn't go. All my classmates went, and Stelle went, because she also knew them. But I couldn't go. I had the mumps. And those're the only two. All my relatives're still around." She hesitated. "It sounds like I'm complaining. But I'm not. I just never knew anyone that died. Except those two kids in high school."

"Jesus," Arbuckle said, "you really are young,

aren't you? I've been to dozens of them. Funerals, I mean. And you've never been to even one."

"Well, it's not my *fault,* Eugene," she said. "I mean, if it was someone I knew, died, and I wasn't sick at the time, naturally I would go. But no one ever did. So far."

"I wasn't saying that," he said, as the waiter brought the pizza. "I didn't mean, you know, I was being mean or anything. You've just been lucky, is all. I think I'm gonna stick with you, kid. You're a lucky charm."

James Saxon sent a letter to Kenneth Farley at his office at Arrow Construction. "I telephoned the United States Attorney on March 2nd to ascertain the status of his investigation. As you may be aware, staff changes have resulted in the promotion of William Pratt to Chief of the Criminal Division. Asst. US Atty. Donald Murphy replaced him as the lead man on the investigation. Murphy told me that he, Pratt, and US Atty. David Curley have examined the records and other evidence carefully in your case, and have recommended to the Department in Washington that prosecution be declined. This is usually, though not always, a *pro forma* procedure, after which the Department as a whole drops the case.

"I therefore conclude that you have no further need of the services of this firm, and I am pleased that this occasion has turned out so well. I enjoyed meeting with you, and I appreciate the candor you displayed in · our discussion."

"There was a bill in there, too," Farley said to John Corey. "In the envelope with the letter."

"For how much?" Corey said.

"Seventy-five hundred American dollars," Farley said.

"You got off easy," Corey said. "I thought he'd whack you twenty."

Steven N. Cole, 31, of Avon, was arrested after State and local police pursued him at speeds exceeding 100 miles per hour through six South Shore towns early in the morning of the first Sunday in March. He was charged with vehicular homicide in the death of Dominic Alta, 53, a security guard returning to his home in Hingham after completing his night shift at the Bristol Freight Company. Cole was also charged with leaving the scene of an accident, driving while under the influence, speeding, driving so as to endanger, assault and battery on a police officer, resisting arrest and operating a motor vehicle without a current inspection sticker. Tpr. Francis Mulcahy told Sgt. Mark Honore that he "couldn't think of anything else to put on the paper. I tell you, when that son of a bitch came out of the car at me, he's lucky I didn't shoot him. I think he wanted me to."

Honore told Mulcahy to calm down. "This should do it," he said. "This should be enough. Besides, if you'd shot him, he'd sue you, even that was what he wanted. Everybody gets just about what they want. It's just, they don't recognize it, they get it. It doesn't look the same as what they had in mind."